Love and Other Consolation Prizes

By Jamie Ford

Hotel on the Corner of Bitter and Sweet

Songs of Willow Frost

Love and Other Consolation Prizes

Love and Other Consolation Prizes

A Novel

JAMIE FORD

Allison & Busby Limited
12 Fitzroy Mews
London W1T 6DW
allisonandbusby.com

First published in Great Britain by Allison & Busby in 2017.

A CIP catalogue record for this book is available from
the British Library.

First Edition

HB ISBN 978-0-7490-2275-4
TPB ISBN 978-0-7490-2280-8

Typeset in 11/18 pt Sabon by
Allison & Busby Ltd.

The paper used for this Allison & Busby publication
has been produced from trees that have been legally sourced
from well-managed and credibly certified forests.

Printed and bound by
CPI Group (UK) Ltd, Croydon, CR0 4YY

For Haley, Karissa, Madison, and Kass.
When you graduated I wanted to skip
'Pomp and Circumstance' and play 'Ride of the Valkyries'.

Pleading moments we knew
I will set them apart
Every word, every sign
Will be burned in my heart.

– from 'Non, je ne regrette rien',
performed by Édith Piaf

Overture

(1962)

Ernest Young stood outside the gates on opening day of the new world's fair, loitering in the shadow of the future. From his lonely vantage point in the VIP parking lot, he could see hundreds of happy people inside, virtually every name in Seattle's *Social Blue Book*, wearing their Sunday best on a cool Saturday afternoon. The gaily dressed men and women barely filled half of Memorial Stadium's raked seating, but they sat together, a waterfall of wool suits and polyester neckties, cut-out dresses and ruffled pillbox hats, cascading down toward a bulwark of patriotic bunting. Ernest saw that the infield had been converted to a speedway for motorboats – an elevated moat, surrounding a dry spot of land where the All-City High School Band had assembled, along with dozens of reporters who milled about smoking cigarettes like lost sailors, marooned on an island of generators and television cameras. As the wind picked up, Ernest could smell gasoline, drying paint, and a hint of sawdust. He could almost hear carpenters tapping finishing nails as the musicians warmed up.

Saying that Ernest wished he could go inside and partake of the celebration was like saying he wished he could dine alone at Canlis restaurant on Valentine's Day, cross the Atlantic by himself aboard the *Queen Mary*, or fly first class on an empty Boeing 707. The scenery and the festive occasion were tempting, but the endeavor itself only highlighted the absence of someone with whom to share those moments.

For Ernest, that person was Gracie, his beloved wife of forty-plus years. They'd known each other since childhood, long before they'd bought a house, joined a church, and raised a family. But now their memories had been scattered like bits of broken glass on wet pavement. Reflections of first kisses, anniversaries, the smiles of toddlers, had become images of a Christmas tree left up past Easter, a package of unlit birthday candles, recollections of doctors and cold hospital waiting rooms.

The truth of the matter was that these days Gracie barely remembered him. Her mind had become a one-way mirror. Ernest could see her clearly, but to Gracie he'd been lost behind her troubled, distorted reflection.

Ernest chewed his lip as he leaned against the vacant Cadillac De Ville that he'd spent the better part of the morning polishing. He felt a sigh of vertigo as he stared up at the newly built Space Needle – the showpiece of the Century 21 Expo – the talk of the town, if not the country, and perhaps the entire world. He was supposed to deliver foreign dignitaries to the opening of the Spanish Village Fiesta, but the visitors had been held up – some kind of dispute with the Department of Immigration and Naturalization Services. So he came anyway, to try to remember the happier times.

Ernest smiled as he listened to Danny Kaye take the microphone and read a credo of some kind. The Official World's Fair Band followed the famous actor as they took over the musical duties for the day and began to play a gliding waltz. Ernest counted the time, *one*-two-three, *one*-two-three, as he popped his knuckles and massaged the joints where arthritis reminded him of his age – sixty-four, sixty-five, sixty-something, no one knew for sure. The birth date listed on his chauffeur's permit had been made up decades earlier, as had the one on his old license with the Gray Top Taxi company. He'd left China as a boy – during a time of war and famine, not record keeping.

Ernest blinked as the waltz ended and a bank of howitzers blasted a twenty-one-gun salute somewhere beyond the main entrance, startling him from his nostalgic debridement. The thundering cannons signaled that President Kennedy had officially opened the world's fair with the closing of a telegraph circuit sent all the way from his desk at the White House. Ernest had read that the signal would be bounced off a distant sun, Cassiopeia, ten thousand light years away. He looked up at the blanket of mush that passed for a north-western sky, and made a wish on an unseen star as people cheered and the orchestra began playing the first brassy strains of 'Bow Down to Washington' while balloons were released, rising like champagne bubbles. Some of the nearby drivers honked their horns as the Space Needle's carillon bells began ringing, heralding the space age, a clarion call that was drowned out by the deafening, crackling roar of a squadron of fighter jets that boomed overhead. Ernest felt the vibration in his bones.

When Mayor Clinton and the City Council had broken ground on the fairgrounds three years ago – when a gathering of reporters had watched those men ceremoniously till the nearby soil with gold-plated shovels – that's also when Gracie began to cry in her sleep. She'd wake and forget where she was. She'd grow fearful and panic.

Dr Luke had told Ernest and their daughters, with tears in his eyes, 'It's a rare type of viral meningitis.' Dr Luke always had a certain sense of decorum, and Ernest knew he was lying for the sake of the girls. Especially since he'd treated Gracie when she was young.

'These things sometimes stay hidden and then come back, decades later,' the doctor had said as the two of them stood on Ernest's front step. 'It's uncommon, but it happens. I've seen it before in other patients. It's not contagious now. It's just—'

'A ghost of red-light districts past,' Ernest had interrupted. 'A ripple from the water trade.' He shook Dr Luke's hand and thanked him profusely for the late-night house call and the doctor's ample discretion regarding Gracie's past.

Ernest remembered how shortly after his wife's diagnosis her condition had worsened. How she'd pulled out her hair and torn at her clothing. How Gracie had been hospitalized and nearly institutionalized a month later, when she'd lost her wits so completely that Ernest had had to fight the specialists who recommended she be given electroshock therapy, or worse – a medieval frontal-lobe castration at Western State Hospital, the asylum famous for its 'ice pick' lobotomies.

Ernest hung on as Dr Luke quietly administered larger doses of penicillin until the madness subsided and Gracie returned to a new version of normal. But the damage had been done. Part of his wife – her memory – was a blackboard that had been scrubbed clean. She still fell asleep while listening to old records by Josephine Baker and Édith Piaf. She still smiled at the sound of rain on the roof, and enjoyed the fragrance of fresh roses from the Cherry Land flower shop. But on most days, Ernest's presence was like fingernails on that blackboard as Gracie recoiled in fits of either hysteria or anger.

I didn't know the month of the world's fair groundbreaking would be our last good month together, Ernest thought as he watched scores of wide-eyed fairgoers – couples, families, busloads of students – pouring through the nearby turnstiles, all smiles and awe, tickets in hand. He heard the stadium crowd cheer as a pyramid of water-skiers whipped around the Aquadrome.

To make matters worse, when Gracie had been in the hospital, agents from the Washington State Highway Department had showed up on Ernest's doorstep. 'Hello, Mr Young,' they'd said. 'We have some difficult news to share. May we come in?'

The officials were kind and respectful – apologetic even. As they informed him that his three-bedroom craftsman home overlooking Chinatown, along with his garden and a row of freshly trimmed lilacs in full bloom – the only home he'd ever owned and the place where his daughters took their first steps – all of it was in the twenty-mile urban construction zone of the Everett–Seattle–Tacoma Freeway. The new interstate highway was a ligature of concrete designed to bind Washington with Oregon and California. In less than a week, he and his neighbors had been awarded fair-market value for their properties, along with ninety days to move out, and the right-of-way auctions began.

The government had wanted the land, Ernest remembered, and our homes were a nuisance. So he'd moved his ailing wife in with his older daughter, Juju, and watched from the sidewalk as entire city blocks were sold. Homes were scooped off their foundations and strapped to flatbed trucks to be moved or demolished. But not before vandals and thieves stripped out the oak paneling that Ernest had installed years ago, along with the light fixtures, the crystalline doorknobs, and even the old hot-water heater that leaked in wintertime. The only thing left standing was a blur of cherry trees that lined the avenue. Ernest recalled watching as a crew arrived with a fleet of roaring diesel trucks and a steam shovel. Blossoms swirled on the breeze as he'd turned and walked away.

As a young man, Ernest had carved his initials onto one of those trees along with Gracie's – and those of another girl too. He hadn't seen her in forever.

As an aerialist rode a motorcycle on a taut cable stretched from the stadium to the Space Needle, Ernest listened to the whooshing and mechanical thrumming of carnival rides. He caught the aroma of freshly spun cotton candy, still warm, and remembered the sticky-sweet magic of candied apples. He felt a pressing wave of déjà vu.

13

The present is merely the past reassembled, Ernest mused as he pictured the two girls and how he'd once strolled with them, arm in arm, on the finely manicured grounds of Seattle's *first* world's fair, the great Alaska–Yukon–Pacific Exposition, back in 1909. When the city first dressed up and turned its best side to the cameras of the world. He remembered a perfect day, when he fell in love with both girls.

But as Ernest walked to the gate and leaned on the cold metal bars, he also smelled smoke. He heard fussy children crying. And his ears were still ringing with the echoes of the celebratory cannons that had scared the birds away.

He drew a deep breath. Memories are narcotic, he thought. Like the array of pill bottles that sit cluttered on my nightstand. Each dose, carefully administered, use as directed. Too much and they become dangerous. Too much and they'll stop your heart.

Raining Stars

(1902)

Yung Kun-ai watched his little *mei mei* struggle to breathe. His newborn sister was only two days old – a half-breed like him, without a father. She mostly slept, but when she did wake, she coughed until she cried. Then cried until she was desperately gasping for air. Her raspy wailing made her seem all the more out of place, unwelcome; not unloved, just tragically unfit for this world.

Yung understood that feeling as his sister stirred and keened again, scaring away a pair of ring-necked crows from a barren lychee tree. The birds cawed, circling. Yung's mother should have been observing her *zuoyuezi*, the traditional time of rest and recovery after childbirth. Instead, she'd staggered into the village cemetery, dug a hole in the earth with her bare hands, and placed his sister's naked, trembling body inside. As Yung stood nearby, he imagined that the ground must have been warm, comforting, since it hadn't rained in months, the clay soil surrounding his unnamed sibling like a blanket. Then he watched his mother pour a bucket of cold ash from the previous night's fire over his sister's body and she stopped crying. Through a cloud of black soot he saw tiny legs jerk, fragile arms go still. Yung didn't look away as his lowly parent smothered his baby sister, or while his mother wearily pushed the dirt back into the hole, burying his *mei mei* by scoops and handfuls. His mother tenderly patted the soil and replaced the sod before pressing her forehead into the grass and dirt, whispering a prayer, begging forgiveness.

Yung swallowed the lump in his throat and became a statue. At five years old, he could do nothing else. The bastard son of a white missionary and a Chinese girl, he was an outcast in both of their worlds. He and his mother were desperately poor, and a drought had only made their bad situation worse. For months they'd been eating soups made from mossy rocks and scraps of boiled shoe leather his mother had scavenged from the dying. When she turned and saw what Yung had witnessed she didn't seem shocked, or apologetic. She didn't bother to wipe away the ashen tears that framed the pockmarked hollows of her cheeks, or the dust and grime that had settled into her scalp where her hair had thinned and fallen out. She merely placed a filigreed hairpin in his hand and folded his tiny fingers around the tarnished copper and jade phoenix that represented the last of their worldly possessions. She knelt and hugged him, squeezed him, ran her dirty fingers through his hair. He felt her bony limbs, the sweet smell of her cool skin as she kissed his face.

'Only two kinds of people in China,' she said. 'The too rich and the too poor.'

He'd remembered combing the harvested fields for single grains of rice, gathering enough to make a tiny handful that they would share while the well-fed children flew kites overhead. His empty stomach reminded him of who he was.

'Stay here and wait for your uncle,' she said. 'He's going to take care of you now. He's going to take you to America. He's going to show you a new world. This is my gift to you.'

Yung's mother addressed him in Cantonese and then in the little bit of English they both understood. She told him he had his father's eyes.

And she spoke about a time when they would be together again. But when she tried to smile her lips trembled.

'*Mm-goi mow hamm*,' Yung said as she turned away. 'Don't cry, Mama.'

Yung wasn't sure if the man he was supposed to wait for was truly his uncle, but he doubted it. The best he could hope was that the man might be one of the rich merchants who specialized in the poison trade or the pig trade, because dealing with men who smuggled opium or people would be preferable to members of the Society of Righteous and Harmonious Fists, the Chinese boxers who had been slaughtering missionaries, foreigners, and their offspring. Equally dangerous were the colonial soldiers sent to put down the rebellion. The villagers, including Yung's father, had been caught in the siege, the melee, and now the maelstrom. That's when his mother must have known that the end of their world was near – when they saw the starving fishermen hauling in their nets, filled with the bodies of the dead.

As Yung watched his mother disappear, leaving him alone in the cemetery, he wanted to yell, 'Ah-ma! Don't leave me!' He wanted to run to her, to cling to her legs, to cry at her feet, begging. But he resisted, even as he whimpered, yearning. He did what he was told as he ached with sadness and loneliness. He had always obeyed her – trusted her. But it seemed as if she had died months earlier, and all that remained was a ghost, a skeleton – a hopeless broken spirit with no place left to wander and no one to haunt.

What little hope she had, she'd bequeathed to him.

So he waited, grieving, as the sun set upon the place where his *mei mei* had been interred. He remembered his Chinese grandmother and how she'd once talked about the Lolos, the tribal people of Southern China who believed that there was a star in the sky for every person on Earth. When that person died, their star would fall.

His ears popped and he heard the familiar booming of mortars and the rattle of gunfire. He watched as the horizon lit up with flares and the flash of cannons. Then the sky was dark again and everywhere he looked, it was raining stars.

Unbound

(1902)

The man who was not his uncle came for Yung in the morning. A white merchant with a ruddy beard, he removed his elegant suit jacket and rolled up his shirtsleeves to reveal an array of old tattoos. He squeezed Yung's arm, pulled his hair, looked in his ears. He then smiled and nodded as his translator, a remarkably fat Chinese man, clapped his hands and shouted, '*Hay sun la!*' waking other children – a host of girls and a handful of boys, who had gathered in and around the cemetery during the night. All of them seemed older than Yung, grade school age at least, or well into their teens. Some had rolls of bedding and carried their belongings in bamboo baskets attached to long sticks, topped with netting, while a few of the older girls wore modest, hand-sewn dresses and tied their hair with red strings. But just as many were like him, in rags, barefoot. And all of them stared at Yung when they realized he was a mixed-blood child. He recognized the look, not one of curiosity or contempt, but an expression that said, *I may have nothing, I may be homeless and starving, but at least I'm not him.*

Yung ignored their attention and tried not to think about his mother as they followed the men away from pillars of black smoke and the sounds of gunfire that were rising in the distance. They walked for hours, Yung taking two steps with his little legs for every one of theirs, as he struggled to keep up. A tributary of sadness flowing into a greater

19

stream of refugees that became a flood of humanity, traveling away from the sound of thunder in a cloudless sky. They boarded a boat, which took them to a city on the Pearl River. When they arrived, in the shadow of a great ship, the salty air made Yung's mouth water, though the only signs of food were the bones of fish that had been recently caught, cooked, and eaten, on the banks of the murky water.

Yung's eyes grew wide as he gazed up at the massive freighter, with four masts and an enormous funneled stack. Everyone spoke of the *Chang Yi*, but he didn't know if that was the ship's name, or if they were referring to the man who was not his uncle.

Swirling black smoke from the stack muddied the sky, turning the sun a ruddy orange, and Yung wondered how such a stout ship could move. Then he felt his legs tremble from the vibrations of a great steam engine. His body was haggard, weary and numb from the march, but he was grateful to be upright as he watched a group of Chinese stevedores pulling an oxcart bearing a dozen elegantly dressed girls with bound feet. Yung heard a shrill whistle as they were unloaded, limping, while a white marine officer parted the crowd and began yelling in broken Chinese, 'Line up and be silent!'

The officer pointed and snapped his fingers as Yung queued up and they were poked and prodded, noses counted.

The officer culled those with rickets or those with stooped backs. That group was herded away from the ship, back toward the heart of the city. Yung watched as the boys and girls obviously stricken with lice and mites were doused in foul-smelling waters, given a change of clothing, and then taken to another vessel.

Yung overheard the sailors chattering back and forth in Chinese, Portuguese, and English, which he understood just enough to gather that they were blackbirders.

His mother had once talked about these men – tailors who sold poor

Chinese to plantations in Hawaii, outlaws who smuggled workers into the western world, and brokers who delivered brides to lonely men in the gold mountains of Gum Shan – the rich and mysterious frontiers of North America.

Despite those warnings, Yung's heart quickened as he began to smell real food – roast chicken, garlic, and other savory spices, emanating from the ship, wafting on the breeze.

The officer yelled boarding instructions, and Yung was ushered on board with his tiny knapsack of clothing. He could see another gangplank leading up to the front of the ship, where the man who was not his uncle had donned a coat and top hat and was hosting elegantly dressed men and women, Asian and Anglo, on a forward deck. There were men in military uniforms and a host of Chinese officials. Yung stared, his mouth watering as he watched them eat, and drink wine from long-stemmed glasses. He and the other children and teens were herded below, through narrow hallways, past crew cabins, and beyond rows of bunks crowded with shirtless Chinese sailors who sported brands on their chests and scars on their backs. Yung followed as they were taken down into what felt like the bottom of the ship, to a cargo hold that smelled of coal dust and stale urine. And there was a constant mechanical thrum coming through the walls that he could feel as well as hear.

As his eyes adjusted to the dimly lit space, Yung could see that the cargo hold had been converted into a living quarters, divided into racks of bunks and rows of low-walled pens, with woolen blankets and straw mattresses. He was assigned to a pen with five other boys, who looked at him warily. A group of peasant girls, some with bound feet, perhaps eight or nine years of age, were put in pens directly across from them, while the teenagers in silk cheongsams and lacy European dresses, with high necks and tight collars, were put in a locked wooden paddock toward the rear of the room. The iron bars suggested the place had previously been used for storing precious cargo. Yung watched the sailors regard the comely girls the way his mother and he used to hungrily stare at street vendors cooking fresh *siu mei*. That's when Yung realized the well-dressed girls had been locked away for their own protection.

'You will sleep here, you will live here, and you will spend the entire month at sea belowdecks,' barked a Caucasian man in a dark blue uniform. He spoke English, which Yung assumed only a handful of children understood. The man removed his cap and rubbed his chin, feeling the blond scruff of a close-cropped beard. He introduced himself as the ship's chief medical officer. 'You will stay here, otherwise you risk catching and spreading a coughing disease.' The doctor pointed to his chest. 'I will conduct daily health inspections. If one of you gets sick, or is stricken with a rash that bleeds, you will not be allowed to threaten the rest of the passengers – you will be thrown overboard. No exceptions. There is no mercy at sea. Is this understood?'

Yung nodded, wide-eyed as a Chinese crewman translated the doctor's words. The boys in his pen, the ones who had been lounging on the floor, immediately sat upright. Yung looked around, wondering who might be sick. He didn't dare sneeze for fear of being dragged back on deck and cast over the side.

There were hushed whispers followed by a nervous pause.

Then a horrible wailing began as the young doctor drew a long, hooked knife from a satchel and went about the room, cutting the soiled cotton bandages that bound the feet of many of the girls, both the rich and the poor. Yung could hear their crying as the girls' painful feet were touched, moved, the popping of bone and cartilage as they tried to flex and put pressure on their lotus-shaped stumps. For the younger ones he could tell that this was a euphoric feeling of freedom and relief, but for the older girls, their feet long since broken again and again, this brought more pain than comfort.

'You will feel better in a few weeks,' the doctor said as he threw the dirty bandages into a wooden bucket. The cotton smelled like blood and herbs and rot.

As girls sobbed, the elegant teens in the paddock sniped at them, 'Stop mewling. You're embarrassing yourselves. Show respect.'

Even as a little boy, Yung recognized their Yue dialect and understood they must be merchants' daughters, of a higher quality than the rest of the children. A few of the poor girls spat back at the teenagers until the sailors began hitting them with rattan sticks.

The older girls looked on, smiling proudly. Better to be a caged peacock, they must have thought, than to live free as a pigeon.

Yung sat down and noticed that the group of peasant girls across from him had kept to themselves. A few of them wiggled their toes for the first time in months and nursed the pale skin on their feet, but none of them cried.

The boys in his pen mocked them and sneered as they shouted, '*lou geoi*,' laughing until a crewman snapped at them.

Yung didn't know what *lou geoi* meant, but he knew the words were an insult of some kind. His mother used to fight back tears whenever Chinese men or European sailors whistled and called her that on the rutted streets of their village.

Yung noted how the girls all styled their hair in long braids and they wore dirty clothing made from hemp and ramie. They looked like the lowest of the low – poor girls whose parents had bound their daughters' feet in an effort to dress them up. Only one of the girls' hair was unbraided, and she also stood out because of her faded blue robe and wide belt.

Yung was beginning to ache for his mother when sailors brought rags and buckets of fresh water to each pen. He waited until the older boys were done cleaning up and then took his turn. As Yung washed his face and teeth, he gazed into the half-empty bucket of dirty water. His reflection rocked back and forth, swaying as the ship began to move.

He glanced around and noticed that one of the older boys had snatched the bucket from the nearby girls, who had just stared back in contempt. Yung thought about the sister he'd had for a brief moment, and then he carried his bucket to the peasant girls' side and offered it to them. They all looked at him strangely, suspiciously as he urged one of them to sit at the edge of the mattress. He knelt, placing one, then both of the girl's feet in the cool water. Yung had once watched his mother treat a cousin this way. He rubbed the arch of her foot; then pushed her toes back, stretching them gently with his small hands. As he washed the girl's feet with the damp cloth, she winced for a moment, inhaled deeply, then relaxed. He wrung out the towel and handed the cloth to another girl, before returning to his pen. There he found an unoccupied corner of the mattress as the boys looked at him with scorn.

That night, Yung woke as the steam engine rumbled loudly along with his empty stomach. He sat up and realized that the other boys were snoring and that the oldest, a stout bully name Jun, had taken many of the blankets, including Yung's, for himself. The cargo hold was cold now, and he clutched his knapsack on his small corner of the shared mattress. And as the ship rocked and swayed on the open sea, he realized that with each minute, each hour, he was being carried farther from his village, away from his mother, forever. He wiped his eyes, and in the glow of a single, wall-mounted lamp, Yung could see that some of the girls across from him were awake, staring back. They whispered among themselves and then lifted a corner of the blanket they were sharing.

'Little brother.' One of the girls motioned. 'Come over here.'

Yung glanced at his sleeping bunkmates. Then he stepped lightly, nervously, with bare feet on the cool wooden floor. He hesitated, worried that this might be some kind of cruel joke. Then one of the girls reached up, tugged his sleeve, and pulled him beneath the covers. They made room as he nestled among them. He felt cold feet next to his, hands and arms, as they patted his chest and shoulders.

'It's okay.' A girl spoke in a small voice. 'You're one of us.'

Yung looked at the girls. 'What do you mean?'

The girl in the blue robe sat up partway and peeked over at him as if the answer were obvious. She spoke Chinese with a thick accent. 'Nobody wants us either.'

Yung swallowed the bitter medicine of truth. He nodded, closed his eyes, and felt the tickling of their hair on his cheeks, on his neck, as they all settled in beneath the covers. Despite the sharing of the wash bucket, their clothing smelled old and musty, like his – reeking of weeks of smoke and dust. Yung didn't mind. Nor did he care what the other boys would think in the morning. He was used to people staring at him on the street – the villagers who'd spat at him or laughed. But for now he felt safely surrounded, comforted, as he drew a deep breath and melted into the girls' kindness.

The Water Trade

(1902)

If Yung had worried about being harassed by his former bunkmates and Jun in the morning, he had little to fear. Seasickness kept everyone in bed, eyes closed, groaning – everyone but Yung, that is.

The doctor told him his sea legs were a natural advantage of being the littlest, the smallest. Yung nodded and watched as the older boys and the young women turned pale and retched up the broth they'd been given. Vomit now speckled their clothing, their shoes, their shimmering gowns.

Yung busied himself by emptying the reeking pails of night soil, washing dinner tins, and ministering to the girls in his pen, helping them take sips of the ginger tea they'd been given to ease their nausea. His new bunkmates were always grateful, whispering, 'Thank you, Little Brother,' which had become his de facto name. They'd introduced themselves one by one as Gwai Ying, Quan Gow Sheung, Wong So, Leung Gin, Fong Muey, Mui-Ji, Hoi, and . . . *something else*, but he couldn't possibly keep track of who was who. They'd explained that the curious girl in the blue robe was Japanese and had been sent to China by her family, sold to an inn where she'd been working as a maid until the owner died and her contract was bought out. The strange girl smiled and spoke Chinese, but when she said her name, Yung couldn't understand the words. He addressed all of them as Big Sister.

On the fourth day, when most were beginning to recover – to sit up and walk about, to play cards or games with string – they were given solid food – the first real meal Yung had tasted in more than a week. The simple offering of sticky rice balls and dried fish made everyone moan with delight. Yung wanted to savor the salty rice, but like everyone else, he ate furiously, almost violently, chewing, swallowing, and gulping as though the food might be snatched from his hands at any moment.

Yung was licking his fingers after dinner when the doctor appeared with a crewman and made his normal round of inspections. Everyone stood as tall as they could, arms at their sides; no one dared to cough or sniffle or even breathe in a manner that might be confused with illness. They waited as the doctor slowly walked by, leather heels squealing on the floor, nostrils flaring. Occasionally he would stop to look into a mouth, or a shirt would be removed so he could examine the skin on a child's back.

Yung chewed his lip as the man, whose breath he could smell, stopped in front of him. Then he lit a cigarette and pushed Yung aside as he directed his attention to the girls, especially the one in the blue robe. He ran his fingers along her neck, removed her wooden hairpins, and toyed with the tresses that hung about her shoulders. He shook his head and then turned back to Yung, who stood out among the girls. The doctor patted him on the shoulder and moved on. Yung listened as the doctor chatted amiably with the other boys, telling them to stay out of trouble. He slapped Jun on the cheek and jerked his ear, playful, but hard enough to make his point. Then the doctor stopped at the paddock of older girls.

They all smiled and kowtowed. He snapped his fingers and said, 'That one.' He pointed to a girl in a lavender dress as a sailor stepped forward with a key and opened the groaning iron door.

27

The merchants' daughters seemed shocked, confused, and then compliant as they stepped away from the tall, slender girl.

'But . . . Sir Doctor, I'm not ill – not even seasick anymore,' the girl in lavender protested, pleading in her native tongue. 'I feel fine, look at me, my skin is perfect, and my hair is shiny and clean.' She tilted her chin as she shook her head and her tasseled earrings swayed back and forth. 'I haven't coughed once.'

The crewman translated as the doctor dropped his cigarette on the deck and snuffed it out with the tip of his shoe. 'I know. That's why you're coming with us.' He smiled politely as his words were translated into Cantonese. 'We will take care of you upstairs. We wouldn't want you wasting away down here.'

The color drained from the girl's face. She smoothed out the lace on her dress and nodded, seemingly resigned. Yung heard the doctor ask the girl, as he led her away, if she liked the taste of *baiju*, rice wine. And then they were gone, leaving nothing but the pregnant silence.

'They're not going to throw her overboard, are they?' Yung asked the girl in the blue robe. She didn't answer or seem to understand the question. But the boys snickered.

That night, after Yung and the girls finished dinner, they piled onto their mattress and played a whisper game. One would whisper something to the person next to her and then that phrase would be passed down the line and back again. It never came back unchanged, and that was the fun. Yung had seen the game played before in his village, but he'd never been included.

He waited, and the girl next to him finally turned and whispered, 'I'm a hairy dog that bites,' in Cantonese. He clapped a hand over his mouth to keep from laughing. He collected himself and then passed the message along to the Japanese girl in the blue robe. She looked confused, furrowed her brow, and did her best to whisper something on to the girl next to her.

The messages went back and forth, from 'My diaper is full' and 'Whipped with a cane' to 'You're my pretty servant' and 'Jun is your ugly lady-boss'. That one made Yung laugh out loud. When it was Yung's turn to make up a phrase, he thought of the silliest thing possible. He said to the girl in blue, 'I'm going to marry you.'

The Japanese girl crinkled her nose, then her eyes grew wide and she laughed.

But the phrase was taken more seriously as the words moved further down the line. The girls murmured it solemnly, sighed wearily, shook their heads, and eventually returned the message as though relaying a bit of bad news. To Yung it felt as though all the joy, all the laughter, had been snuffed out like a candle.

Yung didn't understand the sadness he had caused, even as the Japanese girl turned back and relayed the message that had only slightly changed. She looked embarrassed as she confessed, 'I am sorry. No one will ever marry us.'

Juju Reporting

(1962)

Ernest touched the tarnished band of gold on his ring finger and felt the groove worn into his skin from years of wearing it. He pondered the seaborne episode of his childhood, sipping a cup of oolong tea that had grown cold.

Ernest sighed as he gazed out the third-floor window of his tiny one-room apartment at the Publix Hotel. One aspect of Gracie's dementia was that she didn't tolerate men very well – she had even punched a male orderly at the hospital. Even Ernest was not exempt. As a result, Ernest and Gracie had lived apart for almost three years now. Not the retirement he'd imagined. He visited as often as possible on sunny days – that's what Juju called Gracie's happier, lucid moments – and he wrote to her on cloudy days, when she didn't feel like company. He missed her terribly, even when he was by her side – he ached for who she used to be. He longed for who he used to be as well.

Ernest finished his tea. He could hear passenger trains coming and going, as well as the wind through cracks in the panes of glass that had been covered with masking tape to hold the pieces together and ward off the chill. King Street Station was one block away, and he imagined nattily dressed people streaming from the velvet-curtained Pullman cars, to be embraced by loved ones – the warmth, the smell of familiar cologne or perfume, the rush and excitement that came with a long-awaited reunion. But he also recalled the haunting emptiness of waving goodbye. The sunrise colored by thick, ashy smoke from torched fields and burning buildings. And the depth of sadness plumbed by the remembrance of falling asleep among dozens of seasick children in the belly of a ship that smelled like fear and despair.

Ernest could almost feel the rain and the mist in the evening sky, as much as the melancholy. He stretched his back as he noticed an illuminated spire in the distance that could only be the top of the Space Needle.

He thought about his long-lost mother as he regarded the hairpin she'd given him so many decades before. That tarnished bit of copper – the jade phoenix he now knew as Fenghuang – made him feel guilty for not missing her more, as though sixty years later he had somehow failed her as a son. At least he'd survived. And the sad truth was, he just couldn't remember what she looked like. He didn't possess a single photograph. He could always remember how she smelled, though – sweet, like fresh watermelon, mangoes, and bayberries. While reading a science book years later, he learned that's what a body smells like when it's starving.

Over the years Ernest had always thought more about the many girls on that ship and what might have happened to them – especially whenever he saw an elderly woman in a market in Chinatown, the story of her life written in the lines on her face.

He imagined that if they'd been fortunate, the ones who could walk probably ended up as servants in fancy, ivy-covered manors in Broadmoor or Laurelhurst. Or perhaps they'd found work in a laundry or a sewing factory. The choice few might have been able to earn or marry their way out of their contracts, to eventually have a home on Beacon Hill, and children who would have attended school at Franklin or Garfield High. They would have enjoyed all the trappings of a relatively normal life.

The merchants' daughters, in all likelihood, had ended up as picture brides, married to strangers they'd never seen except in black-and-white photographs.

Unlike the least fortunate of all – the sorrowful girls who had been so kind to him. Like him, they'd been sold by their parents because their families couldn't feed them or didn't want them, or they were mere runaways tricked into thinking they'd get rich in America by working as maids. Many of those girls who came to Seattle ended up at the Aloha, the Tokyo, or the Diamond House, or perhaps the old Eastern Hotel – low-rent brothels. The girls were indentured servants with unfair contracts, who might run away to the police only to be returned, like stray animals, to their owners.

All of these women, Ernest thought – the poor, the merchants' daughters, and the handful of working girls who survived – they'd all be grandmothers by now. With secrets kept, stories hidden, and respectful children who would never dare to ask about their youth.

Ernest's reverie was interrupted by footsteps in the hallway.

He listened as the radiator pinged and hot-water pipes rattled within the walls. As he waited, he drew a deep breath, and then relaxed when he heard the tromping of work boots in the groaning, creaking mahogany stairwell of the old Chinatown hotel.

Perhaps it was his old friend, Pascual Santos, a longtime resident of the Publix who'd helped Ernest move in when he lost his home.

Maybe he's hoping I'll join him for a night out on the town, Ernest thought. He knew he should answer the door, but he didn't feel much like socializing.

In fact, he'd considered moving someplace nicer, but whenever he was woken by chatter in the hallway – greetings in Chinese, Japanese, and Tagalog, some polite, some stern, a few happy, rambling voices that slurred from too much drugstore screw-top wine – Ernest realized that he felt strangely comfortable here. At this pay-by-the-week purgatory, the rooms were tiny, the floors were warped, the bathrooms shared, and the old floral wallpaper was perpetually peeling, but the bar for achievement was remarkably nonexistent, and he was fine with that. Because the Publix was an old workingmen's home, a tobacco-stained hideaway where lost individuals found solace. Where the elderly tended to their gardens on the roof, and the children of the few families who lived here played basketball in the basement. And for Ernest the hotel was also mere miles from all the people he'd grown up with and cared about.

Ernest was about to make a fresh pot of tea when he heard footsteps again, this time the unmistakable rap-tap of a woman's heels on the wooden floor outside his door, and a knock.

'Dad, it's me. Open up.' The voice in the hallway belonged to his daughter Juju. Ernest had been so busy driving people to and from the fair that he'd ignored the small stack of pink While You Were Out messages that had piled up in his mailbox downstairs, courtesy of the hotel's front desk manager. Now he guessed they were from her.

Juju switched to an innocent singsong. 'Da-aaaad, I know you're in there.'

His daughters always worried about him, especially in the years since Gracie had fallen ill. Even Hanny, who lived in Las Vegas, which seemed like a world away, called at least once a week, long-distance charges and all. Ernest rubbed his eyes as he looked in the chipped mirror on the wall. He finger-combed his thinning, salt-and-pepper hair and straightened his well-worn sweater, which had only one button left.

He cleared his throat and donned a smile as he opened the door.

33

'Juju!' he said, wide-eyed. 'Come in and get warm. I'm so sorry I haven't returned your calls. I've been so busy these days – running people around town. Your mom okay? Have you eaten?' As he gave her a hug and she kissed his cheek, he realized that he hadn't shaved.

His daughter loosened her raincoat and stepped inside, groaning as she looked around. She pointed to a patch of old paint blistering on the ceiling and a leaky pipe that dripped into a mop bucket on the floor. 'Dad, if they're not going to fix this place up you should at least let me do it for you. Seriously, how can you live like this? Oh, and I'm pushing forty, so feel free to call me Judy anytime.'

'Hanny doesn't seem to mind—'

Juju interrupted. 'Hannah also wears a three-foot headpiece with ostrich plumes that glitter, and struts around in a sequined G-string for money. Her name doesn't go on a byline like mine does.'

Ernest smiled and tried not to roll his eyes. He couldn't help but be proud of his daughter, a reporter for the *Seattle Post-Intelligencer*. She'd started off at the *Northwest Times*, then landed a job at the big daily, covering the Ladies Garden Club and meetings of the Women's Auxiliary of the King County Library. But somehow Juju (Ernest couldn't bring himself to call her Judy) had fought her way up to a regular beat covering Chinatown, the Central District, and Rainier Beach. Sure, she'd probably landed the assignment because she was ambiguously Asian – and more to the point, because no one else wanted to cover the colored neighborhoods. But her region was also riddled with racial tension, and dubious development deals on every corner and vacant lot – fertile journalistic soil for someone with a sharp, eager plow, and a shoulder for hard work.

Ernest was proud of Hanny too, but it would be an understatement to say that her vocation as a Stardust showgirl (and occasional magician's assistant) had always struck too close to home. He didn't care for her profession the way Howard Hughes didn't care for reporters, or the way Elvis didn't care for the army. Ernest told himself that he was *happy that Hanny was happy*. And honestly, he was impressed that his younger daughter had gotten the job given that she was half-Chinese and didn't look like Jayne Mansfield or the cookie-cutter showgirls he'd seen on postcards. But Hanny was extraordinarily tall (she called it poised) and royally confident (she called it refined) and he guessed that had carried the day.

Occasionally, Ernest worried about her working at places like the Sands, which had made Nat King Cole eat alone in his suite rather than be seen downstairs in the restaurant. But the times were slowly changing. And Hanny seemed immune to controversy. She was Miranda in Shakespeare's *The Tempest*, practically gushing, 'Oh, wonder! How many goodly creatures are there in Las Vegas! How beauteous mankind is! O brave new world, that has such people as Frank Sinatra in't!'

Ernest was less impressed, though he had to admit that he loved to hear about Hanny's run-ins with Billy Daniels and Peter Lawford, even if he had to turn a deaf ear to stories about the drunken marriage proposals she seemed to receive on a nightly basis.

Ernest offered Juju an orange Nesbitt's soda and sat down in his favorite reading chair. He watched as she drank half the bottle in one long swig. She wiped her mouth with the back of her hand and took a seat on his lumpy vinyl chesterfield.

'So what brings you here?' he asked.

'Well,' said Juju, 'I think I found a way to finally get my byline on the front page of the paper. It has to do with you and Mom – but mainly you—'

'Is she okay?' Ernest asked. 'Has she had a relapse? Let me get my shoes on—'

'No, Dad – she's fine. She's, you know, pretty much how she is. She still thinks I'm her nurse half the time, a maid the other half. She's happy, pleasant, in and out of her own world, no nightmares lately,' Juju said with a resigned shrug. 'Better than ever.'

'Then what's the problem?' Ernest asked as he sat back in his chair.

Juju looked at him, one eyebrow raised. 'Oh, it's not a problem. It's just that I convinced my editor to let me write a then-and-now piece about the grand opening of the new world's fair, seen through the eyes of some old-timers who happened to attend the original Alaska–Pacific–Yukon Expo, fifty-something years ago. Granted, that story angle isn't particularly unique, but along the way I dug up some details that could make *my* story stand out above the rest. And since I'm on deadline, I was thinking that I'd fact-check with you about some of the details. Because I remember you talking about how you went to that first expo as a little kid.'

Ernest nodded politely. 'Oh, I don't remember all that much, really.'

'Well, do you remember anything like this, by chance?' Juju reached into her handbag and retrieved a small stack of newspaper clippings. She handed one to her father, who donned a set of reading glasses.

The article was from *The Kennewick Courier* circa 1909 and read:

Seattle – A boy, the charge of the Washington Children's Home Society, was one of the prizes offered at the exposition. His name is Ernest and maybe he will have a surname if the winner, holding the proper ticket, comes to claim him.

Ernest opened his mouth to speak. Closed it. And then opened it again. 'That's interesting . . . I mean . . . they gave away a lot of peculiar things at the fair . . .'

'Dad.' Juju pointed to the name in the article. 'It says *Ernest.*

Was this you? I mean – you once told me how you ended up at the Washington Children's Home after you came here from China. And you said you were given a job as a houseboy after the world's fair. You told me that's where you met Mom.'

Ernest tried to laugh. 'Why would you think that? Ernest is a pretty common name – Ernest Hemingway, Ernest Shackleton, Ernest Borgnine, Ernest—'

'Oh my God, it *is* you.'

'Look . . .'

'Dad, I'm an investigative reporter. This is what I do for a living. I can see the truth written on your face. I can tell just by the tone of your voice.'

Ernest furrowed his brow and drew a deep breath, exhaling slowly. It was one thing to lose himself in memories, but the last thing he wanted to do was share the whole sordid story with his daughter. Let alone one hundred thousand readers of the *Seattle Post-Intelligencer*. He coughed and tried changing the subject.

'Has your mother's memory improved anymore these days?'

'I guess, because she's the one who told me.'

Ernest blinked. 'Told you what?'

'Dad, she's the one who told me that a boy had been raffled off as a prize at the AYP – she said *you* were that boy.' Juju stared back. 'She was listening to the radio and heard a commercial for the new world's fair. Then she started talking to herself. I thought she was spouting nonsense until I looked it up.'

Ernest felt the warmth in his chest grow cold. 'What . . . are you talking about?'

'Mom,' Juju said as she put a hand on his arm. 'She's begun saying things. Most of the time she still doesn't make a lot of sense, but every once in a while – I think she's starting to remember.'

* * *

After his daughter left, Ernest turned on the small Philco swivel-screen he'd gotten on clearance from Hikida Furniture and Appliance, because of a broken dial. It worked fine, though he had to change the channel with a pair of needle-nose pliers. He tried to relax, listening to the hum of the television as the color picture tube warmed up and the distorted image on-screen slowly came into focus.

As far as Juju's questions, Ernest had stalled. He'd bought a little time by saying he was tired and promising to come over tomorrow afternoon to talk. He'd wanted to drop everything and see Gracie tonight, but he knew she'd be going to bed soon and that evenings were when she was most fragile.

Let her rest.

Ernest thought about the people he knew – the ones he'd grown up with as well as his neighbors here at the Publix. He suspected that everyone his age, of his vintage, had a backstory, a secret that they'd never shared. For one it might be a forsaken husband back in Japan. For another it could be a son or daughter from a previous marriage in China. For others perhaps the secret shame was a father they didn't talk to anymore, or a baby they'd given to a neighbor, never to be seen again. Or perhaps a vocational secret – backroom gambling, bringing rum down from Canada during Prohibition, or the personal, private horrors that lay hidden behind the bars, ribbons, and medals of a military record.

We all have things we don't talk about, Ernest thought. Even though, more often than not, those are the things that make us who we are.

Ernest remembered the AYP and wondered how much he could share without giving up Gracie's part of the story. Moreover, he worried about how long it would be before Gracie inadvertently gave herself up. What would Hanny and Juju think if they learned that their mother was once someone else – something else? To him, Gracie would always be more than a survivor of circumstance. She was a person of strength, a woman of fierce independence. But if her past ever got out, her gossipy friends at church, their old neighbors – no one would look at her the same.

Ernest rubbed his temples and watched Ed Sullivan as the show broadcast live from the refurbished Seattle Opera House, which sat adjacent to the new expo's pillarless Coliseum. He offered a warbling introduction to Harry Belafonte and Miriam Makeba, who danced and sang 'Love Tastes Like Strawberries'. That performance was followed by the Amazing Unus, a local equilibrist who could balance anything on one finger – an umbrella, a sword, a padded barstool, even a six-foot scale model of the Space Needle.

Ernest glanced at the clock on the wall, next to a calendar from the Tsue Chong Noodle Company featuring a beautiful Chinese girl in a traditional dress, but with heavy make-up and ruby lips. The calendar was three years old.

He whispered, 'Gracie, where did the time go?'

The Floating World

(1902)

Yung wished that someone had a pocket watch or at least a bundle of timekeeping incense, the kind the Buddhist monks in his village had used to mark the hours of the sun. Instead, the best anyone could muster was a piece of chalk that was used to keep track of the days, according to meals and their regular bedtime. Yung watched as one of the girls made another hash mark and quietly counted to nineteen.

As the ship rocked and the time passed, Yung had mourned his mother terribly – her memory waxing and waning like a ghostly echo. But he'd also been reasonably well fed for the first time in his life, surrounded by big sisters who laughed and smiled. And on his better days, he'd had his impressionable young heart realigned, set on foreign promises: the Hawaiian Islands, tropical sunshine, an endless horizon of warm water, and a beggars' feast of sugarcane. They'd been told that there would be fat stalks everywhere they looked, just waiting to be sliced and peeled and chewed, nectar waiting to be savored. Yung clung to that hope, and the illusion that his mother would survive and that someday he'd grow up and make enough money to send for her. But even his tender imagination suspected that was folly.

And sadly, so were the islands, when a constellation of sores had burst on the chest, arms, and legs of one of the other boys. Because of that illness, the ship was unable to make port in Honolulu. The boy, delirious with fever, had been taken to an isolation room and later his body was buried at sea, as the ship continued to the Northwest.

After that sad event, a rainbow appeared in the form of an oil-stained canvas curtain, which was hung from a rope that kept the nearby boys, Jun included, sequestered from the rest of the children in the steerage hold. The boys had been officially quarantined and were now fed from a separate serving kettle. The doctor paid special attention to them, often checking two or three times each day, though they were as healthy as ever. Or at least as loud as ever – they heckled the girls through the curtain. Especially Jun, who found perpetual amusement in singing vulgar songs, much to the disgust of everyone but the passing sailors. He also teased the girls behind the bars, loudly speculating about which one of them would be taken next. The girls shouted back with cutting words – the kinds of insults that could be hurled only from the safety of their cage.

Yung and the peasant girls stayed out of the fray, giggling until Jun focused his rage in their direction. He ranted until one of the passing sailors shouted in English and everyone laughed and giggled a bit more as they settled down for the night, feeling safe, knowing that despite his bark, Jun's bite was trapped behind the curtain.

Yung fell asleep feeling sorry for the rest of the boys in quarantine.

As Yung slept that night he dreamed about his mother. In his dream he'd come home early from his chores. Hungry and bored, he rummaged through the old opium tin that served as his mother's memory box. Inside was a collection of dried flowers, feathers, shell buttons, and one of his teeth that had fallen out. She'd put it on the roof of their house for a month, an old superstition she believed might make his permanent tooth grow in faster. He was sniffing her empty perfume bottles when he heard his mother's laughter downstairs and that of a strange man. Yung searched frantically for a place to hide as they stumbled into the tiny one-room apartment. In his dream Yung dashed beneath his mother's bed, just in time, as two pairs of shoes entered the room, heavy leather boots and his mother's faded yellow lotus slippers. Yung could smell a mixture of alcohol, tobacco, and sweat. He remained motionless. Silent as clothing fell to the floor, his mother's old mandarin dress and the man's starched white collar. Yung heard the dance of metal as her hairpin fell in front of him. He reached out and grabbed it while the steel springs above him bent as the couple fumbled about the bed. Yung heard muffled sounds that seemed like crying amid the heavy, pained breathing. He gripped the hairpin and imagined shoving the long, sharp needle up into the mattress.

In the darkened hold, Yung opened his eyes, smelled the musty woolen blanket, and heard the thrum of the ship's steam engine. He felt the gentle rocking.

It was only a dream. My mother is gone.

Then Yung heard a timid cry and felt movement next to him. He rolled over and rubbed his eyes, thinking that perhaps he was still dreaming as he saw that Jun had climbed on top of the girl next to him. She was struggling, whimpering, and his hand covered her mouth, while his other hand fumbled with the buttons on her shirt. His large frame draped over her like a blanket, pressing her tiny body into the straw mattress.

Yung's eyes met the larger boy's gaze in the dim lamplight. 'Look away, baby brother,' the boy hissed.

Yung closed his eyes, then opened them. It wasn't a nightmare; it was real.

'And if you tell, I'll do this to the rest of your big sisters. Then I'll do it to you.'

Yung's heart raced. He was confused, terrified as he slowly turned away. Jun was three times his age and five times his size. But Yung's hand moved as though it had a mind of its own as he reached beneath his pillow and pulled out the long brass hairpin. He felt tightness in his chest and a sick sensation of dread in his stomach as he heard the girl struggle, but he was

42

paralyzed with fear. Then Yung saw that the Japanese girl next to him was stirring in the gloaming. He watched her eyes widen, then she snatched the hairpin from his hand and scrambled over him, her bluish robe a blur, flowing water. She raised her arm as though reaching for the ceiling, then she brought it down like a hammer and drove the long copper needle into the flesh of the boy's posterior. It made a sound that could have come from a butcher shop, the slap of a fist on a haunch of meat. The boy screamed. Yung watched as Jun stumbled out of bed, landed hard on the floor, where he curled and writhed in pain, cursing and shouting, crying as tears streamed down his face, '*Lou geoi!* Dirty *lou geoi!*' He continued shouting that she was lower than an alley whore who sold her body for scraps of food.

And as the boy rolled to his knees, Yung watched his mother's keepsake swing about, stuck like a dragonfly on flypaper. He reached for the hairpin, pulling it free as Jun limped about the room clutching the back of his pants.

'I'm not *lou geoi!*' the Japanese girl shouted, spittle flying from her mouth. She was being restrained by the girls who had now woken in equal proportions of confusion, shock, and amusement. Others tended to the girl Jun had attacked.

'I'm *Fahn!*' the Japanese girl yelled, despite being half as tall – a menacing, ferocious eight-year-old screaming in the face of the teenage boy. She shouted again and gritted her teeth as Jun retreated behind the curtain and sailors burst into the room. Then she pointed at her chest. 'I'm Fahn.'

Yung didn't know if that was a nickname. It was a strange word, in a strange dialect. To him the words meant: I'm girl.

As the others let her go, she sat next to Yung and caught her breath. Her eyes welling with emotion, she smiled at him and said, 'Are you still going to marry me?'

Everyone Plays, Nobody Wins

(1962)

The morning after Juju had visited, Ernest found himself dwelling on memories of that night in the cargo hold. He remembered how a few days later the ship finally reached Victoria, British Columbia, where the boys and girls were separated with little fanfare or explanation. I lost my baby sister after two days, Ernest thought. Then I lost my new big sisters in less than four weeks. I didn't even get to tell them goodbye.

Beneath a sliver of a moon he'd been transferred with the other boys to a small sloop, presumably bound for Port Townsend, Washington – a gateway to the salmon canneries and sawmills. Or perhaps the oyster fields. The boys watched as the dark city slid by in the night a few hundred yards away. But they had only a glimpse before they were tied into burlap bags and laid on the deck. The sailors had told them the subterfuge was for the boys' own good, in case the Coast Guard stopped the boat and customs officials wanted to inspect the cargo. They'd been told to lie perfectly still, silent, and not to worry. But on that first night, amid a flurry of ships' horns, yelling, and what sounded like firecrackers, Ernest remembered clutching his mother's hairpin.

In his mind's eye the smugglers were the infamous Ben Ure and Lawrence 'Pirate' Kelly, men known for bringing illegal Chinese workers into Washington via Deception Pass. But now, as a grown man, Ernest knew he'd probably been projecting. Maybe that was something he'd read in a history book – something to explain away the horrible, helpless feeling of being hoisted up and tossed overboard, falling through the air, crashing into the frigid water and tasting the salt. He heard cries for help and then the muffled gurgles of the other boys as they sank. Somehow he'd managed to use that hairpin to rip a hole large enough to fit his fingers through, then his hands, large enough to tear his way free. The other boys had drowned by the time Ernest reached the surface, their shrouded bodies bumping him gently in the darkness, bobbing on the incoming tide like driftwood.

Ernest closed his eyes and remembered lights flickering on the horizon, rising and falling beneath the waves as he dog-paddled to the nearest shore, shivering, his lips and fingers numb. The black water was so cold his skin tingled and then burned.

He saw the search beacon of a Coast Guard vessel in the distance, moving away from him. He was terrified and exhausted, at the point of drowning when a policeman on shore patrol must have spotted him – dove in and pulled him to shore. The policeman shivered as he wrapped Ernest in his coat, which smelled like coffee and cigarettes.

The policeman's name was Ernest, and so Yung had been given his rescuer's name, though he never saw the man again. But he never forgot his words: 'You're a lucky kid. In my twenty years on the job, Dead Man's Bay has always lived up to its title.'

Ernest shook himself out of his daydreams and checked his watch. He grabbed his coat and hat, and went to meet his friend Pascual at Osami's Barbershop.

They both lived at the Publix now, Ernest's three years to Pascual's thirty. With his friend's fluctuating night-time schedule, weeks could go by without them running into one another, so they'd adopted a routine of meeting every week for a shave and a haircut and then a late breakfast at the Linyen, Don Ting, or the Little Three Grand Cafe. His friend was an ardent fan of the many comic books and pulp magazines Osami always had on hand amid the local Asian papers. Pascual called the barbershop his reading room, so Ernest wasn't surprised to walk in and find him already engrossed in an issue of *My Greatest Adventure*. The cover story was titled 'I Was Marooned on Earth!'

That's how Ernest felt.

'*Kuya* Ernest, I almost didn't think you'd show up. What happened, you been avoiding me or something?' his friend asked as he reclined in a red leather chair while the barber slathered menthol-scented shaving cream on Pascual's dark, windburned cheeks and his salt-and-pepper sideburns. 'I went to the Black and Tan last night. That widow, Dolores, was asking about you. Maybe it's time the Lone Ranger got back in the saddle. I know that, technically, you're still married and all, and I know you've done so much for Gracie these past few years. I'm just thinking, maybe it's time. Maybe she would want you to be happy or something.'

Ernest shook his head and smiled at the comforting sound of his friend's Filipino accent, the way the word *thing* came out *ting*. Ernest grabbed a refolded newspaper from a wooden rack and sat in the adjacent chair as the barber's wife rolled down his shirt collar and wrapped a seersucker cape over his shoulders. She pinned the fabric around his neck with a silver clip as he opened the paper. The coupons had already been cut out.

'The usual, Mr Ernest?' she asked.

Ernest nodded and spoke to Pascual, whom he could see in the mirror, both of their images reflected back and forth, shrinking toward infinity. 'I've been busy. Besides, which one is Dolores?'

His friend paused as Osami drew a straight razor across Pascual's left cheek and then wiped the excess shaving cream on a towel draped over his arm. 'So many older, single ladies who remember you from when you used to come with Gracie. I talk to them, but they always just want to know about you. And that's your cruel magic, my handsome friend – you do better than me, even when you're not in the building.'

As the barber's wife put a cloth on Ernest's shoulder and wrapped a steaming towel around his face, Pascual spoke in a more serious tone. 'You know, someone else passed by the club last night. Your daughter Juju – she went around, asked everyone willing to talk, and her questions were all about you, my mysterious *kaibigan*.'

Ernest felt his stomach tighten, and the towel felt suffocating.

'But no worries, no one said too much, mainly because nobody there knows anything. But you know your *bata*, she can be pretty insistent. She kept asking people about your childhood, about the neighborhood you grew up in, where you went to school, if you were adopted or anything, if you ever went by another name. Half the bar knows her from the newspaper or as your daughter, so they just played along, but I think she scared the other half. They probably pegged you for some kind of red spy or something. Which only made you more intriguing to Dolores.' Pascual shook his head. 'Magic, my friend.'

Magic, Ernest thought. That was how Pascual somehow made a living as a full-time gambler and part-time nine-ball hustler at the Palace, a local disturbance in the shape of a pool hall. Pascual had once been a member of the International Longshoremen and Warehousemen's Union, until the national branch called them Communists and tossed everyone out. He couldn't fight the accusations because Filipino workers were being deported for associating with improper organizations. That's how they'd met, more than thirty years ago, both as newly naturalized citizens.

'You didn't tell Juju—' Ernest asked.

Pascual cut him off. 'Nah, I didn't say much. Not that I can remember anyway.' Then he shrugged. 'Aw, I might have said a few things, but then to make sure I didn't spill the beans, I switched to Tagalog, started talking like I just stepped off the boat from Luzon, which isn't too hard after a few whiskey sours. Juju just laughed and went around, kept asking folks, but – you know, she hit the No-No Boys pretty hard back when she was a cub reporter, tore up the whole neighborhood, so even those who know her aren't inclined to say too much. And me, I wouldn't give you up for a million dollars, on my mother's grave.' Pascual crossed himself, then blew a kiss toward the old tin ceiling, painted white. 'Rest in peace, Mama. *Diyos pagpalain*.'

'God bless us all,' the barber's wife said as she removed the towel from Ernest's face and began applying shaving cream to his cheeks with a small boar-bristle brush. Ernest opened the newspaper and flipped through the local news pages, searching until he found her byline: Judy Young. And her piercing photo next to a neighborhood feature titled 'WE MUST SAVE PIKE PLACE MARKET,' SAYS WING LUKE, SEATTLE'S FIRST ORIENTAL CITY COUNCILMAN. The headline seemed fairly benign, but the article about rescuing the market, which had fallen into disrepair after all the Japanese farmers and their families were taken away, didn't pull any punches. The old internment camps were a taboo subject, but Juju had no problem addressing that particular elephant in the room.

Ernest remembered when his daughter had graduated from the University of Washington with a degree in journalism. He'd joked and called her Lois Lane.

She'd said, 'I'd rather you call me Nellie Bly.'

Ernest heard a door chime and lowered the paper as a pair of Chinese boys, probably still in grade school, came into the barbershop with stubby pencils tucked behind their ears. One of them held up a pad of paper that had been printed with grids for Saturday's lottery numbers and stamped by the Sun May Store around the corner.

Ernest said, 'No thanks. I don't play,' while he watched Pascual fill out ten sheets as though each set of numbers was part of a complex math equation, a riddle that could be solved with sound reasoning, cunning, and a pinch of guile. Then he handed the boys a sawbuck from his money clip and flipped them a silver dollar to split between them for running his lottery picks back to the mercantile.

'Hey, Donnie, if I win that ten thousand dollars,' Pascual shouted as they scurried to the shop next door, 'I'll give you each five – no, ten percent, eh!'

Ernest noticed Osami and his wife glancing at one another, eyebrows raised. Then they shook their heads in tandem and continued shaving. He listened as the barber's wife spoke to her husband in Japanese, and then chuckled. She switched back to English and patted Pascual on the shoulder. 'People been playing that lottery ever since I was born.' She extended the word *born* into two even syllables. 'Nobody ever win that big prize money – nobody. And I guarantee, if someone ever does, you can bet it'll be a Sun May cousin.'

Ernest smiled and stared out the window at Chinatown, a neighborhood not without crime or scandal, but no more or less than the Central District, or Fremont, Rainier Beach, or downtown Seattle for that matter. Now Juju was canvassing the neighborhood.

She's tenacious, Ernest thought, just like her mother. Juju was placing small bets all over town, like Pascual playing the lottery, hoping to eventually cash in.

Rising from Grace

(1962)

An hour later Ernest regarded a plastic angel that dangled from the rear-view mirror of Juju's red Volkswagen Beetle. As she drove them from Chinatown to her home on the south side of Seattle's Queen Anne Hill, the ornament swayed back and forth and its golden thread entangled the figure's halo, leaving the heavenly messenger looking as though it had been lynched.

'Since when did you become the outwardly religious type?' Ernest asked.

'It was a gift,' Juju said. 'From one of Mom's old friends from church. You know how they are, everyone's my auntie and all of them are hoping I settle down, find a nice man to take care of me, maybe a doctor or a lawyer – or maybe just their acne-scarred nephew. They want me to have kids, go to PTA meetings, and host cakewalks. Those ladies are always seeking to save my soul, one religious trinket at a time.'

'Amen.' Ernest nodded, remembering the last time he'd heard the bells at the Baptist church on King Street. He hadn't been there in years, mainly because that was always Gracie's church, while Ernest considered himself a deist, agnostic, Shinto Jesuit – a mishmash, a spiritual refugee who had fled an oppressive regime as a child and could never assimilate anywhere else. Though the ladies at church were nice, and he did miss playing bingo, pinochle, and mah-jongg on Tuesday and Thursday nights.

'Now that I've agreed to pick you up,' Juju said, lighting a cigarette and changing the subject, 'you're going to give me the whole story about your childhood, yes?'

Ernest cracked the window and watched her menthol smoke swirl away. He noticed burn marks on the dashboard where Juju's cigarettes had melted the plastic. 'I swear to tell the truth,' he said. 'The whole truth and nothing but the truth . . .'

'So help you God?'

Ernest chuckled. 'So help me and the poor folks at the Black and Tan.'

'So, Uncle Paz told you I made the rounds last night?' Juju asked. 'Sorry, Dad, that's just me doing my job as always, lots of spadework – you understand how that goes. Write hard, die free – rah, rah, rah. Besides, a good reporter never knows what other stories might be uncovered along the way.'

Ernest grimaced.

'Do you know who was the first Asian person to win a Pulitzer?' Juju answered before Ernest could respond. 'Carlos Romulo, in 1941, who went on to become the president of the United Nations General Assembly. Do you know who the first woman was – in the category of Journalism?'

'No.' Ernest felt a tad carsick. 'Though I'm certain you're about to tell me . . .'

'Anne O'Hare McCormick – who went on to join the editorial board at the *New York Times*. And do you know who the first Asian woman was?'

Ernest smiled grimly and said, 'I'm guessing there hasn't been one but the leading candidate works for the *Seattle Post-Intelligencer* and has a habit of shaking down old men who live at the Publix Hotel.'

'Dad – you know me better than that. I'm as careerist as anyone, but this isn't all about me and it's not all about you, it's about what those reporters had in common. They weren't afraid to turn over a few rocks and look at the squishy things underneath. It's about *all* the marginalized people who never get their stories told properly. And, yes, I can understand how, like you, some folks might not be tremendously inclined to talk about the past, but eventually someone will. Might as well be to me – your daughter.' Juju smiled and patted his hand. 'Trust me, I'll make you look good.'

Ernest chewed his lip. *It's not me that I'm worried about.* He watched the green light turn red. He waved absently to a street musician on the corner.

'I'll tell you everything I can,' he hedged, as he allowed himself a little white lie. 'But I think I should talk to your mother first. We haven't had a meaningful conversation in more than a year, and even then . . .'

Ernest sighed. He didn't know how to explain that *his* childhood was also Gracie's childhood. And that whatever indignities he'd suffered through, hers were a thousand times worse – especially in the eyes of their friends and neighbors.

'Do you suppose . . . ?' Ernest hesitated. He didn't want to get his hopes up. 'Do you really think she'll recognize me today? I mean – it's been a while . . .'

Ash fell onto the steering wheel column and Juju stubbed out her cigarette in the ashtray. She coughed and then drew a deep breath, letting the air out slowly in an uneasy sigh that was more of a suppressed groan as she pulled into a steep driveway. Her ivy-covered Victorian home sat perched amid magnolias that had been there since before she was born, overshadowed by an array of new television antennas that towered above the hill, stretching toward the overcast sky.

She wrenched on the parking brake. 'I guess we'll find out.'

* * *

Do you know who I am? Those are the words Ernest said over and over in his mind as he sat across from his wife, who was napping in the living room. Ernest sat fidgeting as though he were a little boy again, curiously regarding the framed photographs that decorated the walls, the end table, and the fireplace mantel. Family portraits, some featuring a younger-looking Gracie, who smiled with a familiar, mischievous sparkle in her eyes. That twinkle shone from their wedding photo, on vacation in San Francisco, at graduation. Juju explained that Dr Luke had recommended surrounding her with photos from her past.

Gracie, in real life, reclined in an easy chair, motionless.

Juju greeted her mother as though she were awake and merely listening with her eyes closed. Ernest watched as his daughter picked up a brush and smoothed out Gracie's thinning hair, tinged with silver. She fixed her mother's coffee-stained pajama top where her buttons had been fastened out of order. Then she gently held the elder woman's hands and whispered something in her ear. Gracie, who hadn't yet opened her eyes, didn't respond.

Juju looked back at Ernest. 'She's kind of stubborn these days. I swear she ignores me just to irritate me.'

'Don't . . .' Gracie said. 'Don't talk about me like I'm not even here.'

Ernest heard the lucidity in her voice.

'Well hello, Ma. I didn't even know you were awake. Dad is here. Ernest, remember? He's the boy you mentioned – the boy who was raffled off at the fair all those years ago. Remember the fair we talked about?' Juju spoke slowly and loudly, as though her mother were hard of hearing. 'Here he is. Look, he's all grown-up now, just like you. And he came all the way over from Chinatown to see you today. I thought you might know some of the same people.' She leaned back and whispered to Ernest, 'I'm expecting the full story when we're done here.'

Gracie nodded pleasantly and stretched her slender arms into a threadbare robe that had been draped across the back of her chair. She said something about the chill as she slipped her feet into mismatched slippers. She blinked at him and then at Juju. Then she turned her attention to the view of Puget Sound, dotted with the V-wakes of pleasure boats, the misty green Olympic Mountains, and a tiny hummingbird that flitted about a bird feeder hanging from a soffit outside the living-room window. She sniffled and seemed to tear up as she pointed a trembling finger at the bird, which zipped up and down, back and forth, like a bumblebee with a long red needle for a beak.

Ernest looked at his daughter and then past the bird, south toward the Century 21 Expo: the silhouette of the new Space Needle towering above the sweeping curve of the monorail, the pyramid-shaped roof of the new Washington State Coliseum, and the colonnades and vaulted arches of the United States Science Pavilion. He'd heard that the trees that were dug up in front of his house had been replanted there. That row of hardwood now lined one of the grand pavilions.

'Ma, Dad is here to talk to you. And chat about the fair,' Juju said.

Her mother blanched at the sound of Juju's words.

'Oh,' Gracie said with surprise. 'We shouldn't talk about the *af-fair.*'

Juju laughed and shook her head. 'No, Ma. Ernest is here to talk about the Alaska–Yukon–Pacific Expo – *the great big world's fair,* remember? He was there, just like you, so I thought you two might have a little visit, become reacquainted. Maybe you can share some of your stories about the old days. How's that sound? He'd love to hear some of your memories, your tall tales. Maybe he can answer some questions – help you fill in the blanks, you know.'

Gracie had ignored him. But when Juju wasn't watching, Ernest could have sworn he saw his wife wink and suppress a knowing smile.

Juju said to Ernest, 'I'll go make us some fresh tea – see if we have some cookies or something.' She switched on a shelf-top Radionette and tuned in to KRAB, where the local balladeer Ron Holden was crooning his hit single 'Love You So'. The song had made headlines for cracking the *Billboard* top ten, but most local stations, like KJR, refused to play it.

'I like your taste in music,' Ernest said. He had a deep abiding weakness for love songs, ballads, and musicians of color.

'What can I say? I am my father's daughter,' Juju said as she turned up the volume. 'I'll be in the kitchen. Just shout if you need me.'

Ernest smiled and pulled his chair up next to Gracie's. She looked so thin. She kept her hair long, as she always had, and her beautiful cheekbones had hollowed a bit. Her eyes looked haggard, though not so unlike his. They'd both seen so much.

Where did you go, my dear sweet girl? After three years of trying, failing to reach his wife, and watching her become terrified, tearful, or practically catatonic at the attempt, Ernest had accepted their situation. But today he wasn't merely going through the motions of a loving caretaker. Or a distant friend. Today he dared to hope.

Ernest cleared his throat and said, 'Hello, Gracious.'

He held his breath as she reached over and held his hand with both of hers. He searched her eyes for a glimmer of recognition.

'It's been a while. Do you remember me?' he asked as he longed for his wife of years ago, before the ringing in her ears, before the sudden headaches and dizziness, before the seizures that took her away.

Gracie nodded and drew a deep breath, sighing. 'It's been too long. No one has called me Gracious in . . .' She blinked, squinting at him, pursing her lips, and shaking her head as though he were a puzzle waiting to be put back together. '. . . in . . . forever.'

Ernest smiled and nodded even though he'd called her that just last week. But she hadn't remembered him then and had told him to go away.

But today, she touched his cheek, felt his stubble. She traced the lines on his face and the bags beneath his weary eyes. In that moment, he ignored how the years had accumulated on Gracie, memories that had left their marks, and the scars, which had piled up like layers of sediment. He felt his own age, though, as his heart seemed like a clock that had come unwound, slowly ticking. And he longed for the years he'd lost and the lifetime that she'd forgotten.

'Ernest,' Gracie whispered, nodding. 'Young.'

He breathed a sigh of relief and choked back a tidal surge of emotion.

'I'm here.' He held her soft warm hands, mottled with veins and spots, mileposts from a life richly lived. He dared to kiss them.

'And just like that . . . here you are,' she said, furrowing her brow and then smiling again. 'I'm not imagining this, am I?'

Ernest shook his head.

She coughed and then tugged at a loose thread on her kimono, pulled the red string, then snapped it off. She dangled it and then dropped the loose bit into an overflowing ashtray, sighing. 'Oh dear . . . I'm so sorry that you're seeing me like this.'

'It's always good to see you, Gracious. You're as beautiful as ever.' Ernest looked toward the kitchen, from where Juju was peeking, smiling. 'And our daughters, they're just like you. You must be so proud . . .'

'And there it goes,' Gracie said as she noticed the hummingbird fly away.

Ernest watched her eyes and saw the lucidity come and go, fading in and out like a television signal during a thunderstorm. He turned off the radio. Then sat back down.

'Do you remember us?' Ernest asked as he held her hand again.

'Oh, I remember you,' Gracie said with a nod, but her furrowed brow said otherwise. 'You were my most . . . devoted friend. How could I ever forget . . . you?'

Ernest turned his attention to their matching wedding bands. 'And you – you were the precocious girl who stole my heart.'

'Mmmm . . .' Gracie sat back and smiled. She seemed lost in wistful thought as she touched her lips. Then she laughed gently and asked, 'Do you want it back?'

Ernest squeezed her hand. 'No, my dear. That's yours to keep, forever.'

He watched as she closed her eyes, seemingly content, patting his hand, comforted. He listened as her breathing slowed and she relaxed, pulling her lap blanket up toward her chin, resting her head on a pillow in Ernest's direction. Then he turned to his daughter, whose smile had evaporated as she walked back into the living room. She shrugged an apology as if to say, *We'll try again some other time*. But Ernest didn't mind. He was happy to sit next to her, to watch Gracie sleep so peacefully. This was the best moment he'd had with her all year.

Ernest sat next to Juju on her small, moss-covered patio and sipped a cup of tea. Her lawn hadn't been mowed in forever, and weeds had taken over the plot that once belonged to a modest garden. He glanced over his shoulder toward the house and back to his daughter. 'Your mother looks fabulous. More clearheaded than she's been in . . . years. Tired, but still, she seems so . . . content. But now that she's more present, she doesn't ever leave on her own or wander off when you're not home?'

'She never does,' Juju said as she tucked her hair behind her ear. 'She's always content with her game shows and happy with her radio and her bird-watching – a perfect roommate. We go for walks around Kerry Park. Or I'll take her shopping at the market. She still gets confused when we run into someone who knows her and she can't remember – she used to get really uncomfortable, agitated even. But lately she's been more relaxed. As though she's rediscovering things. I was thinking that maybe, just maybe, we could take her to the world's fair. Maybe some of that excitement might unlock a few of those closed doors.'

Ernest blinked and mulled that over. Gracie seemed so happy, so peaceful. Would it be better to leave her in her bliss, rather than stir up the past and hope for more? There is good in the past, but there are things that should be left undisturbed.

Juju opened her reporter's notebook, clicked a ballpoint pen.

'Well, my deadline isn't getting any longer.'

Ernest nodded politely. He'd agreed to talk, to share the past.

'From what I've been able to find in newspaper archives and on microfiche at the library, you were what – a newborn, or a toddler?' Juju asked. 'And yet nobody came forth with the winning ticket to claim you, correct?'

Ernest shook his head and looked down at his worn, wrinkled hands – old man's hands. He touched his wedding ring and thought about Gracie sleeping so perfectly, dreaming of better days, as he cleared his throat and looked back at his daughter.

'No, although there was a baby that they tried to give away at the incubator exhibit. I wasn't that baby, or even a toddler. I was quite a bit older. And yes, someone did claim me for their own.'

Native Tongues

(1909)

Seven years after arriving in America, Yung Kun-ai didn't dream in Cantonese anymore. Though he did occasionally have nightmares about the US Immigration Bureau's decrepit holding facility at the northern corner of Elliott Bay. He'd been crammed into that warren for months with fifty or sixty people, Chinese and Japanese, all of them sharing three copper buckets for washing. He'd experienced his first Christmas, with ginger cookies and mince pies that volunteers must have made for the inmates. And there were the strange, festive moments when Japanese women would be married on the spot to migrant workers who came to claim them, with Immigration Bureau employees serving as witnesses. The women always cried, sometimes sobbed, and Ernest could never tell if the new brides were happy or sad, joyful or in a state of mourning.

Yung Kun-ai had grown into a boy whom everyone now called Ernest Young. Neither pure Oriental or Caucasian, nor fully American or Chinese, he left the holding facility and became a ward of the state, drifting through a series of reformatories and state-run boarding schools, where he played sports and studied American textbooks. He dreamed of baseball and hitting the game-winning home run (or at least getting on base). He dreamed about second helpings of tender roast beef with herbed gravy on Sundays. He dreamed of Saturday afternoon field trips to the Seattle Public Library. And he dreamed of wooing the tall, intelligent, adventurous Maud Brewster in Jack London's *The Sea-Wolf*.

Ernest dreamed of all these things, even at 5:15 a.m. as he sat on a frigid toilet in the dark, unheated lavatory of the Holy Word Academy and warmed the porcelain seat for one of the older boys, who would be waking up at 5:30.

Fagging for the senior students was part of the routine prescribed to all of the second-class kids – the half-Indians, the mulattos, the slow and the lame, many of whom had been sponsored by wealthy docents, matrons like Mrs Irvine – Ernest's own patron saint, who had agreed to manage his affairs from a distance. The older woman was polite, but stern, and always quick to remind him of his good fortune and the vastness of her charitable heart. Though her patience and interest seemed to wander as he got older and her attention spread to younger children, who were more easily amused.

So every weekday morning Ernest shined leather shoes with Vici Paste, refreshed linens, made beds, dried towels, refilled tins of tooth powder, heated baths, and brushed wool and linen coats by the dozen. No matter how he was treated at Holy Word, the conditions were infinitely better than his first year in America, when he'd been mistakenly remanded to an Indian school in Tulalip and forbidden to speak anything but English. That's where he had yearned for other things, like a day without having to march around the playground, in the rain, in the snow, while wearing ill-fitting boots. That's where he had dreamed of a better life, or at least an afternoon without being forced to watch other kids whipped for accidentally speaking in Klallam, Okanagan, or Salishan.

A year later, the students' collective dream had come true when the school mysteriously caught fire. The dormitory, the classrooms, the machinery and woodshops, the nursery, all of it burned to the ground. Ernest remembered standing with his knapsack and watching the flames as heat lofted burning planks into the sky, carrying them away like magic carpets. Ernest had stood in awe, still somewhat in shock and disbelief as a man from the school came up to him and pinned a note to Ernest's shirt, then put him on a bus for the Washington Children's Home at Dow's Landing.

There, Ernest rarely thought about the Indian school because his new home was so placid by comparison. He enjoyed an idyllic year, surrounded by white faces filled with hope and vicarious joy. Ernest loved living at that old house on Green Lake, with the geese in the summer, the rare ice-skating parties in winter, the ever-present sound of piano lessons. He didn't care that his friends all found foster homes or farm work while he'd been left behind. He could have lived there forever, but Mrs Irvine eventually came along and chose him from a lineup of mixed-race kids who were considered unadoptable. She determined that since he was half-white, he was worth sending to Holy Word, a boarding school. She paid his tuition so he could attend alongside wealthy children from good families, to make a proper young man out of him. Even if most of the students, teachers, and administrators didn't share that enthusiasm.

Ernest's residency at Holy Word lasted until just before the seventh grade, culminating in the year's fall sponsor review in the school library. Ernest walked into the room and stood at attention before Mrs Irvine, who remained seated. A servant escort, a slender bald man in a dark suit, lingered behind her.

'Hello, Ernest dear.' She held a sheaf of papers in her hand that Ernest knew would be his grades and his progress reports, his running tab of merits and the occasional demerit. 'My, look how much you've grown.'

Ernest tried not to fidget as he smiled. He hadn't seen her in a year – he barely knew her – though he was required to write to her each month with an update of his progress. She never wrote back, except for a general holiday greeting. Nevertheless, he was grateful for her patronage and knew he owed her a tremendous debt.

Mrs Irvine waved the papers about with a flourish. 'I'm so proud of you, young man. You've come so far in just a few years here among the other boys.' She beamed as she dabbed at the corner of her eye with a gloved fingertip.

The routine always made Ernest miss his mother. He also felt homesick, which was confounding because he'd never had a real home, ever.

'Tell me,' Mrs Irvine asked, 'what's been the highlight of your summer? Did you enjoy the boat races and the sailing lessons? What about the salmon bake on Alki Beach? And are you excited for middle school?'

Ernest nodded politely. He didn't want to disappoint her by sharing that he'd been excluded from all those school outings. Instead he'd spent his time here – in the library with the other scholarship children, who had become his friends and outcast confidants, reading, studying, learning for hours on end, sometimes out of curiosity, but other times out of sheer boredom. It didn't matter what the truth was, really, because Ernest's answers were always well rehearsed. A school counselor wrote down recommended responses for Ernest a week before Mrs Irvine's visit and had him practice them. He used to think that the script was to help with his English, but now that he spoke almost as well as the other students, Ernest realized the performance was something else.

'I wonder, Master Ernest . . .' Mrs Irvine cleared her throat as she set the papers aside and accepted a cup of tea from a school secretary. She blew on the steaming liquid and took a sip, then handed the cup to the bald man in the dark suit, who added sugar and a slice of lemon. 'What would you think about working here? Perhaps after the eighth grade I can arrange to have you join the custodial staff. With enough hard work and dedication, you might work your way up to head groundskeeper. Would you like that?'

Ernest found himself nodding, agreeing out of habit, even as he thought how much that would be like graduating to perpetual detention. The other kids talked about high school, and one day continuing their studies at Seattle College, but Ernest had been told that no women or colored students were allowed. He hadn't bothered asking about Orientals.

'Thank you,' Ernest said as he continued standing at attention, trying to remember what he'd been instructed to say. He was flustered with frustration and disappointment, and the words all seemed so pointless. He continued, 'I'm very happy at this fine boarding school. My education and moral upbringing are . . .' He paused. 'Vital to my future, no matter what that future might . . .'

Mrs Irvine smiled and sipped her tea again, nodding her approval to the servant and Ernest. 'Continue,' she said.

'My future . . .' Ernest thought about his morning routine serving the other kids, who were never grateful, the monotony of always being on the outside looking in. He wished he could attend a public school with normal children, go to a real home in the evening. He was grateful for a full belly and a warm bed, content to learn, even if he had to sit in the back of the class, where he often struggled to see the blackboard and the second-class kids were never called on. But it got to the point where most had stopped trying, stopped raising their hands. To the teachers they were invisible, tolerated, but not encouraged to hope for the same things as the other kids.

'My future . . .' Ernest's words drifted off the scripted page

63

he'd memorized. He swallowed and said, 'Mrs Irvine, I'm so very appreciative of all you have done for me.' He felt his disappointment turn to frustration. 'I was wondering . . .'

'Anything,' the elegant woman stated. 'Just ask.'

Ernest breathed a quiet sigh of relief. He smiled and felt emboldened, if only for a fanciful moment. 'Well, ma'am, I was wondering . . .' Ernest looked at his shoes. Then he looked up again. 'Do you think I could leave this place? Perhaps go to another school, or even back to Dow's Landing? I'm not looking for an easy way out, I'd be happy to sell papers on the street corner after school, to wash dishes someplace for room and board. I don't expect anyone to adopt me proper. I was just thinking that I might have greater opportunities someplace else. I don't suppose . . .'

It looked as though Mrs Irvine had bit into her lemon.

'You don't want to stay here?' she asked with a frown, cocking her head. 'This is the most expensive school in five states, I've been paying your tuition . . .'

'It's a wonderful school.' Ernest hoped his face wouldn't reveal the truth. 'It's just that there's a great big world out there, I think I could be happier . . .'

'Happiness is a state of mind, not something you'll find on a map,' she snapped. Then her servant refreshed her tea and leaned in, whispering in her ear.

Ernest watched as they stood up and stepped into the hall. Through the open doorway Ernest saw a passing administrator join the conversation. The man and Mrs Irvine bickered for a moment, talking back and forth. Then the administrator snapped his fingers and called to a secretary, who brought him a newspaper. They pointed to an article on the front page and nodded as they came to some agreement.

Ernest noticed how Mrs Irvine's countenance softened. Her eyes widened. She actually smiled as she came back in, but she didn't sit. She allowed the bald man to help her with her fur coat.

'I have a better idea, young man,' she said. 'Something that might suit your desire to leave my care and also fulfill a pressing need for a civic organization that I belong to.'

Ernest was relieved, but also confused.

'How do you feel about the world's fair?' Mrs Irvine asked. 'The great big Alaska–Yukon–Pacific Exposition that everyone is talking about. I know all of you boys are probably dying to go. I've been and it's breathtaking. And there's a unique opportunity coming up, one you would be perfectly suited for.'

Ernest could hardly believe his good fortune. He'd been reading about the AYP for weeks in the newspaper. Most of the boys had been several times, but the scholarship students rarely left the grounds. Mrs Irvine must have seen the answer in his eyes as he practically bounced up and down with excitement.

'Perfect then.' She beamed. 'I'll take you one week hence, for your birthday – you'll be my most special guest. Oh, and pack your things,' she said with a wave of her gloved hand. 'Because when I take you, young man, you won't be coming back.'

Healthy Boy, Free

(1909)

Ernest Young was told three things by Mrs Irvine on his twelfth birthday: that he would finally be given to a good home, that he would see the president of the United States (albeit from a distance), and that his legal name was now, in fact, Ernest Young.

The first was a surprise. He'd long since given up hope for any sort of adoptive family, especially since he wasn't Chinese enough for an Asian family and wasn't white enough for a Caucasian home. It was true that he didn't look particularly Oriental, but he appeared different enough that no one would want him.

So when Mrs Irvine told him all this on the way to the fair, Ernest had naturally been skeptical about the part involving 'a good home'. The whole thing, particularly the part about being adopted – seemed too good to be real. How had this possibility materialized so suddenly? First a carriage ride – something he'd rarely experienced – and now this strange revelation.

All week long he'd puzzled over Mrs Irvine's parting words – where would he be going after she took him to the fair? He'd worried about being sent to a poor farm, or back to the Indian school; the best he'd hoped for was perhaps being allowed to run away with a circus – and even that was a wistful fantasy, because to tell the truth, a permanent home had always been beyond the grasp of his hopeful imagination.

So with each mile, he watched the city roll by and kept waiting for the grim truth to present itself, like in the gothic fairy tales he'd read – the older, unvarnished versions, where Cinderella's stepsisters had cut off their heels with a hatchet and chopped off their toes in hopes of fitting their feet into the glass slipper. Or where the Pied Piper hadn't been paid for ridding the hamlet of rats and so he returned and took away all the village children, drowning them in a river.

The second thing – seeing President Taft – was exciting, sure, but not so much more than seeing the Alaska–Yukon–Pacific Exposition, where the nation's commander in chief would be appearing. Ernest had spent months yearning to visit the AYP – Seattle's world's fair. He'd listened with palpable envy as the other boys returned to the dormitory on Saturday evenings, recounting tales of animal shows and carnival rides. But as Ernest arrived and followed Mrs Irvine through the boisterous crowd at the south entrance, past all the things he'd daydreamed about – the Fairy Gorge Tickler, the Aero Plunge, and the Dizzle Dazzle – the glittery, sparkling, splendorous, musical reality was far better than the stories he'd heard or the newspaper photos he'd seen. Ernest had eagerly read the daily reviews in the *Seattle Post-Intelligencer.* He'd weighed the possibilities and knew that there was no way the twenty-seventh president could compare to the Hindoo Mystery, the dog eaters of the Igorrotte Village, or Red Men's Day, when hundreds had participated in a mock battle between Indians and militiamen. Ernest read that someone had died during the re-enactment, shot at close range with a wax-tipped blank. He didn't know who had been killed, but he secretly hoped that the unfortunate fellow was a soldier; Ernest had always had to wear a feather when the kids played cowboys and Indians back at Holy Word Academy. And being a onetime resident of the Tulalip school, he was partial to the plight of underdogs in general, and noble savages in particular.

The last thing he'd been told was the least surprising of all. Ernest had never forgotten his ah-ma and the Chinese name his mother had once inscribed in the book of families at the small Buddhist temple in their village near Toisan. Yet in the years since he'd arrived in Washington, he'd often seen his name written as Ernest Young. The fact that it was now official was somewhat confusing, but his new English name wasn't.

As Mrs Irvine guided him toward Klondike Circle, he watched a lost helium balloon career upward, sailing above the newly planted trees – pindrow firs and digger pines, and beyond the gondola ride and the swaying cable that split the blue sky in half. That's how he felt – soaring inside, but sharply divided between the past and the present, between his origin and his destination, caught between joy and the unknown. Still, he couldn't help smiling as he inhaled a rainbow of scents and aromas, and his heart beat faster. He imagined the future, along with the sharp crispness of Hires root beer, waffle sandwiches, crispy and hot, and endless skeins of silky, cottony, fairy floss. Mrs Irvine even bought a small bag and gave him a bite, which was sweet and lighter than air.

This must be what Heaven is like, Ernest thought, as he looked around. Everyone seemed accepted here – embraced by the collective thrill of the moment, as if the future were one endless possibility. Heaven? No – this must be what love feels like.

The idea popped into his head unbidden; Ernest didn't have much experience with affairs of the heart. His mother had once loved him, of course, as had, he believed, the girls on the ship – albeit briefly. Other than that, though, love was still a mystery.

As he walked, Ernest practically begged Mrs Irvine to stop at the Eskimo Village, but evidently she had other plans. She relentlessly parted the crowd like an icebreaker through a polar sea. And when he lagged behind, gawking at the Forestry Building, she took him by the arm and guided him to a perch atop the highest step of the newly built Women's

Building. This was where the crowd was gathering to hear President Taft speak. From there Ernest had a commanding view of the reflecting pool and thousands of visitors milling about expectantly, toting parasols, small American flags, and the occasional whirligig, lazily spinning in the cool September breeze. Mixed in with the rabble were entire companies of infantrymen in russet-colored uniforms. They looked more like soldiers on leave, less intimidating than the mounted cavalry, who pushed through the multitudes wearing steel Brodie helmets and tight spiral puttees, their rifles slung across their chests at the ready.

'Since President McKinley was killed at the Pan-American Expo in Buffalo, the current administration is taking no chances,' Mrs Irvine pointed out as she clutched her purse and checked the time on her silver wristwatch.

Ernest gazed at the surrounding buildings, looking for a sign of the president and his entourage, as Mrs Irvine exchanged pleasantries with those around them. The ladies talked of their hope that the fair would finally cleanse the city of its notorious reputation, using words like *putrescence* and *degradation*, *feculence* and *corruption*. That's when Ernest realized he was the only male present, a standout among the matrons of the Seattle Women's Suffrage Association. He fidgeted with the buttons on his coat as he wondered if he'd be going home with one of the older, prune-faced ladies who smelled like mothballs and liniment. He looked around for someone younger.

He noticed the women appraising him. They smiled politely and whispered, 'Is that him? Is that the boy?' and 'My, he's so tall, what is he?' or 'Quite handsome, actually, like George Primrose without the make-up.'

'Where are you from?' one of the women asked.

Ernest looked at Mrs Irvine, whose expression seemed to say *go on*.

'Um . . . I grew up near Green Lake,' Ernest said, though he wasn't sure if that was the correct answer. 'The Holy Word Academy, I guess.'

'No, dear,' the woman said. 'Where are you really from?'

Mrs Irvine jumped in. 'He came over on a boat from the Far East, but he's only half Oriental. His father was European, and young Ernest speaks English marvelously. And although he's not a Mongoloid, he's not a Caucasoid either. He's . . . unique.'

Embarrassed, Ernest fussed with a loose button and turned toward the marble columns of the massive Government Building across the parkway. He distracted himself with the gentle splashing of the Geyser Basin. He could see the pristine rows of cascading waterfalls and the mirrored reflection of Mount Rainier in the stillness of the outer reflecting pool. He marveled at the crowd – a bonanza of derby hats and bow ties, and a parade of women, who tilted forward in their corsets as though running a race, but were slowed by their hobble skirts, doting endlessly on their mantles and tea jackets. The men strolled at the gentle pace set by the ladies at their arms, and everyone seemed to move in slow motion.

That's when Ernest noticed one nearby face, then two, then a dozen more. All of them were staring in his direction – not just in his direction, *directly at him*. Bewildered, Ernest looked over his shoulder and saw the ladies continuing their conversation, showing each other their tickets. The tickets weren't just for admission into the fair but were for something else. Ernest looked up at the yellow and purple flag atop the building, then down to his trousers. He wondered if his buttons might have come undone.

He turned around and found himself facing Mrs Irvine. She put her hands on his shoulders and whispered in his ear, 'They're all here for you, young man – such a marvelous thing! They've all come out today, rain or shine, to see *you* – to find out who has the special ticket. To find out who the lucky winner is. Isn't this exciting?'

Special ticket? Ernest furrowed his brow and blinked, once, twice. Ever since the AYP had opened, on the first of June, there had been a raffle each day. Today was no exception, and the raffle winner would be selected after President Taft's speech. In fact, Taft himself would draw the winning ticket. Ernest remembered that on Anaconda Day the delegation from Butte, Montana, had given away five thousand copper ingots. On Yakima Day, visitors had won barrels of apples and cruets of cider vinegar. And on Agriculture Day, someone had won a milking shorthorn.

But today is President's Day, Ernest thought. What could they possibly give away on . . . ? Ernest felt his unalloyed joy, his excitement, plummet into the pit of his stomach.

He remembered. This is also Washington Children's Home Day.

'Someone is taking you home with them,' Mrs Irvine said with glee. 'I bet you never thought you'd find a real home, but wishes sometimes do come true.'

He turned toward the crowd and realized that *everyone* was staring at him – thirty thousand people, smiling, laughing, pointing – all of them waiting as Mrs Irvine's words echoed in his mind, *They're all here for you.* Then he noticed the ticket holders. They stood out among the masses, hundreds of them, checking and double-checking their numbers, waving their tickets in the air, fanning themselves with the small slabs of printed cardboard.

'I'm . . . the prize,' Ernest whispered. Those three words hung in the air like that lost helium balloon. I'm to be given away. I belong to one of the ticket holders. Everyone's here for the spectacle, for me, and the president, of course.

As a drum major struck up the band in front of the Government Building, Ernest glanced back at Mrs Irvine, who was smiling, adjusting her President's Day ribbon. Soldiers and policemen marched by, creating a brief reverential mood, until a collective cheer, a full-hearted roar, swept through the crowd.

Ernest watched, too numb from shock to feel awestruck, as ladies curtsied at the sight of President Taft's unmistakably large frame and wide handlebar mustache. Ernest stared into the crowd and wondered what stranger would be taking him away, and to what end, for what purpose? He heard the audience cheer as the president descended the steps of the Government Building in a black tuxedo with long flowing tails and a top hat. One peculiar woman, with a shimmering peacock feather in her gold-colored boater hat, merely smiled and placed a cigarette in her mouth as he approached. Ernest watched in silence, somewhat shocked as the Big Lub himself paused, fished out a silver lighter, and lit the rolled tobacco at the end of her dangling holder. He offered a hearty grin and then continued shaking hands and kissing babies on his way to the bandstand, where he gave a rousing speech in his high-pitched, South Midland voice, about something Ernest barely understood and quickly forgot.

When President Taft was done speaking, the band played 'Hail to the Chief', but the crowd stayed put, cheering and shouting. Ernest watched the man whom Teddy Roosevelt had called Ol' Puzzlehead bask in his hard-fought presidential glory, but Ernest knew full well that the patrons of the fair were merely waiting for yet another prize to be raffled off.

He overheard one of the women behind him. 'Heavens! The gossip and rumors have run amok,' she said. 'People have been saying that the boy must be colored – others that he's an heir to a great fortune. The *Seattle Star* even speculated that the prize was actually a dwarf dressed up as a boy and that the whole affair was a practical joke. Can you believe that?' The other ladies laughed and kept murmuring.

But as Ernest watched President Taft remove his cufflink, push up the dark sleeve of his long-tailed tuxedo jacket, and reach into an enormous birdcage tumbler of ticket stubs, he knew this wasn't a prank. The AYP had one-upped the raffled livestock and barrels of produce given away at fairs in Buffalo and San Francisco.

Ernest held his breath, and for a moment the snare drums sounded like the rattle of gunfire, the thunderous bass became the booming of cannons, the sousaphones blared – lonely boat horns, echoing on the surface of cold, black water. He blinked and saw his mother among all the spectators, a skeleton in a mandarin dress and yellow shoes, touching her heart, slowly waving goodbye. Ernest ached inside, reaching out to her, stepping toward her as she vanished into the crowd, which fell silent.

This is everything you ever wanted for me, Ernest thought.

He exhaled and blinked again as a timpani rolled to a crescendo and the president drew a single, random, destiny-changing, fate-defying bit of paper. He handed it to a man who was introduced as Superintendent L. J. Covington, who announced through a squelching microphone that 'whoever has the matching ticket can immediately claim today's prize as their very own – handsome and dark, clever and strong, donated by the Washington Children's Receiving Home, a healthy boy. Free to a good family!'

Half the audience cheered and the other half laughed or gasped in amazement. There were even a few jeers.

'Can he sing and dance too?' a man yelled. 'Does he do magic tricks?'

'I'll take a girl who can cook!' another man heckled.

'I need a boy with a strong back,' a woman shouted.

'Get on with it!' someone snapped, as the crowd grew restless.

The superintendent raised his arms along with the other half of the winning ticket, which slowly subdued the crowd. He read the numbers into the microphone: 0-9-2-5-7-5. Silence, then the losing ticket holders collectively groaned as chatter spread through the audience. Ernest searched the crowd for someone, anyone to come forward – to shout and holler, to wave his or her hat in the air. But no one appeared. And his mother was gone, forever. Ernest felt utterly alone in a gathering of fashionable strangers.

The superintendent read the numbers again, but now in a tone that seemed more pleading than celebratory, and again, was answered with silence. Then came stirs of confusion, groans of disappointment, and eventually apathy as the president began his exit and the crowd started to disperse, off to the next amusement.

Ernest felt his fear and anxiety dissipate, along with his expectations. He shook his head. It had been terrifying that his fate would be determined by something so random as a raffle, but without his even realizing it, in these few moments, his heart had somehow conjured a glimmer of hope. He'd dared to dream and now suddenly felt like yesterday's news, last week's trivia. After seeing so many children come and go from Dow's Landing, or parents visiting their sons at Holy Word, he'd never allowed himself to aspire for the life the others had, but now his heart had briefly inflated, then burst like a balloon, leaving an aching cavity inside his chest. He rubbed his eyes and swallowed what small pride he had as he realized there would be no winner today, just a solitary loser. He exhaled, long and slow, wiping a tear, as the sun found its usual hiding place among the Seattle rain clouds and the municipal band played the 'Seattle Victory March'. In a fog, he watched the president wave to the crowd once more as his delegation was escorted away. Even for free, as a raffle prize, he was utterly unwanted.

Maybe it was all a joke, Ernest thought. A stunt put on by the newspapers. He hung his head and cursed himself.

Mrs Irvine looked confused, frustrated. She beckoned him to join her, and he slowly descended the steps toward the fountain. They reached the square, where they were confronted by another group of women. To Ernest they seemed younger, hardier, and rowdier, but they were as finely appointed, as well-heeled as the stout, cotton-haired matrons of

74

the Woman's Building. They seemed more colorful in dress and manner – literally, because of the make-up they wore. Ernest watched as a strawberry-haired woman with a plunging neckline tucked a pinch of snuff between her cheek and gum and spat the tobacco residue at the feet of Mrs Irvine. Then the vanguard of ladies parted as the woman Ernest had seen from afar swept to the forefront. She was the woman whose cigarette the president had stopped to light. She looked to be the junior of Mrs Irvine by at least ten years, maybe twenty. She brushed back the plume of the blue and green feather in her hat and then fingered her necklace. The cigarette was still smoking, dangling in the holder that bounced up and down in the corner of her mouth as she spoke.

'Hello, Ida.' The strange woman held up a thick stack of tickets. 'How's your husband?' She puckered her lips and then smiled, showing her back teeth. 'We haven't seen him in our parlor in a while. Let him know that he's always welcome.'

'Florence.' Mrs Irvine nodded a curt greeting and gave the woman an icy stare. 'Only you would have the nerve to ask the president of the United States to light your cigarette when you know they've been outlawed for two years. You just made him an accomplice.'

'You're right,' the woman named Florence replied. 'We're now partners in a crime that no one in the world cares about – but you. Half the judges smoke in their chambers, my dear. Trust me.' She smiled again. 'I would know. And what else have you foisted upon the good people of Seattle? Let's see, it's now illegal for a woman to wear pants in public, saloons must be open to public viewing – oh, and tipping of any kind is no longer allowed within the city limits. My, how you love your rules.'

Mrs Irvine pointed to the tickets. 'And the rules for the raffle very clearly said, *to a good home*. Not a place for a *good time*.' She crossed her arms and scrunched her lips as though she had just tasted something bitter.

75

Florence spread the tickets like a fan and waved them in front of her face, feigning coyness, if only for a moment. She blinked over the tops of the cardboard stubs and then revealed a stern countenance. She sorted out the ticket with the winning numbers and then held it up for all to see. 'It took us a while to find the right one; after all, we have so many. But, as you can see, I'm here now to claim my prize. We both have the same intentions, Ida dear, we just have different methods of getting what we want . . .'

'Don't you dare compare me to . . .'

Ernest listened to the women bicker back and forth about propriety and decorum, interrupting one another, chewing each other's words with their mouths open, their teeth bared, their nostrils flaring, cheeks reddening. As they inched closer to each other, the day seemed to grow more confusing and unreal by the moment. Ernest observed this as their arguing became background noise, blending into the sounds of the fair – a distant rock tumbler, a melodious pipe organ, laughing children on a carousel, the glassy popping of flash powder. He noticed that in this group of painted ladies, the older women had made their faces appear younger, while the younger ones, barely out of their teens, were made up to look older. But there was a certain wit about all of them, like every look was a dare, a threat, and a promise.

They all seemed pleasant enough. Ernest thought that any one of them would be a million times preferable to the monotony of the boarding school. Where life was a song with only one note. No melody, and no chorus, just a flat monotonous tone.

Ernest didn't feel entirely comfortable, but he was at least intrigued by the thought of going home with any one of these gay young ingenues. He wondered where each of them lived, who their husbands were. Did they have other children?

That's when Ernest saw the littlest one – not a woman at all, a young girl, really, and barely a wisp of one at that. Ernest noticed her as she stood on the edge of the verbal melee, in a purple knee-high dress with a monogrammed *M*, fringed with lace, and beguiling blond hair cut so short that she almost looked like a boy – almost. She wore an outrageous hat, similar to that of Miss Florence, the leader of the pack. But instead of peacock feathers this queer girl had a pair of stuffed hummingbirds set atop her brim. Ernest noticed her wide, luminous eyes – pools of blue ice, with freckles of summer generously sprinkled on her nose and cheeks.

They observed each other in a silent staring contest, which lasted only half a minute but stretched to infinity in grade school years, until Ernest's tear ducts burned and he blinked his surrender. The girl rolled her eyes and gazed back. Her confounding expression seemed filled with something like loathing – like a long-held grudge for a sin he hadn't yet committed. She stepped toward him and revealed what appeared to be the world's most perfect candied apple – a treat that looked like a ruby atop a stick. It sparkled and shimmered like the Star of India.

She hadn't yet taken a bite.

Ernest stirred himself from his shocked stupor and waved a polite greeting.

The strange girl regarded him with a glare. Then she looked at the candied apple that he'd clearly admired as though she'd momentarily forgotten the thing was there. She paused and seemed to appreciate her reflection in the hard, candy-coated surface. Then she tipped it upside down, holding the stick with two fingers, like the tail of a dead rat. Ernest watched as she stalked to a nearby garbage can, stared back at him, tilted her head, and dropped the apple in the trash with a hollow thump.

Tenderloin

(1909)

E rnest sat with his knapsack on his lap in the backseat of a lurching taxi, a jostling Model T. He was sandwiched between the large woman with the big hat and the girl who hated him for reasons unknown. Most of the other ladies had opted for the trolley, dinner in the city, and a bit of light shopping, he'd been told.

Not the family I imagined, Ernest thought, as he stared out the window and watched the sun set on the waters of Puget Sound. He felt like a tumbleweed, blown by the wind, rolling to the southern edge of town.

Mrs Irvine had put up a good fight, even though Ernest didn't fully understand her reasons. She had argued, grabbed the tickets, and thrown them into the air. She'd shoved Ernest behind her, and he'd watched the pieces rain down like ticker tape on a parade, which created a peculiar appearance of celebration, a joyful moment amid the bickering, until a broad-bellied man in a wool suit broke up the fracas. He fingered his walrus mustache and then reached deep into his over-stuffed waistcoat, buttons ready to burst, and pulled out a gold badge. Ernest thought he had come to Mrs Irvine's rescue just in time, but she called the man a no-good jackal and a scoundrel. The hollering and caterwauling was the closest he'd ever heard Mrs Irvine come to swearing.

As the taxi veered around a carriage, and Ernest thought about Mrs Irvine possibly being on the wrong side of the law, he was compelled to re-evaluate everything he'd ever been told, to reconsider everything he'd known.

For instance, he'd never been in a motorcar. He'd heard that they were ugly, noisy, graceless, foul-smelling contraptions. But as they passed a brigade of crossing sweepers, cleaning up road apples and swatting flies, Ernest thought otherwise. He settled into the polished leather seats, which smelled better than a saddled horse.

He had never once been near the mysterious part of Seattle that lay south of Yesler Way, a street better known as the Deadline. His teachers had talked for years about sewer rats that plagued the area, and rattlesnakes, and about the wolves that prowled the White Chapel District, waiting to sink their teeth into the good people of Seattle, which a local song had dubbed the Peerless City. Ernest had imagined lanky, sinuous creatures with sharp claws and tangles of mangy fur, but as he looked out at the avenue, all he saw were signs for dance halls and saloons. He even heard a fiddle playing a happy tune in the distance as the gaslights on the street corners flickered to life, turning the damp sidewalks a ruddy orange hue. Everything, from the brick buildings to the sidewalks to the lampposts and park benches, looked polished and new, even the brewers' trucks that seemed to be on every corner.

Ernest looked up at Madam Florence. The woman hadn't bothered to remove her hat, and the feathery plume swept back and forth against the canvas top of the motorcar as she turned her head. He tried to evaluate what kind of creature she must have been in Mrs Irvine's eyes.

She seemed to notice him staring. 'First time *below the line*, I take it?'

Ernest nodded.

The woman smiled and pointed out the window. 'It's not hard to understand when you think about it. North of the line was settled by Arthur Denny – who didn't drink. South of the line was all land owned by Doc Maynard, who, shall we say, "enjoyed his libations". So, young man, to the north you get City Hall, the courts, and the police station, and to the south we have booze, casinos, and all kinds of canoodling. That's Seattle for you, the land of the haves and the why nots?'

Ernest thought her explanation made more sense than the schoolteacher's fables.

'I'm Florence Nettleton, by the way. But you may call me Madam Flora.' She handed him the winning ticket. 'I saved this one for you, a little souvenir of this auspicious day. After all, we're both winners, aren't we?' Then she pointed at the others with her cigarette holder. 'This is Jewel in the front seat. She's one of my newer girls. And that's my baby sister, Margaret – my little hummingbird, but we all call her Maisie May. Say hello, sweetheart.'

'Just Maisie,' the girl answered without bothering to turn away from the nearest window. She removed her hat and wedged it between them.

Ernest hesitated for a moment. There were so many questions he wanted to ask. So much he wanted to know about his new family and about the White Chapel District – like how the neighborhood had gotten its name. As he looked around, he noticed a barber, a haberdasher, and a few tailors – he even saw casinos – but didn't see a single church.

'You'll be living here with me, at Washington Court.' Madam Flora pointed to a four-story brick building on the corner as the car's brakes squealed and the tires ground to a halt. 'Your old friend, Mrs Irvine, once called this part of Seattle a bottomless cauldron of sin and hellfire. The Duwamish Indians, on the other hand, called this area the Crossing-Over Place; that's how I like to think of this neighborhood. What do you think?'

Ernest stared up at the new building and shrugged. 'Looks nice enough to me.'

'My sentiments exactly,' Madam Flora continued. 'You'll be the only boy here, so you'll have your own room – lucky you – but you'll be expected to work hard and earn your keep. Ask for Miss Amber, she's my housekeeper, my managing partner. She's in charge of all the help and a bit of a handful, but her heart is in the right place, even if her temper gets in the way once in a while. She'll see that you're properly taken care of. Run along now, darlings, and I'll catch up with you in the morning. Jewel and I have an appointment with a tailor, so she can get fitted for a very special dress.'

Ernest put the ticket in his pocket and followed Maisie onto the sidewalk. He looked up at the tall building and out at the bustling avenue. The paved street was covered in gravel and streaked with mud from shiny motorcars, polished horse-drawn carriages, electric trolleys, bicyclists, the footfalls of scores of pedestrians – and all of them seemed content to share the road, dodging in and out, weaving around each other. Ernest couldn't understand how so many people moved so quickly in so many different directions without accidentally killing one another. Maybe this was what Mrs Irvine had been so concerned about.

'Welcome to the Tenderloin,' Maisie said. 'Follow me.'

The building's entrance was magnificent, with a glittering voltaic chandelier, the foyer accented with finely polished millwork. Maisie took him on a tour of the rooms on the ground floor, including the cloakroom, the library, something she called the teaching salon, and the smoking den. But it was the splendor of the grand parlor that took Ernest's breath away. Never in his life had he seen a home so opulent. Everywhere he looked there were tapestries, lace-covered walls, plush French furniture in crimson and gold, marble cherubs

81

with bows and arrows, angels, stoic busts of bearded historical figures, and risque statues – bronze gods and plump goddesses he didn't recognize. There were candles, oil lamps, mirrors, and sparkling decanters of wine and spirits. The floors were even and smooth, and the plaster walls and wood trim were freshly painted, unmarred by soot from kerosene lamps. When Ernest did finally catch his breath, he smelled rich perfume and scented tobacco, fresh-cut flowers, candles, and savory spices – sage and thyme – roasting in some unseen kitchen.

A black man in a blue tuxedo with a bow tie hanging untied around his neck was tinkering with a melody on a grand piano. Ernest watched as he'd stop, dip a pen into a bottle of ink, mark a few notes on a sheet of paper, and then resume playing. He sang a few whispered words of rhyme and song here and there, nodding and counting. The man stopped playing when he noticed them.

'Mayflower!' he said as he gave Maisie a hug. 'And this young fellow must be the new houseboy – I mean, the *only* houseboy. You'll make a fine coachman someday, son.'

Ironically, just as he was being called son Ernest realized he hadn't actually been adopted as a son, or a stepbrother, or a member of a real family. They were making a servant out of him – hired help – without causing anyone the trouble of having to hire. He paused, reflecting, excited but nervous, and a tad angry at having been shuffled off once again. But more than anything, he was hopeful.

A job is better than that school any day, Ernest thought. Though he wondered what kinds of chores he'd be doing in such a fancy place. He was terrible at kitchen work.

'Madam Flora's big idea.' Maisie shook her head. 'I wanted another girl, but what do we go and get – a boy.'

'What about me?' the piano player asked. 'I ain't so bad, am I?'

'Yeah, but you go home in the morning,' Maisie reminded him, laughing.

At least she can actually smile, Ernest noted. And she seemed quite popular with a handful of young women in lavish dresses who descended the stairs and kissed Maisie on the cheek or gave her a quick hug, or tousled her hair as they passed by. They all greeted Ernest, waving, or giggling mischievously. They cooed and called him honey and doll. One of them said, 'Look at our darling houseboy, he's just so adorable,' as she hugged him, pressing his cheek into her perfumed bosom. Ernest's palms began to sweat, and though he smiled politely and said he was happy to be working there, he still felt like a stranger at someone else's elegant party. A small part of him was reminded of his weeks on the ship, surrounded by girls who eventually accepted him.

'Those are some of the ladies who live here – you'll get to know them all in time, I'm sure. And I'm Professor Troubadour,' the man said as he shook Ernest's hand and peeked over the rims of his thick glasses. 'But you can just call me True – cause I never, ever, ever tell a lie.'

Ernest paused, wondering what kind of professor the man might be. He'd known only a few colored people, and none were teachers. 'Is True your real name?' he asked.

'It is now.'

'Are you a real professor?'

'You see me, don't you?'

'Will we spend a lot of time together?' Ernest asked.

'I'm a piano player and a singer, but I'm not a fortune-teller, son.' The man laughed as he waved goodbye to the girls. 'I'm afraid the future is entirely up to you.'

Ernest furrowed his brow, bewildered by the thought. He'd hardly ever been allowed to choose anything, ever. From what to wear to what to eat, his life had constantly been spent bobbing on the tides of other people's wishes and expectations. The man's words were the opposite of what Mrs Irvine had told him for years. She'd constantly reminded him that he needed to defer to others, his betters, and that his fate was entirely in their hands or, more specifically, hers.

'What if I want to move away someday?' Ernest asked.

The piano player paused. 'Now I don't know why you'd want to, but I suppose if you needed to go somewhere else badly enough, the front door is never locked.'

Ernest wasn't expecting that. 'And . . . if I don't like my job?'

'Then you go get another one. But this is a pretty special place, if you ask me.'

The freedom of those words seemed magical as the piano player went back to his song and Ernest followed Maisie up a grand mahogany staircase. He looked around, studying the oil paintings on the walls as she pointed to a room on the second floor.

'That's Amber's room. Knock loudly – she sleeps like a bear in winter.'

Without waiting to see if he was able to rouse Amber, she entered another room and closed the door. Ernest heard it lock behind her. As he stood by himself, the hallway felt eerily quiet – a calm that contradicted the lavish decor, as though he were standing in the cavernous lair of some mythical creature. He looked around nervously, cautiously.

As Ernest stared at the heavy wooden door, he wondered, who sleeps in till supper time? Perhaps Miss Amber was ill, or tended to drink too much. He hesitated but didn't know where else to go, or what to do with his belongings. He knocked lightly.

It was to no avail.

Then he finally thumped the door with his whole fist, again and again.

The door swept open, and a large woman with short black hair stood in her nightclothes, rubbing her eyes and blinking down at him. She was much older than he'd expected a Miss Amber to be, and taller as well.

Ernest apologized for waking her. 'Madam Flora told me to check in with you.'

'Jesus, Joseph, and Mary.' She stretched and gazed back. 'You the houseboy?'

Ernest nodded.

'I can't believe that Flora went and pulled it off – she took tickets as cash and cornered the market on *you*. She always did want a son – though God only knows why,' Miss Amber said, shaking her head and popping her knuckles. 'Follow me, kid.' The strange woman didn't bother to don a robe or a changing sacque, she merely sauntered down the corridor in her nightgown and stocking feet. She led him down the hall and around the corner to a tiny room with a single, perfectly made bed, a sink, a chamber pot, a small armoire with a mirror, and a throw rug.

'Welcome to the carriage trade, kid. We'll get you sorted out tomorrow and introduce you to everyone – you'll know the routine by week's end. Best to stay in your room tonight; I suggest you turn in early. Things may be getting busy around here in a few hours, and I don't want you in the way. Come down for breakfast, about eleven-thirty. We like to sleep in around here . . .'

She slammed the door behind him.

Ernest's stomach grumbled. He hadn't had a bite of dinner or supper.

As the last echoes of the fair faded, reality set in. Ernest stared out the lone window into the setting sun and back at the closed door. He patted his shirt and retrieved the winning ticket from his pocket and traced his fingers along the printed numbers and the fine print, the torn edge. His fate had been decided by this simple piece of cardboard. He was the prize, a token for celebration, even though he had no say in the matter. But at least Madam Flora seemed excited about having him, even if the others were mysteries. He tucked the ticket into a corner of the mirror and regarded his face, which had aspects of sadness and relief. Then he sat on the corner of the bed and remembered the dormitory at one of the boarding schools where he'd shared a room with no fewer than five other second-class boys – sometimes as many as a dozen. In fact, he now realized he'd never slept alone in his entire life – not that he could remember.

He found no comfort in the silence of his new home, so he opened the window. He welcomed the sounds of strangers, the embrace of their random conversations, overheard from two stories up. Ernest leaned out and looked up and down the street. He marveled at automobiles and delivery trucks, swerving and veering. He watched horses clip-clopping by, their warm bodies steaming in the cool September air. He heard the yelling of coachmen, and the clanging brass bells of streetcars. He was smack-dab in the beating heart of a crowded city, but as he watched happy couples pass by, arm in arm, pairs that moved as one, he felt empty, confused to be in such modern surroundings, to have such a lavish place to call home yet feeling so alone. He thought for a fleeting moment that the Tenderloin might be too good to be true, that perhaps he should run from this place, try out his new freedom – he could be miles away before anyone noticed he was gone. But he doubted he could find another job in a place as nice as this. Plus, he was hungry. Better to wait at least a week, perhaps even a month, to consider other options.

Not wanting to make waves on his first day (and night), Ernest sighed and closed the window. He found an old newspaper in the armoire and read for an hour. Then he found tooth powder and brushed his teeth. He dressed for bed, but the sheets felt cold and the pillow smelled of soap flakes and blue starch. He closed his eyes and tried to sleep, but the solitude of the room was maddening and the bed was too soft compared to the canvas bunk he'd slept on for the last seven years. He tossed and turned until he heard the piano downstairs – not just practice, but a rousing rendition of the song Professor True had been working on earlier.

Ernest took his blanket and pillow and curled up atop the floor rug next to his bed. He felt warm air seeping in beneath the door but didn't mind the draft, or the hardness of the wooden floor. He wrapped the blanket around his shoulders and closed his eyes again and listened to the murmurs of jovial conversation, the popping of champagne corks, and the clinking of stemware. He heard footfalls and chatter up and down the stairs. He chewed his lip and fell asleep to the sound of laughter.

As Ernest slept he dreamed of the boarding school. He was sitting in the foyer, perched by the window, watching some of the boys leave with their parents at Christmas. Sometimes a whole family would show up, take the tour, listen to the holiday program; other times it would be just a coachman and a waiting carriage – but the end result was always the same. Ernest would be left behind to spend another Christmas alone, eating with the few servants who stayed on as caretakers. Ernest stirred in his sleep, half-waking as he flipped the pillow and scrunched it beneath his head.

'Wake up.' He heard someone whisper in the dark.

He blinked, once, twice, and slowly sat up. He noticed the silvery light that shone through his window, the moon, a streetlight, or a combination of both. He glanced around the room, at the bed, the open wardrobe, all of which remained empty.

Maybe he was still dreaming. He yawned and stretched his back.

His mind groggily searched for a possible source of the voice.

'Pssst . . . are you awake now?'

'I think I am,' Ernest said, though he still couldn't tell where the voice was coming from.

'Good. You were snoring like a buzz saw for a while there.'

It was a girl's voice, but not Maisie's. It was accented.

The strange voice went on. 'I could hear you when I got to my room, even with the music. They said you'd gone to bed. What'd you do, fall asleep on the floor?'

Ernest looked around, bewildered. 'Where – where are you?'

'I'm in the room just below. There's a heating vent in the corner.'

Ernest found a small brass grate nearby and crawled over to the metal duct. He felt a surge of warm air rising, tinged with perfume and tobacco smoke, but saw only a vague shadow in the dimly lit room below.

'I see you,' the girl sang, and then she giggled. Ernest was tired, confused, but he felt comforted to hear a friendly voice.

'Who are you?' As he spoke he heard laughter from downstairs and the sound of the front door opening and closing. He heard the greetings, the hello darlings, the goodnights, and the fond goodbyes. He wondered what time it must be. 'Are you one of Madam Flora's girls?'

She laughed. 'Hardly. I'm not a working girl, I just work here.'

'I beg your pardon?'

'I'm a scullery maid – I work in the kitchen. The servants all sleep downstairs, but since you're a boy I think Amber wanted you upstairs so she could keep an eye on you. You look familiar, by the way. I saw you from the pantry when you first came in and I thought, *Hey, you're just like me*. I couldn't wait to talk to you.'

Ernest wondered what she meant. He tried to imagine how many servants there were in such a big place. He'd seen so many girls earlier. They couldn't all be maids.

'I bet you're starving,' she said.

'What makes you say that?'

'Because we keep pretty strange hours around the Tenderloin. Took me a little while to get used to the way Madam Flora and Miss Amber run things, but this is a wonderful place to work. You'll get the hang of it,' she said. 'Oh, and I'm not supposed to go upstairs at night, but I snuck up anyway and dropped something off. So go open your door and take a look.'

Ernest listened at the keyhole, then carefully turned the knob. As he cracked the door he heard more music, more bawdy laughter. He looked down and found a small package, cheesecloth tied with a piece of red ribbon. He picked it up and quickly closed the door and unwrapped the gift. Inside was a large handful of oatmeal cookies. He devoured one filled with walnuts and raisins. It tasted better than anything in the world at that moment.

'Do you like them?' she whispered while he ate.

'Very much.' Ernest spoke with his mouth full. 'Thank you.'

'You're so welcome. I made them after my duties, just for you.'

Ernest was still confused, but at least his stomach wasn't growling. 'Why are you being so nice to me?' he asked. 'You haven't even met me . . .'

'Because this is a tricky place. Your name is Ernest, right?'

He nodded, then realized she couldn't see him. 'Yes. Ernest Young.'

'Well, young Ernest, as Madam Flora always says, this is a give-and-take business and a give-and-take world. But I wanted to do something for you – out of the goodness of my heart, because I like you already. I think we should stick together. So for now, this is my gift. Though maybe next time I go out of my way to do something nice for you, you'll owe me one. How's that sound?'

'Sounds okay, I guess,' Ernest said as he rubbed his forehead, utterly confused.

'Then it's a deal. Get some sleep, young Ernest. Tomorrow's going to be a very busy day for you – the first of many. I'll see you at breakfast. The servants – we eat together in the kitchen, away from the rest—'

'Is Maisie May one of *the rest*?' Ernest interrupted. He surprised himself at how curious he was about her. 'What does she do here?'

There was no reply.

'Hello?'

He listened intently but heard only the pinging of pipes somewhere in the basement or the boiler room. And at that moment Ernest could have sworn he felt the warm air from the heating vent turn a few degrees cooler.

Then he finally heard the voice grumble, 'Just go to sleep.'

Crusaders of Wappyville

(1909)

In the morning Ernest found a freshly pressed domestic's uniform hanging on his doorknob. The simple black suit seemed much more elegant and grown-up than the uniforms he'd had to wear for school. He put it on happily, then took his mother's pin and attached it to his lapel. After dressing, he followed his nose, and the smell of coffee and baking bread, to a narrow spiral of stairs in the back of the house, all the way down to the tiny servants' dining room and the attached kitchen. There, a stout woman who appeared to be the house cook was bustling around, red-faced from her labors.

'Ah, you must be Ernest, the new man of the house, so to speak. I'm Mrs Blackwell. You're a welcome relief, I tell you what. Them britches fit okay? If not, someone can probably find a set of suspenders around here somewhere – all manner of things get left behind in a place like this, you know.' The woman guffawed as she set out a breakfast of hot rolls, jam, and stiff porridge. She wiped her hands on a flour-spattered apron and urged him to sit as she poured him a cup of coffee. He was apparently the first of the servants to appear for breakfast.

Ernest was grateful not to be wearing corduroy knickerbockers, or the type of puffy Little Lord Fauntleroy shirts that Mrs Irvine had bought for him. The ruffled tops always made him feel like a girl in a frilly dress, two sizes too big.

'Thank you, ma'am. The clothes fit like a glove,' he said.

As he straightened his waistcoat, three young women walked in wearing long white aprons and short, tight bonnets. They looked at him and smiled.

'This is Iris, she's the chambermaid,' Mrs Blackwell said. 'That's Violet, who tends to the parlors and the library; and that's Rose, our laundress. Yes, they're all named after flowers. And no, they're not in any way related. Madam Flora just has a way with colorful names.'

Ernest wondered if they were all adopted as well, and if so, from where.

Mrs Blackwell seemed to notice his questioning gaze. 'They're castaways, just like you, lad. Iris was in an orphans' choir all the way from Boston. She caught the scarlet fever and ended up in a hospital, and her church left her behind. Violet worked at a shoe factory, but couldn't ever make ends meet, and refused the special attention from the floor manager. And Rose . . .' Mrs Blackwell sighed. 'Oh dear, our thorny Rose came to us from Portland, where she'd been wooed by an older gentleman, a rich Prince Charming who she later found out was already married.'

'How was I to know?' Rose protested, wide-eyed. 'He said his wedding band was from his *late* wife and it just wouldn't come off.'

Mrs Blackwell rolled her eyes. 'The girls upstairs too, all of them have stories. But look at us now, the party girls and the serving girls, one big happy family.'

The pretty maids stood all in a row, like in the nursery rhyme. They laughed, teased one another, and spoke about what a nice place the Tenderloin was, that it was a lovely residence to work in, and there were so many interesting dinner parties – so many important visitors.

Ernest nodded and greeted them, though he quietly wondered about the other floweret, Maisie – Madam Flora's Mayflower. And what about the girl who had whispered to him last night?

Mrs Blackwell spoke up. 'You should know, since no men live here – present company excluded – we've never had a need for footmen or even a houseman. And the Professor, bless his heart, is the closest we'll ever have to a butler, but he comes and goes each evening. If we had a stable, I suppose you'd be a stable hand, but we don't, so for now you'll shine shoes, polish boots, run errands, empty cuspidors, and attend to the furnace and the fireplaces – is that clear?'

Ernest agreed and then spoke up. 'Miss Amber said something about the carriage trade? Am I to polish the buggy or tend to the leathers?'

The maids tittered in unison.

Mrs Blackwell smiled sweetly, showing off a dead tooth. She put her hand on his shoulder. 'We don't have any carriages, dear boy.' Ernest looked confused.

'She calls this line of work the carriage trade because the horse-drawn carriages, the screaming steam locomotives, the electric trains, even the jangly motorcars now, come and go, bringing discerning gentlemen who all have business here. They come, they have a glass of cognac or some Baltimore rye or a Cuban cigar, they relax, they're entertained, they attend to their business – and poof, they're gone by morning. You *do* know what kind of house this is, don't you?'

Ernest nodded again, though he had no clue. He'd rarely left the confines of the boarding school. Then he heard music. Not the tinkling of piano keys in the grand parlor but the distant booming of bass drums that sounded like thunder. He heard crashing cymbals and brass horns screeching out a baleful tune.

'Glory, not again,' Violet groaned. 'They're starting earlier and earlier.'

Mrs Blackwell guzzled the last of her coffee, wiped her mouth, and hung up her apron. She stretched her back and then clapped her hands. 'Well, time to get saved, young man,' she said as she raised her eyebrows. 'Come along.'

Ernest followed everyone out the back door to the alley and onto the sidewalk, where he saw a banner with the Salvation Army insignia of Blood and Fire, and a brass band leading a march of smartly dressed women down the middle of Second Avenue. He squeezed to the front to get a better view of the crowd, which ranged three whole blocks, perhaps longer – a field of cotton, a crowd of white-haired matrons and grandmotherly women – perhaps one thousand strong. They carried painted signs that read END THIS VICE, FREEZE THE TOWN, and PUT AN END TO WAPPYVILLE!

Leading the parade was a tall man, a minister by the collar he wore. And at his side was Mrs Irvine in a black robe and a long, wide suffragist suit. She noticed Ernest and called out to him, urging him to leave, but he stood frozen in place as she joined a group of singers who belted out 'Come, Ye Sinners, Poor and Wretched'.

As Ernest watched in awe, some marchers seemed divided, half of them praying and blessing the onlookers in the neighborhood, while the other half cursed and spat at the women on the sidewalk. Ernest looked up and down the street as shuttered windows opened and scores of women in negligees laughed and wheedled, or yelled back, heckling the protesters. Ernest's jaw dropped as dozens of bawdy women slipped their knickers off and tossed them out their windows. Sateen bloomers and pantalets of every color cascaded down, occasionally wafting on the breeze, changing direction before delicately landing on the shoulder of a marching matron who'd recoil and cry out as though struck by burning oil or a poisoned arrow. One rotund, balloon-chested woman in particular strutted out onto her third-story balcony and unfastened her ladies' waist—

'Don't look, young Ernest.'

Ernest recognized her accent as he felt a pair of hands reach from behind to cover his eyes. Her warm fingers were nice against his cold cheeks.

'You're the girl from downstairs, aren't you?' he asked, as he heard the marchers scream in horror, which only prompted more laughter and jeers from above.

'Sorry I missed you at breakfast,' she whispered in his ear. 'Mrs Blackwell sometimes needs me to eat in the kitchen so I can keep an eye on what we're making for lunch – to see that nothing burns or bubbles over.'

Ernest sensed the crowd boiling. 'Who *are* all these people?'

'You're living in the Garment District, young Ernest, but trust me, the only thing that ever gets sewn down here are oats of the most succulent and wild variety.' The girl laughed. 'These crusades are organized by the Reverend Mark Matthews, along with the Mothers of Virtue, and the Rescue and Protection Society, plus a few die-hards from the Volunteers of America. They come marching down here to save our souls, plug slot machines, prevent drinking on Sundays, try and enforce all the blue laws, that kind of thing. Occasionally they drag someone off to be baptized in Lake Washington. But mostly, they just harass single ladies on the street, even the legit ones, for God's sake, and they try and shame the police, which is nonsense if you ask me. Everyone knows that sin taxes fund half of City Hall.'

This, of course, was news to Ernest.

'They're a mix of old biddies, cuckolded wives, and suffragists, who got the vote a few years back and then lost it when they tried to clean up the town. Which, as you can plainly see, only made them even angrier. Most of the district moved a few blocks south of us, even beyond Skid Row, but I guess that wasn't far enough, so they just keep coming back down – at least once a month. They get spun up like a hornets' nest, but all they really end up doing is ruining everyone's beauty sleep – which, for the working girls and peacharinos, really hits 'em where it hurts.'

Ernest heard the marchers shriek even louder. 'What's happening?'

She laughed. 'You do *not* want to see this. Trust me. It would scald your eyes.'

Ernest couldn't see a thing. She held on tight, and his imagination ran away with him, along with what must have been the rest of the woman's clothing. Then his head reeled as he remembered the colorful women in Madam Flora's entourage, the girls who all came downstairs yesterday, teasing him as they sashayed through the parlor.

The crowd roared. Old ladies cursed. Young women whistled.

'You just realized what kind of place the Tenderloin is, didn't you?' the girl covering his eyes asked.

'What makes you say that?' Ernest asked, though indeed he had. He sensed people running in all directions as the band stopped playing, the singers quit singing, and she gently pulled him closer.

'Because I can feel you blushing.'

Ernest removed her hands and turned around. He knew his cheeks were flushed with embarrassment. He felt bewildered, confused, but at the same time filled with strange joy and comfort. He hadn't been this close to anyone, physically, since he was a toddler, and had never even held a girl's hand in his, outside of dancing a waltz or a box step once or twice at a school gathering.

She looked at him with a wide smile, brows raised, tawny eyes expectant.

And he looked back, still holding her hands, which were small and pretty, but rough from working in the kitchen. She appeared to be a few years older, like Maisie, perhaps fifteen to his twelve. And she was a few inches shorter, even with her boots; slender with raven hair, tied in the back. Olive skin, like his, her eyes, dark, like his. Her odd accent now made sense – she was a Celestial, an Oriental. Her smile was radiant.

'*Konichiwa?*' she asked. 'Or do you still prefer *ni hao mah*? Hello, either way. I'm your downstairs neighbor.' She smiled again, beaming as she introduced herself.

Hello, indeed. He thought the words, but they got stuck when he tried to speak with his heart instead of his brain, because she didn't look anything like what he imagined a scullery maid might look like. He guessed she was Japanese. She dressed plainly, wore no make-up, but had a natural beauty that was hard to ignore. And she looked vaguely familiar.

'You can't place me, can you?' she asked. 'Honestly, I didn't recognize you right away either, but this tells me all I need to know.' She patted the hairpin that he'd slipped through the buttonhole on his coat.

Ernest said, 'I'm sorry. I don't remember . . .'

'It's okay. It's been what – seven years – since we came over together on that ship,' she said. 'Oh, and are you still going to marry me?'

Ernest furrowed his brow. Then he gasped as he remembered a group of children sitting in the hold of a cargo ship, a voice whispering in his ear, turning toward it to whisper himself. He remembered the Japanese girl among all the Chinese children, a girl with an odd name and a quick temper. As though he could ever forget.

She covered her mouth and laughed, then put one hand on his waist, leaned forward, tilted her head, closed her eyes, and kissed him. Not a simple, polite peck on the cheek, but on the lips; it tasted sweet, like cotton candy at the fair, a blizzard of warm, sugar-spun snowflakes melting on his tongue.

She stepped back, plum lips parted, silently appraising him. 'You've never been kissed before, have you?'

Ernest was speechless, eyes blinking, slowly shaking his head, his heart racing. He stood there, smiling like a happy fool, in the middle of the red-light district, which had fallen into a swirling mass of hysterical marchers, shrieking women, laughing ladies, hapless singers, lost band members, and the occasional idle policeman, who rolled his eyes and looked at the sky.

Ernest willed his mouth to work. 'What . . . was that . . . for?'

Fahn pinched his cheek. 'Remember what I said last night?'

Ernest furrowed his brow and nodded.

'Well, the cookies were a gift.' She smiled. 'But that kiss was a favor. And now, young Ernest, you owe me.'

Welcome to the Future

(1962)

This is a love story, but so was the tale of Romeo and Juliet. That was the greatest love story of all time. And we all know how that turned out.

Those are the words that Ernest read aloud to no one in the dusty, single-volume library of his mind as he lingered at a typewriter in his tiny apartment. The old relic he'd bought at Barney's Pawnshop in Pioneer Square had cost ten dollars and smelled like cigarettes, rust, and machine oil. But it worked. Though he struggled to put down anything that might be of value to Juju.

After he'd talked to her about the Tenderloin, the floodgates of his memory had been opened. So much, that he decided to try to write it all down – to contain his stray memories, to manage his wayward emotions. And yet he could barely get past the blank page that seemed like an acre of soil he could never properly tend. Weeds and other wild seeds would inevitably take root amid his labors.

He had new respect for Juju's profession as he sighed and removed his reading glasses. He thought about what he should say, could say, and what bits he might stitch together to hide the unsavory details of his and Gracie's peculiar upbringing.

He'd explained how he had ended up at the Tenderloin, and Juju had been enthralled, as well as shocked.

'You mean they actually gave you away?' she had asked, stunned that the rumor she'd pursued had turned out to be true. 'Like a barrel of apples or a bushel of corn. How could people do that? That's beyond ridiculous, that's cruel.'

'It was a vastly different time,' Ernest had told her with a shrug. He'd come over on a ship with children who were later sold into servitude, so being given to someone of means, by whom he'd also been offered a job and a new life – that had seemed marvelous by comparison, a generous gift of circumstance. 'The way I always looked at it,' Ernest had said, 'if I hadn't been taken in by Madam Flora, I might have wound up as a street kid, eventually sent to a poorhouse, or a reform school that was more like a jail, or worse . . .'

'What could possibly be worse?' Juju had asked.

Ernest had smiled sadly, feeling his eyes glisten as he patted his daughter's arm. 'If I didn't end up in the Tenderloin, I might never have met your mother.'

Now, he gave up trying to write. It was too late to attempt to rescript the past. Juju had already begun a comparative piece on what the world was like then and now, from the price of a gallon of milk to how women influenced politics. In addition, she'd tracked down dozens of locals who'd been to the AYP – those who were his age and older, men and women who could offer reflections and commentary on the two spectacles more than fifty years apart. The newspaper had named them Special Ambassadors to the Future.

To Ernest, the fairs were merely bookends, sentinels carved from stone, rooted in bedrock, immovable. His life, Gracie's life, was the mystery caught in between.

That was worth writing about, if only to help Gracie remember the sweet moments, Ernest thought. Not old dirt and certainly not all this new stuff. Not the Cathedral of Science. Not the monorail. Not the Bubble-Sift, Bubbleator, Bubble . . . whatever that elevator-thing was called.

The idea for the fair had originated a few years ago, when *Sputnik* went 'beep-beep-beep' overhead, launching the Space Race. America and Boeing, which was based in Seattle, had been dragged into the future. And what better way to showcase Seattle to the whole wide world (and especially to the Soviets, and the People's Republic of China, and the North Koreans) than by hosting another epic world's fair? That's when the twinges of Ernest's deeply buried, seismic nostalgia had begun to stir.

Worried that an old news article – possibly even the one Juju had found – might drag him into the frenzy, Ernest had fortified his memories against a tsunami of queries and interviews that never came. With each evening-news broadcast that showcased the construction of the fair along with some old-timer who had been around back then, each starry-eyed, gray-haired recollection that came and went without a mention of his name, Ernest relaxed, relented, and embraced the comfort of his anonymity. If his life were a play, his had been a moment in the spotlight, and then an exit with no applause.

He never suspected his older daughter would be the first to come calling.

Ernest was still staring at the blank page when he heard a knock on the door. He thought that perhaps Juju had come back when he heard a familiar '*Pssst!*' from the hallway. Ernest sighed, unbolted the locks, opened the door, and was greeted by Pascual. Ernest noted that his friend was decked out in a dark black suit – his only suit. He also had on a tight V-neck sweater worn over a sharp, pressed dickie and a rockabilly necktie, which usually meant one thing.

'*Kuya*, I'm heading up to the Black and Tan,' Pascual said with a wink.

'I'm pretty busy . . .' Ernest protested.

'That's why I thought you might like to come along, brother – take a break. Besides, a single man our age is just a lonely guy looking for trouble. But a pair of dashing old gents – that's respectable magic.' He reached into his pocket and pulled out a small silver flask. 'We can drink our way over.'

Ernest was about to say no, that he'd much rather stay in and read a good book, when he remembered that he was supposed to meet Juju tomorrow at the site of the first world's fair. Suddenly a strong drink sounded irresistible. He looked at his reflection in the cracked mirror on his bureau and straightened his tie. He adjusted the double Windsor. Why not? Ernest thought as he buttoned his cuffs and grabbed his coat and hat from a single hook near the door.

Meanwhile his friend splashed a little whiskey in the corner of the hallway. 'That's for the demon.' Pascual grinned, looking like a fifty-year-old schoolboy. He offered the flask to Ernest, who took a large gulp, feeling the alcohol burn his throat. Then the two of them headed downstairs and out the front door into the cool night mist, which smelled like fetid leaves and the rotting pinecones that plugged up storm drains on every corner.

They walked against the tide of swing-shift workers carrying their night-time lunch pails to the docks and avoided getting run over by delivery bikes laden with Chinese food as they made their way to the neighborhood's last great jazz club. As they approached, Ernest could hear live music over the sound of rubber tires on wet pavement.

The Black and Tan had been around since the days of Prohibition, neatly tucked away in the basement of the Chikata drugstore and almost invisible on the corner of Twelfth and South Jackson. Ernest and Gracie had once seen headliners like Lionel Hampton, Duke Ellington, and Cab Calloway there, but the lounge had faded since its glory days. Now it was just a cover band who played, more black than tan. They did their best to recreate the bebop of yesteryear amid the footlights and velvet swirls of cigarette smoke.

For hours Ernest sat in a tiny faux-leather banquette, nursing a champagne cocktail, while Pascual had loosened his tie and danced the Watusi with a cadre of inebriated Caucasian women half his age. Ernest watched the happy sway of their cotton print Woolworth dresses, their bouffant hair, which towered over his friend.

'Are you sure you wouldn't like to dance?' The kind woman Ernest recognized as Dolores appeared, smiling. 'Your friend tells me you're a great dancer.'

'I would love to,' Ernest said. 'But I'm saving the last dance for someone else.'

'Oh, is she here?' Dolores asked as she looked around.

'Not yet.' He shook his head. 'But I keep hoping she'll come back someday.'

Dolores regarded him with sad puppy-dog eyes. Then she leaned down and gave him a warm hug and kissed his cheek before returning to the dance floor.

Ernest smiled as he wiped the lipstick off with a napkin. He watched Pascual and occasionally chatted with the barmaids who vaguely knew him, until he ran out of cigarettes and grew restless. He waved goodbye to his friend, who didn't seem to notice.

Ernest walked home in a light rain, past all-night liquor stores and flower carts, around sailors in blue, and high-heeled streetwalkers with umbrellas who were arguing with the shore patrol, uniformed men who wandered the neighborhood in white helmets, twirling their chipped black billy clubs. Ernest drifted silently past the benign façades of mom-and-pop businesses he knew to be fronts for Chinatown's many backroom casinos. He pulled his collar up to ward off the damp April chill, grateful it was only drizzling as he strolled beneath pools of streetlight, steering around mud puddles that reflected forgotten constellations and lonely stars of the northern sky. He wasn't disappointed to have played Dean Martin to Pascual's Jerry Lewis, because Ernest had needed a night out. He'd been burdened by memories all week, and now the past seemed more resplendent than the present. But the past was no man's land. He gave five dollars to panhandlers in front of the Publix, then climbed the creaking stairs to his apartment, thinking again about how to tell Juju the rest of his story.

He was still worrying when he saw two people standing beneath the glow of a single forty-watt bulb that dangled from the hallway ceiling. Amid the riot of blistered paint, there was a couple arguing.

'I don't know why you had to drag me all the way down to this dump,' the man said. 'Couldn't we just meet him at a goddamn restaurant or something?'

Ernest understood. The Publix was an acquired taste. The address alone might have deterred some people, because the neighborhood wasn't what it used to be. Most of the fancy supper clubs were gone, replaced by all-night diners like the Bamboo Cafe. And the neon had faded or burned out. Now the streets from First Avenue to Pioneer Square and on up to Chinatown were illuminated with signs for pawn shops and taverns. Empty, rusting cans of Olympia beer and Brew 66 littered the once glorious cobblestone streets. The avenues, which had been crafted by hand, brick by brick, sculpted around polished streetcar rails, had been buried – slathered beneath a layer of burning asphalt, then strewn with twenty years' worth of losing pull tabs and cigarette butts. Now the stench of despair was so strong even the rain was unable to wash it away.

Then Ernest heard a familiar voice.

'Jeezuz, you were the one who said you wanted to meet my family. Well, this is where my family lives – part of my family, anyway. So deal with it. If you'd rather run off and shoot dice until dawn like you always do, that's fine with me, but the least you can do is take five minutes and meet him like you promised you would. It's a surprise.'

'That's just you being childish.'

'Me?' the woman snapped.

'Yes, you. Eight-year-old girls like surprises,' the man scolded her. 'Grown men hate surprises.'

Ernest cleared his throat. 'Not all grown men.' He stepped into the light and waited for their reaction. The man looked annoyed, the woman confused for a brief moment and then . . .

'Dad!'

'Is there a chorus line somewhere in Las Vegas that's missing its lead dancer right now?' Ernest asked as he removed his hat. 'Hanny, this is a wonderful surprise – the best kind. I don't care what anyone says.' He winked at the strange man, who smiled back, barely concealing his embarrassment.

Hanny squealed as she dropped her purse and threw her arms around him. 'Daddy! I missed you so much – Mom too. Juju called and said that Ma's been coming back around. So I dropped everything and booked the first flight I could find. We just landed an hour ago. Oh, and I have another surprise.'

Hanny put her arm around the tall fellow with perfect auburn hair, flawless teeth, and a cleft in his chin like that of the actor Cary Grant.

Ernest smiled. 'I can only imagine.'

'I'm Rich,' the man interjected as he thrust a hand in Ernest's direction. 'It's a pleasure to finally meet, I've heard a lot about you. Oh, and if you ever need an entertainment attorney, I might know a few – starting with yours truly.'

'Nice to meet you,' Ernest said as he noticed the gemstones on the man's fingers. The largest rock was the size of Ernest's thumbnail. He glanced at Hanny, who was beaming and bouncing with excitement.

'Dad,' Hanny said, 'Rich is a lawyer, but he's also my fiancé.' She held up her fingers and pointed to a tiny diamond of her own. 'It belonged to Rich's grandmother. She survived the sinking of the *Titanic* – can you believe that?'

Ernest paused for a moment, hoping Allen Funt would step out of the janitor's closet with his *Candid Camera* crew in tow. 'Wow, that's a lot to comprehend,' he said.

Then he hugged his daughter, wishing her congratulations as best he could, despite the shock. He shook Rich's hand again, wishing him all the best. Ernest chatted and doted and tried not to imagine what Gracie, lucid or otherwise, might think about this news. He wished she were here and able to say something that would help him make sense of all this, or at least signal a warning to Hanny about the impending iceberg that lay in the path of this relationship. Hanny had always had her choice of suitors – ever since high school – and yet somehow she'd settled for . . . *this guy.*

Ernest realized he was grinding his teeth and relaxed his jaw. Then he drew a deep breath, clapped his hands, and rubbed them together. He wouldn't allow himself to doubt his daughter, to be that cynical.

'You know – I believe Rich is absolutely right,' Ernest said. 'This is no place to celebrate. Why don't we all go out and get a late supper?'

'We flew first class,' Hanny said. 'We had chicken Kiev on the plane. But you know me. I can always go for a little dessert. How about the Jasmine Room?'

Ernest smiled. 'That would be perfect.'

Mayflower Rock

(1909)

Ernest's heart was still racing, his mind still spinning. He swore he could still feel Fahn's kiss, even after eating a bowl of porridge. It had been delicious, topped with grated dark chocolate and toasted coconut. And the dairy – Ernest was astonished at the taste, the rich creamy texture of real milk. All those years at boarding school, he'd rarely drunk anything other than tea and the powdered junket they'd served daily, which was supposed to make them healthy and strong, but tasted like warm milk mixed with chalk.

Ernest wasn't sure what Mrs Irvine had been so worked up about.

I wouldn't leave this place to go to Heaven, Ernest thought, as he tried to catch a glimpse of Fahn, who was busy in the kitchen. She caught his eye, winked, and then disappeared. Ernest waved back at no one, but smiled nonetheless. At the children's home the girls lived in a separate building, and in class they ignored him. But here, his new life was off to a roaring start.

He didn't even mind spending the next hour shoveling coal in the basement. He whistled, hummed, practically danced in the dusty coal bin as he worked. Then he changed his clothes, cleaned himself up, and helped Fahn and Violet set up breakfast for the working girls. Ernest observed the precise way Fahn arranged the polished silverware, the breakfast plates, elegant eggcups, juice glasses, and different sets of china for tea and coffee. He followed along as best he could while Violet arranged the plush chairs, opened the curtains and blinds, and tended to the flower vases set about the formal dining room. She retrimmed the stems that hadn't yet bloomed, then weeded out the wilted and the dead.

Ernest stood at attention as Madam Flora and the rest of the upstairs ladies swept into the room in messaline tea gowns. A baker's dozen, Ernest thought, counting Maisie, who looked her tomboyish best in a porkpie hat too big for her head. Miss Amber followed behind, now elegantly dressed and sporting long auburn tresses.

'You know the rules, girl. No toppers in the house,' Miss Amber snapped. 'Now take that ugly thing back to the lost and found. Someone just might want it back.'

Ernest noticed Fahn rolling her eyes as she sighed wearily at Maisie, Miss Amber, or perhaps both – he didn't know for sure. He looked away, suppressing a laugh.

Meanwhile Madam Flora introduced Ernest to the ladies of the manor: Ruth, Pearl, Lillian, Emma, Josephine, Beatrice, Hilda, Cora, Hattie, Mary Alice – many of whom he'd already met casually when he arrived. Madam Flora beamed as each young lady bowed slightly with a polite smile. 'My Gibson girls: these are the finest women in all of Seattle. Have you ever seen such grace, poise, beauty, and refinement? They are elegance personified, perfection in thought and deed . . .'

Ernest smiled and waved, thinking that they did look like the Gibson girls he'd seen rendered in magazines and on advertisements – fragile but voluptuous, empowered with confidence and high-spirited, yet joyful – the opposite of a traditional suffragist.

'Ah, don't be fooled, boy,' Miss Amber interrupted, laughing. 'They're mutton dressed as lamb, every one of 'em.'

And with that Violet and Fahn took their leave as the ladies set to their breakfast, laughing about the parade and the scene in the street that morning. They giggled and cursed and told jokes Ernest didn't understand. They deliberately slurped their tea, elbowing each other, some of them eating with their hands, stirring their coffee with their butter knives, just to tease Madam Flora, who shook her head and sighed, drumming her painted fingernails on the table.

'I'm afraid the girls are just letting their hair down a bit, so to speak. The ones not wearing wigs.' Madam Flora winked at Miss Amber as she spoke. 'But I assure you, these girls have the most class – literally and figuratively. Now, ladies, eat up – you have elocution lessons in the salon in one hour. Then classwork, then music.'

One older girl tucked her spoon into a soft-boiled egg. 'Aye, aye, Captain Flora. Hear that, girls? Our standing orders from the captain and her first mate – by day we're expanding our minds. And by night we're spreading our—'

'That's quite enough, dear,' Madam Flora interrupted with a wan smile.

'Always the button burster, that one,' Miss Amber grumbled.

Ernest blushed again as the ladies twittered and finished their breakfast.

'And you, young man, I have something important for you to do today.' Madam Flora pursed her lips as she produced a small stack of elegantly addressed letters. 'These are special invitations for this month's festivities. See to it that they're all delivered today. My little Mayflower will show you around, won't you, dear?'

'Thank you, madam, but there's no need to trouble her,' Ernest said. 'Perhaps there's a fellow servant who could show me.'

'Nonsense,' Madam Flora said. 'Maisie can do it one last time.'

Maisie took an enormous bite of bread and then shoved her plate away.

'Go on, girl,' Miss Amber huffed. 'Do as Flora says. You can't be a gamine runabout forever, you know?'

Maisie stared at Miss Amber as she chewed slowly and then swallowed. Then she smiled and said, 'I'd be absolutely delighted to show him around.' Her expression suggested she'd rather pluck a live chicken with her teeth.

Maisie walked so fast down Second Avenue that Ernest almost had to run to keep up with her. He tagged along as she led him through traffic, around parked carriages and swerving, honking automobiles. The slower drivers were accompanied by footmen, who ran ahead of their owners' motorcars with red flags of warning.

Maisie marched through business districts cluttered with knots of power lines, telephone cables, and crowded residential streets that smelled like soap and lye from the clotheslines and hanging laundry. She took strange alleyways, skirting houses with warning signs, quarantined by whooping cough, and backtracked so much he was certain she was trying to confuse him at best and lose him at worst. She ignored the gentlemen on the street who occasionally tipped their hats or nodded as she tromped by, and she seemed annoyed with the little boys on crate scooters who noisily raced past them on the sidewalk.

'Where are we going?' Ernest finally asked, out of breath as they passed the Great Northern Tunnel for a second time and headed back toward Pioneer Square.

'Anywhere and everywhere.' Maisie handed him half of the envelopes. There must have been fifty in all. The white lace invitations had been sealed with scented beeswax, each stamped with an ornate T. 'You met Jewel in the motorcar yesterday. She's turning sixteen and having a coming-out party – all the Tenderloin's best patrons are invited. No traveling businessmen, no good-time Charlies or cellar smellers, and certainly no soldiers or sailors. Madam Flora says *we're not that kind of place.*'

'Coming out?' Ernest had visions of Seattle's elegant Grand Cotillion, of horse-drawn surreys and string quartets. He remembered how the little girls at the children's home would carefully clip out photographs of young women in fancy gowns from the society page of the Sunday paper. They'd play with them like paper dolls. 'Like a debutante ball?' he asked.

'Judas Priest, did you just fall off a turnip wagon?' Maisie snorted as she kept walking. Then she put a hand on her hip and spoke in a deep, breathless voice, imitating the way the older girls cooed. 'It's her sweet sixteen, darlin'. She's going to the highest bidder. Let's just hope he's as handsome as he is rich.'

Ernest stopped in his tracks.

'What's the big deal?' Maisie asked with a shrug. 'Is the carriage trade too much for your delicate sensibilities? Or is the new servant boy suddenly too good for us? I sure hope not, because that would be quite funny considering how we just won you in a cakewalk.'

'It was a raffle.'

Maisie shook her head and kept walking. 'Honestly, I'd been hoping for a pony, but evidently that was given away last week.'

Ernest gave up the last shreds of his denial and followed her up the street and across the Deadline, beguiled by the Tenderloin, which wasn't a fancy hotel or a women's social club, as he'd initially tried to convince himself. In fact, the stately-looking brick building was precisely the kind of place Mrs Irvine had warned him about in their yearly interviews. If children didn't protect their virtue, then their carnal nature would invariably lead them to ruin. And to Mrs Irvine, ruin always looked a lot like the Tenderloin – a crib joint, a sporting home, a den of iniquity, a bawdy house of ill repute.

'It's just a coming-out party,' Maisie said. 'Besides, the age of consent is ten, and half the girls in the city are married off and pregnant by sixteen anyway. Probably up to their eyeballs in dirty diapers by the time they're twenty, living in some Sears mail-order house on the prairie, doting on their drunken, philandering husbands, who backhand their wives to keep them in line. And if they're single, they end up as factory girls working twelve-hour days, being pawed at by some creepy boss, all for five dollars a week, which isn't even enough to live on. Or worst of all, they wind up as old maids – schoolmarms who aren't allowed to date or even let their hair down because they might give their students the wrong idea. The girls at the Tenderloin are the lucky ones, Ernest. They get a proper education, they get to see a doctor whenever they want, and get their teeth taken care of. And they get fifty dollars a day. Plus they get to visit their boyfriends once a week, if they care to have one.'

Ernest wasn't about to argue, so he read the addresses on the envelopes as they walked. He didn't recognize the names, but he began to marvel at some of their titles and was confused all over again. There were benign trades like manager of Western Union. Powerful-sounding jobs like president of Greenwood Logging. But the most surprising – alarming even – were the names of city councilmen and politicians – Republicans, Democrats, prohibitionists, socialists, independence leaguers, and even the rarified, beatified, elected occupation known as Distinguished Mayor of Seattle.

'Madam Flora calls them our patron saints,' Maisie said. 'After the Great Fire, the Tenderloin was one of the first places to be rebuilt – better than ever. Old Madam Lou helped the neighborhood get back on its feet, though she still got run out of town. But Madam Flora knows what she's doing, even if she has poor taste in Miss Amber.'

Ernest noticed as Maisie frowned at the thought of Madam Flora's partner.

'Most of Madam Flora's best patrons are right here, in the heart of downtown.' Maisie pointed as they walked past the McDougal and Southwick Company and the Majestic Theatre. Ernest marveled at a hand-painted poster featuring skaters atop a giant block of ice. 'It's better that we deliver the invitations to their offices than their homes, if you get my meaning?'

Maisie led him from the waterfront up First Hill and back, from Hayes & Hayes Bank to the Rainier Brewery. Finally, curiosity got the best of him and he mustered the courage to ask, 'So . . . is Flora really your sister? I mean, of course she's your house sister – you know what I mean, but perhaps you were adopted like the rest, like the help downstairs?'

Maisie slowed down and for a moment seemed lost, then stopped and looked up at the sky. Ernest almost thought he saw sadness in her pale blue eyes.

'I'm sorry,' he said. Having bounced around for years as a ward of the state, he was used to nonchalantly talking about the comings and goings of parents, grandparents, siblings, and guardians. 'If that's something I shouldn't ask . . .'

'It's okay. It's not a big secret to anyone who lives at the Tenderloin. I suppose it's better to hear it from me than from the maids,' Maisie said as she sniffled and mentioned something about the autumn air, even though the sun was shining.

'In the district there are crib joints and then there are parlor joints, and sometimes Madam Flora cherry-picks new girls that have potential from the bad places – the run-down sporting clubs in the neighborhood. Other girls she's found on the street or rescued years ago. But Flora, in one way or another, has adopted almost everyone at the Tenderloin. And the girls who seem to have a certain spark, Flora puts to work upstairs. It's a fancier life, she has them tutored, and trained, but only if they are cut out to be true Gibson girls. The rest, they end up downstairs, working as maids, and cooks, and housekeepers. No one seems to care or mind very much – we all do what we're told. Everyone sticks together through thick and thin, everyone's happy, and everyone minds her own business. Well, except for Fahn, who is always up to something.'

As she kept talking a dam of silent emotion seemed to be cracking. Ernest followed along, regarding her – Margaret, Maisie May, the Mayflower, Madam Flora's little hummingbird. With her tomboy hair, she seemed destined to work downstairs, but there was something about her blue eyes – great beauty, hiding in plain sight. And she seemed smarter than the rest. He wondered where she'd be in a few years.

'We're like a big happy family at the Tenderloin; Fahn and me are like Irish twins. Even Professor True is like an uncle. But, despite all that, you should know that Madam Flora is most definitely *not* my real sister.'

Ernest looked over at her.

'Madam Flora is my *real mother*.'

Ernest blinked and stepped away from the curb as a bus rumbled by.

'Here's the thing. She doesn't want outsiders to know, because it's bad for business. Back in the day, Madam Flora had plenty of suitors – rich, powerful men, some even wanted to marry her. But . . . then I came along and crashed the party. Amber said my father was some banker. From what I heard, he already had a wife back in Chicago, so when he found out Flora was up the duff he wanted her to get rid of me. He tried to buy her off, but she refused. That's how I know she loves me.'

Ernest stopped in his tracks.

Maisie brushed her long blond bangs from her eyes. 'Amber said that man lost a million dollars the year I was born. And we're guessing he blew what was left in the big Knickerbocker Panic, because right about that time we heard he walked off a pier in New Jersey and was never seen again. Sharks probably got him. Madam Flora hung up her stockings after that, once and for all, breaking the hearts and egos of a lot of wealthy gentlemen. Ever since then Amber's just told everybody that I was Flora's little sister – it's less complicated that way. Plus, I think it makes Flora feel youthful.'

Maisie shrugged again. 'Besides, I doubt that Flora's the first working girl to call her daughter a cousin or baby sister . . .'

'But . . . she's still your mother,' Ernest said. 'You're still her daughter, you're . . .'

'I'm nobody's anything, Ernest.' Maisie cut him off as she handed him the rest of the invitations and walked away. 'I'm not the *Mayflower*.' She turned and patted her chest. 'I'm Plymouth Rock.'

Dragon's Blood

(1909)

After Ernest finished delivering the invitations, he returned to the Tenderloin and found Fahn waiting for him on the front step. She was peeling green apples, cutting them, and dropping the slices into a copper pot filled with water. She wiped her hands on a kitchen towel and shook her head.

'When Miss Amber saw that the *Mayflower* had sailed back without its crewman, she chewed her out something fierce and then sent me off looking for you. I circled around for a few blocks, but I knew you'd figure it out.' Fahn smiled and cocked her head. 'I hoped anyway. Grab the pot and follow me.'

As Ernest trailed behind, he tried not to drip on the carpets or the wooden floor and tried even harder not to think about Maisie, and her stubborn acceptance of her circumstances. He remembered the last time he saw his own mother back in China. Her life – her death – had become more myth than memory. He knew he'd been born near the Pearl River Delta, but now he couldn't even find that place on a map. And he remembered his mother telling him how she could never be a good Chinese wife, could never abide by the three obediences – whatever those were.

He put the pot down on the kitchen counter where a dozen ceramic dishes sat at the ready, lined with fresh piecrusts. He felt heat radiating from the large gas oven.

'Are we baking pies?' Ernest asked. 'I don't know a thing about—'

'Mrs Blackwell must be taking a break,' Fahn cut him off. 'She makes the pies. I do all the grunt work. I don't mind, though, because I was able to save you the best apple in all of Washington – maybe the whole wide world.'

Ernest watched as she hung up her apron, polished a perfectly round apple, chopped it in half, and delicately sliced out the core with a paring knife. Then she took a wooden dipper and drizzled honey over the bare fruit. She handed him one half and then bit into the other, wiping her chin with the back of her hand.

'Miss Amber told me to pick up tins of snuff for the upstairs girls. They use chewing tobacco to lose weight and stay fit. Then I have to go pick up Madam Flora's new medicine,' Fahn said with an excited smile. 'Amber thought that you should come with me so you know where to get it next time.'

Ernest's legs felt tired from trying to keep up with Maisie, and his feet were swollen in his ill-fitting leather shoes, but the apple tasted sweet.

'I'd love to go,' he told her.

Ernest followed Fahn, who mercifully walked at a much slower pace than Maisie's battle march. As they turned left at King Street Station and headed east up South Jackson, she pointed out places of interest, like the Maple Leaf Saloon, the Triangle Bar, and the People's Theatre in the basement on Second Avenue.

'Don't be fooled by the name,' Fahn confided. 'It's not a penny crush. It's a low-rent crib joint with watered-down drinks. If a rich customer happens to wander into a place like that, he's bound to take a sap to the back of the head, wake up down on the mudflats, without his wallet. Madam Flora hates those kinds of places. She says they treat the girls awful and give the Garment District a bad name.'

Ernest was still gawking at the buildings when they passed a newspaper boy who stood on a fruit crate, shouting headlines.

'Ty Cobb wins home run title with ninth home run!' he barked to no one in particular as he held up the paper. 'Only a nickel! Read all about it!'

Fahn smiled at the newsboy. 'Maybe on the way back, hon.'

As they continued east, Ernest noticed the signage above the stores had changed from English to Chinese. But there was also Oriental lettering that he didn't recognize – Japanese, he assumed. He remembered how Mrs Irvine had once taken all the kids from the children's home to the Majestic Theatre for a production of *Jappyland*. But all of the performers, singers, dancers, the emperor, the queen, even the geishas and cuddle-up girls were all just white people in heavy robes and thick Pan-Cake make-up – a contrast to the people he was now passing on the street. Men in woolen suits grew scarce, replaced by Orientals in white collars, black hats, and silken robes with fine Chinese embroidery. Ernest couldn't read the symbols on their clothing but vaguely remembered that the robes and the beads represented rank in the community.

'Where are we going?' he asked as he overheard a group of men arguing in a dialect that reminded him of the village where he'd been born.

Fahn took his hand. 'We're going to the Jue Young Wo herb shop for dried dracaena flowers.' She laced her fingers between his and held on tight. She arched an eyebrow mischievously. 'They use it to make dragon's blood.'

Some sort of illicit drug, Ernest thought as he furrowed his brow and remembered old men on a Chinese waterfront sleeping beneath the thick, meaty, sickly-sweet smell of opium smoke. Or like the herbs some men in China used to boost their virility.

Ernest's heart raced as he glanced surreptitiously at his fingers, interlaced with Fahn's. The simple magic of her touch reminded him of how comfortable he felt at the Tenderloin, how excited, and joyful, a sense of belonging he had only dreamed of all those years at the boarding school. Somehow, he finally fit in. That's when he noticed his and Fahn's reflection in the window of the Gom Hong Grocery, their hands swinging freely between them, connecting them. This stroll into Chinatown was also a homecoming. The people, the faces, the smells and aromas of roasting duck, dove, and waxy sausages preserved with cinnamon wafted over him like remembrance of a lovely dream he'd long forgotten. But the faces of the few Chinese women he saw reminded him of his mother, and the Japanese men reminded him of her warnings.

'Avoid the *law baak tau* at all costs,' she'd told him with a stern look, even though the War of Jiawu had been fought before he'd been born. He'd never seen a Japanese man until he'd come to America, and those he'd met didn't look like daikon heads at all. They looked like him, in a way. If anyone looked like ugly potato heads, they were the bald sailors who'd brought him here.

Ernest felt his chest flood with warmth as Fahn said, 'I like holding your hand. We make a good pair, don't you think?'

He tried to say something charming in response but could muster only 'Thanks.'

He remembered sleeping next to her, a little boy among so many big sisters. She seemed older now, in more than just years. Ernest peeked at her, expecting to see disappointment, but she merely smiled, showing off her perfect cheekbones.

That's when Ernest noticed all the men staring at Fahn as they walked through Chinatown, past baskets of dried fish and wooden casks filled with ice and blue rock crabs. Even the ones playing cards and swimming their hands through mah-jongg tiles, smoking, drinking, all took a moment to let their eyes linger on her. Ernest watched as they gazed from her to him, and then back to her again – some smiled, showing crooked or missing teeth. Others pointed, while many laughed and called out to them in their thick Cantonese accents. Ernest wished he knew what they were saying.

'There aren't many women in Chinatown – just old ladies and a handful of girls, Chinese and Japanese,' Fahn said. 'So that makes me a vaudeville attraction whenever I come here, like the women on display at the Japanese Village at the fair. But my American dress sets me apart. They always think I'm the daughter of Goon Dip, who built most of these buildings, or the teenage bride of some other wealthy merchant, or a businessman's new concubine – wouldn't that be a hoot?'

Ernest nodded as though all of this made perfect sense.

'That's why I'm glad you're here – I feel safer with you as my gentleman companion. Usually it's Professor True who escorts me through this part of town.'

Ernest felt flattered and somewhat disappointed at the same time.

Before he'd begun to wallow in that thought, Fahn pointed to a nearby building on a hill. 'That's the Tangerine – it's strictly low-rent. That's the crib where I was supposed to spend my days . . . and nights, eventually.'

Ernest looked at her quizzically.

'After my employer died in China, I came over with dozens of other girls, poor Japanese picture brides, Chinese from the Pearl River, all of us sold by our parents as *mui tsai* or *karayuki-san* – contracted to be little sisters, house servants. They gave us some other girls' passports to get into America. They had us all sign our names with only our thumbprints, since most of the girls couldn't read or write. And then the sailors herded us into a barracoon on the waterfront, where they cleaned us up. Then they moved us to the basement of some other building and stripped us naked.'

Ernest's eyes widened and he fidgeted, unsure if he wanted to hear more.

'At best, our parents thought they were sending us to be contracted servants in fancy houses or, at worst, workers in some garment factory. And the girls without contracts, the rich ones who looked down on the rest of us, they thought they were meeting their new husbands, who turned out to be the same old men in charge of the rest of us. The same men who auctioned all of us off like cattle. I was only eight years old and ended up over there as a servant and a cleanup girl.' She pointed back to the Tangerine.

'On the ship, the Chinese all called me Fahn, which I guess means girl or something, and the name stuck,' she said. 'So that's what they called me at the Tangerine, where I did laundry, I shined shoes and stuffed them with newspaper, I bathed the older working girls, kept bottles of vinegar near the privy, I even did some cooking. Until Madam Flora had the place raided by the police and she took me in.'

Ernest wanted to know more, but just then the pungent aroma of dried ginger and wormwort overwhelmed them.

'Here we are,' Fahn said, as they walked through an open door.

The small shop felt like a lost chapter of his childhood, though this place was larger and much nicer than the one in his village his mother used to visit for dried yarrow to treat colds and fevers. Ernest watched and listened as Fahn ordered two ounces of dracaena and paid for the red herbs with a new silver dollar. The herbalist carefully measured the dried leaves, weighing them on a druggist's scale, and then spooned them into a cone that he'd rolled from a small piece of newspaper. He folded over the top and handed her the herbs.

'These are flowers from lucky bamboo plants,' Fahn said as she waved the packet beneath Ernest's nose. 'Madam Flora mixes them with red wine and drinks it.'

'Why?'

'To treat an old war wound, she says – nervousness from the job. She has headaches. Dizziness. Forgetfulness.' Fahn shrugged. 'She's tried the latest remedies – Horsford's acid phosphate, tinctures of mercury, and even long, hot baths in mineral salts from Soap Lake, but nothing seems to help. So she read about a Chinese doctor in San Francisco who could cure certain maladies with dried herbs. She wrote and told him about her fits of melancholy, and this is what he recommended.' She lowered the tone of her voice. 'If you ask me, I think she caught the *big casino* back when she was just a working girl. Syphilis is supposed to make you do crazy things as you get older.'

Ernest had no idea what Madam Flora's condition had to do with a casino, big or small. But he had heard that *other* word, and only vaguely knew it as some kind of shameful illness. 'Do the herbs work?'

'Guess we'll find out, won't we?'

As they left the herb shop Ernest felt bold enough to offer his arm, and Fahn took it without ceremony. She talked and talked, occasionally pausing to point out a puffy cloud in the blue sky that looked like a circus animal, or to admire the crispy ducks hanging in the window of a Chinese barbecue, or her favorite blossom, tiger lilies, on a nearby flower cart – the street provided an infinite supply of everyday things to amuse and delight her. At the corner, where they waited for a streetcar to roll by, she even complimented Ernest on his smile.

And when they reached Pioneer Square the paperboy was still there, still hawking today's news – something about a Wright Brothers airplane crashing in France and killing the pilot, and the return of a great comet. Fahn paused, and Ernest watched as she read the paper's headlines, then regarded the boy, who was still standing on his upturned crate. She dropped a nickel into his tin cup as he stepped down to hand her the paper, which she ignored. Instead, she placed her hands on the newsboy's shoulders, stood on her tippy-toes, tilted her head, and kissed him square on the lips.

Then she smiled, took Ernest's hand, and continued walking, leaving the stunned paperboy behind them without a second glance. 'I don't like paying for bad news.'

Ernest looked back at the boy, who seemed dumbfounded. 'But . . . why did you do that? He's a total stranger!'

'Well, we're not *total* strangers, Ernest. I see him on the same corner at least once a week.'

Ernest remembered his own kiss and was even more confused, and a bit jealous.

Fahn seemed to notice his befuddlement. 'Women settle for the admiration of men, which is worthless. A dog will admire trees all day but only respect a sharp stick. That's what Madam Flora always says. She tells us that we need to make our own way in the world and not rely on a man for anything. Sometimes that means we have to take what *we want* for a change. So I kissed him back there because I wanted to add a little something to my collection.'

Ernest felt her squeeze his hand.

'Some people collect pennies or feathers. Others collect commemorative ribbons or stamps of the world. I collect first kisses. But that wasn't his first,' she said, shaking her head. 'Trust me. There are a *lot* of boys in my menagerie, and I can tell by now.'

Ernest held her hand as they walked. Or, more aptly, she held his hand and led him along the avenue. He didn't mind. Not too much, anyway. He was deeply dazzled by this strange place, this happy new life. Though when they got back, as she let go of his hand and bounded up the steps, two at a time, part of him felt sad to be left behind, disappointed that she didn't care to collect second kisses, or thirds.

Old Man on Campus

(1962)

Ernest contemplated the collection of sentimental items that had accumulated in his desk drawer – postcards, souvenir pins, campaign buttons (more losers than winners), and ticket stubs from old movies. And of course Juju's latest news clippings, and programs and lobby cards from Hanny's many performances in Reno and Las Vegas.

Some people yearn for the spotlight, Ernest mused.

While at the Tenderloin, he had often heard about a legendary Japanese woman known as the Arabian Oyae. She always wore bright blue stockings and was said to be the rival of any of the Tenderloin's Gibson girls. Fahn had actually seen Oyae once, on King Street late one night, a regal woman, who was surrounded by a retinue of servants and rich men, who all fought for her attention. That encounter, years before Ernest had arrived, had left an impression on Fahn. She had told him that she wanted more from life than her household duties. She wanted to become the talk of Chinatown, if not the city. Fahn wanted to be like Oyae: she wanted to become the next unbreakable horse.

Ernest sipped his coffee and read the paper. He tried not to worry too much about his daughter's new Caucasian fiancé. Rich the lawyer *was rich*, and handsome and successful, and he'd said all the right things over apple pie à la mode. And he obviously cared about Hanny a great deal, but . . . marriage, a mixed-race one at that – that's a complicated

124

undertaking. Ernest remembered Gracie's favorite magazine, *Ladies' Home Journal*, and its trademark column 'Can This Marriage Be Saved?'

Marriage is easy to untangle in Las Vegas, Ernest thought. Perhaps that's why Hanny is entering this arrangement so suddenly after turning down so many other overtures. Meanwhile, Washington's judicial system refused to acknowledge divorces from Nevada – let alone those from south of the border. What had been so convenient for Katharine Hepburn, Elizabeth Taylor, and even last year for poor Marilyn Monroe and Arthur Miller, would never work in Seattle. Not that Ernest would ever consider divorcing Gracie, no matter what her condition was or if she even remembered him.

Ernest shook his head and went back to his newspaper, where he read about the musical *West Side Story*, which had swept the Academy Awards. He'd watched the movie, alone, at the Atlas Theatre. The story had reminded him of classic romantic tragedies like Pyramus and Thisbe, Odysseus and Penelope, and of course, that famous tale of the daughter of Capulet and the son of Montague, which in turn made him think of his own years of teen angst and heartache with Fahn and Maisie. That was forever ago. He chewed his lip and turned to things more wondrous and less nostalgic. He was reading about a test pilot named Neil Armstrong when the phone rang in the downstairs lobby.

Ernest wished the rooms had their own phones as he heard the hotel manager shouting his name up the stairwell. That's when he realized he was late for his meeting with Juju at the University of Washington – she hoped strolling around the former grounds of the AYP might jog loose a few memories. He grabbed his hat and coat and quickly trundled down the stairs, past the manager, who held the phone out at arm's length.

'Tell her I'm on my way,' Ernest said. The man rolled his eyes and smacked on his unlit cigar, as he went back to reading his *Life* magazine bearing the headline OUT OF THIS WORLD FAIR IN SEATTLE.

* * *

Ernest climbed inside his old black Cadillac, thinking how he'd once made a fine living with the elegant sedan, as the favored driver of visiting jazz musicians, colored celebrities, and the occasional prizefighter. Gracie had always loved this car as well, and he had so many fond memories of road trips, weekend getaways. But Ernest also had recollections of trips to the hospital, and driving Hanny to Sea-Tac Airport last year.

Now she's back, Ernest thought, *I have more people to hide Gracie's secrets from.*

When his wife moved in with Juju and Hanny moved away, Ernest had slipped into marital limbo. He tended a small garden in what used to be Kobe Terrace Park. He volunteered at the Chinese Community Center. And he'd haunted the Seattle Public Library, catching up on scores of books he'd wanted to read. Until he grew restless and paid a visit to Kawaguchi Travel, where Gracie used to work part-time, and on a whim he inquired about visiting Canton. A part of him longed to find the village of his birth, where his mother must have died. But in the end he knew traveling there wasn't an option – visits had been prohibited to US citizens.

So instead, Ernest had been forced to settle for a book of Chinese poetry. As he drove, he thought of the words of the great poet Shijing.

I search but cannot find her,
awake, asleep, thinking of her,
endlessly, endlessly . . .

Ernest's route north to the U-District paralleled the gash of construction that had almost healed, leaving a scar the size of a superhighway through the heart of the city. As he saw the towering figure of George Washington who marked the entrance to the campus, Ernest knew that memories had always loomed over him, connecting him to places and people. He waited at a stoplight near the statue, which had been erected when the grounds were being converted to a university campus at the end of the AYP. He remembered that when he was a boy, the sculpture had sparkled, shining almost cobalt blue. But now the first president had taken on the color of dark ash, and his shoulders were covered in epaulets of pigeon droppings.

We are all a bit worse for wear, Ernest mused.

After he parked, Ernest fed the meter a dime and donned his hat. He walked briskly across the old red-brick plaza now known as Red Square, toward the old Geyser Basin, which had been remodeled and renamed Drumheller Fountain. Ernest used the reflecting pool as a compass to orient himself. The trees had added the growth of fifty summers and the view of Mount Rainier wasn't quite as spectacular as he remembered, but if he squinted he could almost recall the grand vista, the cascading waterfalls that had now been replaced by an unadorned walkway. Now the Court of Honor, the massive Government Building, and the Grand Cupola atop Denny Hall were gone. And most of the turn-of-the-century buildings had been replaced by brick structures of a more modern era, designed to please school administrators instead of visitors from faraway countries.

Students milled about, bicycling from class to class, hurrying from building to building, kissing and making out on the wet grass.

As Ernest baptized himself in memory, he searched for the surviving buildings that he could remember from his days at the fair. A few of the big halls remained, but their Doric columns were now a patchwork of repairs. He kept walking until he finally found the marble steps of a modest building that looked like its two stories had sprouted up in a thicket of tall trees. The sign read CUNNINGHAM HALL, renamed after the famous Seattle photographer, but Ernest remembered standing atop those steps surrounded by elderly matrons of the Woman's Century Club and the Daughters of Saint George, raffled off like the strange, peculiar novelty he was.

He stood there for a moment and looked up at the blanket of wet gray flannel that passed for a Seattle sky, sensing mist on his cheeks, the fresh smell of rain, and the sobering cold that came before the first drops of a heavy spring cloudburst. He watched the hermit sun peek out from behind the clouds, then disappear as though saying *goodbye, farewell, nice knowing you.* And he heard a low rumble of thunder as though timber were splitting and then falling in some faraway forest.

Then he spotted Juju, who waved and crossed the parkway. He watched her fondly, knowing that she didn't just want to meet him at the site of the first world's fair – she wanted to follow him into the past.

Ernest buttoned his coat and walked down the steps, as he'd done five decades earlier.

'I thought you might have stood me up,' Juju said as she met him halfway. They found a quiet, somewhat dry park bench beneath the thick canopy of a red madrona.

'I was tempted,' Ernest confessed. He sat next to her and watched Mount Rainier disappear as rain began to dapple the ground.

'To do what?' Juju teased. 'Run away from your fatherly duty of giving Hanny away in marriage to Lantern Jaw Legal Services of Las Vegas, Nevada?'

Ernest nodded. 'That too, now that you mention it.' He listened to the thrum of the rain on the leaves above them as the sprinkling turned to drizzle. 'I take it you met?'

'I had breakfast with Rich and Hanny this morning. Interesting fellow. I get it. Hanny's not the youngest girl on the block anymore, and her clock is ticking.' Juju rolled her eyes. 'Then Han came over for a while by herself. Mom recognized her right away, which was amazing . . . and surprising . . . and wonderful. Plus Mom keeps talking to me more and more – bits of real, salient conversation. She hasn't been this engaged in – forever. She even suggested we go out for dinner tonight, if you can believe that.'

Ernest was as delighted as he was terrified.

'So, I was thinking,' Juju said. 'We could introduce her to Rich at Ruby Chow's, which was always Mom's hangout of choice – order all her favorite dishes. We can go a few hours early, before the dinner rush. We can sit near the exit in one of those private booths in the back. She hasn't been there in years, but Ruby's staff has known Mom forever, they know all about her condition.'

Not exactly, Ernest thought. 'Are you sure that's not too much for her?' he asked.

'I don't think so,' Juju said as she opened a notebook and licked the lead of her pencil. 'It's more of a baby step – like you telling me what I need for my article.'

'I suppose,' Ernest said as the drizzle turned to heavier rain. 'Do you know what they'd say back in my day? That it wasn't just raining . . . it was raining *pitchforks and mud turtles*. Things were so different then . . .'

'That's the understatement of the year! Especially considering they thought it was okay to raffle off a little boy.' Juju found a blank page in her notebook. 'I want all the details that you can recall – no matter how small or insignificant you think they might be. Because, face it, you're about to become the biggest story of the Century 21 Expo – no one is going to believe this actually happened. Plus my editor bet me a hundred bucks that I couldn't get you to talk, so there's that too.'

'Do I get half if I'm a willing participant?' Ernest asked.

'Absolutely,' Juju said. 'Though we might have to split it three ways if Mom opens up tonight and starts talking as well.'

Ernest nodded. He thought about Hanny and Rich. About Maisie and the Tenderloin. 'Should be a night to remember.'

Precious Jewel

(1909)

Jewel's coming-out party was indeed a grand affair. Ernest had experienced nothing so spectacular during his first month. Not on the normal, frolic-filled weekends, not when Madam Flora had a man from the Seattle Astronomical Society place telescopes on the roof so the girls could watch shooting stars, and not even when she'd hired a seven-piece chamber orchestra to play Vivaldi in the grand parlor to celebrate the autumnal equinox. Ernest supposed that the closest he'd come to such extravagance was reading *Great Expectations*, in which the wealthy and eccentric Miss Havisham had hosted such lavish parties.

Madam Flora had arranged to have out-of-town guests stay at the newly built Sorrento Hotel, where welcome baskets awaited them and a perfumed note from Jewel rested on each of their pillows. She then had the gentlemen picked up in style and delivered to the Tenderloin by 8 p.m. Ernest manned the door, politely greeting dozens of men who arrived in carriages and limousines dressed in their evening finery. Ernest took their top hats, made of gossamer and fur, and their polished canes and silver-handled walking sticks, and waited for the final name on the guest list, Hiram Gill, president of the Third Ward, patron of the First, and charismatic head of the Seattle City Council. He was the last to arrive, and everyone in the neighborhood seemed to know who he was as they called out his name and offered to buy him a drink or a cigar when he stepped out of a chauffeured sedan. Ladies working the street corners shouted, 'Looking good, Mr Councilman, if you run for mayor you got my vote, darling!' Though they *couldn't* vote – not anymore.

Ernest held the door as Hiram Gill smiled and waved, then sauntered inside and loudly proclaimed, 'The esteemed Clara Laughlin likes to say that "well-regulated work is the best kind of fun." Well, ladies and gentlemen of Seattle, I'm afraid dear Clara got it backwards. I say that well-regulated fun is the best kind of work!'

Everyone cheered. Professor True pushed his glasses higher up the bridge of his nose and began a ragtime version of 'I Love, I Love, I Love My Wife – But Oh! You Kid!'

Ernest looked at the guest list, checked all of the names, then helped put coats away as the men gathered in the parlor, where they were served Canadian whiskey and sweetwater oysters from nearby Fanny Bay, steamed in the finest French wine. The elegant ladies from upstairs flitted from guest to guest. Before he'd come to the Tenderloin, in his mind's eye – based on Mrs Irvine's stark admonitions – Ernest would have expected the women to be perched on the men's laps in their underthings, stockings rolled down to their bare ankles, or at least sporting knee-duster skirts. He'd imagined them lighting cigars, drinking to excess, and flouncing about. Instead they all wore floor-length princess dresses of raja silk and smoked machine-rolled tobacco from long, gold-tipped cigarette holders. The women sang along with Professor True, solo, in duets, or in the occasional harmonic trio. And whenever the piano player took a break, the ladies would hold court, putting their elocution lessons to the test. One young woman gave a brief drawing room lecture on Turkish girls and life in a harem. Several took turns elegantly reciting romantic poetry by Lord Byron, Emily Dickinson, and Oscar Wilde, from memory.

Ernest listened and thought of Fahn as one of the girls spoke: 'And there is nothing left to do but to kiss once again, and part, nay, there is nothing we should rue . . .'

Ernest peeked into the kitchen, where Fahn and Mrs Blackwell were hard at work basting stuffed pheasants and garnishing steaming cups of creamed barley soup. Fahn looked up at him, licked butter from her finger, smiled, and blew him a kiss. Ernest quickly shut the Dutch door, adjusted his tie, and sauntered back to the parlor.

He noticed that even Miss Amber had cleaned up splendidly for the occasion. She had donned a wig the shade of pink cotton and wore so much make-up that Ernest hardly recognized her. She smiled at the guests and whispered orders to the servants, moving them around like chess pieces on a board. The only person missing – aside from Jewel, who would be presented later, and Madam Flora, who was waiting in the wings – was Maisie. He'd heard Miss Amber earlier yelling at the Mayflower to put on a dress and act like a lady for once. Ernest smiled at the thought.

As Professor True played 'Meet Me Tonight in Dreamland' and sang, 'Come with the love-light gleaming . . .', Madam Flora made her entrance, descending the grand staircase in a flowing gown of shimmering red and gold sequins. While all eyes were on the matron of the house, Ernest slipped upstairs to retrieve a set of grooming brushes so he could properly tend to the haberdashery. As he passed Maisie's room, he was startled to hear gentle weeping. He hesitated and then peered past the partly opened door. But Maisie wasn't the one in tears. It was Jewel, who sat on the edge of the bed in a simple dressing gown as Maisie held the older girl's hand.

'It's probably cold feet. You just got a case of the morbs.' Maisie spoke softly, gently. 'It's happened to other girls. It's perfectly normal.'

Jewel wiped her eyes.

'When Madam Flora brought you here, you were practically being forced by the county shelter to marry an old widower you didn't want to be with. This is different – this is better. It's just one night, Jewel Box, and you'll be rich tomorrow instead of cleaning up after another woman's children, or out there drifting on your own, hoping some clod treats you to a nice dinner or a string of pearls that you can pawn to pay your rent.'

'I know that' – Jewel sniffled – 'I know I'm so much better off this way. But what if he's some disgusting monster? What if I can't go through with it? Or what if no one wants me, what if no one bids . . . ?'

'Who *wouldn't* want you?' The whispered words slipped out of Ernest's mouth before he could stop himself. He covered his mouth. Both girls froze and looked up at him.

'I'm sorry for eavesdropping,' Ernest whispered, 'I didn't mean to. I came upstairs to get something.'

'You didn't see a thing,' Maisie snapped. 'And you didn't hear a thing.'

Ernest stepped into the room. 'I heard enough. But I would never tell a soul, I promise you that. It's just . . .' He knew exactly how Jewel felt, being put on display, worrying that he was merely part of some terrible joke. He handed his pocket square to Jewel. 'I don't know you all that well, but what I do know is that you're smart, and kind, and beautiful, and honestly, who in the world wouldn't want a girl like you?'

Ernest thought Maisie might groan at the sentiment, but she said nothing.

Jewel dabbed at her eyes with the handkerchief. 'Well aren't you a keeper? You're a regular blue serge, Ernest.'

Ernest wasn't sure what she meant, but her words sounded kind. He wondered where Jewel might go if she didn't go through with it.

And whom she might end up with if she went downstairs.

'They're all rich and educated and come from proper families, but money doesn't automatically make you a gentleman, does it?' Jewel asked of no one in particular. 'If all those fellows were as decent as you, Ernest, this might not be so hard.'

Maisie suppressed a sarcastic snort. 'Unfortunately, he'll probably grow out of it. He'll just be one of *them* eventually, minus the bank account. Come on, let's get you cleaned up,' she told Jewel. 'And, Ernest, I'm sure you're needed downstairs.' She took the damp handkerchief and handed it back to him with a wan smile.

Ernest nodded as he heard the dinner bell ringing from the kitchen. He slipped back downstairs, returning to his station in the dining room just in time for Madam Flora to begin her first toast of the evening – one of many.

After a nine-course meal, which included poached salmon with mousseline sauce, parmentier potatoes, pheasant lyonnaise, cold asparagus vinaigrette, and three courses of wine, the guests were invited to the smoking lounge for a cigarette course and a dessert of fresh fruit, cheese, and Waldorf pudding.

Ernest had never seen so many grown men in distinguished suits titter like schoolboys – they seemed giddier than Ernest after his taste of fairy floss at the AYP. He thought their behavior was merely due to the abundance of alcohol, but he fully understood why such anticipation filled the room when the *real* dessert cart arrived.

Ernest gaped at Jewel as she was wheeled in, lounging atop a polished silver truss. Maisie led the way in a plain dress, showering the room with white rose petals. Jewel looked lovely, innocent yet decadent as she sank her teeth into a Red Delicious apple, staining the fruit with her freshly painted pomegranate lips. Her long auburn hair had been curled so the tips framed her perfectly powdered cheeks. She smiled, the way she'd been trained, and wagged her manicured finger at the men who got too close. She wore a shimmering gown of radium silk, trimmed with Cluny lace and pearls, and a diamond-studded headpiece (which belonged to Madam Flora, according to whispers). The tiara glittered in the lamplight. She seemed to have left her tears and doubts and sadness upstairs as she slowly orbited the room, the guests bowing and gushing their praises. She made eye contact with Ernest for a fleeting moment and then looked away.

Madam Flora offered a toast of tawny port and then proudly announced that the bidding would begin at one hundred dollars. In American currency, she added, noting that one of the guests had come all the way from Vancouver, British Columbia.

That's when Miss Amber asked Ernest to answer a knock on the front door.

As he reluctantly stepped away from the spectacle, past Professor True, who was still playing, Ernest cast his mind over the guest list. Everyone who had sent an RSVP was accounted for. And besides, who would be showing up at this late hour?

As he opened the door he felt a wave of condescension even before he took in the sight of Mrs Irvine, flanked by a dozen hard-nosed matrons of the Mothers of Virtue. Her scowl seemed to soften when she saw him. The other ladies were trying to pass out handbills to strangers on the street, most of whom ignored their attempts. A few of the women carried painted signs condemning Madam Flora and the Tenderloin.

'It's a miracle!' Mrs Irvine said as she regarded Ernest and then cast her eyes toward the gray, overcast sky, the starless night. 'You're alone! This is your chance, Ernest. We ladies have important work to do, but you can leave, *get thee behind me*, and when we're done here I'll take you back to Holy Word, away from this . . . this . . .' She spat the word at Ernest's feet: 'this nightmare.'

Ernest paused, breathless. He thought about the conversation he'd had upstairs, with Jewel. He remembered his placid, servile existence under Mrs Irvine's care, where he'd undoubtedly be for the next year if he were to return. He looked at the signs the women hoisted that condemned *white slavery*, and he remembered how easily they'd put him on the block to be raffled off. He wondered what the difference was. Then he thought about the Tenderloin, about Fahn, and Maisie, about earning real money of his own and about eventually learning to drive a motorcar. He heard the piano calling him. He'd briefly wondered why Jewel didn't leave, and now he had to ask himself the same question.

'What are you waiting for?' Mrs Irvine asked before Ernest could compose himself enough to speak. 'I'm sorry that you ended up here, but if you care a whit for your immortal soul, you should run far and fast, and do it now. Better to live out your days as a beggar in a poorhouse than as a young lord in a house such as this.'

Ernest felt a twinge of guilt, not for being at the Tenderloin but for feeling so excited at the prospect of being a young lord. 'It's good to see you, Mrs Irvine,' he stammered. 'But I have a job to do. And, I'm sorry, you're not on the guest list.'

Mrs Irvine frowned and held up one of the invitations. The envelope had been opened, and she regarded the elegant piece of stationery as though it pained her just to be in its presence. He wondered how she'd come to have it in her possession. 'We came to stop this abomination. And we brought help. We're going to shut this place down eventually – mind my words, young man – and if you're here when that happens, you'll get smeared with the same tar brush.' She cocked her hip as though that was the end of the argument. Then she grabbed a pair of uniformed police officers by the arms as the other ladies practically pushed them up the front steps.

One of the grim-faced policemen tipped his hat at Ernest and shook his head slowly, almost imperceptibly, then turned around to address the crowd.

'Now you ladies go on and head home to your husbands. Let us take care of this ugly piece of business,' the officer said in a calm, commanding tone. 'This isn't the kind of neighborhood you ought to be in after dark. Rest assured, I'll make certain those accountable get what they deserve.'

A police wagon motored up to the curb, and three more officers stepped out and redirected pedestrians on the sidewalk away from the area in front of the Tenderloin.

Satisfied, the women clutched one another and sang a hymn as they held their heads high, marching off into a gathering crowd of gawkers and looky-loos. Mrs Irvine yelled back from somewhere in the street, 'Remember what I said, Ernest! Remember what I said! It's not too late to come back!'

As Ernest watched, the police officers walked past him through the door and into the parlor. The lead officer paused, then yelled, 'What's a guy gotta do to get invited to this kind of party?' The reply was a rousing cheer from the patrons inside.

Ernest walked back in as Miss Amber was handing glasses of port to each of the officers, and the Gibson girls sidled up to each man in uniform.

Madam Flora appeared next to Ernest. 'It's so good to have you with us, dear. Welcome to the sporting life.'

He watched as she placed a cup in Councilman Gill's hand and he offered a toast to the hardest-working police department in the Northwest. Then a few of the officers were led up the grand staircase as the bidding continued.

Ernest felt an arm around his waist and knew that it was Fahn. She'd doffed her apron and kitchen bonnet but still smelled like rosemary and sage.

'I heard that lady talking to you, young Ernest,' Fahn said. 'Madam Flora did too. Maybe that woman – Mrs Irvine – is right. Maybe you should go now while you still can, before you start to enjoy your new life. We've all had a chance to leave this business and no one ever does. Why do you think that is?'

Ernest looked up at the crystal chandelier, the velvet wallpaper, the lacy elegance, the wealth in the room, the power – but the sensation that overwhelmed him was more than prestige and opulence. He sensed Fahn's warmth, the comfort of her touch; he felt charmed and alive, as they stood hip to hip. It was in sharp contrast to Mrs Irvine, who seemed dull, and cold, who found offense in everything she saw, except her own decadence. Maybe that's why the dour old woman never seemed to smile. Ernest thought too about his immortal soul, as Mrs Irvine had described it – the same one he'd learned about in Sunday school, where the children were taught to do good deeds unto others. And yet, those same kids had wrapped up rocks and bricks as gifts and given them to him on his last birthday. Ernest had opened them up quietly, one after another, as everyone laughed. When the teacher arrived, she merely chastised him for making a mess.

As a ward of the state, Ernest had never had a girl as a friend, let alone an actual *girlfriend*. At Dow's Landing the boys all pretended that they hated the girls, and relentlessly teased anyone who acted contrary. And at Holy Word, the second-class kids were rarely allowed at dances or ice cream socials. But as Fahn leaned into him he felt at peace, unjudged. He felt free. He wasn't sure what their relationship was becoming, but whatever the strange connection was, he was caught up in the blatant, unrepentant honesty of the Tenderloin – as naked and bare as the girls upstairs. He let himself drift away on the riptide of new emotions that came with this place on a daily basis. He felt tangled to the point of casual surrender. That's when he thought of Mrs Irvine's words and knew that it was already too late.

'Five hundred dollars!' one of the men shouted.

The women cheered. The men heckled one another, boasted.

'Councilman Gill, are you going to let that kind of offer go unchallenged?' Madam Flora dared as she took the cigar from his mouth and began smoking it, blowing smoke rings across the table. 'You have a reputation to uphold. I don't think you want people thinking you've become some kind of teetotaling Quaker, do you?'

The councilman smiled and yelled, 'Here's to an open city, with open minds, and open wallets. Seven hundred dollars.'

'Seven hundred and fifty,' another shouted as he finished his drink and set his glass down with a sharp retort. 'And open breeches!'

The drunken men roared.

'Eight hundred for this lovely girl,' an older, clean-cut businessman said. 'But for a night of my sterling companionship, *she* should be paying me!'

The men laughed, and more drinks were poured.

Ernest looked at Jewel, who seemed to be eating up the extravagant attention by so many rich and powerful patrons. Her cheeks, which earlier had been streaked with tears, now seemed to be positively glowing as she regarded the bidders. Some might have passed as handsome, ten or twenty years ago. Ernest thought about what Fahn had said about dogs admiring trees.

Ernest lost track of the sum after it passed one thousand dollars and the roaring and cheering all blended into a deafening hurricane of ribald commerce. The music, the bidding, the laughing, the shouting, the lavish fervor was intoxicating. But it was sickening, confounding as well. Being sold at a high price didn't change the fact that a person was being sold like a head of cattle. His heart was numb when the auction finally died down and the last toast was offered. The ladies all sang 'Good Evening, Caroline' as Jewel and the lucky winner ascended the stairs and waved goodbye, as though setting sail aboard the *Mauretania*.

Ernest chewed his lip and shifted uncomfortably at the thought of what they'd be doing hence. Jewel was the youngest of the Gibson girls, which left only him, an assortment of maids, and presumably Maisie, and Fahn, as the residents of the Tenderloin whose virtues remained somewhat intact. As he stared at the grand carpeted staircase and listened to the music, he might have daydreamed for hours if Miss Amber hadn't poked him in the ribs. She handed him a heavy silver bucket with a bottle of wine, overflowing with chipped ice.

'What are you lollygagging about for? Follow them upstairs, and do it quick. And watch your step, that bottle of cuvée is a Ruinart '82, the best in the house – probably worth more than you'll make in two lifetimes.'

Ernest looked at the bottle and did what he was told. He trailed behind the couple, setting the bucket on a table just inside the door to their suite. The winning bidder thanked him happily and then shooed Ernest off with a ten-dollar bill as he unfastened his black suspenders and loosened his white tie.

Jewel stared back at Ernest with quiet eyes. She seemed neither happy nor sad, scared perhaps, just a little, but more resigned than anything else. She didn't even blink as the cork popped and careened off the ceiling. Instead, she merely mouthed the words 'Thank you' to Ernest as he closed the door behind him.

When Ernest looked at the clock it read 2:37 a.m. He'd been busy all night, decanting wine, shining shoes, removing lint from the coats of guests, and fetching cabs as the party slowly wound down to the calm of intimate conversation and a gentle waltz rendered by Professor True. The piano man had loosened his tie and seemed to be playing in his sleep, eyes closed, bent over the ivory keys of his baby grand even as his fingers danced back and forth like puppets on strings.

The policemen had left hours earlier, but not before the girls showered them with wet, lipstick-stained goodbyes and Madam Flora slipped each officer a handful of folding money. She could afford it, as Jewel had brought in over a thousand dollars from a porcine businessman with a cleft in his double chin. If Jewel had objections to her suitor, she'd kept them masterfully hidden. Ernest thought of how she'd cooed and addressed him as though he were the man of her dreams – Prince Charming in a waistcoat one size too small.

'Thirteen hundred dollars was the winning bid. Not by a particularly handsome man, but at least it was a handsome sum,' Fahn had whispered as she collected empty wine glasses.

Ernest had never even seen a hundred-dollar bill, let alone held one. He felt the ten-dollar bill in his pocket, more money than he'd ever possessed at one time. At the Tenderloin, the cash and the stringent rules of polite society ebbed and flowed as freely as the whiskey and the bottles of Bordeaux.

'What's the most anyone's ever paid for one of these nights?' he asked.

'Well – if you can believe it, they say there was a man named Louis J. Turnbull who once bid five thousand dollars.'

'For who?' Ernest asked, wide-eyed. His jaw hung open, slightly. That was a king's ransom. Ernest couldn't comprehend that much money. He was making twenty cents an hour, plus room and board.

'You don't want to know.' Fahn rolled her eyes.

'I do, actually,' Ernest said.

'For the one person who isn't up for sale anymore,' Fahn said. 'I know you heard about how Madam Flora retired. Well, some men didn't think that certain restrictions applied to them, especially Louis Turnbull. He used to spend entire weeks with Flora. I don't know if he was heartbroken when she stopped working, or just upset that there was something in the world his money couldn't buy. Over the years he tried charming her with lavish gifts from around the world, but Amber put a stop to that.'

Ernest tried to imagine that kind of money.

'It's a story for another time – rather ugly. Hey, I'm done in a few minutes. Give me a half hour to freshen up and get out of my uniform, then come up to the empty guest room on the fourth floor. I'm ready to collect on what you owe me.'

Ernest's palms began to sweat, and his heart and stomach seemed to change places. He remembered her long kiss in the street – which had sent lightning bolts from the top of his head to the soles of his feet. That moment had filled his daydreams and had kept him awake at night.

He'd been haunted by her words: *now . . . you owe me.*

But Ernest lingered downstairs and pretended to be busy. Sure, he liked her – he definitely cared for her and was infatuated in a way that he'd thoroughly enjoyed. Yet he wasn't certain about paying back whatever debt she was intending to collect.

A man's raspy voice said, 'You can't avoid her forever, you know.'

Ernest looked over and saw Professor True peeking at him with one eye open. Then the old man smiled, shook his head, and kept playing with his eyes closed as he said, 'Might as well go on up. She's not gonna bite you or nothing, not that one for sure.'

'It's not the biting I'm worried about,' Ernest said. 'It's everything else.'

Professor True chuckled and shook his head. 'Oh, what I wouldn't give to be your age all over again. Then again, back in those days, I was playing on street corners in Kansas City for pennies.'

Ernest wondered, 'How long have you been working here?'

'Longer than you've been alive, son,' the man said. 'Let's just say that I came with the building. And I'll be here, writing, playing, singing, as long as my fingers will allow. But you're just stalling now, aren't you?'

Ernest sighed in agreement and untied his apron.

'There you go,' Professor True said. 'As a wise man with a funny collar and pointy shoes said, *Once more unto the breach, dear friends, once more; Or close up that wall* – something like that. You know what I mean . . .'

Ernest didn't, but the quote sounded like a verse he'd read in school. Probably Shakespeare. And as he took the long walk up the stairs and along the carpet-lined hallway, he heard the now-familiar giggles and laughter from behind closed doors, and the odd rhythm and helpless moans of men and women in the throes of pleasure or anguish – sometimes it was hard to discern which. He passed some of the upstairs girls as they were freshening up with new, painted-on smiles, or winding down. Some even kissed him on the cheek and bid him goodnight.

He brushed the hair from his eyes, cleared his throat, and gently knocked on the guest room door. Words from another play the older kids had once put on at the children's home came rushing back – *Lord, what fools these mortals be!*

Ernest knocked again, and the door pushed open, slightly. Cautiously, he peeked into the room. One small paraffin candle was burning on a corner table. The window was wide open, and a cool breeze blew the curtains back like the sails of a ship with a broken mast, lazily drifting to nowhere in particular.

He called out Fahn's name. Then he heard whispers.

'Out here, young Ernest, on the fire escape.'

Ernest smelled tobacco on the cool draft and heard another,

familiar voice in addition to Fahn's. He closed the door behind him, crept across the room, and held the curtains aside as he climbed through the open window and out into the early-morning air, which felt unseasonably warm.

'Well, well, well,' the other girl's voice called out.

Ernest flinched and then felt bad for recoiling when he saw Maisie – especially as she smiled up at him for the first time ever, and waved benignly.

'Geez, I'm not gonna hit you, Ernest,' she said. 'Relax, willya.'

Both girls had removed their dresses and were sitting on the grating of the fire escape in their long slips, leaning on one of the crossbars, dangling their stocking-covered toes over the edge of the platform, which hovered fifty feet above the alley and the rooftops of the nearby buildings. The girls scooted over in opposite directions, inviting him to sit between them. He double-knotted the laces on his shoes, lest one come loose and tumble to the street below, then sat between them. The metal of the fire escape felt cold and hard, but he didn't care because just to sit – to get off his weary feet – was a welcome relief.

From their perch he could see the flags atop the courthouse and the Alaska Building; he could even make out the shapes of the frescoed walruses, tusks and all, which adorned the crown of the Arctic Club. But the loveliest spectacle was that of the rippling waters of Puget Sound, deckled with lights from piers, boats, cruise ships, and freighters of every kind. He'd never seen a view from a place so high up. Then he smelled coal-fired furnaces, steam plants, and Maisie's cigarette. He looked on, wide-eyed, as she took a deep drag and then offered it to him. He stared at the tip, glowing reddish orange in the breeze. Mrs Irvine had dozens of names for the vice: *little white slavers, dope sticks, devil's toothpicks,* the list went on. Before he could react, Fahn reached over, took the cigarette, put it to her lips, and inhaled as a moth flitted overhead.

She exhaled slowly through her nostrils, and wispy tendrils of gray smoke looped over her lips and swirled into the air. She whispered, 'If you've never been kissed before, then I'm positive that you've never tried a Sweet Caporal.' She put the cigarette to his lips. 'Here – don't try to swallow the smoke, just inhale nice and gentle-like, then slowly let it all out.' Her words were lullaby soft.

Ernest didn't want to, but one little puff seemed simple enough. So he inhaled – then coughed, lurched forward, wheezed, and gagged so much that Fahn nearly dropped the cigarette as he flailed and batted her hand away. His eyes watered and his throat burned while Maisie laughed – no, she practically roared – clutching her stomach and kicking her feet. She patted him on the back, which only made his coughing worse.

Ernest spat to the dark pavement below, caught his breath, and then spat again. He finally cleared his throat and asked Fahn, 'Are we even now?' He didn't know what was worse, embarrassing himself in front of a girl he had strange affections for, or the searing sensation in his throat and lungs. The combined humiliation seemed to magnify both, as if one plus one now equaled three, or four, or ten.

'Don't worry,' Maisie teased, 'everything at the Tenderloin gets better the second or third time around. Practice makes perfect. You'll see. Except Amber, she gets meaner and ornerier with age. She's old wine turned to vinegar.'

Ernest wiped his eyes and thought of Jewel.

'And no, we're not even,' Fahn said. 'You still owe me.'

Ernest picked bits of tobacco off his tongue. 'What exactly do I have to do?'

Fahn smiled, paused, and then raised that mischievous eyebrow again. 'You, young Ernest, have to touch lips with Maisie – the last of the great unkissed.'

Ernest's jaw dropped. He shut his mouth, hesitated, unsure if this precocious girl was joking or not. But as nervous as he felt, he was intrigued by the dare. He found himself willing, after all; beneath her brusque tomboy exterior, Maisie was plainly beautiful. He turned to face her . . .

'Don't even think about it.' Maisie stared back.

At that moment Ernest wanted to jump off the fire escape – to hurl himself into the void. Fahn laughed as she argued with Maisie about being a prude. 'Everyone calls you the *Mayflower* because you're like those Pilgrims on the ship who were just a bunch of stuck-up Puritans,' she jeered. 'Maisie Mayflower can't hold out forever.

'It doesn't *mean* anything,' Fahn added in frustration; then she lifted Ernest's chin and kissed him. 'See?'

The words stung Ernest, and he felt his bubbling affection for Fahn diminishing by the second, fondness leaving his heart like air from a leaking balloon.

He looked at Maisie, who seemed to be taking the teasing in stride, but that didn't exactly make him feel any better. If anything, he was more confused.

'Well,' Fahn said to Ernest, rising to her feet. 'I guess you'll have to pay me back some other way. I'm sure I'll think of something. Anyway, let's hit the hay. I imagine we're going to have our hands full tomorrow.' She slipped through the window and bid them goodnight as she headed through the room and into the hallway.

'What do we have to do tomorrow?' Ernest asked as he and Maisie climbed back into the room. 'We've cleaned up just about everything . . .'

'You'll see,' Maisie said as a serious tone slipped into her voice.

Then she took a final drag and tossed the cigarette butt out the window, watching the ember sink like a falling star. 'Big parties like this tend to take a toll on Madam Flora, even though she's a real Rock of Ages. It's all she can do these days to keep herself together with special teas and crazy medicines and all that, so she can play ringmaster for the night's circus at the Tenderloin. But tomorrow, you'll see. We'll probably need your help, so get some sleep while you can.'

Ernest didn't fully understand, but it was late, and he was exhausted, and more than happy to go to bed. He said goodnight and walked toward the servants' stairs. That's when Maisie called to him from her end of the long hallway.

'Hey, Ernest, don't believe her. Don't listen to Fahn.'

He turned back as she spoke again.

'A first kiss means everything.'

Boston Marriage

(1909)

E rnest thought he was dreaming when he felt someone next to him. He opened his eyes and discovered Fahn sitting on the edge of his bed, still in her nightgown. Her hair was pulled back and she leaned in close, her soft, warm hand on his bare shoulder. His heart lurched from surprise to happiness to panic as he glanced from the open door to the window, saw the sun shining in and realized that it must be late morning. He'd overslept, missed his Sunday morning chores. 'I'm sorry, I'm . . .'

She shushed him. 'It's okay, Ernest – it's okay,' she whispered. 'I didn't want to startle you. I'm sorry to wake you like this, but we're having a bit of an emergency and I need you to get dressed and put on your shoes as quickly as you can, okay?'

Ernest shook off his slumber and bolted upright. 'Is it a fire?' He instinctively sniffed but didn't smell smoke, only tobacco and the dreamy haze of last night's perfume.

'Nothing of the sort.' She touched his arm and calmly spoke. 'Madam Flora is having one of her fits. Miss Amber and Maisie are trying to calm her down, but I need you to run to the herbalist again and get more of that tea. I need you to go right now. I'll turn around so you can put your clothes on.'

She handed him his pants and then stood and faced the door while he got dressed and donned a clean shirt. When she turned back to him, she held up a dollar bill. 'Mrs Blackwell will take care of the downstairs, there's nothing there that you need to trouble yourself with. And the upstairs girls, for the most part, are still sleeping – they have the day off. Everything will be fine, but this is . . .'

Ernest didn't know what *one of her fits* meant exactly. True gentlemen were not privy to many female mysteries, and the proper response was simply not to inquire further. So he took the money, slipped his shoes on without tying them, and ran down the hall. He descended the grand staircase and sprinted out the front door toward Chinatown.

By the time he reached the Jue Young Wo herb shop, Ernest was sweaty and nearly out of breath. To make matters worse, the store was closed, though he could see the old proprietor moving about inside, sweeping the floor and brewing a pot of tea. Ernest banged on the door and shouted until the man finally let him in. The herbalist offered him a cup of ginger tea and began speaking to him in Cantonese.

Ernest shook his head. 'I'm sorry.' He couldn't remember the name of the herb in English or Chinese. He held up the dollar and urgently pointed to the dried red flowers.

When Ernest returned, Fahn was busy making breakfast for the servants. Mrs Blackwell emerged from the kitchen with a kettle of boiling water. 'Follow me,' she said, as she quickly brewed the tea and took the concoction upstairs on a lacquered tray, inlaid with mother-of-pearl, as if this were any other Sunday and she were bringing up a breakfast of toast and apple butter. Ernest did as he was told. If the cook was distressed in any way, she didn't reveal her concern. Instead she handed Ernest a kitchen towel and said, 'I have a feeling you'll need this.'

A few worried girls, still in their nightgowns, had gathered in the hallway near Madam Flora's suite, but Mrs Blackwell shooed them off. From outside Ernest could hear voices, some soothing, some panicked, almost crying. He stepped back as he heard the strange whir and squeak of light machinery.

He said, 'I don't want to be in the way . . .'

'Your chores can wait, lad.' Mrs Blackwell shrugged. 'Time to see the world as it really is – occupational hazards and all.'

Ernest looked back, confused.

'Madam is our matron saint, and we all need to pull together and do what we can,' Mrs Blackwell said as she walked. 'Besides, honest Abe Lincoln suffered from the same affliction. It goes away for decades, but when it comes back – oh my, how that sickness does some terrible things to the mind. Hopefully this stuff works, because it's a frightening way to go – losing your wits, forgetting everyone around you, going blind . . .'

Mrs Blackwell knocked to announce their arrival and then opened the door. Inside the finely appointed room, Madam Flora sat atop a bicycle that had its front wheel propped up so that she was riding in place. The legs of her short, blue silk pajamas had been pulled up to her knees and fluttered as she pedaled.

I must be dreaming, Ernest thought. *I'm having some kind of bizarre nightmare from ingesting too much tobacco smoke.*

He stood paralyzed, towel in hand, staring wide-eyed at the scene of Madam Flora riding, crying, her white legs streaked with thick purple veins. Wigless, Miss Amber held Flora's hand and kissed her cheek.

Standing nearby was Maisie, whose nose and eyes were puffy and wet with tears. She took the cup from Mrs Blackwell and offered it to her mother.

'Please, Mama . . . Flora, just have a sip,' Maisie said. 'It's piping hot, just the way you like it. Please . . .'

Madam Flora swiped the cup away from Maisie with the back of her hand. The red liquid splashed on the wallpaper as the cup shattered. Madam Flora screwed up her face like a toddler forced to drink a spoonful of cod-liver oil as Mrs Blackwell snapped her fingers at Ernest, pointing to the towel. He sprang to life, scrambling on his hands and knees as he wiped up the mess, dabbed at the wall to try to soak up the tea, and collected the broken bits of porcelain.

'I want to go home,' Madam Flora pleaded. 'Please, just let me go home . . .'

Ernest looked back and saw Miss Amber, a kind shadow of her gruff self, softly whispering, 'Ah, you *are* home, my love. You are the heart and soul of the Tenderloin, and we need you. Please come back to us, my dear.'

Ernest watched as Madam Flora stopped pedaling and looked around the room. The front wheel continued to spin, winding down like the slowing of a panicked heart. Then Flora seemed to realize where she was, and hysteria dissolved into confusion. She touched her hair, the disheveled mess, part up, part hanging down in a ratted clump, as though she'd been caught in a transient state between celebration and slumber. The exhausted woman held out her trembling palms when Miss Amber offered her a fresh cup of tea. This time Madam Flora cradled the delicate china cup in both hands and sipped.

'I'm so sorry . . .' Madam Flora whispered as she stared at the tea-stained wall. She looked at Maisie and began to sob. 'My sweet little girl.'

'It's okay now, Mama,' Maisie said as she helped her mother from the bicycle to a velvet settee.

Ernest watched as Maisie melted into her mother's embrace, gently rocking back and forth. Then Madam Flora dried her eyes and regained a modicum of composure. She held her daughter at arm's length, touched her hair appraisingly. She seemed somewhat confused again as she said, 'Look at this one. I know you. You'll always be my little hummingbird.'

Miss Amber interrupted. 'Just drink your tea, my love. I'll always be here for you.' Then she glanced at the others in the room, pointing with her chin toward the door and whispering, 'Out.'

Ernest felt a hand at his elbow as Mrs Blackwell pulled Maisie and him out of the room. He watched Madam Flora recline on the scarlet settee, eyes closed, burying herself in a flocked quilt and Amber's arms as the door closed.

Mrs Blackwell turned on her heel and disappeared down the servants' staircase. Maisie slowly sank to the floor, her legs splayed across the dark red carpet. Ernest sat next to her, and they rested their backs against the wainscoting, hip to hip, hearts still racing. Ernest felt his hand touch Maisie's. Her fingers were shorter than Fahn's, and her nails had been polished, shining like pearls, for last night's soirée. She quickly placed her hands in her lap. She and Ernest stared at the closed door in silence, listening to the two older women cry.

Ernest didn't know which was more confounding, the thought of Madam Flora frantically riding a bicycle to nowhere, the image of the two tragic women cradling each other, or Maisie May showing a vulnerable side. He wanted to speak, but Mrs Irvine had once told him that a gentleman should never ask personal questions of a lady.

Yet Ernest didn't want to move. He didn't want to ruin this moment with Maisie, let alone abandon her. In the month he had known her, she'd been perfectly distant, so far away – angry. Now that they were here, and even if only under duress, he realized that there was a part of her that was so different from Fahn. Unlike Fahn's, Maisie's affections weren't freely given. They had to be earned.

And so they sat in silence.

From the corner of his eye, Ernest could see Maisie wiping an occasional tear. He could hear her sniffling, until the grandfather clock downstairs chimed and she finally drew a deep breath and spoke. 'Can I ask you something, Ernest?'

He nodded.

'Do you know what a Boston marriage is?'

Ernest shook his head.

'A Boston marriage is a kind of arrangement where two old spinsters live together,' Maisie said. 'What do you think of that kind of marriage?'

Ernest stammered, 'I'm . . . I'm not sure what . . .'

'I used to wish that my mother would leave here. I'd go to bed dreaming that Flora would find a man – a husband for her, a father for me. I used to imagine that we'd run away, that we'd escape all of this and have a normal home, become a family, and that she'd see me as a real daughter – that our life would be as simple as the families you see in photographs.'

But you are *her real daughter*, Ernest thought.

She answered before he could speak. 'I think the days of hoping for that are gone.'

He tried to change the subject. 'Miss Amber is a bit of a porcupine, but beneath that outer layer, she doesn't seem all that bad . . .'

Maisie snorted a laugh and wiped her cheek. 'You know, Mrs Blackwell once drank too much kitchen wine and let it slip that Miss Amber had spent a year down in Lakewood at Western Washington Hospital – it's an insane asylum, you know. That's where she got the idea for the bicycle. Mrs Blackwell said that they sometimes treat madness with exercise. But we can't let the great dame, the all-important Madam Flora, be seen on the street like this, can we? They'd lock her up for sure.'

Ernest sighed.

'For a while I assumed Amber had *worked* at the asylum,' Maisie continued. 'But then I heard how she'd been a patient instead – diagnosed with what they called a diabolical obsession. They said that she was somehow "inverted". I didn't know what that meant at the time, but I figured her condition out later. She'd been given the electric cure and later forced to have relations with all the men there, including her doctor, until she declared herself well and was finally released. I don't know if that's better or worse than what I heard they did to the diabolical boys.'

Ernest winced when she made a scissor-cutting gesture with her fingers.

'I have never understood what my mother saw in her,' Maisie said. 'But I think I understand now. What do you think?'

Ernest hesitated. 'I don't understand much . . .' He chose his words the way a man on thin ice chooses his footing. 'But I understand how sadness can make some people bitter, or angry.' And he was starting to understand Maisie's mistrust of men in general and him in particular.

Maisie looked at him, and he wondered for a moment if she somehow knew what he was thinking. She smiled, sadly.

'And I definitely don't know anything about Boston marriages,' Ernest said, 'or Seattle marriages, or arranged marriages, or plain ol' normal I-pronounce-you-husband-and-wife marriages, for that matter. But I know devotion when I see it.'

They listened to the silence, together.

'I wish I knew what that felt like,' Maisie said. 'Because as much as Miss Amber cares about my mother, she doesn't care a whit about me – I'm just extra baggage most days, a haversack full of rocks. And my mother isn't getting better. She's only getting worse. The mother I used to know, that person is going away. The woman who proudly told the world I was her baby sister, I think she's going away too. And the stranger who's left, the great Madam Flora . . . that person hardly recognizes me anymore.'

Stroll on the Pay Streak

(1909)

The next time Ernest saw Madam Flora was on the following Saturday. She swept into the servants' dining room during breakfast, elegantly dressed, hair lofted high into a cascade of curls, fingernails freshly manicured. She acted as though nothing unusual had ever happened beneath her roof, though Ernest knew that she and Amber had abandoned the Tenderloin for a while, leaving everyone, especially Maisie, to wonder and worry all week. There had been speculation about doctors' visits, special treatments, and miraculous remedies.

But now she was back, and despite the gossip, Madam Flora beamed and grandly announced, 'Good morning, everyone. You'll be pleased to know that we're closing our doors for this evening. But we're not locking up our wares – you fine ladies, I mean – because we're taking everyone to Hurrah Day at the fair!'

The servants – Iris, Rose, Violet – and even Mrs Blackwell whooped and cheered. Were they celebrating Madam Flora's return or the day off? Ernest couldn't tell. But as Fahn elbowed him and smiled, he realized that today's closing of the AYP would draw an enormous crowd and that the Tenderloin would practically be deserted anyway.

This was splendid news indeed. After 138 days of festivities, fireworks, parades, races, and grand hoopla, the great Seattle World's

Fair was coming to an end. And their glamorous benefactor seemed to be healthy again.

Madam Flora smiled and said, 'Everyone, even Miss Amber and Professor True, will be going, just as soon as my Gibson girls finish getting properly dressed for the occasion. And we'll stay through the closing ceremony.'

Ernest watched as she delighted in handing out passes along with envelopes containing ten dollars each, a celebratory bonus to their monthly wages.

Ernest looked at the money, which was twice his weekly salary, and examined the strange cardboard admission ticket – a punch card, barely used.

'Don't worry,' Fahn whispered. 'We're not working the fair. Madam had girls running the Klondyke Saloon at the AYP during opening week, but the joint got shut down a month later. We might as well put the passes to good use.'

Forty furious minutes later, everyone had assembled at the nearest streetcar stand, beneath an enormous world's fair pennant that had faded in the sunlight. Ernest noted that the servants all wore simple black and white dresses. Fahn stood apart, wearing a plum robe over her high-collared shirt, which drew whispered comments and sideways glances from the Gibson girls.

'Good morning,' Ernest said, admiring her outfit.

'*Ohayo gozaimasu* to you too,' she said, twirling proudly. 'Do you like it? I bought it in Japantown.'

He nodded and then noticed that the Gibson girls looked stunning, as always, each in a high-waisted, floor-length skirt of rose, yellow, powder blue, or periwinkle, squeezed into a tight bodice, dappled with ruffles and rhinestones. They'd be walking advertisements for the Tenderloin as they toured the fair.

156

Professor True looked elegantly handsome as well, in a checkered waistcoat. And Miss Amber wore a light blue wig that matched Madam Flora's dress.

The standout, though, was Maisie May, who'd been growing her hair longer. Ernest had never seen her in a corset before, and he wondered what battle had been fought to get her into one of those spoon-billed contraptions. He imagined an angry, feral, six-toed cat, with long claws and no tail, hissing while being dunked into icy water.

He said, 'You look absolutely—'

'Don't say it.'

'I was just going to compliment you on your—'

She smacked him with her parasol. Then she pulled back like Honus Wagner, ready for a second turn at bat. 'Don't make me swing for the fence this time.'

Ernest wished there had been a photographer nearby. He would have loved to keep this image forever. They looked like some kind of crazy family, part elegance, part circus, off on a weekend outing.

As Ernest walked from the streetcar terminus to the fairgrounds, he had a magnificent view of the grand arch of the main gate, and a platoon of uniformed ticket takers who stood at attention beneath a row of flags. The Stars and Stripes was interspersed between dozens of banners, every other standard representing one of the nations that were attending the fair. Ernest noticed that there was no Chinese flag, probably because of the Chinese Exclusion Act. But he and Fahn quickly found the Japanese standard, swaying in the breeze.

Madam Flora led the way, pointing with her bumbershoot as her peacock feather rose above a sea of hats by Chester, Knox, and Stetson. The Gibson girls followed, a parade of ducklings in lace-fringed petticoats. Ernest, Maisie, and Fahn kept up, trailed by the other servants, while Professor True and Miss Amber lagged behind, acting as a suspicious-looking rear guard.

Ernest noticed that the soldiers were gone from when he'd been raffled off in the summer. And the remaining policemen looked less serious, more joyful – except for a tall lummox with a wide mustache who had roped off a half-dozen boys covered in mud. Ernest recognized him as the plain-clothes officer who had broken up the spat between Madam Flora and Mrs Irvine earlier.

'That's "Wappy" Wappenstein,' Fahn whispered. 'He used to be the chief of police, until he got caught up in some scandal and got himself fired. We used to have to pay him a "garment" tax – all the crib joints and parlor houses did. Now he's been relegated to security at the fairgrounds and we pay off his replacement.'

The man smiled and tipped his hat at the ladies as they walked by.

Ernest smelled popcorn and waffle cakes. Maybe it was the perfect autumn weather, the morning sun, or the stable of beautiful women he traveled with, but Ernest couldn't remember ever being so happy.

The Tenderloin brigade gathered in the Court of Honor, between the towering Alaska Monument and the magnificent columns of the Government Building, which looked like what Ernest had always imagined Roman architecture to be like. There everyone began drifting, the crowd, his makeshift family, to the right. He turned toward the bright colors and sounds of the Pay Streak – raucous laughing, joyful screaming, and carnival barkers with peculiar accents amid the warbling of a brass band.

But Madam Flora shook her head and smiled. 'My Gibson girls, please consider this the season's final exam on the intricacies of proper manners, decorum, restraint, and etiquette. You are at the fair to be educated and edified by the galleries, the exhibits, and the architecture. There's even to be a thrilling debate between the world's foremost scientists and geologists about who reached the North Pole first – Peary versus Cook – where they'll settle it once and for all.'

The finely dressed girls groaned and a few cursed like sailors, even as a group of society debutantes passed by with their matronly chaperones, noses in the air.

'Just until suppertime,' Miss Amber interrupted. 'Then Madam Flora's leash comes off. And the rest of you – behave yourselves. Enjoy. Remember this day.'

Ernest felt Maisie and Fahn each take one of his arms as they turned and stepped toward the Pay Streak, the sideshows, and the thrilling rides.

'And where does our little Mayflower think she's sailing off to?' asked Madam Flora.

Maisie stopped, hung her head, and stomped her heel. Madam Flora motioned for her to join the Gibson girls. She sulked as she followed behind her mother, looking back to wave farewell like a prisoner being led to the gallows. Ernest felt awful for her. Fahn took his hand and said, 'Three's a crowd,' as she led him away.

Ernest had read that the AYP was a dry exposition, but as he and Fahn worked their way down the crowded Pay Streak avenue, he smelled alcohol every which way he turned. There were delegations of men and women in matching suits, dresses, and uniforms, sporting ribbons from Hawaii, Oregon, and California, celebrating their final day, and sailors from the United States, Japan, and countries he didn't recognize. The street was a delirious, delightful madhouse.

Ernest and Fahn had skipped breakfast in their hurry to leave the Tenderloin, so they used money from their envelopes to buy rice cakes and handfuls of Idaho cherries, spitting pits on the ground, and drank fresh-pressed lemonade from paper cups.

They paid twenty-five cents each and wandered into the John Cort Arena, where they watched a catch-as-catch-can wrestling match

159

between a huge man, Jess Westergaard, and a stout champion named Dr Benjamin Franklin Roller. The doctor was introduced as a professor of physiology at the University of Washington, and he won the bout, taking two out of three falls from the Iowa Giant.

As they left the arena they were nearly run over by a parade of Franklin automobiles. A man from the Seattle Auto Company stood on the hood of the one in the lead and shouted, 'The only car to make it up the Queen Anne Hill Counterbalance in high gear!' As Ernest wandered, Fahn's hand in his, he thrilled to each new attraction, frittering away nickels and dimes at the Foolish House, the Human Laundry, the Land of the Midnight Sun. They even saw the world's largest piano. Ernest noticed Professor True standing in line, whistling a happy tune as he patiently waited for a chance to play the oversize instrument.

Next, Ernest and Fahn took a jinrikisha ride to the Igorrote Village, where a barker introduced the crowd to the primitive and mysterious dog eaters of a distant island nation. They paid twenty-five cents and waited nearly a half hour to get past the curtained entrance, but when they did there were no dogs to be seen, padding about, on a roasting spit, or otherwise. Nor did the short, dark-skinned villagers look fearsome or frightening. Quite the contrary, they vaguely reminded him of the Indian kids he'd known at the Tulalip school, not their features as much as their lack of smiles, the vacant look in their eyes, even when they danced and sang.

As Ernest watched them walk about in nothing more than loincloths, even the women, he recognized a familiar voice and noticed Mrs Irvine and her group. The ladies moved through the crowd, passing out printed handbills and shaming the male attendees for staring at the topless savages. The men pulled their hats down as they tried to ignore the matrons.

Mrs Irvine spotted Ernest and gave him a stern look of disapproval.

He waved and nodded politely as he was led away by Fahn before the older woman could clear a path to reach him.

The two of them continued snacking their merry way from storefront to storefront, sampling roasted peanuts, salted in the shell, and spears of juicy pineapple from South America. With Fahn at his side, Ernest felt a bit older – wiser, more prideful perhaps. In a month and a half at the Tenderloin he felt he'd learned more of the world than he'd ever seen or read about during his previous years at school. He'd been thrust into an adult realm of discovery and responsibility, though deep down he knew that he was just a kid, and Fahn was just a teenage girl, who seemed reckless with her heart. Ernest didn't protest her affections, though he quietly wondered where Maisie was, what she was doing, and if she was thinking about him, even just a little.

'Oooh, this is what I was hoping to see!' Fahn squealed over the calliope music from a carousel and a parade of drummers and wailing bagpipers. She took his hand and led him past men demonstrating gold panning, around the Temple of Palmistry, to the crowded incubator exhibit.

An official-looking gentleman in a lab coat with a clipboard and slicked hair shouted, 'See these pint-size prizefighters battle it out with a bottle for three rounds, while living in a futuristic machine that serves in loco parentis!'

'What is this place?' Ernest asked Fahn.

'Babies,' she said, clapping and hopping up and down. 'You'll see.'

The barker kept up his routine. 'Right here, we've saved the lives of babes from every country – there's a Russian, Italian, German, Syrian, even a little Parsee girl, a Siwash boy, and newborn Oyusha San – a Japanese maid that's as cute as can be!'

Fahn eagerly paid for both of them as they were ushered past a plush red velvet rope, guided through a door and into a room where a dozen metallic and glass-walled contraptions contained infants.

One had a painted sign attached that read: PLEASE, ADOPT ME!

Through the glass, Ernest could see the babies swaddled in blankets of pink and blue. Some cried, some stirred and wiggled, but most slept as nurses checked on them, adjusting temperature gauges on the incubators. At least Ernest thought they were nurses. Another man in a lab coat walked by, and Ernest saw tattoos on his forearm, which made him suspect that they might all be carnies, dressed up as hospital staff. It was impossible to know for sure.

'What do you think?' Ernest asked as Fahn lingered over the newborn Japanese girl. She waved to get the baby's attention, but the infant didn't stir. Ernest was reminded of his long-lost baby sister.

Fahn tore herself away from the sight of the infants and said, smiling, 'I have an idea of what we should do next. It might not be your thing, but if you come with me and go along with it, you can consider your favor repaid.'

Ernest was quietly relieved, happy to leave this place, but still confused as she took his hand and led him out and past a stand selling hot roast beef sandwiches. They went beyond the pagodas of the Chinese Village, which was sponsored by Seattle's Chinatown, to the very end of the Pay Streak, and into a garden with Oriental statuary and fountains and a large building with a sign that read TOKIO CAFE.

Fahn spoke in broken Japanese and English to the women who worked there. The staff all wore the same type of gown as Fahn, though of different prints and finer fabric. Their sleeves were longer, and they had wide, thick, pillowy belts cinched tight around their waists. Their faces were painted white, their lips bright red, and they managed to walk gracefully on what looked like the world's most uncomfortable wooden sandals. He watched Fahn talk with an older woman who wore her hair up and seemed to be in charge. Fahn spoke until the matron smiled and laughed, pointing at Ernest, as Fahn handed her a silver dollar.

'Come,' the woman said. 'Come with me – we help you.'

She led Ernest to the doorway of a small room with paper screens and woven mats, where she bid him to remove his shoes. Then he walked into the room, which was bare except for a single lacquered table, on which rested a vase, a solitary flower blossom, and a host of cups and wooden utensils he didn't recognize.

'Your *gaarufurendo*,' the woman said. 'She's going to show you something special.'

Ernest bit his tongue and waited as the woman left and closed the door.

When it reopened, Fahn had returned.

She didn't speak, but wordlessly acknowledged his presence with her eyes, smiling as she carried a black box and a teapot to the table. She sat, and nodded ever so slightly as she unpacked the container, lit a candle, and gently added rolled incense to a small flame that he realized she was going to use to heat water for tea.

Fahn sat across from him, upright, kneeling before a small kettle. She said, 'I'm performing the *chado* – the way of tea. When I was a little girl in Japan, I used to watch my *okaasan* do this in the house where she worked. So I've always wanted to perform a real tea ceremony, like my mother – for someone special.'

Ernest smiled at her.

'My *okaasan* would say, "Water is Yin. Fire is Yang. And tea is a perfect expression of both."'

'Both?' Ernest asked politely.

'Both sides of life, hot and cold, light and dark, not as opposites, but as complementary parts of each other,' Fahn said, pausing, as though deep in thought. 'Life is about balancing the good and the bad, the past and the present. Madam Flora may not realize it, but she has a certain balance about her. All her girls do. Everyone does.'

Fahn is water, Maisie is fire, Ernest thought. Or is it the other way around?

He watched, enthralled and impressed, as Fahn bowed, then continued.

'Do you miss her?' Ernest asked. Those four words had been a common question often spoken at the various schools where he'd lived. 'Your mother, I mean.' Ernest didn't miss his mother anymore – at least not as much as he missed the mother he knew he would never have. 'Do you ever get mad about being sold by your parents?'

Fahn shook her head. 'I think about my *okaasan*, and my father too. I remember having younger brothers. We were starving. Because I had value, they could eat – they could live. I'm proud to have saved them. And I look forward to having my own daughter one day, because when I do, she'll have a better life. My sacrifice is for her too.'

Ernest felt as though his heart had been recalibrated. He'd never once thought of her situation in such a light. Though he still wished he'd been able to save his mother.

Fahn smiled and changed the subject. 'The ladies gave us these.' She handed him a plate of green sweets. 'A homemade treat.'

Ernest tasted the chewy candy, which smelled and tasted like a cross between steamed rice flour and tea-flavored taffy. He continued to watch Fahn, appreciating each simple gesture as she ladled hot water into a tea bowl and gently stirred it with a bamboo whisk. He watched as she filled a small teacup. She finally presented the tiny vessel to him with both hands. Ernest accepted the porcelain cup and held it up, rotating it in his hand as if to ask, *Like this?*

She nodded, and then he sipped – tasting the tea, which was lighter, softer than the tea his mother had once made for him, or the teas Mrs Irvine had served with honey and dried lemon at boarding school socials. He regarded Fahn as she adjusted the thin kimono she wore. She was beautiful and poised – absolutely enchanting when she chose to be, but fresh, crass, and delightfully demanding as well. He watched Fahn's eyes as she gracefully returned the tea set to its black serving box.

'How did I do?' she asked.

'I'm utterly gobsmacked.' Ernest tried to mimic the modern expression he'd heard the maids use at the parlor house. But it didn't feel right, so he lowered his voice and spoke elegantly, like Madam Flora. 'When it comes to tea, my dear, you win the golden laurel and the silver.'

Ernest heard polite clapping and turned to the door, where the Japanese women were beaming with pride. He didn't need to understand their words to know that they were praising Fahn.

When he turned back to Fahn, she took his hand, leaned across the table, and surprised him by kissing him yet again. He opened his eyes mid embrace, and she opened hers as she gently bit his lower lip.

'You are lovely.' She smiled and sat back on her knees, laughing and wiping her lips with a napkin. The Japanese women looked on in awe at her brazenness.

Fahn smiled and folded her napkin as she teased. 'We make a great pair, young Ernest. Are you still going to marry me?'

Ernest sat upright, trying not to blush as he nervously changed the subject. 'You should show this routine to Madam Flora.'

'I plan to. I just needed someone to practice my skills on. I'll show her when I'm ready. That's when I'll ask to become one of her Gibson girls,' Fahn said with a confident smile. 'But don't be jealous, you'll always be my sweetheart.'

Ernest smiled and nodded, but he felt his brow knotting in discomfort at the idea. He couldn't believe what he was hearing: Fahn's life downstairs seemed so perfect, the best of both worlds. He found himself caring for her, as a friend – but also as more than a friend. The idea of watching her submit to another – to some rich businessman, a stranger – made his head spin. Although the Gibson girls might have boyfriends, Ernest couldn't bear to imagine sharing Fahn's affections with anyone, especially someone who had to pay for them.

That's when he heard a familiar voice. He buttoned his jacket and stood up, quickly, as though he'd been caught in a state of undress.

'The Japanese Village. Hmmm . . . I knew I'd find at least one of you here.'

Ernest turned and saw Maisie standing in the doorway. She'd bought a cheaply woven porkpie hat and wore it cocked at a sly angle. Her blond hair spilled out from beneath the brim. The cavalier look wasn't enough to hide the S-shape of her corset or the ruffled sleeves of the colorful dress she wore. She looked like one of the older girls, pinched waist, accented curves.

Maisie frowned at Fahn and said, 'My turn, toots.'

'Now we're even, young Ernest,' Fahn whispered. She stood up and turned to leave. 'Your debt is paid in full.'

Ernest followed behind, quietly wondering how long Maisie had been standing there. Long enough, he reckoned.

Outside, a large crowd had gathered at the foot of the Pay Streak on the esplanade near the Lake Union steamboat landing. Maisie pointed out a tall ship in the distance, a replica of the *Mayflower* that sat at anchor. But fairgoers were more enamored with the passenger in a long canoe that was being paddled ashore. The crowd buzzed with excitement as a handsome young woman was introduced as Miss Columbia, to cheers, wolf whistles, and a chorus of racy catcalls.

Ernest had heard about the lovely Labradorean Inuit who had panicked the house and beaten out a darling Seattle socialite for the title of Queen of the Carnival. He stood on his tiptoes, trying to catch a glimpse of the dark-haired beauty who wore a sealskin parka and mukluk boots.

The crowd gushed their excitement, but Ernest could hardly see her.

'I'm tired of the exhibits. My brain, it overfloweth,' Maisie moaned. 'Let's go, I want to explore the House Upside Down and ride the Tickler.'

'I'll catch up with you two later,' Fahn said. 'I heard the Eskimo girl is hosting a reception. I have to see this for myself. She got fifty thousand votes. She even won a villa with a nice piece of property – can you imagine?'

Ernest wanted to see this one-woman spectacle as well, but he followed Maisie back to the wilder part of the Pay Streak and then to the carnival rides.

'How were the exhibits?' he asked.

Maisie pretended to yawn. 'You know, once you've seen an elephant made of apples, one million dollars in gold dust, the world's largest display of clams, and a tribe of topless natives at the Smithsonian exhibit, you've pretty much seen it all. Plus so much bunting everywhere – a sea of red, white, and blue. Madam Flora means well, but I was bored to tears.'

They skipped the carousel and went straight to the roller coaster, where Maisie hung her hat, clutched the hem of her dress, and boarded the first car. Until today, Ernest had never been on anything faster than a merry-go-round. He sat next to her, their legs touching.

'You know, I'm glad it's just us,' Maisie said, 'because three's a crowd.'

Ernest smiled at the echoed sentiment.

Maisie looked at him as she twirled her hair with her fingers, and he felt his stomach lurch, rise and fall, his heart racing again as he tried to catch his breath.

Then the roller coaster began to move.

Stars, Falling

(1909)

After waiting in line for what seemed like hours to ride the Ferris Wheel, the Haunted Swing, and the Scenic Railway, Ernest and Maisie split an egg-cream soda at Ezra Meeker's restaurant. Then they found a meadow alongside Rainier Vista, not far from the bubbling fountain and the gentle waterfalls. They lay down on a cool, soft bed of freshly mowed grass and removed their shoes and socks, wiggling their toes in the warm breeze of an Indian summer. Maisie perched her open parasol on the ground, creating a shady spot to rest their heads as they stretched out, their heads nearly touching as they watched puffy clouds slowly migrating across the blue north-western sky. They could hear a band playing, and watched as kids joined hands and danced in wide circles within circles, groups spinning in opposite directions. It matched the way Ernest felt inside.

'Fahn is sweet on you, you know,' Maisie said. The words felt almost like an accusation. 'At first I thought her obsession was because you're both – you know, sort of from the same part of the world, but I think she really does find you . . . interesting. She told me she stole your first kiss – that's her thing. Just don't be in a hurry to throw your heart away for the first girl who might want to punch your ticket; true love is wasted at a place like the Tenderloin.'

Ernest didn't know how to respond. He found himself smitten

with both girls, though he wondered if he was anything more than a convenient companion, like a younger brother who happened to share the same roof. He also wondered if either one would care if they weren't competing with each other.

'I think Fahn likes everyone,' he said. 'Most of all, Fahn likes Fahn.'

They both laughed. Then sighed, tired, but comfortable to be together. They enjoyed the moment, the music in the distance, the chirping of nearby birds, and the squawking of Canada geese flying south in a lopsided V-formation.

'Do you remember the look on your face when you first saw me?' Ernest asked. 'It was right about here. I'll never forget the expression you made.'

'I couldn't help myself. We got all dressed up and came to the fair and didn't get to go on any of the rides! That was so unfair – unjust. All I knew was that we were here to collect some stupid boy. I remember thinking to myself, *What in the world do we need a boy for? We live in a house where rich old codgers come and go and that's more men than I need in my life as is.* But . . .'

'That's okay,' Ernest said. 'I had no idea in the world what I was in for either. Let's call it even.' He offered his hand.

'Handshakes are so grown-up.' She shook his hand and then let go. Then she stretched out on the grass again and closed her eyes.

Ernest smelled something sweet and sat up slowly, glanced around, and quietly put on his shoes. He looked down at Maisie, who looked like Sleeping Beauty, her long dress splayed upon the clover.

She spoke without opening her eyes. 'And where do you think you're going?'

'Stay here,' Ernest said. 'I'll be right back.'

When he returned he lay down next to Maisie and asked her to open her eyes as he presented her with the most perfect candied apple that he could find.

She smiled and cocked her head.

Ernest held the apple as she took the first sticky bite.

As the sun sank into the waters of Puget Sound and the orange-hued clouds grew dim, everyone from the Tenderloin gathered around the Geyser Basin. Electricity flickered on, lighting building after building. Ernest watched, spellbound, as countless glowing bulbs turned the reflecting pool and the cascading waterfalls into a paradise of glimmering, glittering, yellow and white stars. He held up a hand, momentarily blocking the light, his eyes adjusting. The brightly lit Court of Honor made the fair look like a department store Christmas and Independence Day fireworks rolled into one.

Amid the enthralled crowd, the happy, weary residents of the Garment District exchanged stories about what they'd seen and tasted, waiting in anticipation for the closing of the fair. Ernest's senses were overwhelmed, his heart full, but like everyone else, he didn't want to go home.

As he sat on the lip of the fountain, between Maisie and Fahn, arm in arm with both, Ernest had what he believed to be the best idea of the day. He pointed to a captive hot-air balloon that hovered above the fair, a quarter mile up in the sky.

'We should watch the closing ceremony from up there,' he mused.

There was a quiet, appraising moment as the three of them craned their necks and gazed skyward, following the guylines, ropes that trailed up into the night.

'Not on your life,' Fahn said.

'I'll do it,' Maisie said. 'Since when are you scared of anything?'

'The fire escape at the Tenderloin is as high as I'll go. That contraption must be a thousand feet in the air, in the dark, in the wind. If it came loose, who knows where you'd get carried off to?' Fahn shook her head. 'I'm fine right here.'

Ernest and Maisie exchanged glances, then he looked at Fahn. Her expression seemed to say, *Be my guest if you're that crazy.*

As they got up to leave, Fahn gave Ernest a hug and a kiss on the cheek. 'That's in case I never see you again, which I'm guessing is about a fifty-fifty chance. If you die, I want your room.' She smiled grimly at both of them.

Ernest and Maisie walked to Pacific Avenue in the direction of the balloon, where they found the ticket booth for the ride. The flight was expensive – fifty cents, twice the price of admission to the fair itself – but they paid nonetheless, while waiting for the balloon to come down as four men in shirtsleeves tugged on ropes, guiding the descent. The wicker gondola was larger and taller than it looked from below. Ernest watched as the basket settled to the ground and a man opened a small set of wooden double doors and let a couple disembark. They looked exhilarated, joyful as they giggled and clung to each other, grateful to be back on solid footing.

'Next!' the man yelled as he held out his hand for tickets.

Ernest stepped aside and let Maisie hoist her skirt and petticoats and climb in. When she wasn't looking he reached into his pocket and handed the man his twenty-dollar bill. 'Last ride of the night?' Ernest whispered.

The man snatched the money and looked away, muttering. 'She's all yours, kid.'

Ernest stood next to Maisie, peering over the edge of the gondola as the balloon slowly ascended into the darkening sky. He was grateful to be alone with her, but he felt as though his stomach was still on the ground, and he grew light-headed as they drifted into the sky. He drew a deep breath and tasted the cool air. The view was otherworldly.

'Are you okay?' Maisie asked.

'Absolutely,' Ernest lied as he swallowed, feeling his Adam's apple rise and fall against his collar. He loosened the top button and willed himself to relax, exhaling slowly as the balloon drifted in the breeze.

'You?' he asked, as he gripped the lip of the basket with both hands.

'I'm okay if you're okay.'

It was as if they were standing on top of snowy Mount Rainier. From this lofty perch Ernest could fully appreciate the circular design of the fairgrounds, the streets and greenbelts, the lighted buildings, beautifully concentric and symmetrical. He could even see the flags, pennants, and banners, all blowing east, atop the cupolas and pavilions. And he could see the long, glimmering reflection of lights on the blue-black waters of Lake Washington to the east and Lake Union to the west. The Metlakatla Indian Band began playing national airs.

Then he heard a gushing roar and felt the radiant heat of the gas burner ten feet above their heads. The man on the ground had tugged a rope and increased the burn, which lit up the entire balloon like an immense glowing lantern. Just as quickly it flickered out, leaving them in the candle-like glow of the pilot light. Ernest welcomed the warmth as the night grew colder and the wind whispered through the wicker gondola. He offered Maisie his jacket, but instead she discovered a quilt in a shelf-compartment and wrapped it around herself. They stood shoulder to shoulder, peering over the edge of the basket at the great big, small world, hundreds of feet below, listening to the distant sound of music and the blaring of horns from incoming ferries.

'Since we might die at any moment, according to Fahn, do you want to know my theory on life?' Maisie asked.

Ernest felt a cold gust rattle the balloon, and he tried not to let his teeth chatter as he quietly wished they were back on the ground. 'Tell me,' he said, grateful for any distraction.

'My theory,' Maisie said, 'is that the best, worst, happiest, saddest, scariest, and most memorable moments are all connected. Those are the important times, good and bad. The rest is just filler.' She pointed to the balloon. 'The rest is nothing but hot air.'

Ernest didn't quite follow.

'Remember when I first saw you down there? That wasn't exactly a happy moment for me, or you, but here we are. I have a feeling that we'll be together for a very, very long time – our moments are tied together.'

Ernest nodded, mentally adding Fahn to the equation.

'So tell me what your worst moment was – the saddest moment of your whole life – and I'll connect that memory to your best moment,' said Maisie.

Ernest furrowed his brow. The saddest moment was easy. He'd never mentioned his little sister to anyone, not even Fahn, and certainly not Mrs Irvine. He tried to think of an alternative to telling Maisie the truth, but she sensed his hesitation.

'Whatever it is, just say it. I told you about my father and how he died.'

Ernest sighed. 'It's not a pretty story . . .'

'That's the whole point,' Maisie said as the burner fired again, lighting up their world for a brief, warm moment, and the balloon lofted higher, tugging them along, the basket creaking and groaning against the rope anchors.

'It's my last memory of where I was born,' Ernest said. 'When I was five or six years old, I saw something.' He hesitated. 'Something terrible.'

'I've seen my share of good and bad,' Maisie said.

Ernest shook his head.

'It's okay, I can take it.' Maisie held his hand.

'My parents . . . they were never married. And my father had been killed. I barely remember him. So my mother and I were alone, begging, sleeping at the mission home where she used to work.' Ernest paused and then continued. 'We were starving to death. And one night, I watched my mother smother my newborn sister.' He watched Maisie's somber reaction. 'That was my saddest moment.'

Maisie closed her eyes for a moment and then opened them.

Ernest struggled to process the ugly details while gazing down on such a beautiful place. His heart felt torn between the two worlds.

'You okay?' Maisie asked.

Ernest nodded and continued. 'I remember that my mother always kept herself distant from me. It was like a long goodbye. She knew what was happening around us. Everyone was wasting away, and she was dying. She gave up completely, and that's when she arranged for me to go on the ship, and then she buried my sister. I never knew when my mother finally died, though I always hoped there might be someone to give her a proper burial. Someone who would put rocks and stones and thorns on her grave to discourage the stray dogs; after all, they were starving too.'

Ernest stopped talking and regarded Maisie, who was listening in silence. But she nodded and chewed her lip and waited for him to continue.

'I don't know if she sold me or gave me away. But I survived. I made it to America – bouncing from poorhouse to boarding school. No one knew what to do with me; I didn't fit in anywhere. And eventually I was given away all over again.'

'Right down there,' Maisie said.

Ernest nodded and sighed as though a weight were lifting off his shoulders, floating away like the hot-air balloon. 'I guess that ended up being my best moment, even though I didn't know it at the time.'

Maisie wiped her eyes and blamed the wind. 'See – you've proved my point.'

'I've never told that to anyone,' Ernest said. 'I don't think about those days very often. I try to forget, because sometimes I have bad dreams.'

He closed his eyes, and when he opened them again the world had fallen into darkness. The lights had been put out to mark the official closing of the fair. The lit buildings, the streetlamps, every bulb, had vanished into pitch-black, as if the world below them had fallen away, been swallowed whole. He heard the crowd for a moment, then an aching silence followed by a lone bugler, who played a sad melody.

'You know my secret,' Maisie said. 'And now I know yours.'

Ernest sniffled and held his emotions in check as he thought about happier moments – Fahn's oatmeal cookies, her warm, soft kisses, lying next to Maisie on that soft bed of clover, trading bites of a crisp, sugar-coated apple. He tried to take those new memories and the broken pieces of his heart, rearrange them, somehow mend them together, even as his eyes adjusted to the darkness and he strained to find definition in the murky world he was floating in. That's when he felt Maisie slide closer, wrapping the blanket around his shoulders as well. He could feel her warmth through plush, supple layers of fabric. She smelled like perfume and flowers and happiness. Ernest's heart raced as the gondola drifted and they heard wistful strains wafting up from the crowd below. Fifty thousand people began singing 'Auld Lang Syne', and surrounded by emptiness, gently rocking to the sound of melancholy, Ernest and Maisie sang along in whispers.

He turned as she leaned closer and her arms slipped into a quiet embrace. He felt her hair on his cheek, the softness of her breath as his hands found her waist. He was awed at her touch and what the human heart is capable of feeling – such sadness, such shame, but such acceptance, such joy, all at the same time.

The balloon swayed and he said, 'Steady, I've got you.'

'I've got you too,' she whispered.

Then he looked down, noticing flickering lights, the city on the horizon. He marveled at the beautiful, challenging world beneath them, so far away, and he thought: I wonder if the best thing any of us can hope for in life is a soft place to land.

He felt Maisie nod as though she knew his thoughts. He held on tighter.

Then the night exploded.

Their ears filled with the booming echoes of cannon reports as fireworks burst all around them. Blooming peonies and chrysanthemums filled the darkness. Starlike shells rose to greet them, flashing like comets, painting the sky with swashes of sparkling, flickering, glowing embers that slowly rained back down in a beautifully arranged marriage of fire and gravity.

Ernest closed his eyes for a moment and could still see the shimmering display. He could hear the rhythmic, booming cadence of explosions in every direction. Then he opened his eyes again, and it was like they were standing in the heart of a snow globe, a blizzard of white-hot stars, as far as the eye could see.

He felt Maisie's hand on his chest. 'See,' she said, smiling in the afterglow, the flashing, waning colors. 'This life – your life, my life, the happy memories, the sad stories, the hellos, the goodbyes, you, me, Fahn – everything is connected, always.'

Ernest felt her words more than he heard them. Then he sensed the balloon begin to descend slowly beneath the canopy of pyrotechnics, sinking into the darkness, returning them to Earth.

Ruby Chow's

(1962)

I fell for both of them, Ernest typed.

He left the paper in the typewriter like a loaded gun with the safety off, an unlocked cage with something big moving around inside, a lit fuse. Then he grabbed his coat and hat, and headed up the street to Ruby Chow's to meet his family.

As he walked, Ernest thought about his dear wife – but he also thought about Madam Flora, Professor True, and the other girl he'd been with on that magical day. He wondered what her life must be like now.

He remembered a night a few days after the closing of the fair, all those years ago. He'd climbed out onto the fourth-story escapeway of the Tenderloin, up to the roof, and shared a cigarette with Fahn. They'd taken turns watching through a telescope mounted on a wooden tripod as the sky above the lake was lit up with explosions from a re-enactment of both the Boston Tea Party and the sinking of the HMS *Gaspee*, a spectacular that had been sponsored by a wealthy shipwright a week after the closing ceremonies of the AYP.

Fahn and he hadn't been up nearly high enough to see the ship's burning masts fall, but they'd been able to see dozens of shells vault into the dark sky and rain down. He'd seen the flashes, heard the cannons and the grand explosion when the ship burned to the waterline. A cache of black powder ignited in a thunderous eruption that sent pieces of the flaming vessel through the air and rattled windows for miles.

Ernest remembered hearing those on neighboring rooftops who had watched the show shouting 'Huzzah!' Then the Wagner Band had begun playing somewhere in the distance, followed by the fierce wail of the Clan Fraser Highland Pipers.

'I wish I could have seen that before it went off,' Ernest had said.

'You did,' Fahn had replied. 'The ship they just blew up was redecorated for tonight's extravaganza. We all saw her laid at anchor at the fair, remember?'

'What ship?' Ernest had cocked his head, confused.

Fahn had flicked her cigarette butt to the pavement below.

'That was the *Mayflower*.'

Ernest arrived at Ruby Chow's, with its gabled roof and round, pagoda entrance, and savored the comforting smell of freshly roasted duck, the sound of cast-iron woks banging in the kitchen. Inside, he found Juju and Gracie seated beneath an enormous paper lantern, next to an ensconced Buddha, who looked out benignly over their table.

Juju kissed Ernest on the cheek and said, 'Ah, you made it.' Then she excused herself to make the rounds. He didn't know who the people at the adjacent tables were, though a few seemed familiar – perhaps he'd seen them on television or on billboards. Ernest knew that Ruby's was a favorite hangout for businessmen and politicians, so while he was mildly annoyed that his daughter was constantly working, he also marveled, immensely proud of how easily she traveled in such lofty circles.

Ernest sat down next to his wife. 'Hello, Gracious.'

She lit up when he called her that. She smiled and said, 'Ernest.'

'Our daughter certainly is a busy bee, isn't she?' He examined Gracie's curious, childlike expression, hoping for any kind of confirmation that she remembered who he really was or the life they'd once had together. He'd spent these past three years mourning, adapting to a new, benign form of normal. Some married couples his age had separate beds, or slept in separate rooms. He and Gracie lived separate lives.

'Are you happy that Hanny is home?' Ernest asked.

'Oh yes.' Gracie nodded as she slowly looked about the room.

'And you know that she's bringing someone special to dinner? Someone she wants you to meet.' Ernest hesitated and looked around. 'I've met him. Juju met him. He's a decent gentleman, and a lawyer too.'

Gracie said nothing. One of the older bow-tied waiters came by and exchanged pleasantries as he poured tea with one hand and whipped out a silver lighter and lit Ernest's cigarette with the other – two hands, two separate synchronized motions.

Ernest saw that the lighter featured an engraving of the Space Needle.

'Do you remember much about the AYP?' Ernest asked Gracie, as he noticed the menu featured a special lobster dish in honor of the new world's fair.

She nodded again.

'Do you remember our friend from those days?' Ernest probed.

Gracie smiled, almost imperceptibly, and sighed. 'I've been looking for her.'

'You have?' Ernest asked, playing along.

Gracie furrowed her brow as she scanned the room again, going from person to person, face to face. 'Where has she . . . been hiding?'

Ernest shrugged. A part of him knew he shouldn't ask whether she remembered people from the Tenderloin, but another part was dying to know how many of Gracie's memories remained. How much could he – should he – hope for? Dr Luke had stabilized her condition, cured her with antibiotics, a miracle in a bottle. But he said the damage done was irreversible. Gracie wouldn't go back to the way she used to be, although he also said that her brain might eventually find different ways to remember.

Ernest had often talked with her about their marriage – hoping she would remember him, but he'd never once asked her about her childhood. He figured that, like everything else, those memories were lost forever. But as she smiled he asked, 'Do you recall our early days together? The three of us, all those years ago?'

Gracie hesitated, pausing, searching. Then Hanny and Rich walked into the restaurant amid fanfare from the staff – excited compliments about how much Hanny had grown and how beautiful she was. They all wanted to hear about Las Vegas, the celebrities she'd met, run-ins with famous mobsters, and if she really worked topless. They also gushed about how tall and handsome her gentleman friend was. Hanny showed off her engagement ring, and the hostesses squealed.

Ernest watched as Gracie stared at Rich. 'That's Mr Wonderful,' he said. 'He's not a bad guy once you get to know him, I suppose. Unfortunately, I don't know him very well.'

Gracie nodded again and patted Ernest's arm.

After an awkward introduction, Ernest ordered a series of Gracie's favorite dishes to be shared. The first to arrive was a tureen of steaming melon soup with chicken and water chestnuts. A waiter filled their rice bowls amid the small talk. In the background Ernest heard a jingle on the nearby radio that had been played over and over again to promote the new fair: *If you're going to kiss me . . . kiss me there.*

'Ma.' Hanny spoke as though her mother were hard of hearing. 'Rich is my fiancé. We're getting married. Ma, I'm finally going to tie the knot.'

Gracie looked at both of them, nodding solemnly, blowing on her soup.

Ernest saw the worry in Juju's eyes as everyone waited for a response. Gracie smiled and continued eating.

'So, Ernest,' Rich said, to break the awkward silence. 'Juju told me that you used to work as a driver for all the famous types who came to Seattle.'

'Oh, my daughter exaggerates a bit. It wasn't that glamorous, really; they were just nice people who needed a ride,' Ernest demurred. 'I was your basic, garden-variety driver most of my life, but I did get special calls once in a blue moon.'

'Dad, don't be so humble,' Juju said. 'Sugar Ray Robinson came to town and got sick. He wouldn't trust a white doctor, so he found Dr Luke in Chinatown, of all places. Dr Luke gave him my dad's name, and Dad drove the champ all over the place while he was in Seattle. From there, word of mouth did the rest. He ended up driving Floyd Patterson when he was in town, then Louise Beavers, Dinah Washington – the list goes on and on. He'd come home late at night with autographs for us kids, souvenirs. He even drove Billie Holiday.'

'Now you're just making stuff up,' Ernest said. 'That's how simple stories become tall tales. You might be pushing the limits of your journalistic integrity.'

'That's incredible. Sounds like you'd love it out in Vegas – you're used to rubbing elbows with the stars,' Rich said. 'Speaking of stars, Juju said that you're part of a big story for the Century 21 Expo – something about a mysterious boy who was raffled off at an earlier world's fair. I'd love to look into the legalities of that. And she also told us how you grew up in and around Seattle's old red-light district . . .'

Ernest looked at Juju, who shrugged innocently. He glanced at Gracie, who listened intently as she slurped her soup. Meanwhile, Hanny stared back incredulously as if to say, *And you thought my career was bad?*

181

Rich kept talking. 'I guess before Las Vegas there was always Chinatown. Bootleg booze and gambling going all the way back to Prohibition, speakeasies, all kinds of glamorous night-time entertainment.'

'It wasn't Chinatown,' Gracie interrupted, speaking slowly. 'It wasn't Chinatown or even Japantown, it was a parlor joint called . . . the Tenderloin.' Then she went back to her soup as though she'd said something obvious.

Rich looked at Ernest, who spoke softly, hoping to leave Gracie out of the conversation. 'Yes, the Tenderloin was a . . . club for gentlemen.'

Juju continued, 'My father is being coy. The Tenderloin was a famous sporting house run by Dame Florence Nettleton, over by Pioneer Square. No one knows much about her, and any records of her earlier life were probably destroyed in the Great Seattle Fire. Plus, she's been lost in the shadow of her more famous predecessor, Madam Lou Graham, the Queen of the Lava Beds, who I believe ran the Tenderloin before her. And then later by Naughty Nellie Curtis, who ran a crib joint out of the old LaSalle Hotel overlooking Pike Place Market. There's another story there I'm sure . . .'

Ernest sat back, listening, nodding. His daughter had done her research – he was impressed, again.

'So is that where the two of you met?' Rich asked, smiling. 'At this Tenderloin place? I mean, forgive me for being a bit forward with my assumptions, but I do work in a colorful town and I've seen a salacious thing or two in my time. Hollywood's finest come to Vegas to get married or divorced, sometimes in the same trip.' He laughed. 'I'm immune to scandal.'

'What can I say? We were just kids, barely in our teens . . .' Ernest said.

'You were part of Seattle history,' Juju said. 'And you, Dad, you're

practically a living, breathing *Ripley's Believe It or Not!* I know people
of your generation don't like to talk about themselves very much – if
at all – but come on . . .'

Gracie slowly tapped her spoon on the side of her bowl.

Then she looked about the restaurant – at the lamp, the statue, the
diners at other tables and in booths – as though she were remembering
where she was. Smiling.

'Ernest is being . . . modest,' Gracie said. 'He was a coachman, and
a good one. You had . . . driving gloves and a leather coat. You looked
so handsome. How could I ever forget that?'

Everyone waited, holding their breath.

Then Juju added, 'And you worked there too.'

Rich snickered and teased. 'Don't tell me you were a party girl,
Mrs Young.'

Juju frowned at the man. Ernest tried to change the subject,
waving to the bow-tied waiter, who was already on his way with a
platter of preserved beef, braised chicken, and seaweed salad. All of
it served cold.

'Oh no, nothing so romantic,' Gracie said pleasantly. 'I was a
prostitute.' She spoke as though she might have said, *Please pass the
salt* or *How's the weather?*

Rich fell silent for once, addressing his soup without looking up.
Hanny laughed, thinking she'd just caught the tail end of a joke; then
as reality set in she stared at Juju, mouth agape, her face equal parts
shock, confusion, and disbelief. Juju cocked her head toward Ernest,
as if to ask for confirmation.

Angels in the Snow

(1909)

E rnest pulled his red wool scarf up higher to shield his nose against the wind, which was blowing fat snowflakes in every possible direction. His breath was warm, even as his toes felt like ice cubes in his rubber three-button boots. He leaned into the shovel again and again as he worked to clear the dense, wet drifts of mashed-potato snow that piled up on the sidewalks and the front steps of the Tenderloin. Ernest had always loved the idea of a white, picture-postcard Christmas, even if that meant he had to shovel snow all day long on Christmas Eve.

As he caught his breath and stretched his aching back, Ernest heard the jingling of bells on a harness. He waved a mittened hand at a black-bearded man in a long overcoat, who tipped his snow-brimmed top hat as he talked to his team of draft horses as though they were stubborn children. The man shouted words encouraging them, chiding them, and scolding them as they pulled a metal plow down the street, carving a path through the snow-covered city. Shopkeepers swept and shoveled, businessmen in fine suits took turns clearing the trolley platforms, and dozens of stevedores, hired for the day, worked furiously to clear the rail lines again and again so the streetcars might have a chance amid the falling, drifting snow. It was an effort that, to Ernest, seemed as endless and futile as trying to bail out the Pacific Ocean.

As a group of drunken carolers sang an off-tune, wine-soaked version of 'Here We Come A-Wassailing', men and women completed their last holiday errands all around him, hauling Christmas trees, carrying wreaths, toting presents. Icicles, which hung precariously from the lampposts, slowly began to melt as the gaslights flickered on for the evening. The lamps added a warm glow to the fairy lights that deckled the storefronts, the clothiers, and even the pubs and casinos. Ernest thought that the peaceful street scene was like something out of a painting, as though the clock had spun backward ten years, thanks to the absence of chattering automobiles, replaced by the pleasant clip-clop of horse-drawn carriages, Bristol wagons, and the occasional snap of a buggy whip. He watched as another team of bridled horses snorted gusts of steam through flared nostrils as they trotted by, high-stepping in unison, proudly showing the impotent motorcars buried in the snowdrifts that they hadn't yet surrendered their usefulness.

Ernest stomped his feet to try to warm his toes as he wondered what Christmas morning would be like. With Madam Flora's erratic behavior, planning anything had become difficult. And besides, Miss Amber had been busy taking Flora about the city to new doctors all month. In their absence, Mrs Blackwell and the servants had taken charge of putting up a tree and decorating the house. Ernest thought they'd done a yeoman's job (without Miss Amber's normal, stern input), so at least it *looked* like Christmas at the Tenderloin and smelled like a merry holiday. Ernest had learned from the other servants that certain occasions, especially birthdays, were not celebrated – the upstairs girls chose to keep their ages a secret. So he had wondered if the Advent season would be enjoyed beyond the basic trappings.

In anticipation, he'd bought small, hand-painted wooden angels for Fahn and Maisie, and wrapped layered boxes of chocolates and dried fruit, dusted in powdered sugar, to be shared by the maids and the upstairs girls. But would they really get up early and exchange presents? Or would Christmas involve another late night in the casual company of rich, lascivious customers who came and went, and everyone sleeping in past noon, just another day of canoodling, with or without mistletoe?

Ernest worried, because Madam Flora's bouts of hysteria were getting worse. Her episodes had been draining them of the reserve of hope they'd all built up at the fair.

He closed his eyes and remembered how he'd eagerly returned to the fairgrounds with Maisie and Fahn three days after the closing ceremonies. They'd woken early and stolen away on the trolley to see what remained, yearning to savor one more moment.

But when they'd arrived, the lush greenbelts looked brown and trampled, except for tiny forests of dandelions. It had been sad to see the brick walkways strewn with tickets, candy wrappers, cigarette butts, old newspapers, wads of chewing gum and spitting tobacco. Flights of pigeons and gulls fought over the detritus; the remains of treats that had once seemed magical now sat rotting. And the busiest activity they found were hoboes picking their way through the mess – sad, haggard old men with potato sacks who collected brown bottles for their halfpenny deposits.

Ernest recalled that dozens of other kids their age had come back as well. Together they gathered at Ezra Meeker's place, the solitary vendor still open for the week, or until they ran out of beer, whichever came first. Ernest, Maisie, and Fahn ordered a cream soda to share and comforted each other like the living at a wake.

Since then, the only reminder of the fair had been the occasional visits by Mrs Irvine and her well-meaning, riotous band of puritan do-gooders. Her words seemed like polite cannon shots fired across her widening gulf of disapproval. Each time, she asked Ernest to come back, and each time he declined.

As Ernest finished clearing the latest blanket of fresh snow, he did his best to focus on the bright memories of that last day at the AYP.

All these months, he still woke up each morning wondering if the emotions of that day – that night – had vanished with the fair. Had any of it been real enough to last? Maisie had been warmer to him ever since, in direct proportion to Fahn's growing restlessness.

Ernest snapped out of his daydreaming when he spotted a figure walking down the center of the snow-covered street, leaving a single trail of footprints in the virgin powder. The fat man in a red suit, fringed with white, was unmistakable even amid the swirling snowflakes, as he laughed heartily and rang a brass bell. Ernest smiled as though childhood stories had come to life. People on the sidewalks waved and cheered, and some even opened their windows and shouted '*In dulci jubilo!*' in thick European accents. A few ornery teenagers threw snowballs that fortunately sailed clean of their mark.

When the man got closer, Ernest could see this was no ordinary stuffed-coat, department store St Nicholas. Beneath his beard of white was a very dark face. Ernest recognized Professor True's eyes behind his spectacles before the piano man shifted his bag of presents to his other shoulder and bellowed a hearty 'Ho, ho, ho, Ernest. Christmas can officially begin, because Santa Claus has arrived!'

In the parlor, Mrs Blackwell announced what the upstairs girls had hoped – that there would be no customers tonight, or tomorrow. The Tenderloin was officially on holiday through the weekend. Maisie whispered, 'No one ever comes here on Christmas anyway. The desperate, broken-hearted codgers out tonight always hit up the cribs down the street.'

Miss Amber appeared in a silver wig and began to hold court.

She said, 'Ladies, tonight is our Christmas. Tonight is a celebration of our family, together on this cold, snowy evening. And though I know some of you miss the homes and the places you once knew, we're better off than so many others. And to remind us of that fact, and to honor Flora and all she's done for us, we're going to Georgetown to visit the King County Almshouse. We'll sing carols and pass out gifts. Gloves and chocolate for all the moms, and stockings full of candy, peanuts, and oranges for the little ones.'

Professor True hoisted his gift bag.

'Then,' Mrs Blackwell added, 'we'll return home for our own cup of good cheer.'

Ernest looked around, amused, as the upstairs girls clapped and the downstairs help worried about the weather. In a rush of excitement, everyone followed Miss Amber's lead and donned coats and capes, caps and bonnets, mittens and scarves, and, last, their winter boots as they gathered in the foyer, preparing themselves to march fourteen blocks south through the falling, drifting snow.

'All but you, Ernest,' Miss Amber said as she grabbed him by the back of his collar. 'I need someone to stay behind and tend to the fires.'

Crestfallen, Ernest nodded. He reluctantly removed his hat and coat.

'Ho-ho-home for the holiday,' Fahn teased.

'I'm sorry,' Maisie whispered, frowning.

'It's okay,' Ernest said as he donned a pretend smile. 'You'll all be back home soon enough, I suppose. You'll be frozen, but the fires will be roaring.'

Ernest stood outside the doorway, alone atop the stoop, as he watched everyone march away, singing 'It Came upon a Midnight Clear'.

He closed the door and could still hear their voices in the distance. Professor True's whiskey tenor rose above the choir of fallen angels as they sang and laughed and carried the spirit of celebration away with them. Dejected, Ernest trundled down to the basement to check on the boiler and make sure there was an ample supply of coal in the coal bin. Then he carried armloads of split firewood upstairs and restocked the hearths in the master suites. Finally, he sank into a plush chair in the parlor, stoking the main fire, but wondering what kind of merriment he was missing. As he watched bits of tar flare up and listened to the snapping and popping of still-green wood, he realized that the Tenderloin had never been this quiet.

He remembered something his mother had once said to him when he was a little boy. She'd said, 'Everyone should spend one holiday alone. It's good for the soul.' He wondered if this was just something a parent says when she has no presents to give, or if there was truth there. As he sat in the quiet of the parlor, he wasn't sure how the emptiness he felt might make him a better person. Before he found an answer, he heard a rumble outside and the blaring of a car horn. He grabbed his coat and opened the door as a sleek, black Marmon roadster glided to the curb and a tall driver stepped out.

'I'm sorry, we're closed for the evening.' Ernest glanced toward the back of the car. 'The Tenderloin will be open again in a few days.'

'Well, I guess I'm at the right place then. Wasn't sure if I'd be able to find it, what with all the snow,' the driver said. 'Special delivery for Madam Florence.'

'Would you like to come in and get warm? And what exactly are you delivering?'

'Oh, my apologies, young fella, I thought it was rather obvious, I'm delivering . . . *this*.' The driver brushed the snow off the hood of the car with his coat sleeve and handed Ernest a strange-looking silver key. 'That's for the coil box below the steering wheel; the switch is inside. Ever start one of these things in winter?'

'I've never started one of these, ever.' Ernest spoke calmly but could barely contain his excitement. He clapped his hands together as though trying to keep warm.

'Well then, I guess you folks are going to have fun figuring out your new toy. The only other motorcar in the world that I know of that's this nice was a Pierce-Arrow limousine delivered to the White House just last week, even though Taft's a big horse-and-buggy guy.' The driver reached into his coat and handed an envelope to Ernest. The front was addressed to Madam Florence Nettleton, with the initials L. J. T. elegantly pressed into a waxy seal. 'Have a merry Christmas, kid.'

Ernest stared at his Cheshire cat reflection in the wet chrome as the man walked away. The roadster sparkled like a starry night. It was the most beautiful machine he'd ever seen and certainly the most luxurious. Ernest wiped the falling snow off the polished chrome, then sat inside the motorcar and placed his hands atop the padded steering wheel. The pedals and levers were a mystery, one he looked forward to unraveling. But as his breath fogged up the windshield, Ernest grew cold and he went inside.

There he was startled to find Madam Flora, standing in the parlor in a flowing nightgown of pleated lavender. Her matching dressing jacket hung loosely, almost haphazardly, from her shoulders as she stared into the fire.

'I'm sorry,' Ernest apologized, 'I thought you might have gone with the others. Would you like me to fetch you a blanket or a cup of tea?'

The matron of the house didn't reply, didn't blink, as the fire crackled and popped. Ernest began to worry that she was having one of her bad spells and wondered how he would handle her without help from the others. Miss Amber had been keeping her in her room, so the fits of madness had been confined to shouts in the night, blamed on nightmares.

'Do you have something for me?' she asked.

Ernest had forgotten about the envelope in his hand. 'This came for you,' he said, 'along with . . .'

'I saw. It's a very nice automobile.'

He handed her the envelope. She regarded the embossing, and then pitched it into the fire without bothering to open it.

'Some people . . .' She sighed. 'Some people think the world is for sale.'

Ernest looked on in disbelief as the paper lit up, was quickly engulfed in flame, and then crumbled to ash. He wanted to say something, but could only watch as Madam Flora slowly walked away from the hearth, from the warmth. Ascending the grand staircase, her figure disappeared into the darkness like a ghost.

Ernest sat down and waited for the others to return, thinking of the letters that had sealed the envelope, and the name: Louis J. Turnbull.

An hour later the residents of the Tenderloin noisily tromped back inside, a mass of teasing and laughter. Miss Amber immediately went upstairs to check on Madam Flora, while the others kicked snow off their boots and warmed their rosy cheeks and frost-kissed noses in front of the fire. The Gibson girls doffed their coats, and the servants disappeared into the kitchen and returned with platters of sausage and cheese, bishop's bread, black molasses cake, Christmas cookies, dried fruits, and shelled nuts of every kind. Mugs of cider and spiced wine appeared in everyone's wet, cold hands. And Professor True shed his red Santa coat and began warming up his fingers on the piano. The suit's oversize suspenders draped over his woolen button-down shirt as he removed his cufflinks and rolled up his sleeves.

'Do we have a visitor?' Maisie asked Ernest. 'I thought Amber made it perfectly clear that we were closed . . .'

'The automobile was delivered as a Christmas gift,' Ernest said, hesitating. 'I was given a note . . . with the initials . . . L. J. T., but Madam Flora didn't even bother to open the envelope. She just threw it in the fire.'

The Gibson girls overheard as they returned. 'Louis Turnbull is back in our lives, ladies,' one of the girls said with a laugh. 'Funny how the richest fella in town can't seem to buy a hint.' They began decorating the tree with dyed popcorn strings, gilded eggshells, and small, shaded candles. Though some churches banned Christmas trees, Miss Amber had bought the largest one they could find, a towering noble fir.

Maisie frowned at Ernest as her cold, pink cheeks grew pale.

'Is it really all that bad?' he asked. 'Madam Flora had been talking about getting a car for months now.'

'It's not the gift that's the problem,' Fahn said as she handed him a mug of steaming cider with a cinnamon stick. She offered one to Maisie as well, but Maisie shook her head. 'It's what the giver wants in return.'

Ernest was about to ask more when Mrs Blackwell changed the subject. 'Ernest, I wish you could have been there at the almshouse. The children gushed over Santa, the women cried, the volunteers blessed us . . . and then Mrs Irvine showed up mid carol and told them where we all work.'

'You're joking.' Ernest almost spit out his cider.

'Mrs Irvine had her own group of merrymakers, and they looked at us as though Mary Magdalene had stumbled into the manger and kicked her knickers off. As if the Three Wise Men had showed up drunk with a girl on each donkey,' Mrs Blackwell prattled on. 'As if the Christ child were born the color of our St Nick!' It was obvious that she'd already downed a quick glass or two of her famous syllabub made with cream and a potent raspberry wine. 'So . . . after we finished singing, we were politely asked to leave – through the back door, no less. And Miss

Amber and Mrs Irvine certainly exchanged a few choice words . . .'

Fahn cut in, laughing. 'Miss Amber called her a hypocrite to her face. She said Mrs Irvine was a bitter old coot who goes to the doctor for pelvic massages – that she'd rather faradize than fraternize!'

'But' – Mrs Blackwell rolled her eyes – 'I didn't want to cause a ruckus or ruin Christmas for the little ones. So I separated the two of them and we left. I was just happy they didn't make anyone give back the gifts.'

'Of course,' Ernest said. He remembered his own bleak Christmases at the boarding school.

'Well, it was fun while it lasted,' Mrs Blackwell said with a heavy sigh.

'No good deed goes unpunished,' Fahn added. 'At least it's a Christmas we'll never forget. Should be an interesting new year.'

'Maisie May!' A few of the upstairs girls called out to her as they were almost done decorating the tall tree that smelled like Christmas. 'It's tradition, we need you to put the angel on top.' One of the girls held out a kiln-fired cherub painted with hints of sky blue and gold.

'I'm too old for that,' Maisie grumbled. 'Besides, I don't believe in angels anymore.' She turned and headed up the stairs.

Fahn nodded wearily as she handed her cup of warm cider to Ernest and followed Maisie, muttering something about rich devils.

After the party ended and the servants had cleaned up, Ernest lay awake in his bed, tossing and turning. Professor True had read everyone 'The Night Before Christmas', but as Ernest tried to sleep, he didn't think about flying reindeer or sugarplum fairies. He thought about Maisie and how upset she'd been – Fahn too. Were they troubled by the scene at the almshouse, the mysterious gift from Louis Turnbull, or perhaps both? And Ernest wondered about Mr Turnbull himself and what he might think if he caught a glimpse of his obsession in her current deranged state.

Ernest wasn't sure what to do with his vague unease. Then he remembered the painted angels he'd wrapped as gifts.

With a worried sigh, he rolled out of bed and stepped to the window, scratching his head. There were no cars. No carriages. Even the saloons were closed. The entire city was asleep. The downy flakes had stopped falling, and all seemed solemn and still.

Ernest shivered at the thought of the cold and then got dressed. He bundled up in two pairs of pants and three shirts, and doubled his socks. Then he crept down the main staircase, which was carpeted and quieter. He tiptoed to the door, slipped on his boots, his overcoat, hat, and mittens. He wrapped a scarf around his face to keep his neck and cheeks warm.

Once outside, the air was so crisp, so cold it made his eyes water as he crunched through a thin eggshell crust of windborne powder, frozen atop the deep, wet snow. He walked around the building until he stood beneath Maisie's darkened window. He looked across the wide street, which was now covered, with nary a footprint, then up at the window once again and watched his breath steam away into the night sky. Finally he sat down, lay back into that cold desert of fresh powder, spread out his arms, and made a snow angel. He stood up, regarded his work, then took a giant step toward Fahn's side of the building, sat down, and did it all over again. He stepped again and again, up and down, occasionally feeling snow and ice go down his pants or the back of his shirt. He made snow angel after snow angel, covering the street, the sidewalk – anyplace that could be seen from the girls' windows. He caught his breath as he counted three dozen, then four, then five, while his nose ran and his eyebrows froze.

Finally, he crept back inside, warmed himself in front of the fire, adding another piece of thick cordwood and watching it burn. Then he wearily climbed back into bed just before the grandfather clock downstairs sounded three in the morning.

Ernest was exhausted, but he smiled as he fell asleep, imagining the look on Maisie's face at sunrise when she looked out her window, Fahn's face too.

He wondered how many angels he'd made. He had no idea. He'd stopped counting after two hundred.

B Sides

(1962)

Ernest stood on the sidewalk in front of Ruby Chow's impatiently counting the minutes. He'd paid the bill and stepped outside while Juju and Gracie were still chatting with the waitresses – about nothing too revealing, Ernest hoped.

There had been an awkward silence after Gracie dropped her bomb about being a prostitute. Then Juju had deftly stepped in, saying something about having left too many copies of *Whisper* and *Confidential* magazines lying around the house for Gracie to read. Her mother must have misremembered a bit of Hollywood gossip about Veronica Lake or Helen Hayden. Since Gracie's ailment had set in, she'd said plenty of things that didn't make sense, and they'd laughed it off, albeit nervously. Meanwhile Gracie had turned her attention to a nice rock cod, roasted whole with shallots and fresh parsley. She'd put the tender cheek, the choicest part, on Hanny's plate.

Everyone in Chinatown seems to have a B side to his or her character – an untold story – Ernest reasoned as he lit a cigarette and remembered that one of his favorite songs was a Hank Williams flipside record, 'I'm So Lonesome I Could Cry'. That song had seemed to do pretty well. Then again, some say Hank Williams died of a broken heart.

Poor Hanny, Ernest thought. She didn't know what to believe. So she smiled and said nothing. I guess there's comfort in denial.

But Rich knew the truth – Ernest could see that plainly in the man's wide-eyed look of surprise and benign admiration, even as he went on and on about his colorful life in Las Vegas. He told a story about being a law clerk during the raid on Roxie's, a famous western bordello. And about how he'd once met the famous Miss Bluebell, as well as Marli Renfro, the showgirl who'd been Janet Leigh's body double in *Psycho*.

Fortunately for everyone, Hanny and Rich had had to leave before dessert. Rich had to take a phone call with a client who was in jail.

Ernest put out his cigarette and loosened his tie as he looked down the street toward Chinatown, past popcorn stands and Turkish baths, past businessmen in raincoats heading home or to a bar, and past secretaries running to the post office, or meeting their friends for a drink. He could see the old Washington Court Building in the distance – the ascendant home of Madam Lou Graham, then Florence Nettleton. The building was now home to the Union Gospel Mission, one of the few missions that had survived the great flu that wiped most of them out forty years ago. The building now had a neon sign, which read, REACHING OUT AND TOUCHING LIVES.

If there is a God, he's the god of irony, Ernest thought. The angels of Ernest's childhood had been replaced by a scattered crowd of lonely, bearded men who wandered around the sidewalk entrance like pigeons bobbing for crumbs of bread and wobbling, noontime drunks, loaded to the muzzle.

Ernest was still gazing off into the distance when Juju emerged.

'It's all true, isn't it?' she said as she put a gentle hand on his shoulder. 'What Mom said – and that's where you both lived.'

Ernest nodded as his daughter handed him a bag full of pink takeout boxes. Gracie had appeared behind Juju, beneath an awning, buttoning her coat and covering her hair with a floral scarf as the cloudy sky began to drizzle.

'How's she doing?' he asked.

'She's restless,' Juju said. 'She talked to everyone about the new world's fair – says she's dying to go. But she's tired. She hasn't been over to this part of town in forever – so many familiar faces, so much to process, so many . . . things remembered.'

'You're taking this *revelation* about your mom remarkably well.'

Juju shrugged. 'I deal with the lurid side of humanity for a living. Am I shocked? Of course, but she's still my mother – who am I to judge? It was a long time ago, and back then only one in ten girls even graduated from high school. She's probably lucky she ended up at the Tenderloin. Besides, I still have a deadline and a feature to write.'

Ernest cleared his throat.

'Oh, don't get me wrong,' Juju said. 'I'm leaving Mom out of it – I'm not crazy. But you – you're still part of a great story. I still can't quite believe you were raffled off and ended up in a brothel. That's quite a secret.'

Ernest shook his head.

'I was just reading about how Louis Armstrong grew up in a bawdy house in New Orleans, a place just like the Tenderloin. That hasn't hurt his record sales one bit.'

Ernest recalled a decades-old memory of Professor True talking about the urchin boys who grew up in Storyville and how they'd go through the suit coats of customers while the patrons were otherwise engaged, skimming the pocket change. Ernest's life at the Tenderloin had been downright respectable by comparison.

Juju kept talking. 'And, now that I think about it, Mae West practically made her name playing the types of characters you grew up with.'

198

Ernest said, 'Mae West isn't helping your argument.'

'Why's that?' Juju asked as she helped Gracie fix the buttons on her coat.

'Because I remember going to the AYP and watching a dashing musician named Guido Deiro,' Ernest said. 'He went on to be the secret love of Mae West – a scandal that haunted both of their careers.'

'It was a different time then.' Gracie shrugged. 'People move on. Speaking of, we should too. It's starting to rain.'

Ernest looked at his wife, his mouth open. It seemed as if she was really following the conversation. 'I'll go get the car,' he said.

'I'd like to walk,' Gracie interrupted.

Ernest looked at his daughter, and Juju's expression seemed to say, *Why not?*

Despite the cloudy sky, it was a pleasant summer evening. The avenue was clear and the streetlights were flickering to life, reflecting gasoline halos in the wet pavement that surrounded them. Neon shimmered on the damp sidewalks, and gulls bobbed happily, picking out scraps among the litter. As they walked across the street, Gracie slowed and then stopped in the middle. She looked around, her face suddenly flushed with confusion. She pulled the scarf from her head and dropped it to the ground. Ernest felt a jolt of déjà vu as Gracie froze, a statue staring up into the sky as rain began to fall.

'Ma, what's wrong?' Juju asked.

Cars rounded the corner, slowed down, honked, and then swerved around them, bathing the street with their headlights. Ernest dropped the bag of takeout and caught Gracie, as her legs buckled and she collapsed in his arms.

Cloudy Days

(1910)

Ernest was bringing in large tins of coal oil on a rainy Tuesday night when he heard a racket from the third floor. At first he presumed that the banging, door slamming, and caterwauling was Madam Flora having another one of her *bad moments*. But as he set the tins down and ascended the grand staircase, followed by Fahn and Professor True, Ernest heard a heated argument that included a man's voice. And when Ernest reached the landing, he saw Miss Amber down the long hallway, a baseball bat in hand. In her largest, reddest wig, she towered over one of the Tenderloin's new customers, yelling at the man, who stood in a doorway. A gaggle of the upstairs girls still in various states of undress joined in on the shouting match like a chorus of hectoring, henpecking furies. Their voices echoed off the wallpaper that had been painted with doves.

Outnumbered, the man's barks turned to yips as he muttered, 'You're all just a bunch of two-bit harlots anyway.' He hastily collected his hat and necktie and stormed away. Some of the girls threw shoes and hairbrushes after him, and the objects bounced off the walls, the man's head, or both.

Miss Amber cursed and hollered back, 'I don't ever want to see your face again. The last man who caused a stir under my roof ended up in jail. Try explaining that to your boss. Or your wife!'

Ernest and Fahn found Maisie in the hallway; her cheeks were flushed with emotion. 'What happened?' they asked her.

'That jerk got jealous. He wanted Jewel to be his steady.' Maisie shook her head and stared daggers in the man's direction as Professor True followed him downstairs to make sure he found his way out. 'And when Jewel laughed and said no thank you, he slapped her around, started yelling, calling her names. He shoved her head into a wall. Luckily Miss Amber keeps a close eye on all the new gents these days.'

Ernest could barely remember the man's face, let alone his name. Since Madam Flora's health had been failing, business had been slowing as well. Her presence as hostess, emcee, and ringmaster for each evening's entertainments was a crucial ingredient of the Tenderloin's magic. Without her showmanship, a haunting sadness had settled over the place, and customers seemed to sense it. They were staying away. Plus her numerous treatments and clinic visits had been costing a small fortune, even though they'd done little to ease her slide into madness.

In response, Miss Amber had been forced to open the Tenderloin's opulent bedroom doors to strangers. Before that, new customers had been allowed only in the company of a trusted regular, someone vetted and vouched for. Now Professor True, sometimes with Ernest's help, had to toss out a belligerent drunk at least once a week. Ernest felt he'd aged years in the past few months. He was no longer a simple houseboy but seemed to have inherited a man's responsibilities, always on guard, protecting members of their odd little family.

'That fella got lucky,' Maisie said. 'Miss Amber only brought her bat. One of these days she just might shoot a man, or cut him where it counts. A creep like that could end up singing castrato at Squire's Opera House.'

'It'll get better,' Fahn said. 'Madam Flora's bound to come back to her senses.'

Ernest hoped for the best, but he wasn't so sure. Their matron had been having more bad days than good. And even her good days were not the same. She'd occasionally dress up and preside over a Friday evening gala, or introduce a guest poet, or a famous cellist who was in town to play with the symphony. But her time in the spotlight was always tenuous, and her smile barely masked the disquiet that lurked underneath.

As Ernest scratched his head and looked up and down the crowded hallway – at the working girls coming and going in their elegant dresses and silk changing gowns – he couldn't help but wonder. Perhaps the right patron *could* actually change things. Perhaps that person was Louis Turnbull after all. Surely he wasn't the only one who had imagined Flora's old paramour might be the answer to the complicated riddle the Tenderloin had become. But no one mentioned the man's name – at least not in the presence of Miss Amber. Though his gifts kept arriving – cases of Bordeaux from Château Latour, a floor-length coat of Russian sable, an oxblood vase from China, a painting by someone named Sargent.

Did Louis Turnbull even know about Madam Flora's fits of madness? He must have – surely – gossip travels fast. Maybe Turnbull thought he could rescue his lost love from the ghost of a woman that Madam was becoming. Or perhaps he thought her condition was exaggerated in rumors spread by jealous rivals for her affection.

'Okay, get back to work, ladies. I'll take care of everything here,' Miss Amber said as she clapped her hands. 'You too, young man.'

Ernest nodded and slipped by Miss Amber toward the servants' stairs and past the open door to Jewel's bedroom. He peeked inside and saw that Madam Flora was already there, sitting on the edge of the bed, holding the girl, dabbing at her black eye and bruised cheek with a hand towel from the washbasin.

Ernest stepped aside as Maisie slipped into the room and sat next to her mother, who was still in her sleeping gown, with curlers in her hair. Madam Flora put her other arm around Maisie, gently kissing her forehead.

'My ladies are my world,' Madam Flora said as she held both girls and gently rocked back and forth. 'No one will ever hurt you again. I promise.'

Sunny Days

(1910)

Madam Flora was true to her word. The Tenderloin went back to its regulars-only policy, despite dwindling business. And there were no more incidents. Now the only disturbance was the occasional evening when the house was too quiet – just the ironic sound of Professor True playing 'Everybody's Doing It Now'.

But at least spring had arrived. The morning fog had become a memory, and the rain took a brief, unexpected vacation, leaving sunshine to look over Seattle in its absence. As Ernest walked outside, he marveled at the smell: thousands of *sakura* florets had filled the air, swirling on the breeze like pink snowflakes. The flowering buds came once a year, and for only a week or so, but they meant rebirth, another beginning. Just like the new hotel that had opened on the corner of Sixth and Main – where Fahn, Maisie, and Ernest were heading.

'Follow me, I have a little surprise for the both of you,' Fahn had said, as she led Ernest and Maisie through Chinatown, past apple carts and fishmongers, to the thriving Japanese neighborhood to the north. There they wended their way through the flowering cherry trees. Ernest loved the trees' cycles of beauty and then repose, unlike evergreens, which stood constant and dull by comparison.

He remembered reading about cherry saplings that had arrived in Washington DC, gifts from Japan to President Taft's wife – two thousand trees in all. Most had been blighted with some type of disease, the damage had spread, and now all the young trees had been dug up and destroyed before they took root.

Pity, Ernest thought. The young trees in Seattle were marvelous to behold, finally coming into their own, a season away from bearing fruit. They reached toward the sun, potential waiting to be fulfilled.

'What's the surprise? That you're going to try to be the next Gibson girl?' Maisie asked. 'You told bigmouthed Rose, so now everyone knows your plan. Word's probably spread all through the neighborhood, all the way to Aberdeen by now.'

It was only a matter of time, Ernest thought, frowning.

Fahn had been practicing her Japanese tea routine for months. And she always managed to work, clean, and polish the silver within close proximity of the upstairs girls, hoping to improve her already formidable social skills. Fahn had taught herself to charm and flirt, following Jewel around and borrowing her books, like *The Evolution of Modesty* by Henry Havelock Ellis.

'Tut, tut.' Fahn brushed away the comment, parroting Madam Flora. 'A lady does not confirm or deny idle gossip; doing so is like wrestling with a pig: you both get dirty, but the pig enjoys it.' Then she revealed an apple she'd stolen from the cart down the street and took a nonchalant bite. She offered the purloined fruit to Ernest and Maisie, who both declined, frowning. They waited for a convoy of Sternberg trucks to pass, then a trolley, and then they crossed the street.

'No matter,' Fahn said. 'We're almost there.'

As they trundled up the sidewalk, Ernest felt bad for stepping on so many delicate buds that dotted the pavement. But he quickly forgot his worry when they rounded the corner and saw the shining brickwork and polished windows of the hotel that had been named after America's latest international adventure – the Panama Canal. Workers from

Seattle – and everywhere for that matter – had been shipped out to carve a channel from the Pacific to the Atlantic, battling malaria and jungle rot the whole time. Ernest had read in the newspaper that many scientists were worried that the balance of life in each ocean would be forever disrupted when the two systems met. The idea seemed familiar to Ernest, a mixed-breed boy in China, a half-breed in Seattle. He wondered if Fahn ever felt the same way. If so, she never showed it. He also wondered if Maisie felt out of place in this part of town, which Fahn called Nihonmachi.

'Here we are,' Fahn said, out of breath from marching up the steep hill of Sixth Avenue. 'Welcome to the Panama Hotel.'

'And . . . what exactly are we doing here?' Maisie asked, slightly winded.

'Don't be such a Friday face, I didn't bring you all the way up here just to show you the hotel. I brought you here to show you what lurks beneath – the Hashidate-Yu, the finest Japanese bathhouse in Seattle.' Fahn made a grand flourish with her hands, like a magician revealing a stage-crafted mystery, then pointed to a set of steps that led below the street.

Ernest had walked past the steam baths in Pioneer Square that the Scandinavian sailors from Ballard all favored, as well as the other Japanese baths whenever he'd run errands to this part of town – the Shi-moju, the Naruto, the Hinode. But he'd never dared enter – he wasn't even sure what a public bathhouse was, or how it worked.

'Goodie for you, Fahn, but what are *we* doing here?' Maisie asked, her expression a mixture of displeasure and wariness. 'Are we even allowed?'

'That's the beauty of the *sento*,' Fahn said. '*Everyone's* allowed – men and women, the rich and the poor. Follow me. I came here when the hotel first opened last month. I wanted to share it with you; it's

206

lovely and feels wonderful. I used to go to an *onsen* bath each week when I was a little girl in Japan – this is almost as good.'

Ernest followed the two girls down the stairs and through the double doors. He felt a rush of steam and humidity hit his face, making his shirt feel damp and heavy. He inhaled the scent of soap and fresh laundry as he paid twenty cents to get in and took the bath towel and washcloth he was given. He removed his footwear at the behest of a sign. There were a handful of Japanese patrons milling about.

'You're sure about this?' Maisie asked.

'Maybe you two should go without me . . .' Ernest mumbled.

'Relax. There are separate tubs for men and women, boys and girls,' Fahn said. 'Just do what everyone else does, wash first, then soak in the giant pool. If you sit near the wall, we'll be right on the other side, okay?'

'Got it,' Ernest said, but his heart beat warily. From when he was a toddler, he remembered people from Jiangsu frequenting the public bath, but he and his mother had never been allowed. They were too poor. Like most in their village, they bathed in the same cold, muddy river where they washed their clothes, upstream from where people poured their buckets of night soil.

Ernest reluctantly followed an older Japanese man through a curtain into the male side of the bathhouse, to a row of wooden lockers. A half-dozen elderly patrons were in various stages of undress, some toweling off, some soaking, one sitting on a stool scrubbing himself with a wooden brush. Another sat in the corner near a laundry window, wearing a towel around his waist, drinking a Rainier beer and wiping his brow with the cool bottle. Ernest felt self-conscious about his relative youth as he watched the elderly men move slowly, taking careful steps on the wet, tiled floor.

Through the wall he could hear Fahn explaining the rules of the bathhouse to Maisie, and the chatter of older women talking, laughing.

Having watched the other men do the same, Ernest took a tin pan and scooped out hot water from the large bath, then sat on a stool and lathered up with a bar of soap, scrubbed with the washcloth. Afterward, he scooped up another pan of hot water to rinse, again and again until he was clean, his olive skin steaming. Then he stood on the marble riser that surrounded the enormous pool. He slipped over the edge into the water, inch by inch, until he was all the way in and found a seat next to the wall. The clear water, which seemed hot enough to boil an egg, leveled off just below his chin. The heat was incredibly soothing, relaxing, and there was something about the purity of the bath, something magical about soaking in such a finely appointed tub. It made him feel less self-conscious about the shriveled old men who sat across from him, eyes closed, as though sleeping or meditating, or sobering up from a long night of drinking.

Ernest felt the water moving, like the rocking of a cradle. He noticed that through a small rectangular opening in the wall, no larger than a shoe box, water could pass freely between the men's and women's soaking tubs.

That's where he heard Fahn's voice.

'Are you in yet?' she asked him.

'I'm in. Does it have to be so hot?'

'It's just the time of day. The water is at its hottest in the morning. That's when all the old people come to the *sento*. Then after school, mothers bring their children, and then men show up in the evening, after work, and before going out on the town. Late at night, people come here to freshen up before bed. The water gets cooler as the day stretches into night. So what do you think?'

'It's okay,' Ernest said. 'I guess.'

'I haven't bathed with other girls since I was a toddler' came Maisie's voice.

'Try to relax,' Fahn said. 'Clear your mind.'

Ernest closed his eyes. The water felt soothing. He heard light splashing as the other men left the pool, dried off, and began to get dressed. Soon he found himself alone in the large room. Then he heard whispering, the sound barely audible over the dripping tub and the gurgling drain.

'Fine,' Maisie said to Fahn, in response to something. 'Close your eyes, Ernest.'

'They are closed.'

'And you keep them closed,' Fahn added.

He did as they instructed, even as he heard the swish of metal rings on a curtain rod and the faint padding of bare feet on wet tile. Then he felt the hot water rise and ripple against his chin and heard light splashing.

He squinted and saw the two girls climbing in, covering themselves with hands and forearms and their tiny cotton washcloths, their bare skin pink from the hot water.

'Hey! No peeking,' Maisie said.

He covered his face with his wet hands and smiled as he felt them swimming, splashing, then sitting next to him, Maisie on one side, Fahn on the other.

'Surprise,' Fahn whispered, and Maisie giggled.

He opened his eyes as they sat hip to hip with him, water to their chins. He tried to stare directly ahead at the wall, but his eyes wandered through clouds of steam and he couldn't help but notice their long hair floating like lotus leaves on the surface of the bath, their bare legs extended, suspended in the water. Fahn folded her washcloth into a neat square and then rested the small towel on her head. Maisie splashed hot water on her face and let it trickle down past her ears. Then they each held on to one of Ernest's hands to keep from floating away into separate, steamy corners of the deep tub.

'Is this allowed?' Ernest asked, blushing, though he didn't really care. His face was already flushed from the heat, masked by clouds of steam. 'I don't want us to get kicked out of here or anything . . .'

'You worry too much, Ernest,' Fahn said. She sank lower in the tub and her toes surfaced through the clear water, wiggling. 'This is normal where we come from – and I don't mean the Tenderloin. Besides, this is the quiet time. All the old people go home, but school isn't out yet. This is our time.'

An old Japanese woman wandered by, collecting wet towels for the laundry and wiping down the bench seating near a row of wooden lockers and hand-painted advertisements for the Maneki restaurant and the Higo Variety Store. She did a double take when she saw the three of them soaking, likely more surprised by Maisie's blond hair than by the three of them bathing together, but she said nothing.

'Hello there. Pleasant weather we're having,' Ernest said. The girls laughed, but the woman's expression remained unchanged as she continued to the boiler room and closed the door behind her.

Ernest imagined what would happen if Mrs Irvine walked in and saw him now. He pictured her eyes widening, her jaw dropping as she clutched her garments.

Then he felt Fahn let go and slowly drift away. Maisie too. They smiled and floated, spreading out their arms and hands, their feet, their bodies occasionally touching his as he closed his eyes again.

'I can't believe we're doing this,' Maisie said softly, her voice a ripple on the steamy, glassy surface of the water. 'What are you thinking, Ernest?'

He searched for words that could describe this moment, this strange, marvelous joy, filled with intoxicating nervousness and thrilling emotion. The warm ocean of happiness and contentment that washed over him seemed endless. He wished Maisie and Fahn could read his mind – and that it could always be like this.

On the breezy walk home, Ernest stopped near one of the blooming cherry trees and carved a large heart with the sharp end of his hairpin. Inside the heart, he inscribed three sets of initials, while the girls twirled amid the falling blossoms.

Coming Out, Going Away
(1910)

Ernest shoveled a heaping mound of coal into the great iron boiler beneath the Tenderloin, ensuring that there would be plenty of hot water for the Gibson girls' morning baths, though soaking in the clawfoot tubs upstairs couldn't compare to the bliss of skinny-dipping at the *sento*. He closed the groaning furnace door with a worn leather mitt and felt the searing, blinding heat slowly fade away. He grabbed his shirt and put it on, buttons pulling over his broadening chest.

Ernest cleared the coal chute, restocked the supply bin, and then cleaned himself up for breakfast. When he finally made his way to the servants' dining room, Iris, Rose, and Violet were already there, enjoying a fresh pot of tea. He greeted the ladies and took his seat at the far end of the long table. He ate a hash of last night's ham, corn, and creamed potatoes while poring over a wrinkled copy of the *Seattle Star*. There was an article about a working girl named Hazel Moore, who'd been arrested and was fighting back. Her series, 'My Confession', had become popular with the upstairs girls. Ernest skimmed her tale of woe, from rural farm girl to a budding actress in musical theater. She eventually became the mistress of a wealthy man. He was now serving time on McNeil Island while her fate remained unsettled, much like what had remained of Madam Flora's memory.

But even those troublesome tales had become lost in the latest topic of the day.

He turned the page, and Rose read over his shoulder, 'Astronomers in England say the tail of Halley's Comet is millions of miles long and made of cyanogen and could kill every one of us when the Earth passes through that poisonous gas.' She gave him a look of wide-eyed worry as she pointed to the article. 'If you ask me, it's all an omen of something terrible.'

Violet rolled her eyes, while Iris said, 'What you're suggestionizing is preposterous. It's just a big shooting star, dear, like the Daylight Comet we saw in January. Make a wish and be done with it. The real news, Rosie, is that you're a ninny.'

Rose sputtered as she held up the newspaper. 'Every time it reappears, terrible things happen. Look at England – their king is on his deathbed. And this lady, Madame de Thebes, says there will be flooding in Paris.' Rose put her hand on her hip and cocked her head as if that settled the argument.

Of all the maids, Rose had been the most caught up in the worldwide fervor about comets, spirits, and astrology. She'd gone to see Alexander: The Man Who Knows at the Pantages Theatre. She'd even bought a Ouija board and scared half the upstairs girls out of their wits until Miss Amber made her get rid of the parlor game.

As Fahn joined them at the table, Ernest listened to their bickering, imagining Madam Flora as their personal star, streaking across the sky in a fading trail of light.

It was *their* end of the world: Madam's declining health and her declining capacity for joy, business sense, poise, and charm.

While Violet and Iris went on to discuss their duties for the day, and Rose and Fahn compared notes on the handsome patrons from the night before, Ernest wondered if they too had noticed that the hysterics had become more frequent. Did they hear the flustered chatter at night, the banging on the floor, the struggle by Miss Amber to keep Madam Flora in her room when she was out of her mind and going off like a church bell? Or the sullen way Maisie carried the burden of losing her mother, echoing the cycle of good and bad days? Instead, as if determinedly looking away from what was going on in their own house, everyone seemed to talk only about sensational stories of the latest race riots, Jack Johnson carrying on with a white woman, or aeroplanes and world's records. Though also about the motorcar and the gifts that kept arriving.

'I still can't believe that thing!' Rose said to no one in particular. 'Most men send flowers or Swiss chocolates, or maybe silk scarves, but this fellow buys us a brand-new car. Too bad he didn't just send cash!'

Ernest looked about the room and noticed the nervous glances.

'Louis Turnbull is nothing to worry about,' said Maisie. 'That old fool wasn't content with his slice and now he wants the whole pie. Let him take a good bite and see how Madam Flora tastes now. He'll turn tail and run – the feckless coward.'

'And how is your big promotion going, lad?' Mrs Blackwell shouted from the kitchen, snapping Ernest out of his wandering thoughts. 'Madam always wanted a real coachman. And once Professor gets done teaching you how to operate that contraption, you can take us all out for Sunday jaunts on the regular. Oh, how I'd love to soak my bunions at Green Lake Park.'

'Bring your bathing suit and we'll make a day of it,' Ernest promised.

The ladies laughed and Ernest smiled. Professor True had already given him three weeks' worth of driving lessons. His most recent had been a starting, stopping, stalling, lurching journey in which they'd traveled a whole twelve blocks to J. Redelsheimer & Co., where he'd been fitted for a leather driving coat, butter-soft gloves, goggles, and a cap. He knew Madam Flora couldn't afford it, but she had insisted.

He'd been told that when he passed his twelve-question driving test, he'd begin taking Madam Flora and Miss Amber to their numerous weekly doctor appointments all around the city.

Meanwhile some of the Gibson girls were less eager to start riding in the car. They'd read articles in respectable magazines regarding the fact that traveling at such high speeds – as fast as twenty miles per hour – might cause acute mental suffering, nervous excitement, and circulatory problems in women. Other articles questioned the propriety of a man and a woman traveling together in an automobile.

But as Maisie had said, 'What does Madam Flora have to lose either way?' She'd laughed broadly and asked Ernest to start the car.

That day the roads were bone dry and the sun was shining, so Miss Amber sent Ernest out with Professor True for another lesson – another battle, really. Ernest tenderly retarded the spark plug so he could start the thing, only to wrestle with the pedals and the gearbox, the throttle and the brake lever.

'And take our darling ragamuffin twins with you, while you're at it,' Miss Amber had said. Ernest felt nervous but excited about finally taking them for a spin.

'Don't think of us as passengers,' Maisie teased. 'Think of us as victims.'

'Survivors,' Fahn said. 'We're safer here than on the sidewalk!'

They sat in the back, laughing and crowing, but seemed more apprehensive than when they'd waited in line for the Fairy Gorge Tickler. They kept finding things inside the motorcar to hold on to, looking for ways to brace themselves.

'How do you know so much about driving, Professor?' Fahn asked as the musician cranked the starter rod. If he minded playing mechanic

215

while still wearing his evening tuxedo, he didn't show his displeasure.

The Professor shouted above the roar of the engine, 'I don't! But I know how to work an engine, baby doll. Spent a winter helping my brother operate an ice cutter back in the day, made from a repurposed motor. The rest . . . ah, we'll keep figuring it out together.' He jumped into the front passenger seat next to Ernest and patted him on the back. 'What's the worst that can happen?'

Ernest tried not to think about the car turning turtle on the sidewalk, or crashing into a bus. He was more mature, at least, than some of the other chauffeurs on the road. Boys as young as eleven were being enlisted as drivers all over the city.

'When do I get a turn?' Maisie asked.

'Right about the time I run for president,' Professor True said. 'You know Madam and Miss Amber: there are some things a proper woman just doesn't do, and driving an automobile is one of 'em.'

Ernest refrained from noting the irony of things a proper woman at the Tenderloin *doesn't do*.

'Well, when I get the vote,' Maisie argued, 'I'm going to make sure women can drive anytime they want . . .'

'As fast as we want,' Fahn added.

'Why would you want to drive when you've got me as your chauffeur?' Ernest interrupted as he stepped on a pedal, lurching the roadster into high gear. Then the car stalled in the middle of the street as another car veered around them. 'Don't answer that.'

'Things are gonna change,' Maisie said. 'You just wait and see . . .'

'Now you sound like Mrs Irvine,' Ernest said as he started the car again and they motored up First Avenue, around the Bon Marche, Frederick & Nelson, and Knosher's clothier. Then he pulled hard on the brake lever as he turned a corner and had to swerve to avoid hitting an oncoming trolley. Professor True held on to his hat while singing the melody of 'The Longest Way 'Round Is the Sweetest Way Home'.

As Ernest straightened the wheel, Fahn wrapped her arms around his neck and sang the chorus into his ear, 'Two young lovers strolled down by the stream, said the maid with a smile, as they crossed o'er the stile . . .'

'Keep it in one piece, son,' Professor True said as Ernest drifted one tire up onto the sidewalk and back down again. Fahn stopped singing and let go, laughing.

'Madam might need this thing,' Professor True added. 'Sounds as though she and Miss Amber will be taking a cruise to San Francisco to see some special doctors – might be down there a few months, and this kind of newfangled medicine don't come on the cheap. Money is tight without Madam Flora at her fighting best, so they're talking about maybe selling this car to pay for the trip.'

Ernest was both surprised and relieved to hear someone finally speak frankly and openly about Madam Flora's condition. He blew a spot of dust from the dashboard, disappointed at the thought of losing such an amazing new machine right when he was getting the hang of things. He wasn't sure what to believe.

'When did you hear this?' Maisie asked. She held down the hem of her dress as the fabric blew in the wind. 'Who told you that?'

'Miss Amber told me last night, Mayflower. I thought you knew.'

Before breakfast Ernest had overheard Mrs Blackwell mention there'd be some kind of announcement tonight. He assumed the big news was another dinner party like the Victorian, rose-themed Valentine's Day gala. Or the bawdy Easter egg hunt Madam Flora had celebrated upstairs. Though some of the servants had been murmuring about possible wage cuts or longer weekend hours.

Ernest slowed down and honked, tipping his hat to a group of ladies on the street who waved as they trundled across. *Why send me out for driving lessons if they planned to sell the car?* he wondered.

Then he felt Fahn's hands on his shoulders again as she leaned forward and whispered, 'This is my big chance, young Ernest.'

That afternoon, after lunch and their midday duties were attended to, Ernest sat with Maisie taking a break on his fire escape, sipping glasses of fresh, tart lemonade. They dangled their bare feet as they watched a steamship, probably loaded with millworkers and bindle punks, chugging toward Bainbridge Island beneath a trailing cloud of smoke. They counted the vessels in the mosquito fleet as well as the smaller boats, which shuttled downtowners to Alki Point and families to Luna Park.

Ernest stretched his back. The weather was unusually nice. The rains of March had been absent and the warm sunshine felt like a gift. Now that Maisie's blond hair was longer, it fluttered in the breeze, and curls brushed Ernest's face, tickling his cheek.

'Sorry,' she said as she tied her hair back with a piece of ribbon. 'I'm not allowed to cut my hair, by order of Madam Flora and Miss Amber, all part of their conspiracy to make a lady out of me, the next grande dame. Like I'd want *their* jobs . . .'

As Ernest watched the silver-hulled Bainbridge ferry slowly turn against the tide and the breeze, he thought about Maisie and her quiet transformation. Gone were the dungarees, the suspenders, and the porkpie hats. Now she wore dresses and French make-up every day. But those weren't the only changes he noticed. As a Christmas present, for instance, Madam Flora, in a moment of clarity (or madness), had given her little hummingbird private dance lessons with Anna Pavlova, a famous ballerina who was visiting the city. Maisie had turned her nose up at the gift, but shortly after the lesson Ernest had caught her practicing her pointe, more than once. She'd been attending elocution lessons with the other girls, lectures on politics and women's suffrage, and had even studied the pros and cons of the latest temperance movements.

There was no doubt in Ernest's mind that Madam Flora was preparing her daughter to one day become *Madam* Maisie. After all, the sons of doctors often followed their fathers into medicine, and the sons of accountants often one day added their signatures to their fathers' ledgers. Why wouldn't a daughter follow her wildly successful mother as a captain of late-night industry?

Ernest tried not to stare at the girl who could make his heart turn inside out merely by tying her hair up in a bow, just as much as whenever Fahn kissed him. Instead he appreciated the cloudless azure sky. It felt as though summer had come early and with the sun's arrival, a promise of comfort, acceptance, and opportunity. He breathed a sigh of relief that anything seemed possible and every good thing seemed within his grasp.

'You know what Fahn is up to, don't you?' Maisie asked.

Ernest sighed. 'I have a pretty good idea.'

'She's serious . . .' Maisie shook her head. 'She's with Madam Flora and Amber right now, trying to convince them to let her follow Jewel and become the next *belle de Tenderloin*. Why would she do such a stupid thing?'

Maisie kept talking, not waiting for a reply. 'She has a great life. She gets to live here without really *working* here, if you know what I mean. She could grow up and manage any house – not just in the Garment District, but any house in the county. There's always a position for an expert domestic, and even Miss Amber would give her a decent reference. She's crazy to want to be turned out as just another working *quiff*.'

Ernest had never heard the word, but it was easy to partake of its meaning. He shook his head. 'She thinks she's selling herself, but she's just giving herself away.'

Maisie nodded and then stopped abruptly. 'You fancy her, don't you?'

'It's not that,' Ernest dodged. 'Well, maybe a little. But it doesn't matter, does it? She has other plans.'

Maisie looked disappointed, a tad jealous, then they heard shouting from the alley, where a group of teenage boys had gathered, heckling Maisie about showing off her legs. They hurled obscenities as she tucked the fabric of her long dress beneath her.

'Hey, pretty bird!' one of the boys shouted. 'I thought you whores weren't supposed to come out in the daytime.'

The other boys laughed and joined in. One boy even unbuttoned his trousers and dropped them to his ankles.

Maisie razzed the boys back, but Ernest could see her face flush as tears began to well up in the corners of her blue eyes. He took one last sip of his lemonade and then emptied the rest onto the heads of the young men below. They cursed and shouted even louder as they wiped their arms and faces with handkerchiefs.

'You're being too nice,' Maisie said as she took aim and then dropped her entire glass, contents and all. She smiled as the glass shattered atop the head of the pantless boy with a satisfying popping sound, spraying lemonade and broken shards in all directions.

Maisie stood up and wiped her tears. 'Let's go inside.'

'To see about the announcement?'

'No,' Maisie said. 'To see what else we can find to drop on their lousy heads.'

Ernest smiled. 'Maybe Professor can help us with the piano.'

After the servants ate dinner that night, Miss Amber gathered the residents of the Tenderloin in the grand parlor. They were all there –

the upstairs ladies as well as the working staff and Professor True – for the announcement everyone had been murmuring about.

Ernest sat on a plush purple chaise between Fahn and Maisie, trying not to tap his feet on the wooden floor while Miss Amber paced back and forth like a reluctant field marshal in a violet wig, about to address her ragtag, misfit army before they fixed bayonets and charged into battle.

'Where's Madam?' Rose asked, walking in late as though she didn't know.

There was a suppressed groan from the rest of the staff.

'What?' Rose asked, as she looked around, wide-eyed.

'Quiet!' Miss Amber stepped in before the staff began to argue. 'Well, I'll get right to it. The big news is . . .'

'I told you,' Rose exclaimed. 'It's the comet, isn't it? I knew it . . .'

Miss Amber stared at Rose until she fell silent.

'No, dear.' Madam Flora appeared from atop the staircase, much to everyone's surprise. From the look on her face, even Miss Amber was taken aback. Madam Flora descended slowly as she said, 'I can assure you – it's not the comet.'

Ernest smiled. He noticed that her hair was less than perfect and her make-up nearly absent, but her poise and natural magnetism made up for it. She knew how to make an entrance, Ernest thought, even when sickly.

After a brief, whispered exchange with Miss Amber, the grande dame smiled and then spoke as she gazed about the crowded parlor. 'Thank you, my dears, for your patience these past few months, your loyalty as well as your discretion. As many of you have heard or read, the big news *outside* our doors is that Councilman Gill is the leading candidate for mayor, which means that we'll soon have a friend and patron in a very high place. Our livelihoods are assured.'

Ernest drew a deep breath, exhaled, and waited.

'The bad news, though, is that . . . How shall we say this? I haven't been myself for some time now – months in fact. Some of the older girls have recognized the change in my constitution for what it is, and you may as well know . . .' Her words trailed off, as her normally regal voice choked with emotion.

Miss Amber chimed in, 'What Madam Flora is saying is that she has a serious condition, which isn't getting any better, no matter what we've tried. Her ailment is a frightful one, caused by this daft business, and only made worse by how hard she's worked on behalf of all of us. And so now it's our turn to do what we can, before this thing becomes permanent, left untreated . . .'

Ernest felt Fahn take his hand as he listened. She was trying desperately not to look full of anticipation, a stark contrast to Maisie, who looked worried. Ernest held her hand too as they waited for Flora and Amber to get to the point. He couldn't help hoping for good news – something unexpected and wonderful, though he couldn't imagine what that would be. Certainly not what Fahn was hoping for.

Ernest glanced about at all the faces – happy, sad, and in between – they'd become his family. He had come to love his new life. It wasn't without ugliness, but it felt so much more true and honest, richer and more satisfying than life under Mrs Irvine and the custodial care of the state.

Madam Flora regained her composure and spoke, though her energy seemed to be waning. 'The good news . . . is that there is a Prussian doctor . . .'

Miss Amber spoke up. 'His name is Dr Erhlich, and he practices at the Royal Institute for Experimental Therapy. He specializes in a new serum cure. But his clinic is located in Germany, so we will need to travel there and live abroad until Madam Flora is treated.'

Everyone looked stricken, especially since Germany had not been favored in the news as of late.

Everyone except Maisie, who lit up. She leaned over to Ernest and whispered, teasing, 'I'm going to miss you, Ernest. I'll send you a picture postcard. And if we don't come back soon, you better come join us, okay? I'm not leaving you to Fahn's wicked imagination.'

Ernest had barely begun to take in the thought of the Tenderloin without Maisie when Miss Amber cleared her throat to get his and Maisie's attention.

'No one knows the future,' Miss Amber said. 'Not even Professor True.'

Everyone laughed a little, and wore their bravery in their smiles.

'But I *am* hopeful,' Miss Amber said, 'that we'll be back by summer's end and that Madam Flora will be hitting on all sixes again.' She drew a deep breath and exhaled, as though she were shouldering a terrible burden. 'That being said, the treatment is expensive. So to fund this little escapade we've decided to throw one more grand party.'

Ernest felt Fahn squeeze his hand.

Miss Amber continued, 'It will be one more coming-out soirée. And with the money raised, we'll be able to travel to the Royal Institute and live there until we sort this thing out. In the meantime, the Tenderloin will be open for business as usual. Mrs Blackwell and Professor True will be in charge until we return.'

'We won't let you down, ma'am,' Mrs Blackwell said.

'But who's coming out?' Rose interrupted as she looked around the parlor. 'We haven't had a new girl since Jewel.'

'Don't look at me,' Jewel said, wagging her finger and tossing her skirts and petticoats. 'That ship sailed, sister. Bon voyage, boys.'

Ernest felt Fahn squeeze his hand again and sit up proudly, brushing the hair from her eyes. She licked her lips, which had been freshly reddened with carmine dye.

'When it comes to parties, we have thrown some humdingers,' Miss Amber said. Then she added a layer of drama to her voice, doing her best to recreate the circus atmosphere Madam Flora was always known for. 'But this next party, this grand gala, will be a masterpiece for our jammiest bit of jam. This will be the greatest celebration for a special, one-of-a-kind coming out,' Miss Amber trumpeted. 'And I can assure you, Madam Flora and I did *not* come to this decision lightly.'

Fahn smiled, beaming as Madam Flora nodded along.

Miss Amber adjusted her wig as she spoke. 'And so, I'm happy – no, I'm more than happy, I'm downright proud to announce . . .'

Everyone else held a collective breath in anticipation.

'That our own *Mayflower* will sail her maiden voyage in three weeks!'

Ernest felt Maisie's hand go limp. Fahn let go of Ernest's other hand as well, slumping back into her seat, her face a mask of stunned bewilderment. Then she stood up and stormed out of the room, past a startled Mrs Blackwell. The slamming door punctuated the silence.

All eyes immediately returned to Maisie as Miss Amber took her arm and helped her to her feet. Ernest stared helplessly into her wide pools of blue, as she blinked and looked away for a moment, attempting to hide her own shock. Then she recovered and smiled timidly, politely, as the room clapped and then cheered and congratulated her on such a gallant contribution. Jewel clapped the loudest. Ernest gaped at Madam Flora, who had stood like a statue through the announcement and now wiped a tear from her eye and clapped along, her hands in tea-length gloves.

Ernest looked at the empty spot where Fahn had been and back at Maisie. He was so relieved on behalf of one girl and furious on behalf of the other. He was also stunned by Maisie's tacit acceptance of this news. He wanted to rescue her, to stand up and argue with Miss Amber and what was left of Madam Flora. He wanted to shake everyone in the room until they came to their senses. He wanted to condemn every man who walked through the front door. He'd seen Jewel and the others reluctantly surrender, but the Mayflower – *his* Maisie, this was unthinkable.

He rose to his feet, and Maisie nodded back at him. Her sad eyes seemed to be saying, *It's okay. I'm okay.* She gamely went along with the charade, gently thanking the upstairs girls for their good wishes, bravely playing her part.

Anger Is Your Currency

(1910)

After the announcement, everyone at the Tenderloin went to neutral corners. The servants gathered in their dining room to gossip, the Gibson girls all went outside to smoke, while Professor True retired to his piano and began singing 'Heaven Will Protect the Working Girl'.

Ernest listened to the Professor sing his own rendition: 'A village maid was leaving home; with tears her eyes were wet. Her mother dear was standing near the spot. She says to Maisie dear, I hope you won't forget, that I'm the only mother you've got . . .'

Ernest was worried about Maisie, who had gone upstairs with Amber and Madam Flora. He went looking for them, but heard more doors slamming, and reluctantly followed the noise. He found Fahn in her room, packing her clothing and personal belongings into a bamboo picnic basket that she must have taken from the basement pantry. She stuffed in everything but her dark domestic's dress, her white collars, and her aprons, pausing occasionally to wipe her eyes.

'Don't trouble yourself, Ernest,' Fahn said when she saw him standing in her doorway. 'I'm done, I tell you. I QUIT!' She yelled the word as though that single syllable were a rush of air from a bellows onto hot coals, bursting everything combustible into white-hot flame. 'I'm moving someplace where I'll be properly appreciated. In fact, why don't you come with me?'

Ernest stared back in horror and disbelief. He couldn't comprehend how Fahn could be so enraged, all because Maisie was being turned out instead of her. Her best friend was about to be auctioned off to the highest bidder – albeit as part of a glamorous party, surrounded by wealthy men – but that didn't change the fact that she'd be becoming . . . an upstairs girl. Ernest couldn't bring himself to use the word the boys in the alley had used. That term had always been reserved for the girls who worked at other places. But when you boiled it all down, wasn't that what Maisie was becoming? How could Fahn so desperately want that life? How could she react as though she'd missed out on the promotion of a lifetime?

'Don't look at me that way,' Fahn snapped as though she could read his mind.

Ernest imagined his aching heart ripped from his chest and wrung through a taffy puller. He was surprised by how deeply he cared – about both girls – his care made manifest by how hurt he felt. He was losing Maisie, about to watch her sacrifice herself. Consumed into the belly of this confounding business that was like all the people he ever knew, from his mother to Mrs Irvine, from Madam Flora to Miss Amber – joyful and awful, so free at times and yet so broken. And now Fahn was abandoning ship – simply because she couldn't have what Maisie didn't want.

'I can't leave, not like this. And you shouldn't either.' Ernest shook his head and struggled to remain calm. 'Are you out of your mind? You're only fifteen, and you actually want to sell yourself to the highest bidder? Just think about what you're doing!'

Ernest argued, bargained, and grappled with denial as he tried to talk some sense into her. He stopped short of shouting, *You stole my first kiss! You can't leave because I'll miss you too much. I can't lose you and Maisie too.* But he hesitated, surprised as the words rose from the center of his chest but got stuck in his gullet. And then he remembered what Maisie had once said – true love is always wasted, distorted, lost in the funhouse mirrors of the red-light district.

Ernest sat down. 'Are you truly going to leave us because the upstairs girls get a few favorable nods? That's how the world works – you're a servant, for God's sake, and well paid at that. I wouldn't trade my job for all the expensive clothing and fancy dinners in the world! I'd rather be shoveling coal and peeling potatoes all day than counting ceiling tiles all night long, no matter how much they pay me.'

Mrs Blackwell appeared in the doorway. 'He's right, you know.'

'I don't want to be an old maid,' Fahn said, looking directly at Mrs Blackwell. 'In fact, I don't want to be a cook or a maid at all. We live in steerage while they're in first class. I want what they have – respect.'

'But they don't have real respect, dear. Can't you umble-cum-stumble anything? What they have is an illusion, crafted by Madam Flora.' Mrs Blackwell rolled her eyes and removed her cooking bonnet. 'Oh, they have such beauty, don't they? And charm to spare, and the well-polished veneer of high society. But as a form of currency, dear, that beauty *fades*. You have beauty too – so much it hurts, I know. But you're also so self-absorbed, girl, you possess so much anger, which scares the dickens out of me. If anger is your currency, then you're one rich bitch.'

Ernest blinked.

Fahn froze.

For a moment he felt relief, thinking the words of the dowdy old cook had found purchase in the jagged reaches of Fahn's imagination. Then she fastened the top of the basket and stared back at Mrs Blackwell and nodded at Ernest.

'You don't need to worry about me. I'll find my own way. The Tangerine will want me back now that I'm all grown up. Or the Aloha Club.'

'But . . . those are just run-down cribs,' Ernest said.

'We all have to start off somewhere,' she said as she stormed past him.

He could smell perfume, something she must have stolen from upstairs.

'If you leave us, child, you know there's no coming through that door again,' Mrs Blackwell said. 'If Madam Flora hadn't lost her wits, things might be different, but you know Miss Amber – she refuses to stand for this kind of nonsense, especially from the help, of all people. She won't take you back and she won't give you a recommend to your next employer when you come to your senses. Please, just calm down, girl – think about what you're doing.'

Fahn continued without looking back, down the hallway, across the foyer, past a startled Professor True, and toward the front door.

Ernest sprinted upstairs to find Maisie. He hoped she could talk some sense into Fahn, but the Mayflower wasn't in her room. He ran to his bedroom and threw open a window, from which he could see Fahn wending her way around drunks in the street.

'Fahn!' he called out past throngs of bewildered onlookers. He wanted to give chase, but he couldn't. As upset as he was, he was also worried about Maisie.

'Fahn, please . . . come back!' Ernest drew a deep breath and was about to shout again when he noticed everyone on the street staring up at him, regarding the queer sight of a young man hollering from the third-story window of the most famous brothel in the Garment District.

And he fell silent.

Fahn turned and shifted the basket to her other arm. She looked as lovely as ever, but breathtakingly sad. Even from a distance he could see that her cheeks were wet from tears. She touched her heart and then blew him a kiss, staring back at the Tenderloin as though soaking it all in, as though proudly, stubbornly saying goodbye for good.

Ernest heard someone behind him. He turned and saw Jewel standing in the doorway. 'At least you tried, Ernest.'

When he looked back out the window, Fahn was gone.

Ernest hurried down the hallway in search of Maisie. Her door was ajar, her room still empty, so he followed the sounds of shouting and crying, which led him to Madam Flora's room. Maisie was in tears, arguing with Miss Amber, while Madam Flora sat at her rolltop desk, which was open and littered with documents, invitations, and bundles of cash. The grande dame appeared to have fallen into a stupor, a tangle of confusion and detachment. She looked neither happy nor sad, present nor particularly absent – she just stared at her desk, absently touching papers as though searching for something she'd lost.

Ernest felt relief wash over him that Maisie was at least fighting back now.

'You're just going to scare her,' Miss Amber was arguing.

'Mama,' Maisie kept calling. 'Mama, it's me.' She was trying to push her way past Miss Amber, reaching for her mother, but Miss Amber held her back.

Madam Flora turned her head slowly and looked on in surprise.

Miss Amber pulled Maisie back. 'Stop this ruckus and stop being so selfish. She doesn't even know you anymore, girl – you'll only set her off. She barely knows *me* in her present state. This is why we couldn't ask you, we had to *tell* you. Her treatment will cost a bloody fortune, but it's her only hope.'

Maisie kept struggling.

'You have to do this – for all of us – there's no other way.' Miss Amber held Maisie by the shoulders and spun her around so she faced Madam Flora. 'Look at her!'

'She's my mother!' Maisie shouted. 'She'd never do this to me! She'd never turn me out like one of the other girls – I'm her hummingbird . . .'

Maisie broke free and shook her mother, yelling, 'MAMA!'

Madam Flora grimaced, put her hands up, and recoiled in fear – her wide, panicked eyes rolling away as she curled up into her chair.

Miss Amber grabbed Maisie by an arm and by the hair on the back of her head and wrestled her, kicking and screaming, until the girl stumbled and fell to her hands and knees.

'Don't you do this to her,' Miss Amber hissed as she towered over the fallen girl and reached for a leather belt. 'You're only making it worse.'

Ernest jumped between them.

'Oh, get out of the way,' Miss Amber said, more annoyed than angry.

Ernest drew a deep breath and stared back, unmoving.

Miss Amber coiled the end of the belt around her fist and raised the dangling, buckled strap high in the air. 'I'll fire you.'

Ernest slowly shook his head.

Miss Amber hesitated, her arm trembling in anger before she realized her bluff had been called. She gritted her teeth in frustration and then dropped the belt. She walked away with her hands on her wide hips. 'Glory, what a spectacle we've become. And look at you. The truth is, girl,' Miss Amber said, '*Flora didn't even want you* – do you know that? But she had you and she kept you around, hoping to get more money later. When that fool went flat broke her plan got washed away. You should count your lucky stars that she kept you, somehow grew to love you, because you owe her everything, from the roof over your head to the custom-tailored clothes on your back, to your pretty little figure and your dimples and your button nose – everything.'

Ernest helped Maisie to her feet. From the look on her face, he could see Miss Amber's words had wounded her more deeply than the belt ever could. She shook off his arm.

'What about the man who gave us the motorcar?' Ernest interrupted. 'Fahn once said that he offered thousands of dollars—'

'For Maisie,' Miss Amber cut him off. 'Louis J. Turnbull offered five thousand dollars for Madam Flora's *little sister*. Five. Thousand. Dollars.'

Ernest watched the fight drain from Maisie's face.

Miss Amber kept speaking. 'For you, dear – he couldn't have Flora, so he wanted the next best thing – he wanted you when you came of age. And Flora said no. She protected you. She always protected you, didn't she? But these are desperate times. Just look at her – now she's all but lost to us, and the bloody French disease has gone to her head. And you're right – the great, elegant, magnanimous Madam Florence Nettleton would never do such an unthinkable thing on her own, would she? So I had to make the hard, thankless decision for all of us.'

Maisie stared back, her shoulders rising and falling with each weary breath.

'But you're so stubborn, so mule-headed. We both know I can't do this to you if you don't agree to go along willingly.' Miss Amber rubbed her scalp beneath her wig, her voice trembling with emotion. 'So there it is, I've said my piece. I said what I think should happen, and it's the only way I know to make this better, the only way to save her. That's why you must decide for yourself now. Whether she sees the proper doctors, goes to a decent hospital, whether she lives or dies – it's all on you now.'

'Maisie, you don't have to do anything you don't want to,' Ernest said quickly. 'There's got to be some other way – we'll sell the car . . .'

Maisie approached her mother again, and this time Miss Amber didn't stop her. Slowly, lovingly, Maisie reached out and placed her hands atop her mother's hands.

Madam Flora smiled. She held her daughter and then ran her fingers through Maisie's hair as though she were a porcelain doll, a child's plaything to be dressed up and served finger sandwiches and petits fours at make-believe tea parties.

Ernest watched Maisie look into her mother's eyes, seeking recognition in Madam Flora's vacant expression.

'Mama, don't you know who I am?'

Madam Flora smiled and nodded. She took a deep breath and exhaled. 'Of course, my dear, I'm going to take care of you. My girls are my family.'

'Who am I, Mama?' Maisie asked. 'Say my name.'

'I know who you are.'

'Who am I?'

Madam Flora looked at Miss Amber, then back at Maisie.

'You're the new girl. And I'm going to make a proper lady out of you.'

Bedside

(1962)

Dr Luke politely knocked on the half-open door to Gracie's hospital room. 'How's our young lady doing this afternoon?' he asked as he walked in. He found her chart at the foot of the bed and began flipping through the pages.

'I'm not sure how to answer that,' Ernest said as his eyes wandered from his sleeping wife to the pale blue walls, the gray ceiling, the dull overhead lights. 'The good news is that she's starting to remember things. The bad news . . . well . . . is she's starting to remember things.' Ernest held Gracie's hand, which felt warm but limp. She'd been sedated in the ambulance and once more when they reached the emergency room. She'd been sleeping peacefully ever since, despite the assortment of tubes and wires, the IV, the heart monitor, the hissing oxygen mask.

There was another tap on the door, and a redheaded nurse came in and attended to Gracie's roommate. Ernest regarded the other patient, who was sleeping as well – an elderly Asian woman whose bedside table boasted an array of flowers. The adjacent wall was covered with get-well cards, letters, crayon drawings, Polaroid photographs, and a red and gold tasseled scroll with Chinese characters that Ernest could barely see and couldn't read – he thought it said something about longevity.

As the nurse opened the blinds on the window, she mentioned

that Gracie had a large group of visitors, who had gathered in the waiting room. 'Looks like they're going to be there awhile. They're having a potluck.'

'I guess that means the ladies from church have heard the latest news,' Ernest said. 'What do you suppose I should tell them this time?'

'Well,' Dr Luke said as the nurse left and closed the door, 'from the blood work there doesn't seem to be a problem – at least not the problem we'd worried about.'

'Are you sure?' Ernest asked.

'I'm absolutely positive. All of her lab work is clean. Honestly, she's in great health for a woman her age, despite the neurosyphilis that's been asymptomatic for most of her life. Ever since she was treated as a young woman, it's been dormant, which is why you never got it, why it never showed up during childbirth. And we took care of the recurrence with those heavy antibiotics three years ago – still gone, completely – not a trace. As you know, though, residual damage can be severe, even mimicking Alzheimer's disease.' Dr Luke tapped his forehead. 'But the human body is a marvelous work and a wonder. While the damage to the front, temporal part of Gracie's brain was permanent, our neurological will has some sneaky, unexpected, and not entirely understood ways of reconnecting those cognitive pathways.'

'So, you're saying . . .'

'I'm saying she's fine. She's just . . . being overstimulated with memories that are flooding back,' Dr Luke explained. 'Like waking up from a dream and realizing that dream was real.'

'Or a nightmare,' Ernest added.

'That too.' Dr Luke nodded, frowning. 'I'm sorry, Ernest.'

When Ernest stepped out of the hospital room, he found Pascual sitting in a padded armchair in the hallway. His friend looked up from a dog-eared Doc Savage paperback and grinned. 'About time you came out, *kuya*. Too bright in there – you want me to have someone close the light?'

Ernest shook his head as his senses adjusted to the dimly lit hallway.

'Juju and Hanny are downstairs entertaining folks in the waiting room. Those church ladies mean well, but they kinda drive me crazy, so I figured I'd hang out up here.' Pascual closed the book, marking his place with a lottery stub from the Sun May Store. Then he clasped his dark, scarred workingman's mitts around Ernest's hand and touched the back of it to his forehead, a gesture that Ernest had seen his friend use often with elders in the neighborhood. His friend's arms, with their assortment of scars, burns, and faded, blurry tattoos, told the story of Pascual's life – coming from the Philippines as a boy, working the canneries in Alaska, the orchards in Yakima, and then back to Seattle and the loading docks along the waterfront. Ernest thought about the IV taped to his wife's wrist, which told a different tale, the ending yet unwritten.

'This place got nothing on the Chateau Marmont,' Pascual said as he scratched his unshaven face and winked at one of the candy stripers passing by with a cart of fresh linens.

Harborview Medical Center. The crown jewel of First Hill. Ernest felt awash in the irony that Gracie was being cared for in a hospital founded by the Reverend Matthews, one of the many people who had helped the late Mrs Irvine put an end to the Garment District all those years ago. The fancy hospital was a far cry from the old Yesler Home – a mass of pink stucco that catered to wayward women after the red lights faded. Gracie must have been able to see the old building from Juju's living room, until the place had been condemned and flattened to make room for the new world's fair.

Pascual pointed toward the nurses' station with his pursed lips. 'I tried to get them to transfer you guys to the Edgewater Inn; that way we can spend Gracie's recovery time fishing for coho salmon right out your window, instead of being cooped up here.' He shrugged. 'But they said the new hotel is booked solid for the world's fair. Oh, and I got your car home from where it was parked near Ruby Chow's. I'll keep an eye on your place – get your mail, water your plants, as long as you need.'

Ernest thanked his friend and said goodbye. Then he sat thinking about Gracie, about Madam Flora, and the nights of his youth, filled with celebration and echoes of madness. He remembered running through Chinatown in search of dried bamboo flowers that would be mixed with red wine, just one of many home remedies, strange concoctions born out of desperation. He thought about visiting an herbalist in the morning to get foxglove tea and red yeast rice and all the other things old men and women in the neighborhood used these days to treat a nervous condition, even bouts of hysteria.

Tomorrow, Gracie would be sent home, wherever that was. And he was at a complete loss about what else he could do to help her.

Cardboard and Lace

(1910)

Fahn had left the only real home she'd ever known, leaving Ernest alone to console Maisie about her fate. If she was still upset, though, she didn't let those emotions show anymore. Not since that tearful breakdown days ago with Madam Flora.

'You don't have to do this,' Ernest argued. 'Miss Amber is just using you to solve her problems. Madam Flora – your mother, if she were able to think clearly – you know she wouldn't make you go through with this.'

Maisie sat at her mirrored vanity, brushing her hair. She'd taken to wearing parlor dresses regularly now, and Ernest could hardly remember the tomboy she used to be.

'No one can make me do anything I don't want to,' Maisie said. 'It's my choice and it's just one night. I can tolerate anything for one night. Especially if it means getting my mother the treatment she needs – the medicine, the specialists, whatever is required. And if I can help keep a roof over the heads of everyone else, so be it.'

Ernest knew next to nothing about Louis Turnbull, but he now hated the man. If he was so rich – so vastly wealthy – and if he cared that much about Madam Flora, why didn't he help her without strings attached?

Ernest asked, 'And what if *I* don't want you to go through with it?' He remembered how she had felt standing next to him, high above the city.

Maisie stopped brushing her hair and stared back at Ernest. Her words cut like blades. 'It's just one night, Ernest. One night doesn't mean anything.'

Ernest thought about Maisie's words as he worried about Fahn. He missed her terribly. She'd been gone only a few days, but no one had seen her, no one had heard from her. Everyone hoped for the best – certain that she'd calm down and return. But Ernest had scoured the neighborhood, to no avail.

In the meantime there were preparations to be made for Maisie's big night. And if the finest parlor joint in Seattle was hard-pressed for money, Miss Amber didn't acknowledge such concerns as she gave Ernest precise instructions. Maisie was not to settle for a frilly one-piece sorority dress, even the elegant kind offered at Frederick & Nelson. Instead a tailor at J. A. Baillargeon's would take care of her personally.

When they arrived at the clothier, Ernest parked the motorcar out front and opened the door for Maisie. He helped her alight to the curb like he'd been taught by Professor True, and he tipped his hat to the uniformed valet who ushered them along a purple carpet on the sidewalk and through the double doors into the posh clothier. Ernest's leather heels clicked on the polished wooden floor, and his dark uniform stood out in sharp contrast to the rows of glass display cases, and the columns of white marble that supported a pressed tin ceiling. Dozens of elegantly dressed mannequins stood in repose beneath an array of crystal tulip lighting, backlit by sconces that looked like glowing seashells.

Ernest stood next to Maisie, hands behind his back, feeling conspicuously out of place as she handed Madam Flora's calling card to a slender man who wore a monocle around his neck.

He bowed and then kissed Maisie's outstretched hand. 'You must be the one and only Miss Margaret Nettleton – I've been so looking forward to meeting you. For years I've worked with Flora, and it is such an honor to meet her spirited little sister.' He fished out a silver pocket watch. 'And you're right on time.'

'Please, call me Maisie.'

The man then said, 'Your boy can wait outside.'

'This is my driver and colleague, Ernest Young,' said Maisie. 'He has excellent taste, so I value his opinion. I'm sure you won't mind if he has a seat.'

Ernest smiled, silently cheering Maisie for her refusal to be pushed around. Even as the clothier sneered down his nose at Ernest's outfit, his black leather gloves, and the driver's cap, which he'd removed and tucked beneath his arm.

'Of course, be my guest,' the tailor chirped as he donned an obliging smile, one reserved for wealth. 'Let's begin this little adventure of ours.'

Ernest sat on a tall stool and watched as the tailor put a shellac record on a windup Victrola, playing an Italian ballad. Maisie was offered a cup of English tea with milk and honey as the slender man discussed her preferences. Then the real work began as she stood on a platform and was measured in every way imaginable. Ernest looked on as Maisie disappeared behind a large Coromandel screen, followed by a trio of seamstresses, who attended to her like a flock of fairy godmothers.

Maisie periodically reappeared, each time wearing a gown more elegant than before. Ernest loved them all, even the heavy white linen dresses that Maisie rolled her eyes at. She finally settled on an elegant design of white satin. Over her bare skin she wore a guimpe of lace that had been held in place by pearl-topped dress pins. The sheen of the new machine-made fabric was all the rage, and made her lightly freckled skin look like creamy silk, almost translucent, shimmering beneath the humming electric glow of the store.

Ernest watched Maisie become more beautiful with each incarnation of fabric and sequined lace. He almost forgot that she wasn't dressing for him.

'What do you think?' Maisie asked.

He opened his mouth but found his capacity for rational thought to be temporarily impaired. He tried not to imagine who would eventually be removing Maisie's party dress. Or Fahn's silk robe, for that matter. The girl whom he had shared a balloon ride with was drifting away. And the girl who had stolen his first kiss was expanding her collection.

'Ernest, your opinion please?'

'You don't really want to know what I'm thinking.'

'You're a man,' the slender man said. 'Your opinion always matters.'

'If my opinion mattered, this wouldn't be happening.' He tried to reconcile his feelings – balancing what he wanted so much with how little he actually could attain. 'I think you're perfect just the way you are. It doesn't matter what you wear.'

'And . . . spoken like a man,' the tailor said with a groan.

'Thanks.' Maisie shook her head. 'You're a big help.'

Ernest stared at Maisie, her reflections – facets in the many mirrors that surrounded her. She wore no make-up, no eye shadow or lip rouge. Her hair wasn't curled or pressed like that of the upstairs girls. She looked like the stubborn Mayflower he'd always known, but with longer tresses now and a ballroom dress that made her look like royalty. Through the kaleidoscope of Ernest's imagination, she looked more beautiful than all the Jewels in all the Tenderloins in all the red-light districts in the whole world. But in this moment, he found himself feeling guilty for admiring her. As if doing so made him complicit, somehow in league with the men who would be bidding.

The world is upside down, spinning backward, Ernest thought. *And*

241

what about Fahn? She was somewhere, selling herself as well, though deprived of such luxury.

The slender man snapped his fingers and left to get something. Maisie posed in front of Ernest, one hand on her hip, her head cocked to the side. She pursed her lips and batted her eyes.

'How much would *you* pay for me?'

Ernest felt tongue-tied.

'Why so quiet? What's there to think about?'

Ernest smiled and looked away.

Maisie laughed. 'Aside from that.'

Ernest finally laughed as well. 'I was worth a cardboard ticket when they raffled me off – the going rate for a novelty. But for you, I suppose I'd pay the going rate – plus a nickel,' he said.

'And what would you want in return?' Maisie asked casually. Her eyes reminded him of the way she had looked floating above the world, amid the fireworks.

Ernest shook his head. 'Nothing.'

'You wouldn't want anything?'

All I want is everything.

He shook his head again.

He kept his mouth shut and took a deep breath, exhaling from a place in his chest that ached with sadness and longing. He couldn't bring himself to speak about things he wanted, things he could never have, either for himself or for the people he loved, so he turned away. He pretended to be interested in a display of fur coats made from mink and fox, though he couldn't look at them without remembering the wild and beautiful things that had been trapped to make them.

Five Thousand Reasons

(1910)

After dinner, Ernest sat next to Professor True on his well-worn piano bench and watched the musician's long fingers dance across the polished ivories playing the hit song 'Chinatown, My Chinatown'. When the Professor reached the chorus he drew a deep breath and crooned, 'Where the lights are low, hearts that know no other land, drifting . . . drifting to and fro . . .'

Ernest listened and touched the spot on the mantel that used to belong to an old windup metronome. He remembered seeing it earlier in the week, atop Madam Flora's messy desk – Miss Amber had placed it there so that the tick-tock motion would soothe the grande dame. Ernest had watched, fascinated by Madam Flora's twitching eyes as the swaying arm of the oaken box enthralled her. Ernest found himself squarely jealous of her madness, which insulated her from the world more than Miss Amber ever could.

Bliss, Ernest thought. Madam found her own bliss at the Tenderloin.

Meanwhile Ernest had found his heart torn between Fahn – lo headstrong and hot-tempered, but fearless, daring to do what she wanted – and Maisie, who was willing to sacrifice herself for a mother who didn't know her anymore. Fahn had been given nothing in life but the short straw at every turn, while Maisie, in comparison, had had so much, at least until now. Both struggled to do what they thought was best, even for him.

Maisie and Fahn had known Ernest's secrets, all except for the one he'd thought was obvious – that he was in love with both girls. But what did that matter now?

As Ernest listened, he noticed that the Professor changed the ending of the melancholy song, finishing up-tempo, with a blizzard of stinging quarter notes. 'That there was for you, my boy,' he said.

Ernest nodded. He tried to smile, but the expression came out as more of a polite grimace. He wished Fahn were here so the girls could talk to each other. He had a hard time talking *to* Maisie *about* Maisie. But he hadn't given up.

Professor True began playing something jazzy and modern called the 'Comet Rag', but Ernest barely batted an eyelash.

'My playing that bad tonight?'

'Sorry. It's not you,' Ernest said. 'I'm just, you know . . .'

'Man, if you're nervous . . .' Professor True began playing a sad tune Ernest didn't recognize. 'I can only imagine how the Mayflower must feel about what's happening in just a few days. I'm all for parties, but this one . . .'

Ernest had tried not to obsess about Maisie and Fahn, but the more he tried, the more he worried, fretted, felt helpless. He had lain awake each evening staring out the window, where the cloudy sky held wishing stars for ransom.

'How's that new job of yours working out?' the Professor asked.

'Gets better every day.' Ernest sighed as he released the top button of his coachman's uniform and tried to relax. One of his new tasks was to drive a carload of Gibson girls about town, late in the afternoon, decked out in their voluptuously corseted finery. The girls would bare their shoulders and wave their gloved hands as they blew kisses at gentlemen on the streets in a wanton display of advertising. Though lately they'd been pilloried by the Ladies Relief Society, the Women's

Christian Temperance Union, and Mrs Irvine's Mothers of Virtue, who would heckle and throw rotting food at them as they passed, leaving Ernest to wash the car each day and pick bits of eggshell off the chrome.

But the worst was the long, anguished afternoon he'd spent alone in that fancy black car, delivering invitations for Maisie's coming-out gala. He'd driven around downtown, then to select gentlemen's clubs in Wedgwood, Ravenna Heights, and Seward Park. Ernest had somberly read the important-sounding names on the sealed envelopes, which had been addressed by Miss Amber – though he'd seen Madam Flora signing the cards, personally, in a moment of silent lucidity.

Despite visiting fancy town clubs, the city treasurer's office, and even the executive floor of Dexter Horton Bank, Ernest knew who the real guest of honor would be. He had delivered an extra-large envelope to the Turnbull Shipwright Corporation. He'd come so close to pitching all of the invitations out the window, or burning them, or sinking them to the murky bottom of Lake Union, even at the risk of getting fired and kicked out into the street. But it didn't matter. He knew that Miss Amber wouldn't be put off that easily. She'd just have someone else send out a fresh batch of invitations. Besides, all the driving allowed Ernest to look for Fahn.

'Do you know much about this Turnbull gentleman?' Ernest asked Professor True. His curiosity was dark, morbid, and painful. He felt the way he had when reading about an avalanche that had made an entire Great Northern passenger train disappear last month. The train cars had fallen 150 feet into the Tye River near Wellington. Hundreds of passengers were missing – all of them probably dead, and no one could lift a finger to search until the snow melted.

That's how Ernest felt. Helplessly counting the days.

'Oh, Turnbull's well known around these parts,' Professor True said as he played an ominous chord. 'Louis Josiah Turnbull was one of the founders of the Arctic Brotherhood. He made his name when he was just a boy, running loads of gelignite up to Alaska, and piloting riverboats up the Yukon River during the first years of the Klondike Gold Rush. Then he placed his newly built fortune on the stern of a ship-building concern, named after himself, of course, and got lucky when his wharf was the only one left standing in the wake of the Great Seattle Fire. He went on to become the biggest shipbuilder in the Northwest – and owned a few ships too, importing goods from all over the globe. Now he's a fellow with enough cash to buy the whole world. I suppose for a fellow like L. J. Turnbull, being denied something that he wants just makes him want it even more.'

Ernest nodded.

Professor True said, 'Turnbull was still a fairly youthful man when his health started failing, and since he was from a consumptive family, his doctors gave him a year to live. So what does he do? He builds the biggest house anyone has ever seen – a place to spend his waning months. Named the mansion Speedwell. But instead, his wife dies of the hundred days' cough, and here it is ten years later and Ol' Louis Turnbull is still going strong. He was smitten with Madam Flora back in the day. And when he found out she'd retired, he started asking when the Mayflower would be up for bid – sister, daughter, I don't think he cares – next best thing, I guess. Rich men get spoiled, or go crazy, a little of both I suppose. Grown men who should know better, I've seen them fall hard, like tripping down stairs, head over teakettle for some of the working girls, and then they can't understand why the girls don't fall right back.'

Ernest felt the anger and helplessness surge through him again. 'I guess there's a difference between the body and the soul. You can buy a body, but the heart . . .' He shook his head. 'The heart, you can't even rent.'

* * *

Those were the words that lingered in Ernest's mind as he scoured his room for every nickel, dime, and wheat penny. He'd saved most of his wages since he had begun working as a houseboy last year, and now he earned tips as a coachman – sometimes large ones. He'd drive home patrons who'd had too much to drink, and they were loose with their wallets.

He counted $128. He paused for a moment, astonished, after not having had even a penny for so many years. But then, chagrined, he remembered his savings were but a pittance compared to the enormous wads of folding money that the regulars would be throwing about at the party on Saturday night.

Ernest also took out the ticket from the fair – his prize-winning ticket – that humble piece of cardboard that had put his future in the generous, magnanimous, but now-quaking hands of Madam Flora. For a moment he wondered what his life would have been like had someone else claimed him. Where would he be? As torn as he was about Fahn's and Maisie's fates, he wouldn't have wished to be anywhere else.

Last, and with much reluctance, he added the gold hairpin topped with jade that had once belonged to his mother. When he wasn't wearing it on his lapel, he'd kept the piece of jewelry hidden in an old sock in the bottom of his dresser. That slender piece of soft, tarnished gold was his only earthly reminder of his time in China, those dark moments with his ah-ma.

Ernest gathered everything and walked down the hall to Miss Amber's room, where the door stood partially open. He peered inside, where she stood in a casual evening dress, smoking a cigarette and tending to one of her many wigs, as though the nest of golden hair were a small terrier in need of grooming.

'What now?' she snapped, blowing out the candle that she had used to heat a curling iron. 'Let me guess. A few gents come early tonight? Tell 'em I'll be right down.'

Ernest shook his head. 'No one is here yet. It's just me. I have a question . . .'

'Speak your mind, kid, but make it quick. You're wasting time and I'm sure there are things you need to busy yourself with downstairs. Is the car gassed up and ready? I have a few gentlemen who might need a ride tonight.'

Ernest nodded. He cleared his throat as he searched for the right combination of words that could somehow change Miss Amber's mind. Then he held out his money and the winning ticket. 'I know you're only doing what's best for Madam Flora. And I understand how sick she is and all, and that if we don't do something quick, she'll only get worse, and no one wants that. But . . .'

'Ah, geez Louise . . .'

Ernest spoke faster. 'There must be another answer. I don't have much . . .' He handed her his money and the gold pin. Then he held up the ticket. 'Maybe we could figure out an arrangement. I could work here for free, for as long as it takes to pay off the amount that the Tenderloin would be making for Maisie.'

'You want her?' Miss Amber stared at him, confused.

'Yes. I mean, no,' Ernest stammered. 'It's not that. I don't want her to do this at all. You could even sell my services, maybe Mr Turnbull needs a houseboy or a driver – I could ask him to loan you the money you need for Madam Flora's treatment. Then I would work without pay, for as long as it takes . . .'

Miss Amber took a long final drag on her cigarette and then snuffed it out. 'That's a sweet idea, kid, and the sentiment isn't lost on me. I think my heart skipped a beat. Wait . . . there it goes – it's beating again. See, you almost killed me.'

Ernest stared back, frustrated, loathing her.

She shook her head. 'Look, I live in the real world. Besides, Louis

248

Turnbull could buy a hundred other girls and a hundred thousand servants like you. *But that's not what he's after* – he wants the Mayflower, so he gets the Mayflower. Understand? Trust me, we're just lucky that we happen to have something he wants so badly. The way I see it, this is fate paying back a kindness to Flora for not giving up Maisie in the first place.'

She lit another cigarette and put on her wig. She spoke to Ernest, addressing his reflection in a three-way mirror. 'I only needed one good reason to turn Maisie out, and that's our Madam Flora's well-being. But this man has given me *five thousand* reasons.'

'This' – she waved her hand at the ticket – 'this doesn't even come close.'

Ernest put the cash, the pin, the ticket, back into his pocket.

'You're too late anyway. I already closed the deal.'

Ernest stared at her three reflections in the dressing mirrors as they moved in unison; he felt equally confused by each one.

'Kid, no one – and I mean no one on God's green Earth – was going to outbid Louis Turnbull, so I called and we settled things on the telephone, quick and proper. He won't grace us with his presence, but we'll have a coming-out party for the Mayflower nonetheless – she'll have her big, showy entrance, descend the staircase, and get her moment in society's grand spotlight – then *whoosh*, out the door she goes. I'll make sure that the upstairs girls treat the guests to something special for showing up, everyone will have a swell time in the style and fashion that the Tenderloin is known for, and Maisie gets to have her own party. All I need from you is to keep your wits about you and deliver her to his mansion in Windermere, with a bottle of our finest bubbly, of course.' Miss Amber winked and smiled through tobacco-stained teeth. 'Compliments of Madam Flora.'

All I Have to Give

(1910)

To Ernest, Maisie's coming-out ceremony was a blur of silk, lost in a haze of cigar smoke, tainted with the smell of brandy and Canadian rye. She wasn't wheeled in atop a silver cart like Jewel; instead she walked on her own two feet, gilded in her expertly tailored dress. Ernest was simultaneously awestruck and heartbroken as she slowly descended the grand staircase in shimmering high-heeled shoes that made her seem much older than her fifteen and a half years. As she made her entrance she was flanked and feted by every Gibson girl, who smiled as they fanned her with plumes of ostrich feathers, while Professor True played a waltz.

Compared to Maisie, Ernest thought, the others looked like last year's models.

All of the wealthy men in attendance, with slick hair and waxed mustaches, who wore tuxedos with open collars and sparkling cufflinks, cheered. A few of the younger gents dared to kiss the back of Maisie's gloved hand, but none ventured further, not even for a peck on the cheek. Ernest wondered, wryly, if there was some unspoken etiquette regarding virgins on their nights of deflowering. Or perhaps the distance in Maisie's smile was enough to keep the wolves at bay.

Like the sober banker who said, 'I'll pay you one hundred dollars for a kiss on the lips, dollface. How 'bout it, sweetheart?'

Or the sloppily drunk man who heckled, 'How about five hundred for a bumpy ride in the back of my new car?'

Maisie deflected each offer with a piercing stare and a smile that might have killed had she not lowered its intensity.

Ernest waited along the far wall and listened to the music. The rest of the help were quick to fill an empty drink, replace a full ashtray, or fetch the humidor for a fresh cigarillo. Professor True broke into an original song he had composed for the occasion as Maisie made her way, turning her attention to one patron and then quickly to another, flitting like a hummingbird through the room. The working girls all swayed, mooning over the sweet, gentle music, but Ernest knew that when the song ended, Maisie would be leaving. To his weary heart it sounded like a funeral dirge.

As Maisie orbited the room once more, stoking the fires in the bellies of rich men for the other girls, Miss Amber snapped her fingers toward him. For Maisie, the party was ending. Ernest donned his driving gloves and worked his way to the foyer. Her very presence – her magnetic beauty coupled with her coy aloofness – teased the gentlemen who looked on. They knew they'd been outbid and who the lucky winner was. They raised their glasses and drained them as they toasted their misfortune and jokingly cursed Louis Turnbull.

'Here's to Old Man Turnbull, the only fellow I know who succeeds at everything he sets his mind to . . . with the exception of dying!' one bearded fellow yelled above the crowd. 'He knows how to pick 'em. Let's just hope he remembers what to do with 'em!'

Ernest gritted his teeth and stared at his shoes, trying not to think about the age of the man awaiting Maisie in his mansion. In his mind's eye all he saw was a gray-haired Methuselah in moth-eaten robes, with a face of wrinkles, a tongue darting to the corners of old, cracked lips.

Maybe he'll have heart failure. Ernest smiled grimly as he regarded a few of the older gentlemen in the room. His eyes wandered back up the stairs.

Ernest had hoped Madam Flora might marshal some of her wits in reserve and find her way down to the party, where she'd perform a miracle by postponing Maisie's fate the way Governor Hay might have offered a stay of execution.

But no last-minute rescue came.

Instead, Miss Amber held court as best she could. She wasn't regal, or well spoken, like her flamboyant business partner, but the free-flowing Canadian whiskey and Kentucky bourbon worked well enough. The men laughed and raised their glasses to Madam Flora in absentia.

And then Miss Amber announced that it was time for the belle of the ball to take her leave. The men cheered once again.

Ernest knew that Amber and Flora would be leaving by train soon after the party ended, for New York City, followed by the journey by sea to Europe. And as some of the men began to ascend the stairs with their girls of choice for the evening, it became obvious that they knew as well, as they wished the grande dame bon voyage.

Ernest stood by as the rest of the upstairs girls hugged Maisie. They whispered in her ear, and Ernest could only imagine their congratulations, condolences, words of advice perhaps. Maisie smiled and laughed.

And then the downstairs servants took their turn near the door, forming a makeshift receiving line, though the Mayflower wasn't a bride.

Mrs Blackwell, Violet, Iris shared a toast of purloined champagne in servants' teacups, all but Rose, who barely restrained her sobs, as though she somehow knew that Maisie's departure foretold the ending of an era.

Ernest, who was drifting in the barrel of his imagination, toward the lip of his own emotional Niagara Falls, had almost forgotten that the end of Maisie's childhood was almost too much to bear for everyone else as well. For a moment, he wondered why there had been so much vested emotion for Maisie but not for Fahn. He worried that they all knew something he didn't, that Louis Turnbull was some kind of sadistic creature. Then he realized that in the minds of the downstairs help, if Maisie was leaving, Madam Flora must truly be lost, and no one knew when she'd ever come back. The big heart and little soul of the Tenderloin were both leaving within one sweep of the clock hand.

Ernest stood at the curb and put Maisie's small overnight valise into the trunk of the roadster. He warmed up the car and watched as Maisie slowly descended the steps. He got out and held the door, helping her inside, offering her a blanket, which she gratefully took to ward off the chill. She sank into the plush leather and closed her eyes, as if leaving had been the hardest part of the evening.

Ernest honked the horn and waved goodbye to a tearful Mrs Blackwell.

In the rear-view mirror he could see that Maisie was smiling but also dabbing at the corners of her eyes with the lace fringe of her long sleeves.

Ernest hesitated and then asked, 'Did you say goodbye to Madam Flora?'

Maisie shook her head and composed herself. She took a deep breath, held it, and then let it out slowly. 'No need. I'll see her when she returns. And it wouldn't matter right now anyway.'

Ernest turned north toward the Turnbull estate. 'I'm so sorry.'

'It's fine.'

Ernest glanced over his shoulder. 'Last chance,' he said soberly. 'Just say the word and we'll light out for them hills. I could be Wild Bill Hickok and you can be Calamity Jane. We'll search the cribs until we find Fahn, we'll rob a few banks, and they'll never bring us back alive.'

Maisie smiled back, but said nothing.

After that, Ernest didn't say another word. He drove in silence, his feelings of love, loss, regret, and remorse drowned out by the roar of an eighty-horsepower engine.

He could see Lake Washington in the distance as they entered Windermere and passed the massive marble gateways that led to stately mansions with names like Lochkelden, Summerport, and Islesworth. Beyond the gates were long drives through manicured gardens where lamplighters had kept the roads illuminated.

But the largest home, a sprawling gaslit mansion in white, with endless balconies beneath the high arches of a black-tile roof, was the home of Louis Turnbull.

No sign or demarcation was necessary. The five-story manor known as Speedwell was by far the largest house in the area, and it adorned the highest hill, with a commanding lake view. Ernest took special care not to graze the sculpted topiary that lined the road as he wended his way up the long, serpentine driveway. He finally pulled into a grand porte cochere. The Italian architecture, the fountains, the shrubbery trimmed into the likenesses of soaring birds and leaping fish made the opulence of the Tenderloin look like a second-hand store in a shantytown.

A butler must have noted their approach, for he stood at attention at the top of the steps near the rear entrance. Ernest idled the engine as a pair of uniformed footmen also appeared. One was quick to hold the car door open for Maisie, while the other attended to her small linen suitcase on the other side and that bottle of wine from Miss Amber.

Ernest looked in the rear-view mirror, waiting, as Maisie sat with her eyes closed. He silently hoped, begged for her to close the door and ask him to drive away. But then she seemed to awake and took the footman's hand without so much as a glance in Ernest's direction. She didn't say a word of goodbye, and maybe it was better that way.

'Someone will call in the morning for you to come and pick

her up,' said one of the footmen. Ernest watched her walk toward the manor, the hem of her dress skimming the wide marble as she ascended the steps. Maisie became a silhouette in the glow of the open door, and her long shadow seemed to reach out to him as the light of a chandelier emanated from the entrance of the mansion. Then the wooden sway closed.

Just like Fahn, Maisie was gone too.

Ernest loosened his collar and surrendered an aching sigh, his throat so tight he found it hard to swallow. He chewed his lip and shifted gears and felt the rumbling engine as he slowly began to motor back down the long, winding driveway. Then he heard a shout over the pistons. He glanced back toward Speedwell and saw a light between the hedges. He couldn't turn the roadster around on the narrow road, so he slammed on the brakes, opened the door, and stepped to the pavement. He saw a figure in white – Maisie, it had to be – running toward him in stocking feet, her blond hair cascading off her shoulders. Ernest removed his chauffeur's cap as she threw her arms around his neck, nearly tipping him over as she kissed him on the lips. She tasted like lipstick and sparkling wine. He held her tight, pressed so close that he could feel her heart racing through their layers of silk and cotton and sticky sateen. His hand found a soft spot at the nape of her neck, and he heard a sigh float away on the breeze. And when he finally, reluctantly let go, it was only to exhale his surprise.

'You deserve that more than anyone,' she whispered as she hugged him again, clinging to him, and then letting go. 'I'm sorry that's all I have to give.'

Crossroads

(1910)

A first kiss means everything.

Those were the words that echoed in Ernest's mind as he drove home in a fresh downpour, to the sound of speeding tires on wet pavement, the growl of automobile engines, and the lonely bell of a late-night trolley.

Ernest touched his lips. He felt torn, twisted, pulled between his perpetual longing for Fahn, who knew him better than anyone, and Maisie, who had just surrendered a part of her heart. And yet he couldn't be with either girl.

He turned the car south, toward the center of the city, and folded the front window down. As he drove into the cold night, he wanted to feel the wind, the chill; he wanted to feel something – anything to assuage the enormous vacancy in the roadster's passenger seat, the cavity in his chest. But all he found was the dank smell of horses leaving their marks on the muddy streets, the stench of low tide and rotting fish.

As Ernest drove through downtown, he was in no hurry to return to the Tenderloin. He didn't have to be back until 11 p.m. to take Madam Flora and Miss Amber to the train station. So he cruised along the waterfront, past piers nine and ten, where the US Navy's Great White Fleet sat at anchor, running lights aglow. He veered west in the shadow of the glittering Orpheum Theatre, where Maisie and the Gibson girls had seen productions of *Misalliance* and *The Shadow of the Glen*, gossipy plays that stretched the definitions of love and dissected the politics of the day, temperance issues, the suffrage movement, labor, socialism, and the union battles that dominated the headlines.

Ernest now realized this had all been part of Maisie's education, calculated planning by Madam Flora and Miss Amber. And as he regarded a long line of theatergoers paired up beneath dark umbrellas, he saw that tonight's featured production was *At the Old Cross Roads*, a show about the child of an octoroon. It was an odd happenstance, since a crib joint called the Octoroon House sat four blocks away on the fringes of the Garment District.

Ernest had always wondered about that place. Almost as much as about Weed's Pharmacy on Jackson Street. He glanced at his reflection in the shop window as he motored past. Weed's was where the girls went each month for illegal discourses on womanhood and how to avoid pregnancy. Mrs Irvine and her group often stood outside the store with signs on Sunday afternoons, protesting.

When Ernest finally arrived back at the Tenderloin, he expected to see preparations for a grand send-off for Madam Flora and Miss Amber. Yet all he heard were honking cars and music from nearby saloons. The upstairs girls were all in their rooms with customers. And the servants had busied themselves elsewhere. Their absence spoke more than a pretend smile ever could, and revealed how much resentment had built up toward their once beloved leader and her business partner.

The only people who said goodbye were Mrs Blackwell, who held an umbrella for Madam Flora, and Professor True, who was there to help with the luggage, as moisture from a sudden downpour fogged up his glasses.

Ernest expected Miss Amber to ask about Maisie or Louis Turnbull, but all she said was 'King Street Station. Be quick about it.'

Madam Flora said nothing.

At the nearby station the Empire Builder was waiting, the flagship locomotive of the Great Northern Railway, a midnight train bound for Chicago. In the City of Broad Shoulders they'd switch trains for New York, where they would board an ocean liner, and then sail beyond the horizon of the Americas.

Ernest watched as Madam Flora, eyelids drooping from laudanum, boarded a Pullman car designed for sleeping, while black porters, all named George, helped with the luggage. After Madam Flora and Miss Amber were aboard, he stood on the platform as others blew kisses and crowds of well-wishers waved at the departing train with a flurry of white handkerchiefs.

Ernest watched Miss Amber disappear without so much as a glance in his direction, or back toward the Tenderloin. He lingered long after the train had departed and the station became as quiet as a library on Sunday morning, nothing but the sound of the rain and the occasional clip-clop of a leather heel on the marble floor.

When Ernest finally walked back outside, he saw that all the cars had stopped, idling in the street, as a team of horses nearby grew restless, braying in their harness. Ernest stepped to the roadster and climbed atop the running board to see what the commotion was. He saw a crowd of people in front of Billy the Mugs, a popular saloon where men drank buckets of beer and often fought in the alley. The vaudeville musicians in the basement had also come up to the street. The fiends who haunted the stoop of a nearby drugstore had even stopped their begging to watch.

Despite the rain, another crowd had gathered on the opposite sidewalk: finely dressed women, holding folded newspapers above their heads to keep their hats from getting wet. That's when he spotted Mrs Irvine and a dozen other matrons from the Mothers of Virtue, protest signs in hand, warning of the evils of John Barleycorn. The ladies were mixed in with uniformed men and women from the Stranger's Rest and Olive Branch Missions a few blocks away. But the crowds weren't shouting at each other. They were silent as a tintype photograph, luminescent in their intensity as they stared at someone between them in the middle of the street, a woman – a girl.

Ernest recognized her immediately from a block away. He recognized her despite the rain, despite the flickering glow of gaslights and the veering, reaching, clawing shadows cast by the headlamps of the motorcars that honked and veered around her.

Fahn.

She was naked. Barefoot. Limping down the middle of the street in the pouring rain.

Some men whistled, others heckled and jeered, laughing.

The missionary women gasped, clutching their pearls.

Ernest felt his heart in his throat as he pushed his way through the crowd, running toward her, shouting her name. But she was confused and didn't seem to recognize him. Her skin was so pale she looked cadaverous, dazed, staring ahead in the direction of the Tenderloin. The street was littered with cigarette butts and broken glass from discarded bottles of beer, and her feet were cut, bleeding, leaving ruddy footprints on the pavement. Ernest removed his coat as she fell to her knees. He wrapped the long woolen shell around her shoulders. Her wet, tangled hair reeked of smoke. She held out a clenched fist and slowly opened her fingers like flower petals blooming. She stared down at a handful of quarters, then dropped them. The bits of silver clattered to the pavement and rolled away, skittering toward the gutters and the feet of a group of women who were crossing themselves and saying silent prayers.

Ernest looked up at the ladies, many of whom shielded their eyes with their hats or their scarves, receding into the shadows. 'Help me!' he shouted as he heard bells in the distance. 'She's hurt! Help me get her to a doctor.'

The women stared back in silence, shaking their heads with pity.

'Call a doctor!' Ernest shouted again. Then he saw Mrs Irvine. She looked him in the eye and said, 'The wages of sin.' Then she turned her back and disappeared into the crowd.

Ernest struggled to his feet with Fahn cradled in his arms. Her body was cold, and as she went limp, he heard the wail of a siren. He thought it was a motorized police wagon until he saw flames erupt from the windows of a building five blocks away, tongues of flame illuminating old brick, licking the sky as clouds continued to weep. It was a crib joint, the Tangerine.

The fire brigade arrived shouting, 'Move!' and 'Make way!' as more bells rang.

Women shrieked and fled; dozens of men with axes and buckets, a horse-drawn steamer, a hose wagon, and a new motorized chemical engine made their way up the crowded avenue.

Ernest opened the passenger door to the car and set Fahn in the backseat as gently as possible. He found all the driving robes and covered her shivering body. With a small lap blanket, he tried to dry her long hair, which clung to her face like swashes of ink, strange letters, foreboding characters. Her lips were pale, and she began to shake.

'It's going to be okay,' Ernest said, though he wasn't sure.

Then Fahn drew a deep, shuddering breath, as though she'd kicked her way to the surface of the ocean, released from the grasp of a hidden current. She blinked and looked around. She stared, recognizing him as the rain dripped from her bangs down her cheeks. She swallowed and cleared her throat, smiling, trembling as she spoke. 'A-a-are you still going to marry m-m-me?'

Still

(1962)

Ernest sat in his apartment at the Publix while Gracie slept in the bedroom.

After his arguing with his daughters at the hospital about where she should go, Gracie herself spoke up. 'If you don't mind . . . I'd like to go home with young Ernest,' she said with tired eyes. 'He always took excellent care of me.'

I did, Ernest thought.

From that moment I found her bleeding in the street, I never let go again.

Juju had been furious – at the doctors who murmured about Gracie's unstable behavior and how she'd be better off in a mental hospital. And at Ernest for thinking Gracie would be fine back in Chinatown and not at Juju's house on Queen Anne Hill.

But as Ernest stared through the cracked window toward King Street Station, he knew that while his apartment was certainly lacking, Gracie's home was with him. That had always been true, except for the time when she'd become lost to herself. And to him. At least the neighborhood still had a certain familiarity. Despite the good and the bad, there was also peace. In the end Gracie had chosen to be here, and she seemed more comfortable now. Though she didn't always remember him as her husband, she now always remembered Ernest as her friend – a beacon, a safe harbor. After a day of sporadic rest, always waking up with him nearby, that was still the case.

Even Juju had to relent then.

Ernest stretched his back and tried to relax as he read the Sunday *Seattle Times*. It was the World's Fair Souvenir Edition, THE LARGEST EDITION IN THE PAPER'S HISTORY, or so a front-page headline declared in bold black and blue type.

Gracie still wanted to go to the expo. In her waking moments, that was all she talked about – often mixing up the new fair and the old.

Ernest skimmed articles about pencils and postcards being given away; stories about livestock judges from France; the Spacearama featuring twenty-five UFO experts and astronomers from around the world; even photos of the feathered, high-heeled showgirls who would be performing *Salute to Ziegfeld*. Nothing surprised him anymore, not even reading about the Russian cosmonaut Gherman Titov, who'd visited the fair last week and had offended everyone by stating that he didn't believe in God. 'I,' he declared, 'believe in man and science and the future.'

The future, Ernest thought. Everyone in town seemed to be happily abuzz, even at the hospital, where silk-screened Century 21 decals had been slapped on doors and windows. It was a collective celebration – the future was here, ready or not. Meanwhile a part of Gracie was still marooned on an island somewhere in the past.

Ernest was finishing the paper, reading about abstract paintings that had been hung sideways at the Fine Arts Pavilion, when Rich, Hanny, and Juju arrived. They carried an enormous basket of flowers and a bouquet of helium balloons that swayed and twirled beneath the ceiling fan. Ernest watched their strings slowly twist into a knot.

'Someone from church sent these,' Hanny said with a smile. 'The manager downstairs asked me to bring them up.' She put them in a corner of the room where other arrangements from the hospital had already begun to wilt.

Ernest smelled something savory and was surprised to see that Rich had a familiar carton on his lap, tied with twine. Hanny's fiancé undid the string and folded back the lid, tilting the box so Ernest could see inside.

'The Lun Ting Bakery?' Ernest asked in disbelief.

'Hanny said these were your wife's favorite comfort food.'

'Mine too,' Ernest said as he took one of the *bau*. It felt warm as he peeled the wax paper from the bottom and bit into the pillowy pastry, a barbecue-pork-filled cloud. He could smell the mushrooms, the scallions, even before his taste buds could react to the filling. The buns were a welcome change from the bland hospital meals he'd been subsisting on for the past few days.

'How's Mom reacting to her new surroundings after her little setback?' Hanny asked. She reached into her purse for a pack of Winstons. Ernest watched as she lit a cigarette with a matchbook from the Golden Apple Nightclub down the street.

Setback? Ernest thought. He was grateful she had seen only her mother resting in the hospital, not her collapse in the street.

'Maybe tomorrow we should bring her buckwheat udon from Maneki? Ma always loved that place,' Hanny said to Rich. 'She even worked there as a hostess once upon a time, long before the war. She used to tell us stories of how all the women would read poetry and sing folk songs to homesick Japanese boys, who called them *nihonjin tori*. Ma was one of those Japanese birds who raised enough money to fund the Japantown library.'

Ernest checked on Gracie, who was still napping as their daughters reminisced about their mother volunteering at the Betsuin Buddhist

Temple and the Japanese Community Center, how she used to lead dances in the street during Obon each summer.

Meanwhile, Rich was busy exploring the tiny apartment, examining the faded prints on his walls, the books in Ernest's bookcase. He tilted his head as he read the titles: *America Is in the Heart* by Carlos Bulosan and *Nisei Daughter* by Monica Sone; romantic novels by Longus, *Cheri* by Colette, and Henry De Vere Stacpoole; and volumes of translated poetry by Li Bai and Cao Xueqin. Ernest listened as Rich read the title of Stephen Crane's *Maggie: A Girl of the Streets*.

'Seems like your apartment is nothing but books,' Rich said.

'A terrible habit.' Ernest smiled. 'Picked it up in my youth.'

Rich furrowed his brow. 'It's like books are your religion.'

'Well, my mother was a Confucian, and I believe my father was a Methodist,' Ernest answered with a shrug. 'But I didn't see either one again after I was four or five.'

Rich nodded and clicked his jaw. He seemed to consider this as he drifted to Ernest's makeshift kitchen, examining photos on the refrigerator of Hanny and Juju as little girls, playing in a plastic swimming pool, drinking from a garden hose.

'What's the story with this morbid-looking thing?' Rich held up a picture postcard of an oil painting that stood out from the black-and-white smiles of the photographs. The postcard's flat colors depicted a woman with a book and a cigarette. A sad, partially decorated tree, surrounded by faceless women, haunted the background.

'Let me guess, Matisse?' Rich asked.

Ernest shook his head. 'That's Edvard Munch.'

'The Norwegian guy who painted *The Scream*?' Juju asked.

Ernest nodded.

'So what's it called then?' Rich raised his eyebrows, unimpressed. '*Boring Lady in a Bar Painted by a Second Grader?*'

Ernest sighed and ran his fingers through his graying hair. 'That particular piece was created when the artist was somewhat down on his luck, and drinking too much. Hanging out in low places. He titled that painting *Christmas in the Brothel.*'

Hanny glanced toward the kitchen as she lit a cigarette.

'Like that Tenderloin place where you and your wife grew up?' Rich asked.

Ernest nodded. 'Sort of an inside joke, if you will, from an old friend.'

'From Uncle Paz?' Juju asked.

Ernest shook his head as he regarded his old typewriter.

The stack of blank pages, layers of onionskin. He'd tried writing something – anything, weaving memories together for Gracie's benefit, but the few mottled pages he'd typed were little more than awkward attempts, rambling sentences filled with typos, imperfections that had been corrected with Liquid Paper, leaving bumps on the smooth surface that stood out like benign tumors.

Rich turned the postcard over. He touched the stamp, which had been postmarked in North Seattle. He read the back and casually looked up. 'So, who's Margaret Turnbull?'

Faded

(1910)

Ernest opened his eyes as a sharp, metallic ring jarred him awake. He mistook it for another fire alarm before he realized the sound was coming from the telephone in Miss Amber's room. He heard the ringing again and again as he sat up. His first confused, panicked thoughts were of Fahn.

Ernest had parked in the alley and carried her in through the Tenderloin's servants' entrance – much to the shock and bewilderment of Mrs Blackwell, who'd frantically found Professor True. Together they'd managed to get Fahn, barely conscious, to her old bedroom. Meanwhile, the Tenderloin's customers were streaming out of the building. The upstairs girls leaned out the windows, watching the commotion up the street, wary of the blaze spreading in their direction. Fortunately the rain and the new pump engine were able to contain the fire.

Iris, Violet, and Rose helped get Fahn into a hot bath, washing the smoke and soot from her hair. They dressed her for bed, bandaged her feet. Ernest had made elderberry tea, and Mrs Blackwell heated a bowl of beef bone soup with onion syrup.

Fahn had begun running a fever and said very little as they tried to feed her.

'I just . . . wanted . . . to say goodbye to Maisie,' she had murmured.

She had said even less after Mrs Blackwell gave her a generous mug of warm brandy.

'The girls found marks on her arm,' Mrs Blackwell had whispered as Fahn drifted off to sleep. The stout cook pointed to a spot on her own sleeve near the pit of her elbow. 'Some kind of poison, I tell you. Probably a morphine gun. Some cribs do that. I hope she burned every last one of them along with that wretched place.'

Ernest heard the telephone ringing again. He squinted at the morning sunlight streaming through the windows. He regarded his chauffeur's uniform, now terribly wrinkled, then trundled down the hall in the direction of the sound, knowing that most of the upstairs girls would still be in bed.

Ernest thought about what Mrs Blackwell had said. He understood what she meant as she'd made an injecting motion – more of a recollection, really. While at the US Immigration Bureau, Ernest had been given shots, but he'd also seen tins of opium confiscated from men and women alike. He vaguely recalled the toothless beggars that his mother always steered him away from and the sugary smell that came from the long pipes the delirious men and women had smoked.

'I'll report them. Madam Flora always had those vile places broken up by the police. Though without her around . . .' Mrs Blackwell's conviction had trailed off along with her voice. 'In the meantime we will all take turns watching our prodigal daughter. If her fever gets much higher we'll have to take her down to the Wayside.'

Ernest remembered the abandoned paddle-wheel steamer *Idaho*, which had been converted into an emergency hospital for the poor.

Fahn had come by boat, he thought, and she might be leaving the same way.

As Ernest passed Maisie's empty bedroom, he noticed someone had turned down the covers and left a tiny box of chocolates with a pink bow from Stokes Confectioner atop her pillow. There was a large, hand-decorated card as well, signed by all the Gibson girls, welcoming her to the sisterhood.

As Ernest continued to hear the phone ringing, he finally realized who must be calling. He slipped into Miss Amber's vacant room and answered.

'Good morning, sir,' a deep, raspy voice said on the other end. 'This is Mr Waterbury, I'm the butler of Speedwell. Mr Turnbull asked that I call to let you know that you can retrieve Miss Nettleton at your earliest convenience.'

'Of course,' Ernest stammered. 'I'll be right . . .'

'He also asked that you might stop at his favorite bakery on the way. He says he's tired of breakfasting here and would like a special meal after a special night.'

Mr Waterbury waited patiently for Ernest to retrieve a pad and pencil before he dictated a long, detailed list of things to pick up en route. Then the butler thanked him and hung up before Ernest could respond.

Ernest tamped down his rage, listened, then hung up and went back to his room. He tied his shoes, finger-combed his hair, and went downstairs, where he found his dark coat hanging up in Fahn's room. He'd gone upstairs to rest after her fever had finally broken and had fallen fast asleep. Now Jewel was there, curled up in an armchair, wrapped in a quilt, both girls sleeping. Ernest smiled when he saw that the color had returned to Fahn's cheeks. Her face was as peaceful as the surface of a lake on a windless day, but he wondered what creatures were slumbering at the bottom, buried in the muck. He didn't want to imagine whom or what Fahn must have endured these past few weeks.

I'll be right back, Ernest thought as he gently closed the door.

* * *

After taking a number at Blitzner's Bakery and waiting in line for ten minutes that seemed like ten hours, Ernest arrived back in Windermere, motoring in behind elegant horse-drawn carriages, delivery trucks, and dozens of colored servants who walked to work in their freshly pressed uniforms. As he finally returned to the Turnbull estate, there was a coachman waiting to wash the roadster while Ernest was escorted inside, his arms laden with a gaudy assortment of walnut tarts, orange meringue cookies, a dozen bolivars, a white raisin cake, plus a Vienna stritzel with a side of fresh Devonshire cream.

Ernest hastened as he was led down a long gallery, strangely devoid of paintings or photographs. The hall connected to an area that looked more like the atrium of a grand hotel than a home. He was dumbfounded by a three-story pipe organ that reached toward the vaulted ceiling, which had been painted like the sky.

'This is a special place, isn't it?' Mr Waterbury said. 'Though sadly, the pipe organ hasn't played a note since the lady of the house passed away all those years ago. Mr Turnbull also had all of the art in the galleries removed at that time. He is of the opinion now that artwork competes with the view of the lake. He did keep the Tiffany chandeliers in the library, which was certainly commendable.'

Ernest listened as Chinese women in kitchen aprons transferred the baked goods from their paper boxes to a silver cart and arranged them on covered serving trays. The women then added a service of hot tea, coffee, and apple juice. Mr Waterbury himself topped the whole thing off with a crisp copy of the Sunday *Seattle Times*.

'Mr Turnbull asked that you deliver breakfast in person,' the butler said. 'I gather that he would like to meet you, for reasons that I do not quite comprehend. Nevertheless . . .' He waved Ernest toward a waiting elevator.

Ernest had never seen an elevator. The only one he knew of was the lift at the Butterworth & Sons Mortuary on First Avenue. And that particular device was used only to move bodies in heavy oaken caskets.

Ernest thanked the tuxedoed man, bewildered that the servants could pretend there was nothing unusual about a young girl being delivered and later retrieved from the bedroom of a rich old man. He held his tongue as he wheeled the serving dolly inside the elevator, nodded to the black operator. The chandelier inside the lift swayed and jingled like glass chimes as the operator closed a brass gate. Ernest held on as the small, elegant room began to rise.

When he regained his bearings and stepped off on the top floor with the serving cart, he felt as though they'd been transported to an even richer, more gilded world, half again as decadent as the foyer below. The operator tipped his velvet cap and directed Ernest to a set of double doors at the end of a long, lushly carpeted hallway.

Ernest began to wonder how many beautiful young women had journeyed down the plum-colored corridor. How many like Maisie had walked past the slender tables adorned with Oriental vases full of fresh flowers, past the rosy cheeks of painted cherubs that adorned the inside of the arched ceiling and peeked out from the ornately carved lintels. Ernest smelled the flowers and noticed thorns on the roses. Remembering Fahn recovering in her bed, he reached out to one of the stems, jabbing his thumb directly onto one of the briers. He felt the sharp, distracting, invigorating pain; he watched the warm trickle of crimson. He wiped the blood on his handkerchief before wheeling the serving cart to the double doors and reaching for the knocker. He paused, closed his eyes as though making a wish, and then made his arrival known. He heard footsteps, then the door was opened by yet another servant.

Part of Ernest had expected to find Maisie strewn across a bed, half-naked as if from a scene out of *One Thousand and One Nights*, guarded by turbaned eunuchs with scimitars. He was relieved to see that she wore the same dress as last night, the same shoes, though her hair was now down and her lipstick had long since faded. She sat on an ornate chair, hands on her valise, smiling casually, slightly impatient, as though she were waiting in the lobby of a bank perhaps. Ernest cocked his head as he noticed a sparkling strand of tiny diamonds draped around her neck.

'There you are. You're right on time.' Maisie stood and smoothed the creases of her dress with a tremendous sigh, like that of a tree bent by the wind, now leaning back toward sunlight. She approached the breakfast cart, tore off a piece of stritzel, dipped the pastry in the whipped cream, and then popped it in her mouth, chewing and giggling.

She smiled as she spoke with her mouth full. 'Come live with me and be my love, and we will all the pleasures prove. That valleys, groves, hills, and fields, woods or steepy mountain yields.' The line from the poem was something the Gibson girls liked to recite.

Ernest straightened his tie. 'Shall we go?'

The servant who had begun pouring coffee stopped and stood at attention. Ernest heard humming as Mr Turnbull strolled out of an adjoining dressing chamber.

Ernest nodded to the man, who looked to be a hale fellow in his early fifties. He wore a short beard, the color of honey, tinged with silver. Turnbull was already dressed in a dark brown suit with a waistcoat and starched white collar.

'Oh, there you are. This intriguing young man must be Ernest,' Mr Turnbull said. Ernest noticed that Maisie's wealthy sponsor had tattoos on his forearms, a sailor's resume peeking out from beneath his buttoned shirtsleeves. There was something odd about the fellow – a familiarity, perhaps. Ernest tried to reconcile where he'd seen the man.

Had this gentleman been to the Tenderloin unbeknownst to Ernest?

Ernest furrowed his brow as Mr Turnbull thanked Maisie, kissed her on the cheek, and said, 'Until next time. Don't forget my offer, dear.' The servant escorted Maisie out and then closed the door behind them before Ernest could follow. Mr Turnbull reached for the newspaper and found his seat behind an enormous mahogany reading desk. He sipped his coffee, smiled, and sampled a meringue cookie. Brushing away crumbs, he gestured for Ernest to help himself to the breakfast offerings.

'Oh, what a world we share,' Mr Turnbull remarked as he looked up from the page.

'I'll show myself out,' Ernest said.

'Nonsense. Stay a moment.' The man tapped the paper. 'Look at this. Ballington Booth, the former head of the Salvation Army, went to London and told everyone that we are rapidly approaching the end times. Fire and tarnation! For some reason every generation thinks the world is coming to an end. What do you think, young man?'

Ernest was sorely confused. And weary. *I must still be dreaming*, he thought.

'I'm not exactly sure what you're asking me,' Ernest said. He kept his anger in check, but his patience was thinning. He needed to get Maisie home. He needed to check on Fahn.

'The arrogance astounds.' Mr Turnbull shook his head as he looked up and asked, 'How did you sleep last night?'

Ernest heard himself say, 'Quite poorly.'

'That's too bad. I, on the other hand, slept like a lamb. It's the bedding, made from the finest Japanese silk. And of course, I would be lying if I said the company was not . . . remarkable.' The peculiar old man set the paper down and broke into a singsong rhyme: 'Round as an apple, eyes deep as a cup, the whole Mississippi can't fill them up.' He looked up at Ernest with a wink. 'My apologies to Mother Goose . . .'

'I'm sorry, sir . . .'

'No, no, no . . . I am the one who needs to apologize, young man, that we haven't met sooner. You see, we have something deeply, *profoundly* in common, you and me.'

Ernest waited impatiently as the man took another bite and then continued.

'Young Margaret told me how you two met at the fair in the wake of President Taft's visit – how you came to find yourself in the employ of the magnificent Florence Nettleton. I insisted that she tell me all about this person she ran from my doorstep to say goodbye to. Flora always found the most amazing people to bring into her fold.'

Ernest couldn't help but notice that as the man spoke of Madam Flora, the twinkle of admiration grew from a spark to a flame. It was an odd respect that he proffered, mingled with his infatuation.

Mr Turnbull kept talking, rambling, drumming his fingers on his desk as he spoke. 'Ever since my late wife, Millie, left this world, I have been . . . consumed with Flora Nettleton, despite her being the Mother Jones of madams – you know, the wrinkled old bird who likes to chirp, "Women don't need the vote to raise a little hell." Well, maybe Mother Jones is right though, because Madam Flora is one heck of a woman.' The man stroked his beard and took a deep, clarifying breath. 'Pity that she's so unavailable now. She was a smart one though, perhaps the smartest woman I've ever known. That's why I'm not surprised she cornered the market on you that day at the AYP.'

Ernest began to wonder what Maisie might be doing downstairs. Perhaps she was outside, kicking the tires of the motorcar by now.

'The point that I'm trying to make,' Mr Turnbull said, 'is that I wanted to meet you in person, to see the good things – the promise, in a young man like yourself, especially from someone of such humble, provincial beginnings.'

'Because I was won at the fair?' Ernest asked. He couldn't understand where this was heading.

'Not just that.' Mr Turnbull laughed as though he'd been crystal clear and somehow Ernest hadn't been paying attention. 'I wanted to meet you – yes, you – because you came to this country as a lowly child from the Far East – from a territory that was rent asunder, torn apart by war, by rebellion.'

'Because I came from China?'

'Exactly. Now we understand each other. I called my executive secretary and had him look up the manifests at one of my offices this morning, and lo and behold.' Mr Turnbull took another sip and then pointed at Ernest with his cup of coffee. 'There's a decent chance, young man, that you came over on one of my ships. What are the odds?'

Ernest opened his mouth, about to speak, and then closed it. His head spun, and lurid memories returned. Images of the unsavory men in China, the ship's doctor, the blackbirders who'd passed themselves off as merchants, silk-clad girls in cages, Jun and the other boys who drowned after they were transferred to the care of smugglers.

'I was on a few of those voyages myself,' Mr Turnbull said, as he casually tugged up his shirtsleeves, revealing a blur of faded ink.

Ernest remembered a morning in a cemetery.

Refugee children waking up.

Being herded away from his ruined village.

The sound of gunfire. A man in an elegant coat.

Louis J. Turnbull.

Ernest stared at the man as he kept speaking.

Louis J. Turnbull was the man who was not my uncle.

The rich man went on and on about his business ventures in the Orient, the ships he built, the fleet he owned, the precious cargo they'd carried.

Ernest could almost smell the smoke, the fetid mud, and his mother's peculiar fragrance before she wandered off to die.

'Now look at you.' The man slurped his coffee as Ernest woke from his strange memory. 'You're an upright figure, a model citizen, as Western as can be. I know what you are thinking – that you should thank me . . .'

Ernest's mouth hung open as spoken words vanished into the dull throbbing at his temples, the pulsing of his heart as he imagined hundreds of people, perhaps thousands, lied to, tricked, bought and sold, shipped overseas, offered to the highest bidder, indentured. While others were cast off, given away. Bodies bobbing on the surf like driftwood, flotsam and jetsam, women and children.

'If anyone, I should be thanking you, my young fellow,' Mr Turnbull continued. 'I started off with lowly, penal colony riffraff from the darker parts of Australia and Fiji, but Canton changed my fortunes.' He waved a hand, looking about the room. 'All of this, everything I have, was built on the idea that despite the unfair labor laws, the damnable exclusion act designed to keep your kind out – bringing people like you to this country was a profitable, charitable, and even humanitarian transaction.'

To Ernest the man seemed so full of himself, his waistcoat looked ready to burst.

'Just seeing what has become of you' – Mr Turnbull smiled broadly – 'that's all the thanks I will ever need. You're living proof that my life's work has been a noble adventure. Gold is folly, ships – they sail away. But fresh humanity, that is still the ultimate commodity.'

Ernest thought about Fahn, staggering home in the rain. He imagined all the girls like her, who never found someone like Madam Flora. And even Flora, succumbing to the tolls of her labors.

Ernest watched as Mr Turnbull returned to his morning paper.

The man spoke without looking up. 'And now John D. Rockefeller Junior has retired to become a full-time philanthropist.' He turned the page. 'Meanwhile half a world away, China has abolished slavery. How about that? If you ask me, it sounds like the slaves have broken their chains of bondage on two shores.' He laughed to himself as he looked up. 'It was a pleasure meeting you. I'm sure you can find your way out.'

Ernest left without saying goodbye. He was barely able to depart without grabbing the man and throttling him. But he'd be of no use to Maisie and Fahn in jail.

Beyond the elevator a servant showed Ernest to the door and down the steps to where he found Maisie next to the roadster, eyes closed, sunning on the grass, legs crossed, arms spread, her fingers amid the clover. When Ernest's shadow fell on her, she opened her eyes and squinted up at him. 'He told you, huh?'

'Told me what?'

'That he was the one who brought you over here.'

Ernest nodded. 'And Fahn too. She was on that ship as well.'

Maisie closed her eyes. 'Just like I said. The good. The bad. It's all connected. It's like fate – that's what our darling Rose would call this. The herbalist in Chinatown would call our tangled lives the red thread. Madam Flora would call it . . . destiny.'

Ernest looked at her. He was lost for words.

'Don't look so sad,' Maisie said as she sat up.

Ernest swallowed. 'Why are you so happy?'

'I'm happy because Louis Turnbull made me the offer of a lifetime.

He doesn't have a wife anymore, no children to speak of, so he wants me to become his ward. Can you believe that? He said he'd take me abroad – I can go anywhere, do anything. I can find my mother. I can pay for whatever she needs.' Maisie gushed her enthusiasm with a vigor that wounded. 'And the best part is, he said I could bring you along as a servant. We could all sail for Europe together. Spread our wings. How does that sound?'

Like he's never stopped buying and selling people. Ernest sighed.

'Maybe you should take some time and think it over,' he said.

'What's there to consider? Don't you see how perfect this is? We can leave this week. The two of us. Just think about where we could go, what we could see.'

Ernest fell silent, though a part of him was screaming to join her.

'Well, the three of us, actually.' Maisie shrugged with a smile. 'But I'm sure Turnbull will be occupied most of the time, doing other things, running his business.'

Ernest cared about Maisie, so much that it hurt. But as much as he wanted to be with her, to travel the world in her company, to share the life she'd have, he knew he could never accept that kind of offer. He'd been given away, twice. And in that moment, he swore he would never give himself up that way again.

Maisie stepped closer and placed her hands on his shoulders. She pursed her lips and leaned forward, then paused. She looked into his eyes, as though she were about to speak, as though important, convincing words lingered on the tip of her tongue. Magical whispers. Secret promises. Stories with happy endings.

But she fell silent.

'I can't,' Ernest said.

He held her hands.

'You can't?' Maisie asked. 'Or you won't?'

Ernest imagined a sunset at sea. The smell of the ocean. The sound of the waves, crashing. Then he remembered the cold rain last night.

'Fahn is back.' Just speaking Fahn's name, knowing she was safe again, filled him with hope, satisfaction, and joy. 'She needs me.'

Maisie nodded and let go. She wearily climbed into the backseat and closed her eyes. She didn't stir when he started the noisy car. She hardly moved as he drove back to the Tenderloin in silence.

Unspoken

(1910)

The next morning Maisie was gone.

She didn't leave a note, but she did leave her necklace in lieu of a goodbye, on a pillow next to Fahn as she slept. Ernest found the strand of diamonds in the morning, when he brought Fahn tea and soft-boiled eggs for breakfast.

Fahn had recovered just enough to fully understand the significance of her friend's absence, as Ernest explained that Maisie had left to become the ward of Louis Turnbull. He also told her that it was Turnbull who in all likelihood had helped bring him and Fahn across the Pacific. The words sounded like fiction as Ernest described Maisie's plan to travel to Europe to find her mother – and how she'd invited Ernest along.

'Why didn't you go?' Fahn asked, holding the necklace.

He could sense the strange admiration and jealousy of the upstairs girls that had driven Fahn to such disastrous choices. But he could also now see a greater wisdom in her eyes, a validation. She knew what such choices could cost; whether they involved a crib joint or a gilded cage – the price was always the same.

'Because . . .' Ernest stirred milk and honey into Fahn's tea. Then he handed her the cup. 'I thought you were still going to marry me someday.'

A small part of him regretted not going with Maisie. It would have been nice to travel the globe. But this was his world now – she was his world.

Fahn held his hand. 'Be careful what you wish for, young Ernest.'

When supper time came, Fahn dressed for dinner. She limped to the servants' table, sat next to Ernest, and chatted amiably with the maids and Mrs Blackwell as though little had changed. She even joked about becoming a Gibson girl after all, now that the Mayflower had left a vacancy – which made Ernest nearly choke on his Welsh rarebit. Violet and Iris laughed, albeit nervously. No one dared to ask what had happened at the Tangerine, about the fire, and whether Fahn had had anything to do with that calamity. At least until Rose walked in, late from cleaning Maisie's now-empty room.

'I went up the street today to pick up mending for the girls,' Rose gushed. 'I just had to take a detour to the crib that caught fire. Lord, it's a wreck! Just beams and part of a staircase – like looking at the carcass of a whale, bones burned black. Workmen on the avenues were saying it's a miracle no one got hurt.'

Ernest noticed how everyone in the servants' dining room was doing their level best not to look in Fahn's direction. He couldn't help but see her again in memory, stumbling down the street in the rain. Bloody footprints. Laughter.

'I don't suppose you had anything to do with that fire, did you?' Rose asked, glancing at Fahn before tucking her napkin into her lap. Then she noticed the condemning stares. 'Oh my. I said something out of turn again, didn't I?'

The room fell so silent that Ernest could hear the thrum of the electric lightbulbs flickering overhead, the sound of someone's stomach gurgling through layers of silk, cotton, and wool, the muffled footfalls of the ladies upstairs, heels on carpet.

Fahn set aside her knife and fork. She delicately wiped her chin. 'What do *you* think, thorny Rose?' she said as she adjusted the wick on the oil lamp in the center of the table, turning a brass knob up and down and making the flame hiss.

Then she asked Ernest to pass the bread.

There was no doubt in Ernest's mind that Fahn had set fire to the place. And he didn't blame her one bit. What he could not allow, though, was for her to work upstairs.

That evening, Ernest stoically manned the front door, greeted the night's patrons, and gathered the gentlemen's woolen overcoats, their pearl-handled walking sticks, and their hats for brushing and cleaning. He showed the guests into the grand parlor, where they were welcomed by the ladies and treated to their usual glasses of sparkling wine served on silver platters. They were rich gentlemen, Ernest had seen some of them many times before, but he had stopped caring to remember their names.

'Don't look so grim,' Professor True said as he sat down at his piano.

'Is it that obvious?'

'It's election night, so things are bound to be slow around here. But beyond that, if you really want to know the truth, young man . . .'

Ernest knew the Professor only wanted to help, that he wanted to add some kind of thoughtful, fatherly advice – a verbal salve to ease the outbreak of melancholy caused by Maisie's departure and Fahn's return. But Ernest wasn't in the mood to listen.

'I'm sorry, Professor,' he said as he walked away. 'But I've got all the truth I can handle right now.'

Ernest returned to the cloakroom wishing his circumstances could change. That's when the lights went out, quite literally, and he heard the Gibson girls shrieking and hooting in amusement. Ernest stepped into the gloom and saw that the electric chandeliers that lit the foyer and the parlors were all off, and the belt-driven ceiling fans that cooled the building were winding to a halt, squeaking in the darkness. Mrs Blackwell barked orders to the maids, who fetched candles and matches to light the oil lamps in each room. Meanwhile, Professor True kept playing, barely skipping a beat.

'Well, I guess we know who our new mayor is,' Mrs Blackwell muttered to Ernest as he opened the blinds to let in the glow of the gaslit street. Councilman Gill had been a vocal critic of Seattle's Department of Lighting and Water Works, and it seemed as if the upstart utility had shut down their services in protest of his election.

'How long do you think we'll be without electricity?' Ernest asked.

'Not long,' Mrs Blackwell said. 'Just long enough to make a point, lad.'

Ernest peered out the window and saw that the nearby saloons were emptying drunken patrons into the street, bottles in hand, filling the sidewalks of the Garment District. Traffic came to a halt as coachmen redoubled the grip on their reins, idling their horses as motorcars honked their horns in vain at the electric streetcars, frozen in place beneath a cobweb of power lines. Despite the blackout, people in the neighborhood shouted and cheered, celebrating the victory of Mayor Gill.

'Politics, lad,' Mrs Blackwell mused. 'It's still mired in the shuffling of people, from one place to another. According to the rumors I heard, Gill's campaigners trucked in hundreds of unemployed men from Wenatchee, Yakima, and Cle Elum, from wherever they could find them. They boarded them all over the district, then ushered the entire lot to the polls as newly registered voters. Half of 'em probably can't even read or sign their names properly.'

Ernest stared out into evening, benumbed. The new mayor was now free to harvest the ripe fruit of the open town policy from the wild seeds he'd sown as a councilman. Ernest knew that in all likelihood business would be better in the long run. The bars and taverns would be allowed to stay open all night now, all week long, and bands would be playing, even on Sundays. How it would affect the Tenderloin was anyone's guess.

Ernest squinted and rubbed his eyes as the electricity flickered and hummed, and the lights came back on. Everyone cheered, and the Gibson girls toasted their customers and one another. That's when Ernest saw Fahn across the crowded parlor in her black maid's uniform and apron. But she wore her hair down like the upstairs girls, in a way that made her look older, and she wore the diamond necklace that Maisie had left. She chatted with the guests, then looked over her shoulder, found Ernest, and tried her best to smile.

Ernest stood in the basement, where he liked to go to collect his thoughts. The dank, musty boiler room, with new electrical wires and old groaning pipes, was as far away as he could get and still technically be performing his duties.

I used to be scared of this place, Ernest thought, remembering how he had hated to be alone in such an eerie, cavernous room. Now this was his sanctuary.

He tied his handkerchief, covering his nose and mouth, feeling the warmth of his breath as his eyes adjusted to the darkness. Then he found his way to the coal bin and the boiler, which radiated so much heat his forehead began to perspire.

In a fog of frustration, Ernest reached to open the furnace door, forgetting to put on his gloves first. He felt the searing metal handle burn his palm. He cursed and snatched his hand back, gritting his teeth. His fingers felt icy and hot all at once, and his eyes watered with the pain. He sniffled and examined his swelling hand in the dimly lit room, touching his swollen skin where a blister or two would surely appear. Eventually the pain began to subside and with it, a measure of his sadness.

Ernest shook his head at his foolishness and settled onto an old crate. He looked at the marks on his hand and remembered once catching a glimpse of mysterious cuts along Miss Amber's upper arm, the old scars that she kept hidden by wearing long sleeves. When Ernest had mentioned what he'd seen to Mrs Blackwell, she'd called those marks the wrinkles of past suffering, but she'd also said that the men at Western Washington Hospital called Amber's pernicious habit of cutting herself in her youth a partial suicide. The term seemed absurd, but now, with Fahn's departure and return, he understood how a part of you could perish. As he stared into the radiant heat, watching the flaring embers, he felt how easy it could be to slip from a place of warmth to a place of engulfing fire.

Whispers of Calliope

(1910)

The following Sunday, Ernest stood next to Fahn on the breezy upper passenger deck of the ferry *City of Seattle*, staring across the murky blue-green waters of Elliott Bay as the vessel steered toward the tidal flats of Duwamish Head and Alki Beach.

In months past, their days off had been spent in the Garment District, strictly below the line, since so many businesses, theaters, and penny arcades were closed on Sunday. But since Mayor Gill's election a week ago, Luna Park, the Coney Island of the West, was open every day, just like the many bars and taverns across the city. In fact, Ernest had heard the saloon at Luna Park boasted the largest and best-stocked bar in all of Seattle – a fact that probably didn't sit well with the amusement park's sleepy West Seattle neighbors.

As the ferry swayed, he strained to hear the faint sound of a roller coaster and the calliope music of a carousel.

'So, young Ernest, what would you like to do first?' Fahn asked as the ferry slowed on its approach. She leaned on his shoulder as the wooden deck gently rocked, the engine idled, and seabirds circled overhead, squawking, swooping, and diving.

Ernest inhaled the salty air.

This.

He imagined wrapping his arms around her.

And this.

As he'd lean down and kiss each cheek, rosy and cool from the breeze.

And finally this.

He pictured himself whispering.

Something to undo the past.

Then the ferry blared its horn and interrupted his daydreaming.

'The Canals of Venice sound nice,' he said as she took his arm and they joined the crowds and the horses that disembarked from the ferry. They took their time and strolled the mossy boardwalk toward Seattle's own Midway Plaisance, past freshly painted sandwich boards advertising LaSousa's Minstrel Band, a Water Carnival, and Madame Schelle the Lion Tamer. They both smirked at the word *madame*.

Ernest enjoyed the comforting echoes of their visit to the fair. Even some of the attractions were the same, including the hot-air balloon. And he'd also heard that Luna Park was in the process of relocating the Fairy Gorge Tickler, which they had purchased to bolster their own special assortment of thrill rides: the Chute-the-Chutes, the Joy Wheel, the Cave of Mystery, and the enormous Figure Eight Roller Coaster, which was advertised as being a half mile high.

As Ernest squinted up at the wooden framework from across the amusement park, he could tell that the rumored height was an exaggeration, though the loud screams of the riders told everyone within earshot that the ride was high enough.

Ernest pulled Fahn aside to let a clown with a tremendous purple wig walk by; the clown pulled a pig in a tiny Studebaker. Then they boarded a long black gondola and floated through the park's Venetian canals, past string musicians in black tuxedos and a woman in a lofted wig who sang in Italian. Ernest sat back in the red leather seat, warm from the afternoon sun, and wrapped his arm around Fahn's shoulder the way the couples in the other boats did. As they drifted, Fahn talked about how much she missed Maisie. Ernest felt the same emptiness. He didn't really believe it – nor did he think Fahn did – but they both agreed that their friend was probably better off. They told themselves that no one could make the Mayflower do anything she didn't want to do. And as the gondola finally drifted to a stop, they were helped out of the boat.

Fahn brightened as she pointed to a ride off in the distance. 'Look, a carousel.'

Ernest heard the pipe organ and chased after her as she ran toward the menagerie of painted horses. They slowed, and she climbed aboard, where she wended her way through a forest of animals – mares mostly, but also bears, buffalo, and even a striped tiger covered in glass jewels. Ernest caught up to her as the previous riders were stepping off and men and women, some still in their Sunday finery, boarded the carousel. He climbed atop a black stallion with a tail made from real horsehair as Fahn sat facing him, sidesaddle, legs crossed, on a matching steed, the lace fringe of her simple yellow dress cresting just below her knees. Ernest paid the operator a dime for the both of them and held on to the striped pole as the music played and the roundabout began to move. As they spun in merry circles, their mounts rising and falling, Fahn's figure was dappled and reflected a thousand times in the mirrored mosaic at the center of the ride. To Ernest she looked like a girl again, a happy teenager, cheeks flushed with joy, hair pulled back in a bow. And in that moment – that perfect, breathtaking minute, he felt so lucky. He opened his mouth to speak when she looked down at her feet and he saw that her childlike smile had vanished.

'What's the matter?' he asked.

She didn't say anything as the festive music continued to play and the world of Luna Park orbited past their field of vision. That's when Ernest saw people in uniforms. No one in particular, a group of men, sailors. There were plenty such men to be found on a sunny day. They were pointing to an exhibit where a bear was drinking from a baby bottle. Then one of them glanced over and tipped his cap and leered.

When Ernest turned back, Fahn's horse was empty. He glimpsed a blur of yellow as the carousel kept spinning. He jumped off and orbited the ride until he found the direction he'd seen Fahn running. As he slipped through the oncoming crowd, he caught another glimpse of her dress and realized she was heading back toward the ferry landing. When he caught up to her near the entrance, she was standing still, staring at the ground, her shoulders rising and falling as she caught her breath.

To Ernest she looked like a rock as a river of people flowed around her. He smiled wanly at the children who passed, laughing.

He took her hand and tried to look into her downcast eyes. 'We don't have to leave so soon,' he said. 'Why don't we just take a break, grab a lemonade and go for a walk?'

Her eyes darted as she glanced up at him and then out toward the ferry, which arrived every thirty minutes. 'I'm sorry, Ernest. I know we just got here, but I can't stay. I don't think I belong here . . .'

Ernest didn't know what he could say to make things better. She had all the confidence in the world within the confines of the Tenderloin, but out here, in the sunshine . . . 'I don't belong anywhere.' He shrugged. 'But here I am.'

She closed her eyes and rubbed her forehead. 'I was hoping to tell you in a better way. But Mrs Blackwell sent a telegram to Miss Amber, care of the Great Northern Railway. She told her about how Maisie had left and how I'd come back.'

Ernest imagined the mixed reactions to those bits of news.

'She got a reply this morning,' Fahn said. 'Amber didn't mention Maisie at all. But she insisted that if I stayed at the Tenderloin, I would have to earn my keep by working upstairs. I know I once told everyone I wanted—'

'You don't have to,' Ernest said. 'Surely, Mrs Blackwell—'

'I won't put her job at risk.'

Fahn pulled her hat down lower, shading her eyes. 'I'll manage somehow. Let's just go home.' She walked out of the park toward the incoming ferry.

Before Ernest could argue or convince her otherwise, he heard the steam whistle blaring from the inbound vessel. And then he heard the peculiar, yet unmistakable strains of collective voices, singing. The song wasn't from one of the operatic divas featured at the amusement park but was coming from a choir that had assembled on the forecastle of the ferry *West Seattle*. Even from a distance Ernest recognized the dour countenances of ministers in black robes and ladies bearing signs condemning drinking on the Sabbath. Evidently Mayor Gill's opponents, the Mothers of Virtue and a sister group, the Forces of Decency, hadn't been willing to submit. The election had stirred up the hornets' nest.

Fahn buried her face in her hands.

'Follow me.' Ernest took her arm and spirited her across the parkway to a nearby trolley platform for Seattle Electric Railway's Alki line. He hastily bought tickets and they boarded the car just in time. He sat Fahn with her back toward the ferry. The protesters disembarked and they began their parade into the amusement park as the trolley rolled away. He held on while they cruised down toward the tidal flats and across the muddy trestles of a bridge that would take them in the direction of home.

After switching trolleys on Spokane Street, they glided back into Pioneer Square. Ernest took Fahn's hand and helped her off at the platform nearest to the Garment District. She looked tired – not just tired, but lost in shadow.

Ernest couldn't bear to go back to the Tenderloin in that moment.

But as he scanned the neighborhood, he could see there was no peace and quiet to be had, not in theaters, noisy restaurants and saloons. Plus the streets seemed more crowded than usual, as cars and delivery wagons slowed down and more picketers were gathering for what appeared to be another rally against the newly elected mayor. Ernest spotted Mrs Irvine addressing the crowd with a megaphone from atop a flatbed truck.

The AYP had revealed Seattle to the whole nation – the good, the bad, the outrageous. But now the wild, open town that Mayor Gill had supported was being put to the test, from its own citizens. Plus the return of Halley's Comet had aroused yet more doomsday superstitions, worrying parishioners back into church pews, where they hedged their bets with acts of repentance. And those who already had a desire to save souls caught fire and had been joining Mrs Irvine by the hundreds. A blessed unrest was flooding the Garment District, and Ernest wasn't sure what might happen at the Tenderloin without Madam Flora or Miss Amber there to defend against the pious incursions.

He led Fahn across the street to the quietest spot he could find, H. J. Ellison's Bookstore, a favorite hideaway, which was peaceful inside and smelled like coffee and leather. He led her to a row of popular novels, far from the front of the store.

'I really don't feel up to another lesson on French literature,' Fahn mumbled as she absently browsed recent books by Harold MacGrath and Joseph Conrad. 'This is my day off. Why don't we just go home and I'll sleep until I have to work?'

Ernest watched through the bookshop window as the crowds migrated toward the Tenderloin and the motorcars and carriages began moving again.

'Anything I can help you with?' the proprietor asked.

Ernest nodded to the man, who sat at a desk near the back of the store oiling a typewriter. A pipe dangled from the corner of his mouth.

'Pick something,' Ernest whispered to Fahn despite her protestations. 'Pick something for enjoyment, not schooling. Let me buy it for you.'

As though in a fog, Fahn chose a hardback by an author named Stacpoole. She absently handed the book to Ernest, who stepped to the counter and presented the owner with a silver dollar, waiting patiently for his change.

'Ah, excellent choice,' the man said as the pipe bounced up and down from the corner of his mouth. 'The book is in its seventh printing already – a bestseller. The story's about two kids like you, marooned on a tropical island.'

Ernest paged through the book as he inhaled the scent of fresh printer's ink and the man's grape-flavored tobacco. *Perfect.* Ernest looked back at Fahn, who was now a silhouette, a beautiful mannequin that stood near the store window as the world streamed by. He thanked the owner, then led her gently, as though she were sleepwalking, out of the store and away from the crowds, upstream to the entrance of a triangle-shaped building, on the fringes of the red-light district. A giant electric sign sat atop the roof, emblazoned with letters twenty feet tall that spelled out HOTEL SEATTLE.

Ernest stared at their reflections in the polished glass door.

Why not?

He saw the resigned look in Fahn's eyes as he led her inside and paid for a room in what had once been the Occidental Hotel. She seemed disappointed to not be going home, though somewhat expectant as well, as though this were just another chapter in the sad chronicle of her life. Ernest held her hand and walked her up the winding staircase to a room on the fifth floor overlooking the street. She sat on the bed and he took off her shoes, whispering that he could order room service, but she said she wasn't hungry. Then Ernest loosened his tie and looked outside as he watched police officers on horseback riding into the district. There were fights in the streets, and people were throwing bottles and rocks. But from above, the scrum seemed a world away, the people like actors in a silent film. From the top of this world Ernest had a commanding view of the construction of the new Smith Tower and beyond that, the sparkling blue-green waters of Puget Sound. From here he could see trains coming and going, he could watch the ships at sail, steam billowing from their stacks, but all he could hear were the gusts of wind on panes of glass and the sound of his leather heels on the wooden floor. And even that was muffled by the carpets as he stepped back toward the bed.

Ernest propped up a pillow and urged Fahn to lie back, to relax, and to close her eyes if she wanted to. Then he took the great feather duvet and tucked it around her shoulders. He pulled up an easy chair next to the bed and sat down.

'You're safe now,' he said.

'You're not getting into bed with me?'

Ernest blinked. He slowly shook his head.

There was an awkward silence.

He drew a deep breath, entranced by the way her dark hair fell across the white duvet. Fahn stared back at him, searching his face for understanding.

'You know you can, if you want to,' she said. 'It's okay . . .'

Ernest reached out and touched her hand. 'It's not okay. And I don't care what Miss Amber says. If she's going to try to make you work as an upstairs girl to earn your keep, then I'm going to pay for your time – all of it, every night. Just like this.'

He patted the book, then opened to the first page. He cleared his throat and began to read aloud, pausing every so often to look up at

Fahn. Her eyes were closed, and she looked tired, weary, but she also smiled as she curled beneath the covers. He hoped she was warm enough.

Ernest got comfortable and read until the evening, until Fahn fell asleep.

And then he read one more paragraph to himself:

Here it made the air a crystal, through which the gazer saw the loveliness of the land and reef, the green of palm, the white of coral, the wheeling gulls, the blue lagoon, all sharply outlined – burning, coloured, arrogant, yet tender – heartbreakingly beautiful, for the spirit of eternal morning was here, eternal happiness . . .

He closed the book and whispered, 'I love you. I will always love you,' softly so he wouldn't wake her. Then he put his feet up and closed his eyes as well.

Lit the Fire

(1962)

Ernest sat next to Gracie as she curled up on his chesterfield beneath an old blue afghan. Gracie had crocheted the blanket years ago, and although she probably didn't remember its origin now, its vague familiarity seemed to bring her something beyond physical comfort. Just like the book that Ernest held in his lap, the same well-worn hardback he'd bought for her fifty years ago. Together, they must have read forty or fifty novels during the long year that Gracie had been required to work upstairs as a Gibson girl. But this book had always been her favorite – Ernest's too. As he turned the pages to the last chapter, he smiled, detecting a hint of tobacco, and the burnt-almond scent of old paper.

'Keep reading,' Gracie said. 'You can't stop now.'

Ernest obliged, knowing that although they'd read this book a half-dozen times, the story was now brand-new to her. By her eagerness, Ernest could tell that Gracie didn't seem to remember that the romantic adventure ended in tragedy for the main characters. The two young lovers had finally been rescued from their deserted island, but only after consuming handfuls of poisonous berries, just when they'd thought all hope had been lost.

As Ernest read the final page, he cleared his throat, drew a deep breath, and changed the ending. He gave Gracie what he thought she needed, a grand rescue at sunset and a happily ever after for good measure.

She furrowed her brow as he closed the book.

'People don't find real happiness in the end, do they, young Ernest?'

He regarded the wrinkles on his hands, the loose skin. He didn't feel so young anymore. 'I found you, all over again – that makes me happy.'

Gracie pursed her lips and stared into the past.

'I remember . . .' She paused. 'I remember you and Maisie. I miss her.'

'That was a long time ago,' Ernest said. 'I miss her too.'

They sat in silence for an endless minute, as Gracie continued searching, weighing something in her mind. Ernest heard a siren in the distance.

'You . . . should have been with the Mayflower,' she said. 'She offered you the whole world. And you missed your chance . . . somehow . . . I messed things up, didn't I?'

Ernest watched as Gracie's gaze swept the small room, the old books, the sepia photographs, the magazines that featured the Century 21 Expo, the newspapers with Juju's bylines, Hanny's latest head shots, Rich's business card, her own reflection in a glass of water, distorted and yet transparent, like her memories.

Gracie fidgeted with the button on her blouse. 'You never asked what happened at the Tangerine.'

Ernest nodded – she was right about that. Over the years he had never wanted to engage in that particular conversation – it was ancient history as far as he was concerned. But he also realized that those tarnished memories were cobwebs now, blocking Gracie's view. She needed to acknowledge them if she was to have any chance at moving forward, cleaning them from the sills of her mind.

'I didn't need to know,' Ernest said. 'And I never asked because I didn't want you to have to relive a moment of what happened.'

Gracie nodded and stared out the window as though she were only partially listening. 'I remember the strangest things, you know.

I remember the way Madam Flora wore those feathered hats. Miss Amber's wigs. I remember laboring in the kitchen . . . the warmth of the oven, the smell of freshly baked bread, the scent of coal oil and perfume, the wine bottles and old, dusty carpets and drapes. But that wasn't the Tangerine, was it? That place smelled like . . . lye. And vinegar. That place . . . was run by a man named Jun.' Gracie paused, then she shook her head. 'That's not right either, is it? Whoever they were – I never knew their names, but they seemed nice at first.'

'Gracious.' Ernest held her hand and shook his head. 'You don't have to . . .'

But she ignored him, kept talking, kept trying to remember. 'They charged us rent, gave us . . . second-hand clothes. They told us that we owed them for the cost. The other girls . . . were working on contracts that never seemed to end.'

Gracie stood and looked into a dressing mirror. She reached out, touched her reflection. 'At first . . . I sleepwalked through the men, dozens of them, sailors, cannery workers – their hands smelled like salmon and fish oil.'

She touched her cheek as though recognizing herself. 'But my pride couldn't keep up with my body. So I said I wanted to leave . . . I wanted to go home. They refused.'

Ernest watched as Gracie drew a deep breath. Then another.

'They . . . locked me in my room. And when I banged on the door for hours, they gave me something . . . that made me . . . sleepy. When the medicine wore off, I said . . . I was going to run away, shouted that I was going to call the police. Said that I knew people. That's when they took my clothes. They kept me in a room with nothing more than a lamp and a bottle of poison. I suppose most of the girls just ended it there.'

'But you're not most girls,' Ernest said.

Gracie slowly shook her head. 'With my memories, I lit the fire. I

297

thought of you and Maisie as I took the lamp oil, and I splashed the walls, the carpet, and I set the bed aflame. I felt the heat on my bare skin, tasted the smoke. I thought that if I was going to die I was going to bring the roof down around me. That's when the owners came bursting into the room with buckets of sand, yelling . . . and I ran.'

You're still running, Ernest thought.

'I burned that filthy place to the ground, didn't I?'

Ernest nodded, oddly proud of her. He remembered worrying that someone might have been hurt, or killed in the blaze. That the police would come around and arrest her. But no one had ever come. He later realized that they'd have been upset only if the Tenderloin had burned.

Gracie glanced around the room. She cocked her head as she looked out the window. 'What am I doing here, young Ernest? What is this place?'

'We're . . . together, like we've always been.'

'No . . .' She shook her head. 'What are you doing with me? You shouldn't be with me. I'm . . . holding you back. You should be with Maisie.'

Ernest sighed. 'That ship sailed a very long time ago.'

Gracie furrowed her brow. 'She goes by Margaret.'

'We're all grown-up now,' Ernest said, nodding. 'We survived.'

As Ernest watched her struggle to reconcile the past with the present, he thought about the book he'd read to her once again – about tragic endings that couldn't ever be fixed. But that's when Ernest understood. Sometimes you need to feel the sadness, you need to feel everything to finally leave it behind, to have peace.

Happiness. Sadness. Like all things, they both come to an end.

Vagrants

(1911)

Ernest helped Professor True haul an enormous, dripping block of ice into the kitchen from a delivery wagon in the alley. The man gripped his end of the block, which was the size of a small steamer trunk, with giant metal tongs, and hefted it into the top cabinet of the icebox. Ernest felt the radiating coolness of the ice on his face, wet from perspiration. Then he latched the lid and followed the Professor back out through the alley and around to the front of the building, where they sat on the steps and basked in the glorious spring sunshine, stretching their backs and warming up their hands.

'You heard from the Mayflower lately?' Professor True asked as he pushed his glasses up onto his forehead and lit a cigar with a kitchen match, puffing away.

Ernest shook his head. He knew that like most everyone else, the Professor had been slow to accept that Maisie in all likelihood wasn't coming back. A year had passed, yet he kept asking, kept hoping for some postcard, or bicycle messenger to show up with a telegram from Germany, or Seattle, or . . . somewhere.

Ernest remembered how a few weeks after she'd moved out, Maisie had called Mrs Blackwell to announce her travel arrangements, but she didn't ask for him or Fahn. The Gibson girls had gone down to the King Street Station, where they gave the Mayflower a balsam wreath with ribbon candy and waved goodbye. Even after all these months, they still talked about how Maisie had been dolled up in a long mink coat, toting an angora-trimmed handbag as she stepped out of a long white sedan. Servants from Speedwell had arrived as well, portering a small mountain of luggage onto the train as they accompanied Maisie and Turnbull on their journey.

Ernest and Fahn decided not to go – they were too afraid a farewell would be goodbye forever. In that strange way, they held out hope. They imagined Maisie taking on the world, though the upstairs girls never once mentioned if she smiled or not.

From the Gibson girls' superficial reactions, Ernest realized that to them, Maisie had unwittingly hit the bull's-eye that Madam Flora had encouraged all her charges to aim for. It was not quite true freedom, he supposed, but a form of social dependence so elevated and grandiose that it looked like freedom to them.

Was this any different than party girls trading favors for silk stockings, bottles of brandy, and dinners in fancy restaurants – or society girls carefully doling out pleasure for the promise of a colorful courtship and a proper wedding?

Ernest had lain awake many nights and wondered. Girls were complicated, women confounding, their challenges almost insurmountable. The world was a rigged game, stacked against them. But maybe Maisie had played to her advantage.

'No one's heard from her. Not a word.' Ernest stretched the truth, just a tad. He *had* received a note from Maisie a week after she left; she was in New York City at the time, about to board a steamer to London. She'd said she felt as if she were living in a fairy tale, a world that couldn't reflect her previous life. She regretted not giving him or Fahn a proper goodbye. And she left a mailing address care of Louis Turnbull. But when Ernest had replied with a picture postcard of himself and Fahn holding hands at the Milwaukee Pier, Maisie never wrote back.

Ernest thought Fahn might have received a note in reply, but if she did, she never mentioned such a thing. And a few days later she moved upstairs into Maisie's room.

Ernest suspected that whether Maisie found her mother or not, the *Mayflower* had set sail for good and was never coming back. She'd sealed her deal with her silence.

That revelation was finally confirmed when Mrs Blackwell discovered Maisie's wedding announcement a few months later in the society pages of the *Seattle Times*.

'It says here that Louis J. Turnbull and his young ward, the lovely Margaret N. Turnbull, have returned, after a European courtship and a marriage at sea, with plans for a honeymoon cruise around the world.' Mrs Blackwell had sat down for once, as though the truth wearied her. Though the maids and the upstairs girls almost swooned.

The article didn't mention Madam Flora. Not that Ernest was surprised.

'What is it with robber barons and their young puppy wives?' Mrs Blackwell asked rhetorically. 'First it was the copper king, William Clark, and his young ward, Anna Eugenia, now our Mayflower. God bless 'em all.'

Since hearing of Maisie's nuptials, Ernest would occasionally notice her in the newspaper, where writers would describe her elegant dresses, her curled hair, dyed a light pink at the tips, an indulgence in the latest fashion craze, and the glittering diamond necklaces and bracelets she wore to yacht races or tennis matches at Viretta Park. But the articles on Seattle's newest continental debutante never once mentioned her humble beginnings. It was as though Margaret Turnbull had been conjured out of thin air.

'She's someone else these days,' Ernest said.

Professor True said, 'There are people in our lives whom we love, and lose, and forever long for. They orbit our hearts like Halley's Comet, crossing into our universe only once, or if we're lucky, twice in a lifetime. And when they do, they affect our gravity.' He said, 'You know what I mean? These people are special.'

Ernest nodded. Halley's Comet had come and gone and the world hadn't ended. But it wasn't ever the same again. And if he ever missed Maisie, he only had to console himself by walking past the less glamorous places where she might have ended up, the cribs that Madam Flora had tried to shut down.

As Ernest thought about the police, he realized he hadn't seen an officer on foot in weeks. Not even to stop by the Tenderloin to 'ticket everyone for vagrancy', which was merely a way of taxing the business. In the past Mrs Blackwell would have cheerfully taken the papers from the officer, paid him the fines out of petty cash, offered him a slice of fresh-baked apple pie and a cup of coffee, and then tossed the tickets into the fireplace.

No more.

As Ernest looked up and down the street, searching for an officer in uniform, he heard bells ringing, cheering, and the roar of a crowd several blocks away. Then he heard singing – voices that sounded more like an army on the move.

'They never give up,' the Professor said as he pointed to a parade of women in black who were marching down the middle of Third Avenue.

From three blocks away, Ernest recognized Mrs Irvine – the mother of the Mothers of Virtue. They were back, louder than ever, and in greater numbers than he'd ever seen, even though business had been quiet in the Garment District.

Rose and Violet came outside to watch the rally as they always did. As the women marched closer, Ernest could plainly read their banners and signs, the same ones that called for an end to the crib joints, casinos, saloons, taverns, bars, dance halls, and even the social drinking clubs. The normal rhetoric.

But this time he also saw that Mrs Irvine was shouldering an ax.

'Hoo-boy, we're in trouble, aren't we?' Rose asked no one in particular.

'I read the latest in the paper this morning,' Violet said. 'Since us women got the vote back, the suffragists have been reorganizing. They've formed a giant group. They're on a new crusade – twenty thousand strong.'

'Looks like they're all here.' Professor True pointed.

Ernest hadn't seen that many people in one place since the closing of the world's fair. He stood and backed up as the sea of women kept pouring down the street.

Many of the marchers carried brooms and yelled that they were here to 'clean up' the Garment District. But just as many carried axes, sickles, and crowbars. Others stormed into saloons, past shocked, drunken patrons. Then they rolled out kegs of beer and smashed them open in the street with picks and hammers, like angry birds pecking a larger animal to death. Others flocked to the alleys, where they'd never gone before, knocking on doors and breaking up dice games.

Ernest noticed that the bawdy ladies who normally heckled the marchers peeked out from their second- and third-story windows and then retreated inside, closing their shutters or drawing their curtains and blinds to block out the horde.

As the marchers paraded past the Tenderloin's front entrance, Mrs Irvine sauntered over, ax in hand. 'Where's the lady of the house?' she demanded. 'I have a little present I'd like to give to her personally –

it's been long overdue.' She reached into her deep dress pocket and withdrew a rolled-up paper.

'Who are you, Carry Nation?' Rose said, before Violet shushed her.

'I'm sorry, ma'am,' Professor True said, removing his hat and speaking gently. 'But Madam Flora and Miss Amber are still gone, taking care of things overseas. She'll be back soon. In the meantime, I'll be happy to let her know that you paid us a visit.'

Mrs Irvine smiled. 'Well, in that case.' She handed the paper to Ernest. 'Why don't you take this, young man? And pass it along to everyone here with my regards. Oh, and Ernest, you do know that I'm a forgiving sort, so you're always welcome to come back. As for the rest of this sorry lot . . .'

She turned on her heel and marched off singing a hymn.

'What's it say?' Rose asked.

Ernest unrolled the paper. It was a legal notice, along with a page torn from the *Seattle Star*. The headline read: MAYOR GILL LOSES IN RECALL ELECTION. A NEW DAY FOR SEATTLE AS WOMEN UNITE TO MAKE THEIR VOICES HEARD.

The Professor took the paper, skimmed the headlines, and then translated the bad news. 'Well, boy and girls, looks like the mayor and the police chief got caught with their pants down, financing that crib joint of theirs on lower Beacon Hill. So the city is busting up the neighborhood – all of the parlors and cribs. Thirty days' notice hereby given.'

Rose asked, 'What's that mean?'

'It means we're all out of a job,' the Professor said. 'And a home too, for that matter. The mayor's been kicked out of office, effective this week. And Wappenstein got reinstated as chief of police just in time to get himself arrested. The City Council is giving us a month to move out, or they'll come down here with paddy wagons and take us away. Either way, says here there's an unpaid lien on our building, plus a hefty fine against Miss Amber for operating all these years without a liquor license.' Professor True shook his head. 'Now it's illegal for you ladies to work anywhere that serves a touch of alcohol.'

Ernest thought of endless bottles of whiskey, brandy, port, and the cases of wine – and the men, the city officials who drank it.

'They can't do this!' Rose looked as though she were about to storm into the parade and start swinging, but Violet held her back. 'Miss Amber won't allow it!'

That's when Ernest heard Mrs Blackwell from behind them. 'It's done, dear.' The cook removed her apron and bonnet and let them fall to the ground. 'All of us, done for – it's over.' In her other hand she held a wrinkled slip of yellow paper. Her face was ashen. 'I couldn't bring myself to tell anyone. A messenger boy came to the servants' entrance with a telegram three months ago with news from Miss Amber. I didn't want to be the bearer of bad tidings. But in light of things . . .'

The sounds of protest seemed to fade to a dull ringing as Mrs Blackwell read the telegram aloud.

'Madam Flora succumbed to syphilis, God rest her soul. Too heartbroken to ever come back. Yours, Miss Amber.'

Prize and Consolations

(1911)

One month later the finest parlor joint in Seattle and the most orderly disorderly house in the Northwest had emptied. The Tenderloin's fine brickwork, gabled ceilings, and ornate crown molding were now nothing more than a skeleton that had been picked clean by vultures. With the lien, the King County auditor's office had called for a commissioned estate auction, which did away with most of the hanging artwork, the Turkish and Oriental rugs, the stained-glass lamps, and the French furnishings, all with the sound of a gavel. And then a foreclosure on the building by Hayes & Hayes Bank turned the remaining bones into soup as liquidators removed everything that wasn't nailed down, including the carpets, light fixtures, and the nouveau chandeliers.

Ernest stood by, waiting for Fahn to return from a job interview, as the last of the statuary, a smooth, bare-breasted marble sculpture of the Greek goddess Calypso, was wrapped, crated, and then lugged out the front door. The upstairs girls had called that statue Madam Damnable, in honor of Seattle's first madam, who ran the Felker House, a lifetime ago. Legend had it that when the rain forced the city to relocate the bodies from the old Seattle Cemetery up the hill to Lake View, the dainty old madam had turned to stone and her casket weighed two thousand pounds.

A very tall tale, Ernest thought. A heavy one too. But he understood

306

the burden that was one's personal reputation. Everyone associated with the Tenderloin now felt that weight, that pressure, that collective shame – which wasn't really shame at all, just the consternation and condemnation from others.

The only item that had somehow been spared the liquidation was the Marmon Roadster. The shiny black automobile had never officially been placed in Madam Flora's name, so to the authorities it didn't exist. Mrs Blackwell and Professor True had agreed that Ernest should have it. The Professor told him to keep the coachman's uniform and use his experience to make a living. Ernest gratefully accepted.

As he went inside, he was sad to be leaving the people he'd come to care about, but he was more hopeful for whatever life he and Fahn could create outside of a world where people were bought and sold. He'd been charmed, for a while, but the illusion had faded. And deep down, Ernest knew that his angular life could never fit back into a traditional box. He recognized that as he watched Violet, Iris, and Rose emerge from the kitchen holding on to one another, a real-life frieze of the Three Graces that Madam Flora had taught the upstairs girls about. Though the faces of the maids were masks of sadness, melancholy, and apprehension, rather than splendor, mirth, and good cheer.

The servants would have the biggest challenge. They were leaving a house of ill repute, without a reference, turned out into a city that was undergoing a moral cleansing. The righteous, upstanding women who had forced Mayor Gill from office would hold no desire to hire domestics who bore the stain of the red-light district. And Ernest was sure the men who'd gladly partaken of the Tenderloin's services would not be of help to the servants in finding placements. Ernest had known unkindness, he'd known outright hatred, but he'd never fully understood hypocrisy until now.

The servants had waited, hoping to eke out a few more days until the water and electricity were shut off. Now he figured that most of them would find menial jobs at poor farms or in flophouses. Mrs Blackwell had found employment running the kitchen at the halfway house on Beacon Hill known as the Lazy Husband Ranch. Ernest knew, because he'd driven the old cook to her new job at the Municipal Workhouse and Stockade. He'd hugged her and then waved farewell.

As he embraced each of the maids and said goodbye, they promised to be in touch once they landed on their feet. But when they walked out the door, he didn't hold out hope that he would ever see any of them again.

That's the one consistent pattern to my life, Ernest thought. *When people say goodbye, they mean it.*

That's how it had been with his mother and with Madam Flora and Miss Amber. He wished the same wouldn't be true with Maisie. He hoped that their threads of happiness and sadness, joy and grief, would somehow intertwine again. But he also understood that his loss might have been her gain, and he struggled to accept his part of that equation.

Ernest thought about the good times as he wandered past his packed suitcase in the foyer to the empty salon and then the smoking room, vacant of everything but the scent of tobacco. He lingered in the library, now absent of books. And he inhaled the stale air of the formal dining room, which – stripped of the tin ceiling and the wainscoting – seemed more bare than any of the girls had ever been. The only things that remained were the piano and a smattering of cases, hatboxes, and steamer trunks that belonged to the upstairs girls.

Most of the older ladies were moving on to sporting houses in Tacoma, while the younger ones had found work on the Levee in Chicago. And Nellie Curtis, who dared to set herself up as Seattle's next great madam, despite the chilly moral climate, had taken in a handful of the girls. She was already establishing a name for herself at the Camp Hotel on First Avenue, flouting the county's new policies and Seattle's new mayor, George Dilling. Word on the street, though, was that Naughty Nellie was all business and had no interest in helping the girls elevate their status in society.

'She's not interested in the parlor life,' Professor True had grumbled, shaking his head. 'She's just running an ordinary crib.'

Ernest had bid each of the remaining Gibson girls farewell as they descended the grand staircase one last time. Their mournfulness, like their expensive perfume, lingered long after they'd departed. As Ernest hugged Jewel, last to leave, he knew that of all the upstairs girls, he'd miss her the most.

'And where are you off to?' he asked.

'Ladies' choice.' She held up a stack of cards and letters, bound with a red ribbon. 'I'm going to check into a fine hotel, order a bottle of wine, draw a nice long bubble bath, put my feet up, and slowly read all the marriage proposals I've received in the last year. One of them is bound to be a keeper. Though to be honest, Ernest, if you were a little bit older, darling – you'd be my first pick.'

'And if my heart were my own . . .' He smiled.

Jewel put a gloved finger to Ernest's heart. 'But it's not, is it?' She planted a long, lingering kiss on his surprised lips. Then she kissed Professor True on both cheeks as he walked into the room. She smiled, grabbed her suitcase, and bounded down the steps.

'That one will do just fine,' the Professor said, fanning himself with his hat. 'Give her enough time and she might get herself elected mayor.'

'She's got my vote,' Ernest said.

'Mine too.'

The working girls will keep on working one way or another, Ernest thought. If not, there's the White Shield Home in Tacoma, a refuge he'd suggested to Fahn. But she had other plans. Besides, she couldn't bear to leave the neighborhood.

As sunset approached, Ernest helped Professor True and a group of colored men load the piano up a steep ramp and onto a flatbed hay truck, where they covered it with a canvas tarp and long stretches of heavy rope.

'Time for me to fly, young man – wish I could take you with.'

'And where might that be?' Ernest asked.

'Vancouver, British Columbia, for a month of gigs at the Patrician nightclub. Then we head east to Chicago. I've never been, but I've heard things – some good, some bad, but sounds like there's plenty of work. I hooked up with a hot band traveling through town led by a man named Ferdinand LaMothe. He just lost one of his crew – married a local girl – so off I go in his place . . .' Professor True reached up and pulled part of the canvas away from the keyboard and played a one-handed stinger on the piano, which was already slipping out of tune.

Ernest said, 'Good luck. I'll be right here with Fahn. I guess we're sticking together for a while.'

Professor True raised an eyebrow and climbed into the back of the truck. Then he smiled as he sat down on a bale of hay and began singing 'Movin' Man, Don't Take My Baby Grand'. The truck drove away in a cloud of dust, leaving behind streets that were less crowded than ever before, and eerily quiet, with just the distant clanging of a trolley and the chatter of gulls to keep Ernest company.

Alone in the house now, Ernest walked back upstairs and peeked into Miss Amber's room, which had long been vacant. It was now empty, the window cracked. He went to Madam Flora's master suite, which was also bare except for tea stains on the wall. He sighed and finally, reluctantly, went to say goodbye to the room that had been

Maisie's, then Fahn's. In the hallway, he paused where some of the ladies had been piling up the things they were leaving behind. There was a small mound of discarded clothing, broken hatboxes, and empty tins of make-up. Ernest took his raffle ticket from the AYP out of his shirt pocket and left it behind on the pile.

Then he went back downstairs, retrieved his suitcase, and stepped out into the mist. He looked up at the four-story edifice that had been his only real home. As the gaslights flickered to life, he found a dry spot beneath the awning and sat alone atop his valise. He listened to the patter of the rain as it showered the streets, turning the dusty pavement black and luminescent. He surveyed the boarded-up buildings, the darkened neon signs as he patiently waited for Fahn, who showed up twenty minutes later. She was soaking wet but beaming.

'I got a job!' she shouted. 'Two actually. I got hired as a waitress,' she gushed. 'But when the owner found out I spoke English, she also referred me to the Japanese Language School – that's what took me so long. After a tour and a short test, they hired me on the spot. It'll probably take me a year to make what the upstairs girls were earning in a month, but it's a fresh start, and you have your savings. They even suggested using me to reach out to some of the displaced girls in the neighborhood.'

Ernest cocked his head.

'Well . . .' Fahn said. 'I had to lie about where I'd worked. But Mrs Blackwell said she'd cover for me. She gave me a marvelous reference. And since I told them we had a motorcar, they said they'd pay us to use it to retrieve some of the girls.'

'We?' Ernest asked. 'You told them about me? About us?'

'I had to,' Fahn said. 'A single woman arouses a certain suspicion around here – I couldn't risk that, not right now. I doubt they would have hired me. And it'll be tough for us to rent an apartment together unless we play along, even here in the colored neighborhoods. So I told a fib. There was no other way, not out there in the real world. I hope you don't mind me pretending to be Mrs Ernest Young, at least for a while?'

Ernest smiled as he felt warmth spreading from the center of his chest. He was almost fifteen and could pass for marrying age. And Fahn was nearly eighteen.

'We could . . .' He hesitated. Then he took her hands. 'We could make it official. We could go to the courthouse . . .'

'I can't believe you *still* want to marry me . . .'

'Why? What's wrong with that?'

She shook her head. 'Nothing. Nothing at all. A part of me would like that, Ernest.' She spoke the affirming words, but her eyes were filled with apologies as she let go. 'I love the thought of a life together, with someone, anyone, but especially with you. I dream of that sometimes. But . . . I'm not the girl you marry. I never was and I never will be. I don't think I'm the marrying kind.'

'I do.'

Fahn turned her back toward the Tenderloin. 'Then I guess we'll see what happens. The world is changing. Maybe I'll be allowed to change as well.'

Ernest picked up his suitcase and stared at the vacant street, the darkened buildings. Everything was quiet. He could hear birds calling on the rooftops, the clip-clop of a distant horse. The faint sound of a church choir.

Ernest thought about the future and sighed. 'Goodness, gracious.'

Love and Marriage

(1962)

Ernest left Gracie at the apartment, engrossed in a live television program about the Century 21 Expo and the opening of the Space Needle. He walked east on South Weller, beyond a vacant lot where an old abandoned building had been torn down and past the smoky entrance of the Consistory Legionarios del Trabajo. He'd visited the lodge with Pascual on occasion, whenever the Filipino-American brethren were serving *lechon*.

As he passed, he didn't smell the telltale aroma of lemongrass and vinegar, so he kept going on across the street to the humble Crescent Cafe. Inside there were burgers frying, chili simmering, and coffee noisily percolating behind the counter. He found a booth by the window and rested his elbows on the chipped Formica tabletop, hands in front of his face as though in prayer. He thought about Maisie and Fahn – better known these days as Margaret and Gracie. As if in answer to his silent invocation, a waitress brought him a glass of water and a menu.

Ernest glanced at his wristwatch and then looked outside at the creeping shadows of the setting sun. As he waited for Juju, pedestrians walked up and down the sidewalk beneath the awnings of the Red Front Tavern, the Manila Cafe, and the Victory Laundry & Bath.

He'd told Juju all of his recollections regarding the great Alaska–Yukon–Pacific Exposition. He'd shared how Madam Flora and

Miss Amber had traveled abroad and never returned, how Fahn had run away to a less reputable establishment, and how Maisie had eventually transcended her social status. But as his reporter daughter walked through the door, he knew that he had to answer whatever other lingering questions she might have, if only to keep Gracie from surprising her on a regular basis.

'Wow, Dad, charming place you picked out. It's almost as nice as the Publix,' Juju said as she hung up her coat and settled into the booth across from him.

'Some people go out to be seen,' Ernest said. 'I prefer to be unseen.'

'Yeah, you and Sasquatch.'

Ernest motioned to the waitress, who brought them a fresh pot of tea, steaming hot. He swirled the pot and then poured for both of them. He observed how the bits of leaves settled at the bottom of each cup, and he wondered what secrets might be foretold, past and future. 'What are Hanny and Rich up to this evening?'

Juju opened her reporter's notebook. 'Han said they'd meet us back at your lovely apartment after dinner; she wanted to spend some more time with Mom before they fly back.' Then she shifted on the cracked vinyl of her seat. 'How's she doing?'

'Better,' Ernest said with a nod. 'I think she's getting a little bit better every day. Though occasionally she'll ask where old friends are – most of whom have long since passed away. But we're together again, so that's something—'

'Dad, I told Hanny the truth about Mom's situation,' Juju interrupted.

Ernest paused and slowly sipped his tea. 'And . . . how did that go?'

'Oh, she already knew.' Juju rolled her eyes. 'Han works in Las Vegas as a showgirl. She's around gangsters and gamblers and topless dancers all the time – she's not that naïve, trust me. She just doesn't like to dwell on the thought of her mom working as a – what was that word you used?'

314

Ernest cleared his throat. 'The Chinese called them *mui tsai*. The Caucasian girls had other, less interesting terms for ladies who were caught up in that line of work. Your mother was what they called a *karayuki-san*. And while she only worked for a brief time, it had a lasting effect, as you well know, mental, physical. Sometimes the girls were lucky, they only worked as maids – domestic servants. But others . . .'

'Yeah, that,' Juju said with an exasperated sigh. 'It's hard to sort it all out. Though I did find this article.' She unfolded a newspaper, a yellowed, brittle copy of the *Seattle Times* from 1901. She pointed to a small headline about Chinese and Japanese children sold as domestic servants. She'd highlighted the line

These women, these children were auctioned off like cattle for four hundred dollars each, with discounts for buying in quantity.

She tapped the newspaper. 'This was big business. Almost forty years after slavery was abolished, this was still going on. Here I am trying to write about the world's fair and cotton candy and roller coasters and cosmonauts, now all of a sudden my story leads directly to the seedy underbelly of the Garment District, to the Tenderloin. And to *other* places.' She shuddered. 'From what I've gathered the whole *mui tsai* system was spotlighted by . . .' She looked down at her notes. 'Winston Churchill. He railed against the selling of people as servants and prostitutes. And then the whole thing collapsed. The circus of that odious business was dismantled by the League of Nations. You could say that was one of the fringe benefits of the Great Depression – too many workers, even in red-light districts. The demand dried up. No profit. So no more supply from overseas.'

The waitress reappeared, and Juju ordered a bowl of clam chowder.

Ernest ordered a red Reuben and watched in silence as Juju paged through her copious notes.

'And now no one talks about it,' he said. 'It's as though . . .'

'It never happened,' Juju finished.

'So are you still going to write about me? About your mother?'

'I'm not sure I'm the right person to write anything,' Juju said. 'I know I barreled in here like a bull in a china shop, but now it's obvious why you were so reluctant to talk. It's very personal. I need to turn in something for my deadline, though.'

Ernest nodded.

'In the meantime,' Juju said. 'I do have one other question. Something that's been bugging me ever since I started digging around. I mean – I have friends who work in City Hall, good friends, people who can get me old records. So I've been pulling on loose threads, trying to track down every detail about you and Mom.'

'You're worried,' Ernest said, 'that I'm not telling you everything. You think I'm covering for Maisie – the great widowed heiress, Margaret Turnbull. She's a popular Seattleite now, a society page regular. She's in the news almost every day . . .'

Juju looked up from her notes. 'Well, yeah. That too, now that you mention it. But actually, what I'm trying to figure out – and it's something silly, but I'm curious . . . because I can't seem to find a record of you and Mom ever getting married.'

Ernest smiled and finished his tea. 'That's because we're not.'

Juju coughed and then reached for her water glass.

'What do you mean you're not married? I'm looking at your wedding ring.'

Ernest regarded the bit of gold he wore. He thought about the matching band on Gracie's ring finger. 'We told everyone we were married. Back in the day. The fiction of being married was a necessity at first – the only way anyone would rent us an apartment. Most landlords demanded to see a marriage certificate, but we managed to fudge it. A few years later we were basically living as a young husband and wife, and I proposed – believe me, I did – again and again, but your mother is quite stubborn.' Ernest drummed his fingers on the table. 'She decided that we were as good as wedded, even though there's no common-law marriage here in Washington State. And, well, as the years turned into decades, it seemed too late. If we had gotten married, the legal announcement would have been in the paper, right next to the police blotter and the obituaries.'

'You're serious,' Juju said.

'Then everyone would know we'd been deceiving them – they'd have questions and we wouldn't have suitable answers. It was easier to just leave well enough alone.'

Juju closed her notebook and set down her pencil.

'But it was more than that.' Ernest smiled, though he felt like crying. 'I think she felt unworthy of the sanctity of marriage, somehow. It was a way for your mother to pay some kind of sad penance for her former life. None of it was her fault, I should have done more to protect her – every day I wished I had, but we were just . . . teenagers. When she went to the Tangerine, I was fourteen, your mother seventeen. We were complicit, willing participants, and our lives were wonderful and they were horrible and everything was painful and true, the good, the bad, together.'

'So . . . to this day . . .'

He nodded. 'To this day . . .'

'You've been living together.'

'In sin?'

Ernest looked into his daughter's eyes – Gracie's eyes, Fahn's eyes, Madam Flora's eyes, his mother's weary, desperate eyes, the eyes of the

317

little sister he'd known for only two days. 'Parents always have a story that their children don't really know,' Ernest said. 'I guess this is mine.'

As Ernest and his daughter walked up the wooden stairs to his apartment at the Publix, Juju kept going on about how she couldn't believe that she and Hanny had been born out of wedlock. Their whole adult lives, their mother had chided them about how they should settle down, get married.

'After a while, marriage just didn't matter,' Ernest said. 'It's not a big deal.'

'Well, it matters now,' she said. 'What if Mom does something crazy again? What if the doctors find out? They won't let you make medical decisions on her behalf . . .'

'Dr Luke has treated patients in this neighborhood forever,' Ernest said as they passed strangers in the hallway. 'He understands.'

As Ernest reached for his keys he noticed that his apartment door was ajar. Hanny was standing inside, coat and purse in hand. An audience on the TV was laughing.

'Hello. Sorry we're late.' Ernest glanced about. 'Where's Rich?'

'He said he had a late-night meeting. Rich is always on the go, he said he was pitching a new client who might do business in Nevada. So, where's Ma?' Hanny looked around wide-eyed; she opened the bedroom door, peeked into the bathroom.

'What do you mean, where's Ma?' Juju said as she double-checked the tiny bedroom, opened the closet door. 'She's supposed to be here with you.'

Hanny smiled and cocked her head as though she thought her sister was teasing. Then she grew serious. 'Wait, she didn't go out to dinner with the two of you?'

Meet Me at the Fair

(1962)

Hanny telephoned her hotel and left a message for Rich. Then she immediately set off for Juju's house on Queen Anne Hill. If her mother wasn't there, she planned to call the police and report Gracie as a missing person. Then she'd sit by the phone. Meanwhile Juju had left to canvas the Betsuin Buddhist Temple, the Japanese Baptist Church, the *sento* beneath the Panama Hotel, Ruby Chow's, and any other place she could think of where her mother might have wandered. That left Ernest to visit the nearby train stations and the Union Gospel Mission, where the Tenderloin used to be. They'd check, then call Hanny and leave messages, doing their best to coordinate their search.

A part of Ernest suspected where Gracie was really headed, though, even before Pascual met him in the hallway. A woman Ernest vaguely recognized from the Black and Tan hung on his friend's arm, smiling.

'*Kuya*, what's up? We popped by earlier and Gracie was heading out, all alone. I knew that probably wasn't a good idea, but she seemed – you know – pretty well put together. I tried to stop and talk to her, but she wouldn't listen. She just handed me this note to give to you and boom, out the door. I figured maybe one of your daughters was waiting for her downstairs. From the look on your face, I'm guessing I was wrong.'

Ernest unfolded the note, which read:

Dear Ernest, I've gone to the fair. It's been too long. I'm going to make things better now. Go to the Space Needle and you'll understand. Yours, Gracie.

He found Juju's business card in his wallet and handed it to his friend. 'Call my daughter – her number's on the back – let her know that I've found Gracie.' Then he tucked the note in his pocket and headed downstairs.

Pascual leaned over the banister. '*Kuya,* wait, where are you going?'

Ernest had worried that the new Alweg Monorail would still be jam-packed – overflowing with tourists, even in the early evening – so he skipped the electric sky train and parked as near as he could to the Century 21 Expo's south entrance, which was mercifully uncrowded. He paid $1.60 for a general admission ticket and pushed his way through the turnstile while hundreds of bells chimed in the distance. Once inside, he felt like a desperate kid again. Everything smelled new, like sawdust, concrete, and blooming flowers, with a hint of cotton candy and candied apples lingering on the breeze.

Ernest inhaled the haunting scents and walked as fast as he could among the thicket of people. He weaved his way through the crowds, past the Interior Design and Fashion pavilion and beyond the snarling stuffed polar bears of the Alaska Exhibit, covered in fake snow. He felt a wave of nostalgia. So much had changed, beyond the location. The long, elegant dresses, petticoats, and colorful parasols were gone, replaced with a rainbow of short dresses and leather boots. Cinched waists had become soft, bare midriffs. Dark French curls had given way to frosted beehives and soaring bleached bouffants. And the decorum of suits and hats had been updated with Bermuda shorts, denim, and sunglasses.

320

The elaborate neoclassical architecture, the Grecian columns and faux marble arches that decorated his memories had been replaced as well, supplanted with visions of the future made manifest in painted steel and soaring walls of pastel concrete.

The expo made Ernest feel as if he'd stumbled out of H. G. Wells's time machine and into a strange future where he didn't quite fit in. He was a Morlock in a world of Eloi, more of a workhorse than a show horse, as he wended his way through the throngs of beautiful, chattering, modern people, who all seemed to be speaking in different languages – Chinese, Japanese, the romantic languages of Europe, sprinkled among the assortment of American accents.

Fortunately the Space Needle made it easy to orient himself as he saw a line of visitors trailing away from the base of the new landmark – hundreds of people, so many that they blocked the entrances of the IBM Center and the General Electric Building, and the sleek rocket-shaped concept cars in front of the geodesic dome of the Ford Pavilion. After fighting his way through the crowd that loitered near a bank of lockers and a row of seashell pay phones, Ernest found the ticket window.

'I've lost someone,' he said to the clerk, as he scanned the crowd. 'I think she might have wandered up to the observation deck. She's not well, plus she's afraid of heights. My whole family is out looking for her, if I could just . . .'

The clerk looked at him as though he'd heard a million excuses to cut in line and a million more sob stories about missing children and misplaced wallets and purses. Then the man lit a cigarette and checked his clipboard. 'Name?'

'Ernest Young, looking for Gracie Young.'

The clerk flipped to the end of his paperwork and then said, 'No need for the sob story, pal. You're on will call.' He handed Ernest a VIP ticket and shouted, 'Next!'

Ernest regarded the ticket, confused but grateful, as he walked to the entrance to the elevators. While waiting, he gazed up at the rotating restaurant that sat atop the pitched columns, five hundred feet above them. Thousands of feet higher, rivers of clouds stretched across the sky, slowly drifting beyond the tip of the needle, which made the spire appear to lean, as though millions of square feet of concrete and iron were falling. Ernest had to look away to keep from feeling dizzy.

'Gracie, what are you doing?' he whispered to himself as he watched the golden elevator capsules, one descending, and one rising. He could see faces in the elevator windows, some happy, some nervous and scared.

Once inside the building, he crowded into the lift as a tall elevator operator in a short dress welcomed their group with a cheery smile and a brief introduction. As they ascended beyond the ground-level visitors' center, Ernest heard a rhythmic booming, drumming, and the brassy strains of trumpets and trombones. The World's Fair Band emerged into view below, dressed in white and yellow, parading down the street. The musicians seemed like a throwback to Ernest's first fair, except their caps were now emblazoned with the spiraling pattern of a hydrogen atom. As though on cue, a pair of fighter jets streaked across the sky, split in different directions, and wiggled their wings at the fairgoers below, who waved pennants and caps. Ernest swallowed, remembering how an identical jet had flown overhead and crashed on opening day. A married couple on the ground had been killed.

Ernest closed his eyes as the ground fell away beneath them. Then he opened them and for a moment was transported to 1909. He was back in the hot-air balloon, rising above an entire world that was celebrating the future.

He blinked as the elevator slowed and the view from the window portals was blocked by steel girders and slabs of concrete. When the doors slid open, Ernest stepped out into a crowded black-tie party, where finely dressed men and women were celebrating with glasses of champagne. Ernest felt underdressed and certainly uninvited as he scanned the room for any sign of Gracie. He worked his way through the room and around a grand piano. He held his breath as he stepped into the open air of the observation deck, felt the wind, appreciated the towering height. The sun was setting, kissing the tops of the Olympic Mountains, as boats on Lake Washington and Puget Sound switched on their red and green running lights. People milled about with cameras, elegant couples, posing, smiling, waving exposed squares of Polaroid film. Ernest searched for Gracie as guests and dignitaries mingled together, waiting for their snapshot smiles to develop. He circumnavigated the deck, ignoring the view of the fair below as he searched.

Then he saw a familiar woman, but much older, in a pearled gown as white as her hair. The spitting image of Madam Flora, she was walking toward him, also scanning the crowd. Her blue eyes lit up when she saw him, greeting him with open arms and a smile that he'd never forgotten.

Maisie.

They met amid the current of people, two stones in a river that eddied and swirled about them. The lines of age, the extra curves and wrinkles, the heaviness of time and circumstance had caught up to the Mayflower, just as those years had accumulated on him. Her hair was short, like when they'd first met. And instead of a hummingbird hat she wore a faded antique ribbon pinned to her shimmering dress. He recognized it as a commemorative souvenir from Hurrah Day.

'Hurrah,' she said, but the word came out more as a question.

'What are you doing here?' Ernest asked. He stood stunned, gazing at the smiling face he hadn't seen in decades. 'And do I call you Margaret now?'

She beamed. 'You can always call me Maisie if you want to. No need to stand on ceremony. I'm too old to care what people think of me now. And I was about to ask what made you call me after all these years, but . . .'

Neither one spoke. Instead they hugged each other, held on as though each couldn't believe the other person was real. Then they hugged again.

'Well, I can see by the look in your eyes, this meeting is a surprise to you,' Maisie said. 'Just like the first time we met . . .'

'All those years ago.'

'I've always wanted to see you,' she said. 'I've wondered how this would go, after all this time. But, I'm guessing this meeting is someone else's doing, isn't it?'

Ernest looked around, expecting to find Gracie lurking nearby, smiling, giggling, happy or heartbroken, lucid or delusional, he wasn't sure. But she was nowhere to be found. 'Fahn goes by Gracie these days.'

'And she's still your . . . wife?'

Ernest drew a deep breath and exhaled, nodding. 'Something like that.'

Maisie smiled, but Ernest could feel the disappointment.

'And you're married again?' he asked.

'Oh, I'm long since widowed,' Maisie said. 'Twice over.'

'I'm so sorry to hear that. You look beautiful, as you always did. And it's so wonderful to see you in person. I've followed you in the newspaper over the years – the society page might as well be dedicated to you. It's just that . . .' Ernest hesitated.

Maisie held his hand. 'It's okay. I'm happy to see you. My secretary said someone called and wanted to meet me here. When I saw your name – honestly, it was like a wish come true. And I thought, *Lucky me*. Ever since they began construction on the new fairgrounds, I haven't been able to stop thinking about those days, those nights, and . . . our precious time together. There was something magical back then, amid that strange world, and I left it all behind.' She squeezed his hand. 'I left you behind.'

Ernest noticed that she wore an impressive array of sparkling diamonds, but that she wasn't wearing a wedding ring. 'We were just kids,' he said. 'You've grown up just fine. Flora would be so proud. Even Miss Amber would be impressed.'

Maisie nodded slowly and looked around the elegant party, at all the important guests in ballgowns and tuxedos, the vintage champagne, the magnificent view of the city. 'I got everything I wanted,' she said. 'And nothing that I needed.'

She dabbed a bit of mascara from the corner of her eye. 'And look at me now. Throwing a gala and adding your name to the guest list.'

'I'm glad you did.'

'I found your address in the phone book and sent you notes over the last few years,' Maisie said. 'But you never wrote back, so I wasn't sure if you'd actually received them. Or perhaps you were mad at me for leaving. And now look at you – look at us, you're here and I'm so happy.' Then she let go. 'And also so very sad.'

Ernest apologized. 'This must be Gracie's doing. I showed her your postcard. She must have called and set this up,' he said. 'She hasn't been herself for a while. Now she's reliving the past, maybe trying to rewrite it somehow.'

'Ah,' said Maisie, collecting herself. 'Fahn did always think . . . Anyway, I'd love to see her. Is she here?'

Ernest shook his head as he looked around. 'I don't think so.' He drifted to the lip of the observation railing. He gripped the cold metal, and the breeze took his breath away as he looked down at the spinning carnival rides, the illuminated fountains, the long tendrils of shadow

325

cast by the setting sun as it seemed to melt into the horizon. He noticed a garish swash of neon in the far corner of the fairgrounds as well as a row of flags marking the entrance to the International Plaza.

Then he hugged his dear old friend once more, sad to be leaving, but hopeful as well. 'I'm so sorry, but I have to find her. I wouldn't show up and then run off if it wasn't important – I think I know where she is.'

'It's okay,' Maisie said. 'Go.'

Ernest kissed her on the cheek. 'We'll talk again soon. I promise.'

Secrets of Show Street

(1962)

E rnest took a shortcut through the old Armory building, where he had once gone dancing with Gracie when they were in their twenties. The place had been turned into the Food Circus, and it smelled like fried sausage, fried fish, fried dough, fried everything. He checked the nurses' station and the dispensary while he was there, just in case, then exited the other side and crossed United Nations Way. Ernest felt the spray and mist from the International Fountain as hundreds of nozzles shot geysers of water into the air in elegant rhythmic patterns that seemed almost hypnotic. In the main courtyard he detoured around a troupe of spinning Russian dancers, and avoided being run over by a honking Fairliner tram and a swarm of Electricabs.

Ernest passed a first-aid station and then scanned the crowd, looking for a familiar face, hoping that by some miracle he'd catch a glimpse of Gracie on the move. Then he worked his way through the knots of tourists and passed the enormous Opera House, where an illuminated sign announced that Rod Serling and Ray Bradbury were discussing the future. He passed the Fine Arts Pavilion and the new Playhouse, and finally ended up in the center courtyard of the International Mall, which was bustling with costumed hosts from the Republic of China, Brazil, Denmark, Thailand, Korea, the Philippines, Sweden, the United Arab Republic, Mexico, Canada, Great Britain, and even the city of

Berlin. Everything was abuzz except for the Spanish Fiesta Village, which was still closed.

'Where is it, Gracie?' he muttered to himself as he looked for the Japanese Village, which he thought he'd glimpsed from the Space Needle. 'Where are you?'

Ernest noticed the Union 76 Skyride passing overhead. The cable car carried fairgoers back and forth above the expo. One little boy even waved. Then Ernest crossed the avenue, searching, until he heard a bawdy saxophone. He followed the curious music until he saw the flashing red neon in the distance and realized there was another place she might be.

Gracie, no.

The glittering lights marked the entrance to Show Street, the scandalous adults-only section of the Century 21 Expo.

Ernest waded through an eager coterie of curious couples, sailors, and college-age boys – thousands of people, all heading in the same direction. He paused to let a group of Lummi dancers parade by in full regalia, singing, drumming, and banging sets of rhythm sticks. He gazed up at the humming neon sign that was occasionally obscured by smoke that smelled like alder wood, cedar, and fresh salmon from the nearby Indian Village. Then he drifted again with the motley tide of people flowing toward the mysterious, nighttime-only corner of the world's fair.

Ernest kept his eyes peeled – searching for any sign of Gracie as he passed an adults-only wax museum, whose teasing placards stretched his already-ripe imagination. He lingered at the entrance of the busy show hall, where Sid and Marty Krofft were putting on a topless puppet revue – the same routine that Pascual had talked so much about. Ernest kept walking as scalpers worked the margins of the crowd.

The volume of visitors seemed overwhelming, and Ernest wondered if perhaps his hunch was off. But as he debated whether or not to leave, the crowd parted and he saw the entrance to Gracie Hansen's Night in Paradise, an enormous dinner theater topped by a giant neon apple with a bite missing.

Another Gracie, Ernest thought. Could *his* be inside the racy revue, with scantily clad showgirls and blue comedians? He didn't think so – he'd read it had been sold out all week.

That left the Girls of the Galaxy exhibit and the seedy Backstage USA, where ticket buyers could spy into the dressing rooms of off-duty performers between sets, in various states of undress. Though rumor had it that the ladies were often just knitting or reading, or mending their feathered costumes. Ernest opted for the former and paid to enter the darkened auditorium, where a dozen topless pinup models were posing in space-age costumes. He felt like a visitor to the set of *Forbidden Planet* as he heard warbling, futuristic sound effects and beheld a bizarre tableau of red-light science fiction come to life. He searched the audience as the stage rotated every few minutes to reveal a new scene, and Jose Duarte – the Man with a Million Voices – played emcee, introducing each new girl and her costume, or lack thereof, while concessionaires mingled through the crowd selling film and renting cameras.

This is the future? Ernest frowned as he scanned the crowd – single men of every age, couples, groups of curious ladies, and foreign visitors. His head ached as he noticed a familiar figure, though it was not Gracie. Alone in the front row, perched near a velvet rope.

'And here we have Sally the Saturness,' the emcee droned over the loudspeaker.

'Having a good time?' Ernest asked as he found a spot at the rail, standing next to Hanny's fiancé. A flashbulb went off from one of the back rows, and he heard the battery-powered whir of a camera.

'You could say that again,' Rich said, then he did a double take as he recognized Ernest. He stammered, 'Wait, Mr Young – what on earth are you doing here?'

Ernest smiled politely.

Rich looked about the room. 'Honestly, it's not what you think. I was down here for research. Legal reasons, actually. I heard that the city tried to shut down all the cabarets for too much shimmying, can you imagine? So, I had to see the show in person – just to appraise the legal footing. For future reference.' Rich seemed to relax a bit as he realized that Hanny wasn't in the room. 'Now the girls here have to pose like statues, which is completely dull. Am I right?'

Ernest tried not to shake his head. 'I'm here looking for someone.'

The emcee chimed in again, 'And behold, the Heavenly Body of Venus.'

'Really?' Rich smiled and tried to contain his surprise. 'Well, I don't blame you one bit. And for what it's worth, you got here just in time. They told me this place reopened a few days ago and already they're closing the show down again. They're padlocking the doors at midnight. What's a fella to do in a city like this?' Rich patted Ernest on the back and waved to a girl wearing purple pasties, whose skin and hair had been dyed green. The stage lights went out and the theater was filled with polite applause and an occasional wolf whistle. Then the lights came back on as more maidens of the galaxy struck high-heeled poses in sparkling metallic outfits, with towering wigs and painted skin.

Ernest sighed, and left Rich in the dark without saying goodbye.

Twice in a Lifetime

(1962)

Ernest stepped outside into the carnival world of glitter-filled balloons, flashing neon, and music. A bank of sun guns lit up the underside of the Space Needle as everyone celebrated nighttime at the fair.

He blinked as he heard a commotion; then he saw a group of elderly women and for a moment thought the ghost of Mrs Irvine was back on the march. But the group was only the Grandmother's Kitchen Band, happily playing washboards and tin buckets. Ernest stepped back to let the procession pass, listening to the banging of pots and pans and the buzzing of hundreds of kazoos.

The world keeps on spinning.

Ernest had almost given up hope of finding Gracie anywhere at the expo when he noticed a guide to the fairgrounds in an overflowing garbage can. He unfolded the discarded map and scanned the page, skimming over the Christian Science Exhibit, the Hall of Industry, and the Antique Car Ride, until he finally found the Japanese Village, near the Islands of Hawaii Pavilion, adjacent to the entrance of the Gayway.

He followed the map, walking past the rumbling compressor engines and hissing hydraulic pistons of the new carnival rides, the Giant Wheel, the Wild Mouse, and the Flight to Mars. He also heard the heckling, taunting seductions of midway barkers offering stuffed bears and Kewpie dolls.

Then, nestled between newly planted trees, he spotted an arched torii that marked the Japanese Village. Ernest walked beneath the gate and approached the kimono-clad girls at the entrance, struggling to communicate in his best, broken Japanese. 'Hi . . . *Konichiwa*. Um . . . *shusshin wa dochira desu ka?*'

The workers stared back, brows furrowed.

'Where are you all from?' he asked. 'What prefecture?'

The Japanese girls looked at one another in confusion, then back at Ernest as they smiled and shrugged and tried not to laugh.

'Um, look, mister, I'm from Bothell,' one of the girls said in perfect English.

'Yeah, we just work here,' another said. 'I'm a sophomore at Franklin High.'

'And I'm from Garfield,' the last girl said. 'Go Bulldogs.'

American Zen, Ernest thought, as he paid to go inside.

He passed a few tourists who were leaving as he followed the girls, who clip-clopped in their geta footwear into the heart of the Japanese Pavilion, where a hidden garden was nestled beyond tatami mats and behind shoji screens. In that quiet, serene space, far from the whirl and bustle of crowds and carnival rides, he finally found Gracie, kneeling at a small table with a lacquered tea set, the box partially open in front of her. She looked at the cups, the teapot, and held the ladle as though trying to remember the proper order of the ceremony she had once been so proud of.

Ernest thanked the hostess and approached Gracie, who smiled slightly, seemingly confused.

'Hello, Gracious.'

She looked up, surprised to see him.

'Oh . . . didn't you get my message?' she said. She touched her pockets as though she might have misplaced it somewhere. 'It said that you're supposed to go to the Space Needle – up there, where I'm . . . too afraid to go.'

'I went,' Ernest said. 'And then I came all the way back down to find you.'

'Was Maisie there?'

'Maisie has always been there,' Ernest said. 'But she's not who I'm looking for.'

Gracie gazed back at him. 'Are you mad at me?'

'Of course not.'

She straightened the collar on her blouse and checked her pearl buttons. Then she noticed her mismatched shoes, one blue, one brown. 'I'm still a foolish old woman,' she said, shaking her head. 'I just wanted you to be happy.'

'I am. You've always made me that way. From the day we first met.' Ernest removed his jacket and sat down across from her. 'Can I help you with this?'

Gracie set down the ladle. 'Please.'

Ernest regarded the elegant tea set, then looked around and spotted a stout earthenware bottle with a wide mouth on a nearby table. He reached over and retrieved the carafe, then gently moved the tea box aside. He sat upright and softly, reverently placed two wide cups in front of them.

'But that's . . . not tea,' Gracie protested. 'That's . . .' She touched the bottle as she remembered. 'That's sake. Rice wine. That's used for . . .'

'Weddings,' Ernest whispered as he offered her a teacup with both hands.

She took the cup in hers, fingers trembling. 'You . . . still want to marry me?'

Ernest nodded and began to pour.

Closing Ceremonies

(1962)

Two months later Ernest and Gracie went back to the world's fair, on the night of the Century 21 Exposition's grand finale. They weren't among the thirteen thousand lucky men and women who squeezed into Memorial Stadium to hear the mayor give his closing ceremony speech, or watch the Police Department Drill Team, or listen to every high school band in the city perform. Instead, they arrived just before sunset, well after the record-breaking crowd had thinned – eager people who'd packed the fairgrounds on this last day, hoping for one more ride on the Space Wheel, one antipodal sermon of science, one final taste of a strawberry waffle cone, or one more last-minute bargain-priced, half-off, souvenir statue of the Space Needle.

'Maybe they'll raffle you off all over again,' Gracie teased as they walked slowly, hand in hand, along a row of transplanted cherry trees. The blossoms, like her memories, had returned in fits and starts since the opening of the fair. Some fresh and lovely, others fallen, swept up, or blown away.

'Doubtful,' Ernest said. 'They already had to shut down one of the concessionaires on the Gayway for giving away poodles. Too cruel, they said. Besides, who would want me? I'm just a consolation prize at best.'

She squeezed his hand.

'I remember you as much more than that.'

Gracie's memory was like a jigsaw puzzle with parts that didn't always fit, but she'd found the all-important edge pieces. She was beginning to reframe her life – their life. It was a work in progress, but the image was coming together.

'It's too bad Juju didn't write her story,' Gracie said.

Ernest laughed. He thought about the old typewriter in their apartment. Maybe *he'd* write their story. Then he thought about his other daughter.

'It's too bad Hanny returned Rich's ring,' Ernest said, though he was far more relieved than disappointed.

'True.' Gracie smiled. 'She should have pawned it.'

As they walked near the monorail terminal, they examined each tree, searching for a loosely carved heart, etched with their initials fifty years ago. Pascual thought he'd seen it and had told them where the tree was. Ernest and Gracie finally found it as the streetlamps flickered to life. Their remembrance, etched in sakura bark so many years ago, was now just one of many, as dozens of other fairgoers had added their names, their initials, their professions of undying love.

'I can't believe you finally married me, young Ernest.'

'And I'd do it all over again,' he said. 'Maybe tomorrow, or yesterday.'

A week after their impromptu tea ceremony, their daughters had found a simple wedding gown, and done their mother's hair and make-up. Pascual had stood at Ernest's side, his best man, in a modest service held at Kobe Terrace Park, with a handful of old friends from the neighborhood. Ernest didn't care what anyone thought about his spur-of-the-moment nuptials. Nor did Gracie as she proudly carried a bouquet of roses – white and lavender – when she strolled down a simple aisle of silk and gave herself away. Ernest had beamed with happiness as he did the same.

Pascual had finally won the neighborhood lottery, Ernest thought, but he was the one who felt like the luckiest man alive.

'It's almost time,' Gracie said. 'I can't wait to see her.'

Ernest blinked and looked up the avenue, searching for Maisie, who'd been unable to attend their wedding. But she'd told them that she would meet them here, tonight. That she'd be able to leave the closing ceremonies and join them as soon as she'd made a final appearance, shaken the governor's hand, introduced some dignitaries.

Madam Flora would be pleased, Ernest thought.

Then he saw Maisie turn the corner. A long-lost love. A living, breathing embodiment of what might have been. She stood apart from the remaining tourists in an elegant dress. He watched as she and Gracie embraced, without hesitation, or restraint, or regret. They held each other, smiled and laughed, wiped the corners of their eyes.

Then the three of them lay on the cool grass and waited, shoulder to shoulder, hand in hand, children again. They watched the crackling, cascading fireworks as a band played Tchaikovsky, as another twenty-one-gun salute boomed. As bells rang, bagpipers piped, and a light rain began to fall, gently washing away the past.

Author's Note

Someone recently asked, 'Do you have a muse who inspires your writing?' This immediately conjured images from the movie *Xanadu*, where Olivia Newton-John played a glittering, roller-skating, disco-singing muse who falls in love with a struggling artist on the verge of giving up.

Needless to say, I *wish* I had a glittering, roller-skating, disco muse.

Instead of Terpsichore, the goddess of dance as played by Olivia, my de facto muse seems to be a never-ending appetite for lost history – the need to constantly turn over rocks and look at the squishy things underneath.

One of those metaphorical rocks happened to be the great Alaska–Yukon–Pacific Exposition of 1909 – Seattle's forgotten world's fair. I stumbled upon an old article about race and the AYP and how China had declined to sponsor an exhibit because delegates had been harassed at previous world's fairs, and how ethnographic displays were immensely popular, like the Igorrote exhibit, a mock village of grass huts, which was basically a human zoo.

As I kept digging, I was intrigued to learn that 1909 was also the height of Washington State's suffrage movement. Both the Washington Equal Suffrage Association and the National American Woman Suffrage Association held conventions in Seattle to take advantage of the publicity of the AYP. And a large group of suffragists climbed Mount Rainier. Led by Dr Cora Smith Eaton, who flew a 'Votes For Women' pennant atop the 14,409-ft summit, alongside an AYP flag.

But curiously, 1909 was also the peak of Seattle's social evils – described as 'dance halls, bagnios, crib houses, opium dens, and noodle joints . . . openly advertised in the full glare of electric light' – a major concern for the host city.

But what haunted my imagination more than anything, among articles about a 'world of wonder' with a wireless telephone, incubators for premature babies, and a machine that could butcher salmon (patented as the Iron Chink) was finding a *Seattle Times* clipping that proclaimed SOMEBODY WILL DRAW BABY AS PRIZE and a sad 1909 follow-up in the *Kennewick Courier*, where a man who was in charge of the giveaway said, 'No one had claimed the baby (yet).'

Much to my authorly delight (and parental mortification) that story turned out to be true.

The Washington Children's Home Society did indeed donate a baby boy to be raffled off. And yes, his name in all the newspapers was Ernest. Ironically, he was offered up under the auspices of then-director L. J. Covington, who fought tirelessly against the moral plagues of his time but apparently had no problem giving away a child.

Oddly enough, I also found a letter in the *Leavenworth Echo* from July 10, 1910, with the headline WANTS TO ADOPT UGLY BOY. A woman named Anna M. Sampson wrote, 'You may send me the ugliest, biggest, most ungainly looking boy you have. I think I know how to bring out the best that is in such a lad.'

The letter was received by M. A. Covington, superintendent of the Spokane district of the Washington Children's Home Society, who responded: 'I have a boy who is not the ugliest and who is only ten years old, but I believe he will suit.'

This begs the question: were there two different Covingtons giving away children? Were they related? Or was this perhaps the same person, confounded by a typographical error? I'm still not sure.

But what I am certain of is that all of this happened during the tail end of the orphan train era, when children were given away with aplomb. And while it's clear that a baby boy was offered as a prize at the AYP, it's likely that no one claimed him, and his subsequent fate is unknown. And I like the unknown.

That's when I decided to write this story.

Because of mysteries like these, Ernest became yet another one of my imaginary friends. And on the blank canvas of his life, I set off to render his tale, which in my world begins in Southern China during a time when workers were being smuggled into North America despite the Chinese Exclusion Act of 1882. Young women were still being sold as *Mui Tsai* in China, or *Karayuki-san* in Japan, often ending up in the United States, where they worked as slaves or indentured servants, more than fifty years after the Emancipation Proclamation.

Due to prejudice, and perhaps barriers of language and culture, the plight of these girls was ignored by all but the most intrepid of heroes, like Donaldina Cameron, who rescued more than three thousand Asian girls in San Francisco. The 'Angry Angel of Chinatown' would remain busy until 1910 when the Mann Act made it a crime to transport white women across borders for the purpose of debauchery.

In reality, the Mann Act was used to prevent interracial relationships. World champion heavyweight boxer Jack Johnson was prosecuted under the Mann Act for dating white women.

Sadly, only after the Mann Act did women of color catch a break.

The tragically true stories of these women inspired Fahn and Gracie. Together they represent a lost generation of women who endured unspeakable hardships.

Someone braver than me should kick over that particular rock and write a novel about this darker side, the one explored in the play *Broken Blossoms*, or the powerful Japanese film *Sandakan No. 8.*

I'm afraid my heart's not up to the task.

Instead, I went down the velveteen rabbit hole of Seattle's Garment District, where the confluence of an early suffrage movement and the lifestyles of high-paid sophisticates created a river of new possibilities.

Seattle's red-light district was a gray area of morality and economics, as elite companionship was somewhat acceptable, while a four-hundred-room crib joint built by Mayor Hiram Gill and his chief of police, Charles 'Wappy' Wappenstein, was not.

Or as the great Western philosophers Cheap Trick once sang, 'Surrender, but don't give yourself away.'

These are the murky waters where Dame Florence Nettleton came to life, loosely based on the notorious Seattle madam Lou Graham, who, for decades, occupied a special rung on the ladders of business and governance.

I had a vague understanding of the red-light district, mainly from taking a tour of the Seattle Underground – a network of old tunnels and basements – and hearing stories about Seattle's most famous madam.

I'd later read how Madam Lou, known as the 'Queen of the Lava Beds', had created 'a discreet establishment for the silk-top-hat-and-frock-coat set to indulge in good drink, lively political discussions, and, upstairs, ribald pleasures – all free to government representatives.'

Madam Lou, along with her 'housekeeper', Amber, held court in a lavish brothel in the heart of Seattle's Pioneer Square. They also had a daughter, Ulna, who was left behind when her guardians moved to San Francisco. When Madam Lou died a month later of a mysterious ailment (rumored to be an occupational disease), the absence of a will meant that Amber got nothing, and Ulna ended up in a convent.

Meanwhile, Lou's entire fortune, estimated at $200,000 – roughly $5 million today – was donated to the King County school system.

You're welcome, kids.

That's the legend, and the stories about Madam Lou tend to focus on her wealth, her connections to banks, and her propriety – if you will – in that she supported the continued education of the women who worked for her.

But in general, the stories were all about Madam Lou.

What I hadn't explored were the social conventions that might lead a woman (or young girl) into the employ of a place like the Tenderloin, or the Tangerine, beyond the stereotypes of addiction, abuse, or mental illness, which are often exaggerated for effect as much as the tall tales of Madam Lou's vast financial empire.

In reading *The Story of Yamada Waka: From Prostitute to Feminist Pioneer*, and also *Twice Sold, Twice Ransomed*, the autobiography of Mrs L. P. Ray (a former slave who ministered to the homeless in Seattle), it's clear that there's no definitive answer. But instead a rogue's gallery of societal pressures that contributed in varying proportions to the difficulty of simply being born without a Y chromosome in the early twentieth century – abject poverty, lack of education, an appalling age of consent (as low as ten years old), religious condemnation, tribal shaming toward unmarried women who dared to (gasp) be sexually active, illegality of information pertaining to birth control, vicious wage gaps.

Oh, and racism.

While Madam Lou made a killing in the stock market, the Japanese and Chinese cribs often worked their girls, literally, to death – and local police looked the other way.

But beyond the peculiar and glamorous world of Madam Lou Graham and the red-light district was a revelation and a question.

Why did frontier cities in the West have the most successful suffrage campaigns while also being hotbeds for vice?

It's a challenging, mind-bending question.

While you're thinking about that, I should mention that I once had a job interview in the Washington Court Building, the brick establishment built by Madam Lou and the physical blueprint for the Tenderloin.

It's a nice place, but it could really use a piano.

Finally, there's the metaphorical moon-rock of the Century 21 Expo, which featured the likes of Elvis, Bobby Kennedy, Ray Bradbury, Rod Serling, and John Glenn.

Both fairs heralded a new economic age: the Gold Rush in 1909 and the Jet Age in 1962. Both showcased the latest technology of their times, from dirigibles and aeroplanes, to satellites and cosmonauts. Both events attracted politicians (Taft, Nixon), celebrities (Buffalo Bill, John Wayne), foreign delegations and visitors from around the world. Both were sources of national pride, and each served as a coming-out party for a humble city tucked away in the great northwest.

But the AYP was starkly different in that there was an undeniable aspect of exploitation that boggles the mind by today's standards. The AYP sensationalized humans – Igorrote villagers – whose attire drew the ire of the Women's Christian Temperance Union. The WCTU asked Reverend Mark Matthews, a Presbyterian minister known for his moral crusades, to look into the matter. The concern was not that there were fifty villagers being exploited for their strange ethnicity, but that their loincloths might be inauthentic, designed for titillation.

There were exhibits of Siberians, Flathead Indians, Arabian women – not showcased to celebrate their cultures as much as to gawk at their otherness. Plus there were Eskimo children on display and, of course, the raffling off of a boy named Ernest.

By comparison, the Century 21 Expo gave away poodles, and even that was met with harsh criticism.

Though the Century 21 Expo was not without its own strange wrinkle – an institutionalized sexism that would make Don Draper twitch.

At Seattle's second showcase to the world, the demonstrators at the National Science Pavilion were all women, were required to have a certain look, and included five Seafair princesses and a former Miss Alaska. They were given a quick course in biology to provide them with enough information to answer questions from guests. The Library of the Future exhibit sent out a call for the sexiest librarians. (Hey, Batgirl was a librarian.) And the elevator operators at the Space Needle were all female, required to be at least five feet six inches, Junoesque in proportion, and possess 'the kind of personality that typified Seattle girls.'

While AYP organizers worried about the city's red-light district and banned alcohol, the Century 21 Expo allowed libations to flow freely, and a bottle of Jim Beam in the shape of the Space Needle was quite popular.

But the most surprising difference was Show Street, the topless corner of Seattle's second world's fair, where fairgoers could rent Polaroid cameras to snap photos of showgirls in various stages of undress.

In this adults-only section of the fair, a charismatic promoter, Gracie Hansen, created attractions that would make Madam Lou proud. I guess the more things change, the more things stay the same, and the more young women are expected to wear green body paint and pose in bikinis.

I doubt Madam Flora would have approved.

Speaking of the Century 21 Expo, I often wonder if the real Ernest ever visited, and what he must have thought. Did he reconcile this glimpse of the future with his own humble past? Did he even know he was once a prize? And did anyone claim him?

These questions remain unanswered.

The real Ernest, as of the publication of this book, would be a centenarian, so it's doubtful that he's reading this. But perhaps someone knew him. And if they do, I hope they'll contact me.

I'm on Twitter: @jamieford.

In the meantime, I'll be here in my office, staring at a blank screen, contemplating my next book, turning over more rocks and waiting for my muse. As much as I'd like to be visited by Erato, the muse of romantic poetry, it'll more likely just be Clio, the muse of history. And we'll do this dance all over again.

Though a part of me still holds out hope for Olivia. Roller skates and all.

Acknowledgments

First and foremost, thank you to my readers and fans (yikes, I have fans). Especially that one lovely woman who has been to seven of my book events and the guy who asked me to sign his abs – you know who you are.

Without readers, authors would be trees that fall in the forest, unheard. So thank you for sharing this journey with me once again, and for passing this novel to a friend, pitching it to your book club, posting about it on Goodreads, or just setting it on your coffee table as a reminder that the written word still has a place in the wonderful world of Netflix.

Then there are all the amazing indie bookstores out there that have been so good to me. As Neil Gaiman once said, 'I do not believe there is a wrong way to buy books. I think that the *best* way to buy books is from a local indie bookshop, if you have one.'

In my travels, I've visited stores in nearly every state in the Union (coming for you soon, Mississippi and West Virginia). But the one that is near and dear to my heart these days is Cassiopeia Books here in my adopted hometown of Great Falls, run by Andrew Guschausky – part bookseller, part therapist, Andrew regularly opens my mind to books and music, simply by using the algorithm of his imagination.

In that same vein, thank you to all of my librarian friends, using your superpowers for good. You are a sacred order, the Knights Templar, the men and women of the Night's Watch, guarding us from a 1,000-year Kardashian winter. I was privileged to give a keynote talk last year to the Kentucky Library Association, which only underscored my immense respect and admiration for both your profession, and your bourbon.

Then there are those who might not think I remember – a small group of readers on Lummi Island, in particular: Isabel Gates, Paula Chu, Henry Chu, Margaret Lyons, Jennifer Hansen, Stephanie Inslee, Cindy Maxwell, Christina Claassen. Thanks for letting me share part of an early draft, and for your gracious feedback.

Research-wise, I'm hopelessly indebted to the authors of these books in particular for letting me stand on their shoulders and take in the view regarding:

THE HISTORY OF THE AYP AND THE CENTURY 21 EXPO: *Picturing the Alaska–Yukon–Pacific Exposition* by Nicolette Bromberg and John Stamets; *The Future Remembered: The 1962 Seattle World's Fair and Its Legacy* by Paula Becker, Alan J. Stein, and The HistoryLink Staff; *Senate Documents of the 61st Congress, 3rd Session, Vol. 29.* (This was the complete report by Board and Managers of the Alaska–Yukon–Pacific Exposition. Yes, I actually read this stuff. I know – it's a sickness.)

LOST DETAILS ABOUT SEATTLE: *Sons of the Profits* by William C. Speidel; *Seattle Past to Present* by Roger Sale; *On the Harbor* by John C. Hughes and Ryan Teague Beckwith; *Echoes of Puget Sound* by Captain Torger Birkeland; *Seattle Vice* by Rick Anderson; *Only the Drums Remembered* by Ralph Chaplin; *Skid Road* by Murray Morgan; and the *Social Blue Book, Seattle, 1958–1959.*

ASIAN AMERICAN HISTORY, because I can never get enough: *Dim Sum – The Seattle ABC (American Born Chinese) Dream* by Vera Ing; *Unbound Feet* by Judy Yung; *Fierce Compassion – The Life of Abolitionist Donaldina Cameron* by Kristin and Kathryn Wong; *Chinatown's Angry Angel* by Mildred Crowl Martin.

THE ROLES OF WOMEN IN PRE-EDWARDIAN AMERICA: *Manners, Culture, and Dress of the Best American Society* by Richard A. Wells, 1891, where I learned 'A lady cannot shake off an improper acquaintance with the same facility as a gentleman.' Sadly, the same rules still apply on Facebook. And *What Can a Woman Do* by Mrs M. L. Rayne. (This was a used book from 1884, and pressed inside was a long-forgotten four-leaf clover. Here's hoping there's no statute of limitations on luck.)

PROSTITUTION AND SEATTLE'S SUFFRAGE MOVEMENT: *The Story of Yamada Waka: From Prostitute to Feminist Pioneer* by Tomoko Yamazaki; *Twice Sold, Twice Ransomed* by Mrs Emma J. Ray.

Speaking of, I owe a whisper of thanks to Maggie McNeil, former librarian and current sex-work advocate, for confirming the assumptions of my research into Seattle's red-light district and for disabusing me of other notions about her profession.

Then there are the institutions that I rely on for inspiration as much as confirmation: The Wing Luke Museum of the Asian Pacific American Experience, Seattle's Museum of History and Industry (MOHAI), Historylink.org, the Seattle Public Library, and the University of Washington's Special Collections.

Of course, there's my amazing team at Penguin Random House (who missed a chance to work for a company called Random Penguin): Kara Welsh, Kim Hovey, Jennifer Garza, Anne Speyer,

Anastasia Whalen, Samantha Leach, Quinne Rogers, Vincent La Scala, and Libby McGuire – you are missed, Libby, but godspeed in your new adventures.

And lest I forget, the lovely folks at Allison & Busby who make me look better than I deserve including Lesley Crooks, Susie Dunlop and Emma Finnigan.

Finally, there is the holy trinity of my writing life.

My über-agent, Kristin Nelson. Back in the day, I had offers from four other agents, all in NYC. But I went with my heart and an up-and-coming agent based out of Denver who saw the publishing world differently. Now a force in the industry, Kristin has forty *NYT* bestsellers to her name. (I think I made the right call.)

My amazing editor, Jennifer Hershey, for her patience as my deadlines *whooshed* by, and for her prolific insight. When writing, I'm sometimes like a person on the dance floor, using so many moves that bystanders think I'm having a seizure. Somehow Jennifer saw the rhythm worth salvaging.

My lovely wife, Leesha, with her Red Pen of Destiny, who tolerates my abuse of the Oxford comma, as well as my never-ending book travels, even when I'm home, up in my office, staring into space, wandering off somewhere in my mind.

Jamie Ford
Montana, February 2017

The old Seattle landmark has been boarded up for decades, but now the new owner has made a startling discovery in the basement: personal belongings stored away by Japanese families sent to internment camps during World War II.

Among the fascinated crowd gathering outside the hotel stands Henry Lee who, as the owner unfurls a distinctive parasol, is flooded by memories of his childhood.

He wonders if by some miracle, in amongst the boxes of dusty treasures, lies a link to the Okabe family, and the girl he lost his heart to so many years ago.

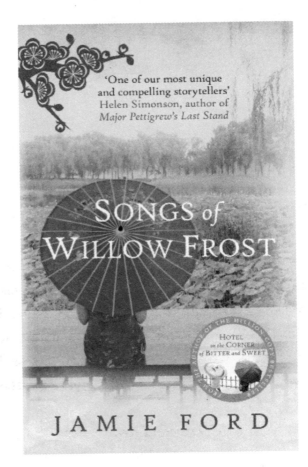

'One of our most unique and compelling storytellers' Helen Simonson, author of *Major Pettigrew's Last Stand*

SONGS *of* WILLOW FROST

HOTEL *on the* CORNER *of* BITTER *and* SWEET

JAMIE FORD

William Eng has lived at Seattle's Sacred Heart Orphanage for five long years, ever since his mother's listless body was carried from their Chinatown apartment. When, during a trip to the movie theatre, William glimpses an actress on the silver screen, he is immediately struck by her features.

Because Willow Frost is many things – a singer, a dancer, a movie star – but most of all, William is convinced, she is his mother. Determined to find her, William attempts to confront the mysteries of his past. But the story of Willow Frost is far more complicated than any Hollywood fantasy . . .

JAMIE FORD grew up in Seattle's Chinatown and found professional success as an art director and copywriter before turning his attention to fiction, becoming an award-winning short story writer. His debut novel, *Hotel on the Corner of Bitter and Sweet*, became an international bestseller. It was inspired by the 'I am Chinese' button his father mentioned wearing as a child after the bombing of Pearl Harbour.

jamieford.com